W9-CPL-815

"Paul Attaway's riveting debut novel introduces readers to the genteel South of the mid-twentieth century and then rips off that façade to reveal a treacherous underbelly of greed, deceit, violence, and bigotry. Attaway's gripping tale unfolds through richly drawn characters that will engage readers and keep them enthralled through one suspenseful chapter after another. This is a story that will stay with you long after you close the final page."

— **Jeff Andrews,** author of *The Freedom Star* and *The Gandy Dancer*

"Aspiring southern socialite Rose Atkins adores her adolescent son Walker — but views older son Eli with contempt. Try as he may, good-hearted dad Monty can't keep his family's dysfunction from spiraling out of control. The result is an emotional psychological drama, a compelling murder plot, and enough twists and turns to keep us riveted."

— **David Aretha**, award-winning author and editor

"A thrilling story with the ambiance and texture that you only find in the deep South. A family that feels so real, it could be yours, but they have secrets to keep. Paul's fantastic storytelling pulls you in and holds onto you, right up to the climactic end. Highly recommended!"

— **Erin and Jim Essert**, avid mystery readers

"Paul Attaway's novel, *Blood in the Lowlands*, is nearly flawless. His smooth, crisp writing style, richly layered characters, and superbly constructed plot leave the reader breathless to the end. A masterpiece of modern writing."

— **Andrea Vanryken,** writer/contributor for Popsugar

"*Blood in the Low Country* is an impressive novelistic debut. It's a good 'read', a crime novel with a plot that propels you forward. Its characters are smartly drawn. Its themes are resonant, provoking. And there's an authorial intelligence throughout that reminds you time and again that this will not be Paul Attaway's one and only book. Not if we're lucky."

— **Jay Boyer**, Professor Emeritus, Creative Writing Program, Arizona State University, Author and Playwright

BLOOD

in the

LOW COUNTRY

"The past isn't dead. It isn't even past."

Gavin Stevens in *Requiem for a Nun* by William Faulkner

A tension-filled family saga of betrayal

BLOOD
in the
LOW COUNTRY

PAUL ATTAWAY

LINKSLAND
PUBLISHING

Copyright © 2020 by Paul Attaway

This is a work of fiction. Unless otherwise indicated, all the names, characters, businesses, places, events and incidents in this book are either the product of the author's imagination or used in a fictitious manner. Any resemblance to actual persons, living or dead, or actual events is purely coincidental.

All rights reserved. No part of this publication may be reproduced or transmitted in any form or by any electronic, mechanical, recording, or other means except as allowed under Section 107 or 108 of the 1976 United States Copyright Act, without the prior written permission of the author.

Twenty-Four Frames
Words and Music by Michael Jason Isbell
Copyright © 2015 Southeastern Records Publishing
All Rights Administered by Downtown Music Publishing LLC
All Rights Reserved Used by Permission
Reprinted by Permission of Hal Leonard LLC

The Man Comes Around
Words and Music by John R. Cash
Copyright © 2002 Song of Cash, Inc.
All Rights Administered by BMG Rights Management (US) LLC
All Rights Reserved Used by Permission
Reprinted by Permission of Hal Leonard LLC

Published by Linksland Publishing

All Bible scriptures are from the English Standard Version.

Library of Congress Control Number: 2020913952

Paperback ISBN: 978-1-7354016-2-1
Hardback ISBN: 978-1-7354016-1-4
Ebook ISBN: 978-1-7354016-0-7
EPUB ISBN: 978-1-7354016-3-8

Book Design: Authorsupport.com

Printed in the United States of America

This book is dedicated to Lyn. An extraordinary person and wonderful wife, daughter, mother, and friend. Thank you for your encouragement, love, and support along the way.

Contents

PART ONE

Come now, you who say, "Today or tomorrow we will go into such and such a town and spend a year there and trade and make a profit"— yet you do not know what tomorrow will bring. What is your life? For you are a mist that appears for a little time and then vanishes.

JAMES 4:13-14

CHAPTER 1

Second Place, Again

KIAWAH ISLAND, SOUTH CAROLINA; OCTOBER 1977

The crisp morning sunlight pierced the amber mist that blanketed the horizon like a gentle, cotton shawl. Gone was the haze that accompanied the oppressive heat of a low country summer, replaced by the cool fragrance of damp salt air dancing off the marsh.

Walker, kneeling to retie his shoes, spied his father in the distance. *Why did he have to come?* Walker thought. *He said he was going to play golf.* But there he was, shaking hands with Eddie's dad. Walker fed off his father's approval, but it came at a steep price.

His father never hesitated to tell him he loved him, but it was always in the same breath in which he told him how proud he was of him. Were the two thoughts severable? Could he love him if he weren't proud of him? If Walker didn't perform? If he didn't win? The pressure. The pressure to succeed weighed on every moment of every day, and the cost of losing far surpassed the joy of winning.

And then there was Eli. Always, Eli. Eli was counting on him.

Walker looked about, sizing up the competition. The Kiawah Challenge was the first cross-country meet of the season, and a chance to gauge the strength of the other teams. Bishop High School always fielded a strong squad, but he'd beaten their best last year, and he knew he'd beat them again this year. But the runners from the other schools were never his primary concern. No, the runner who stood between Walker and medaling first was, and always had been, Eddie Wentworth.

Edward Theodore Wentworth.

Walker didn't hate Eddie; no one did. If there was a word that described Eddie it was effortless. Everything came naturally for him. He shot up in height earlier than most of the boys in class but then filled out quickly, thus avoiding the awkward years. His voice changed seemingly overnight. His blond hair, made more so by the hours he spent in the sun, was unkept but naturally so. The only physical feature not preordained by the gods were his eyes. One was blue and one was green, but the effect made him all the more memorable. But at the end of the day, what stood Eddie apart from the others was the grace with which he carried himself, seemingly unaware that others always noticed him.

Walker didn't dislike Eddie; everyone liked Eddie. But resent? Yes. Look down on? Yes. But why? Jealousy. It all came so easily for Eddie. Walker worked for his accomplishments. How could his successes not be more significant, more meaningful, more deserving? This year would be different. He had trained harder than ever before. This year Walker would not be defeated. This year Walker would beat Eddie. Walker would make Eli proud, his father too.

The race would begin at the end of a dirt road on a thin finger of land bordered by the Kiawah River to the north and marshland to the south. The road extended westward and connected to the Kiawah Island mainland. Kiawah is a barrier island off the coast of South Carolina and was so named for the Kiawah Indians, who had populated the island, by explorers and fortune hunters dispatched in 1670 by England's King Charles II.

The marshal fired the gun, and the boys were off. Walker was not a fast starter, but with three miles ahead of them, and across a gently rolling, predominantly flat terrain, a quick start was not necessary. The runners jockeyed for position over the first few hundred yards before settling into a pace.

The boys ran down the dirt road, the sun rising over their shoulders. Walker knew the course well. His family had rented the same beach house every summer, and there wasn't a corner of the island nor a stretch of beach he had not explored.

As the course turned south, the sights and sounds changed. The smell of the pungent salt air dissipated, and the marsh, populated by blue herons and long-legged great egrets, was replaced by live oaks and the occasional deer. Kiawah Island was a magnificent living testimony to the majesty and diversity of God's creation. Rivers, marshland, tidal pools, the ocean, a maritime forest, and the accompanying ecosystem of each habitat formed a veritable Garden of Eden created by millions of years of shifting tides. Walker's father said that the island, along with baseball and shrimp 'n' grits, was more proof God loved us.

Walker ran comfortably toward the front of the pack. A mile into the race, the runners began to separate. A half dozen runners were ahead of Walker, none of them Eddie. He didn't look back. He didn't have to. He knew Eddie was there, always in striking distance.

Walker waited patiently until the race turned westward. They were on the coolest part of the course, shaded by trees, and due to an early morning overcast sky, the temperature had been in the low sixties when the race began. The dirt road softened as it left the forest and rolled up to the edge of the beach on the south side of the island, and Walker knew the combination of the sun breaking through and the soft sand would slow the pace. For now, though, the cooler temperatures lulled the front-runners into too quick of a pace. Walker was content to wait. So was Eddie.

The dirt roads were not built for cars and, in some areas of the island, were barely wide enough for two-lane traffic. Efforts to develop the island had begun in the 1950s but proceeded haphazardly over the years. Most of the development occurred on the Atlantic-facing south side of the island where homes could be found on Eugenia Avenue, the island's main road.

He spent his summers following Eli and his friends around the island, fishing, crabbing, sailing, and reenacting battles between the pirate Blackbeard and the English Royal Navy. Walker idolized his older brother, and Eli, despite his open complaints, loved having him along.

Preparing for his move, Walker stayed back as the pack of front-runners sped out of the cover of the oak trees and turned westward onto the beach. As they turned, coming from behind, he shot down to the water's edge, knowing the sand would be harder and therefore easier and faster to run across. He had checked the tide the day before and knew it would be at its lowest in the morning, leaving the beach surface hard and compact closer to the surf.

Walker grabbed the lead before the other boys, slogging away in the heavier sand, could comprehend what had happened. They ran toward the harder-packed sand to catch Walker, but it was too late. Walker knew he would not merely hold his lead but increase it and win the race running away. A well-conceived plan. A well-executed race.

But over his shoulder, he caught sight of Eddie, still running along the edge of the forest. Walker couldn't understand it; everyone else had fallen in behind him. Then it made sense. The wind. It had picked up, and before he knew it, he was running into a severe headwind. Eddie, however, running along the edge of the forest, was shielded from the wind and ran unhindered. Out of nowhere, the wind became the biggest factor in the race.

Eddie held back from the front of the pack and waited patiently for the story of the race to unfold. As the course reached the end of the forest trail, Eddie saw the clouds moving more quickly across the sky and a flock of seagulls rise and bank upwards on the shoulder of a strong eastward-blowing wind. So, seeking shelter from the wind, he shortened his stride and stuck to the heavier sand.

Walker reached Eugenia Avenue first, but the stretch on the beach had taken it out of him. It looked like Eddie, close on his heels, was running easily as Walker labored to hold his pace. With only a few hundred yards to go, the race would finish in the parking lot of the Cougar Point Golf Course. Walker's legs burned as he struggled to hold the lead. Eddie pulled even, his gait long and relaxed. Walker pushed himself harder and stayed with him as Eddie sped up ever so slightly. But Walker's legs felt heavy and lifeless. He had nothing left and his shoulders ached. Eddie eased across the finish line with Walker lunging behind him, falling just short.

As the other runners crossed the finish line and huddled, hands on their knees, with teammates, congratulations were handed out to all who had finished. Walker was stunned—not broken but demoralized, not sure what more he could have done.

And there Dad was again, but this time with his arms crossed and his lips pursed, standing off to himself.

I've embarrassed him, thought Walker.

Monty left quickly and trudged off to his car with just enough time to make it to the first tee. He was at a loss for what to say to his son. He hurt for Walker every time he fell short, knowing how hard his son trained. But

Monty was pulled between his desire to counsel and yet encourage his son and his duty to stand by his wife, Walker's mother, who relentlessly pressured Walker to excel. Monty felt she pushed him too hard but when he spoke up, she accused him of taking sides against her. Monty wished he knew what to do and say, and not knowing, the silence defined his relationship with his son, Walker. The resulting tension had opened a gulf between father and son, and Monty feared losing Walker too.

Walker could barely focus on what was happening around him. A small crowd of runners, family members, coaches, and a few girlfriends gathered at the far end of the parking lot. Still, in the fog of his exhausted, oxygen-deprived brain, he made out the words of the race marshal. "And taking second place, Walker Atkins, from Porter-Gaud."

Second place, again.

Chapter 2

Steak & Potatoes

At the Atkins house, dinner was a time-honored tradition. The family would gather around the dining room table bustling with the fine china, glassware, serving platters and trays, pitchers, and more knives, forks, and spoons than either Monty or Walker had any use for. Monty's wife, Rose, loved putting on airs, which Monty would tolerate most nights. But on a beautiful Saturday night, such as it was, he'd hold his ground, and they would enjoy a casual meal on the screened-in porch.

Every Saturday night was steak and potatoes, always a big deal with Monty, and Walker loved it. Tonight, Monty was standing in front of the grill absentmindedly flipping the steaks. He was wearing blue Sansabelt slacks and a white golf shirt. A transistor radio poked out of his shirt pocket, and he was intently listening to the local sports show as the announcer gave a wrap-up of the day's college football scores. College football was in full swing, and Alabama, Monty's alma mater, looked unbeatable. "The Bear has the boys playing at a high level," he exclaimed. He was a longtime fan of Alabama's legendary coach, Bear Bryant.

Everyone always said Walker was a chip off the old block. He definitely took after his father in both looks and mannerisms. Monty and Walker had the same thin, angular face made all the more apparent by their tendency to cock their head to one side for almost any reason, whether perturbed, interested, in deep concentration, or just when intently listening. Where they differed was in height. While Monty was of average height, Walker took after his mom's side of the family and was well on his way to being over six feet tall. Both father and son ran on the slim side despite their legendary appetites. Monty, in particular, could eat whatever he wanted and never put on weight. They both had thin hair, Walker's sandy brown and Monty's dark. But Monty had started losing his hair shortly after college and today he was bald on top. Most men would have felt self-conscious about losing their hair at such a young age but Monty could not have cared less. His lax attitude about his appearance carried over to his dress. It's not that he was a bad dresser; he just rarely gave what he wore much thought.

Walker's mom, Rose, however, was very concerned about appearances and chided Monty about his. "Monty," she'd say, "you're such a good-looking man, I don't know why you won't dress the part!" Monty would laugh and joke how he'd landed the prettiest girl on campus, so he must have had something working.

While Monty tended to the grill, Mom toiled in the kitchen. A large pot of water on the stove was filled with Lipton tea bags coming to a boil.

"One big scoop of sugar for every cup of water," she'd tell anyone who'd listen. "And add the sugar while the water's hot. Too cold and the sugar will settle on the bottom; that's the kind of sweet tea you'll get in the North if you can call it tea. But let it sit too long at a boil, and you'll burn the flavor right off. Just bring it to a boil and let it steep for a few minutes."

The baked potatoes were keeping warm in the oven. When Walker's older brother, Eli, was still at home, after dinner they would wad up the Reynolds Wrap the potatoes had been baked in and run around the house pelting each other with their foil weapons, with Mom screaming at the top of her lungs for them to stop. Monty would sit in his recliner after the meal, watching the Braves on TV, unable to muster a reason to end the boys' shenanigans until Rose's exasperated instructions became more than he could stand. Then, with one loud "BOYS!" they'd stop and sneak off to find some other mischief.

Now Mom was putting the finishing touches on the fried green tomatoes and the squash casserole. Rose Atkins, like her mother before her, took great pride in feeding her family from her garden.

The table was set, complete with glasses filled high with ice for the still warm sweet tea to be poured over, and Walker brought in the plate of steaks and placed them on the kitchen counter. They grabbed their plates, picked out their steaks and potatoes, and piled the vegetables high. The bread was hot out of the oven and smothered with a generous helping of butter. They took their assigned seats at the patio table, held hands, and bowed their heads, then Dad said grace.

Heads lifted and Monty, as he reached for a piece of bread and ripped it apart, slowed, looked at Walker, and said, "Second place, huh? Umph."

Walker's father had a way of saying "Umph" that expressed exasperation, frustration, disappointment, empathy, and unfulfilled expectations all at once. Sometimes he'd slam the palm of his hand against his forehead and exclaim something like "Golly Pete!"

Monty had a never-ending collection of southern colloquialisms. For Pete's sake! Dagnabbit! Son of a biscuit! Not one to swear, Monty wouldn't tolerate it in Walker either. Not that it was a problem for Walker, for he loved his father fiercely, and would never do anything to disappoint or embarrass him. But that "Umph"—well, for Walker, it all amounted to just one thing: He had disappointed his father.

"Well, I know you've logged a lot of miles over the summer getting ready for the season," his father stated. "What could you have done differently?"

"Run faster."

"Don't get smart with your father," snapped Mother.

"I'm not. I just don't know what you want me to say. Just like last year, Eddie passes me at the end."

"Could you get some speed work in this week?" asked Monty with a genuine concerned look, his head slightly cocked.

Walker, mindful of neither wanting to sound sarcastic nor wanting to let down those around him, simply said, "Yes, sir. I'll have to. I'll need a bigger lead next time."

Walker's mom proclaimed, "It's okay, Walker, honey. I know how disappointed you must be. I know I am." Walker winced as if reacting to the quick jab of a stiletto. "I told all the ladies at the garden club yesterday how hard you worked all summer. They were so excited to hear about it. You make me so proud, you know that?"

Again, and deeper, the weight of expectations puncturing any sense of joy.

"Mom, I wish you wouldn't brag that way. It only makes it worse."

"Shush. It's a mother's prerogative. The worst part was Trudy Weathers reminding everyone how many records Edward Theodore Wentworth has. She lords it over everyone, and she's not even a Wentworth. She's just a cousin!"

When Rose Walker said "Edward Theodore Wentworth," she did so in an intentionally haughty voice, head cocked upward and to the side, rolling her eyes. All very dramatic and intended to demonstrate how Rose imagined the Wentworths must have looked down on those around them.

"Yep, thinks she's better than everyone else," echoed Dad. "What about Eleanor Wentworth? I'll bet she was snortin' like a blue-ribbon hog."

"She was indeed but pretends it's no big thing. She'll turn and ask about you and your children. It is *so* annoying."

"Maybe she means it. Maybe she really is interested," Walker remarked.

"Trust me. She's not. Oh, Walker, you can be so naive, do you know that? You make me so proud. She only asks about your children in the hopes you'll ask about hers. I know the type, but I don't give her the satisfaction. She thinks we're all *sooo* interested in her life. He's not popular, is he? Not like you. Must be tough on Eddie."

Eddie was the most popular kid in school but was oblivious to all of it. A big man on campus and didn't know it. Kind to everyone, funny, easygoing, and a gifted athlete. He was good-looking, without being gorgeous.

"Don't think so. He's pretty cool about everything. He's just faster than everyone," said Walker.

"Remember what we've talked about, Son," Monty said. "'Philippians 4:13—I can do all things through Him who strengthens me.'"

"Yes, sir," said Walker, nodding dutifully.

*　　*　　*

The screen door slammed against the frame, bounced, slammed again twice more, quieter each time before coming to a rest, as Walker bolted out the back. Halfway to his car, he shouted over his shoulder, "I'm goin' out."

"Walker Greer, you come here this instant," insisted Rose, as she stood at the top of the back stairs, apron still on and hands on her hips.

"Mom! What?" moaned an exasperated Walker.

"Just where do you think you're going?"

"Out."

"You said that. But where?"

"I don't know. Just out...with friends."

"I don't like you spending so much time with that girl, Isabelle."

"Who says that's who I'm seein'? Besides, we're just friends."

"Well, you keep it that way. You can do better. The Dawsons are climbers. Always have been, and she's just using you. Don't forget, after church tomorrow we're having lunch at the club with the Beauchamps. Connie will be there, and I want you looking and behaving your best. She's the kind of girl you should be spending time with. There will be no mention of Isabelle. Especially in front of the Beauchamps, of all people. Now don't you embarrass your mother."

"I'll be there," he said, sighing as he got into his car and drove off to see Isabelle, with the cassette tape deck playing Glen Campbell's "Southern Nights."

CHAPTER 3

Isabelle

Isabelle Dawson, the only daughter and one of seven children born to Quaid and Mirabelle Dawson, was the granddaughter of Bartholomew Dawson, one-half of the famous South Carolina bootlegging brothers, Bartholomew and Nathaniel Dawson.

In the early 1900s, Bartholomew and Nathaniel made moonshine, as did most folks raised in Hell Hole Swamp, a stretch of land along the Santee River running from Jamestown to Moncks Corner on the Cooper River. Francis Marion was the famed militia commander who helped the colonies repel the British in winning the Revolutionary War. He was nicknamed the "Swamp Fox" for his ability to disappear in these very swamps and elude the British Redcoats. The area became home to wealthy rice plantation owners during the days of slavery, but after the Civil War the plantation owners couldn't pay enough to attract labor and the plantations collapsed. The folks who stayed were a hard, uneducated, and fiercely independent lot, prone to superstition and suspicious of outsiders.

For years, inhabitants of Hell Hole Swamp made corn whiskey for their personal consumption. However, Prohibition sired an unquenchable demand for their product in the cities of Charleston, Savannah, Memphis,

Chicago, New York, and all points in between. The Dawson brothers sold equipment to the moonshiners building stills in the swamp and then purchased the moonshine and sold it to distributors like the notorious Chicago gangster Al Capone.

In the 1920s, the Dawsons were making a fortune and did so with no fear from the authorities. Hell, they owned most the cops and a few senators to boot. Everyone was in on it and doing well. Capone heard that the Dawsons were gaining more power and planned to sell to his rivals, so Capone refused to pay for a large shipment of the moonshine to remind the Dawsons who was in charge. The Dawsons retaliated and refused to supply Capone with product until he paid what he owed. Capone sent several carloads of his toughest enforcers down to South Carolina to settle matters. These men pursued the Dawsons deep into the Low Country swamps, never to be seen again, reinforcing why outsiders fared so poorly in Hell Hole Swamp.

When the Twenty-First Amendment ending Prohibition passed in 1933, the Dawsons went straight and acquired several profitable liquor distributorships. These distributorships funded a lavish lifestyle for the Dawson brothers and for generations to come. However, try as they might, neither Bartholomew nor Nathaniel could shake their reputations as bootleggers. They were shunned by polite society and excluded from the best clubs and homes in Charleston's toniest neighborhood, South of Broad. Nathaniel retreated to the swamps and drank himself to death while Bartholomew tried in vain to shake the poor, white-trash label off his back so long associated with anyone from the swamps.

Quaid Dawson witnessed his father, Bartholomew, grow old and bitter despite his financial success because he never could buy the respectability that he so craved. Quaid was thus determined to live life not caring what others thought, and that is precisely what he did. The quick temper of his father, a first-generation Irish immigrant, did not haunt Quaid's doorstep. He married Mirabelle, an Italian beauty, and they sired seven boys and, finally, a girl, Isabelle.

Quaid did not run from his family heritage but embraced it and made no apologies. He was extremely likable and charmed any and all critics with his aw-shucks humility. However, Quaid was not to be underestimated and proved to be an excellent businessman. The liquor distributorships he inherited grew in size and profitability under his guidance. You would never know it, though, from how he lived. Quaid and Mirabelle were content to live simple lives, organized around their children and their faith in the Lord's love for them.

*   *   *

Despite it all, the moonshining backstory was too much for Rose Atkins, and she looked down on the lot of them for no other reason. But Walker was head over heels for Isabelle and Isabelle for Walker. They'd been inseparable since June, boyfriend and girlfriend, and it drove Rose to fits. Rose would deny their close relationship when asked by others and worked tirelessly to forge a romantic relationship between Walker and young Constance Beauchamp, the debutante daughter of one of Charleston's most prominent families. In the end, there was nothing she could do about it. Walker and Isabelle were in love, as in love as high school kids could be.

Isabelle was sitting in a rocking chair on the front porch reading a book, her bare feet curled up under her, when Walker pulled up the driveway. She was wearing a white sundress and no makeup. Her hair was dark, thick, and lustrous, like her mother's; her eyes green, like her father's. She wore the confidence of a young girl who knew she was beautiful, who knew the effect she had on boys. But her confidence was tempered by a grace associated with a much older, wiser person. Walker had fallen for her the first time he set eyes on her.

But Isabelle worried about Walker. Tonight, she could tell, before he even said a word, as he slowly approached the porch, chin and eyes set, that he'd been brooding about something. Isabelle knew no one more obsessed with their future and with succeeding than Walker. While she admired ambition, what afflicted Walker was more than dreams; it was a need, a hunger, an obsession.

"Hey, Walkie Talkie. What took you so long? It's Saturday night and I'm just sittin' here." Isabelle set her book down and cast a warm smile at Walker as he mounted the last stair.

Walker had earned the nickname "Walkie Talkie" from his brother Eli because Walker talked so much as a child. He had so badly wanted to keep up with Eli that he walked and talked earlier than most. Now, Isabelle was the only one who called him Walkie Talkie, and Isabelle was the only one Walker spoke to about Eli, where he might be and what had happened to him.

"Hey, Izzy." Walker's voice was discouraged, resigned, angry.

"Tell me what's wrong, Walker."

"I have to get out of here. I can't take it anymore. She's driving me crazy."

"I know. Come sit next to me."

"I can't wait till high school is over," said Walker.

"But we're only juniors. What are you going to do?" asked Isabelle.

"I don't know. Run away, maybe?"

"I can see how that is tempting for you. But seriously."

"I don't know. I'm dying, though. She thinks my life is hers to live. She never lets up. And Dad? He sits there in his silence, taking her side. Why can't he come to my rescue? Just once? When I'm in college, I'll be free. Free of her, free of her smothering, free of having to please her all the time. Free."

"I hope you will be. I truly do. But I fear it's not as simple as that. Are you still determined to go to Georgetown?"

"You know I am. And then I want to live overseas. As far from here as possible. You'll come with me, won't you, Izzy?"

"Oh, Walker. Let's see how things unfold. Let's see what life has in store for us. Why do you feel as if you have to plan it all? But yes, Walker, I will."

CHAPTER 4

Brothers

JAMES ISLAND, SOUTH CAROLINA; MAY 1969

Eli and Walker bolted from their classrooms and raced toward the parking lot where Mom waited with the other mothers for after-school pickup. The summer break was a few weeks away, and the boys could hardly wait. Eli was finishing the eighth grade and Walker the second. Their summer would be filled with baseball, fishing, crabbing, days at the beach, and, for the first time, vacationing on Kiawah Island and staying in a rental home.

Walker hopped into his usual place in the back seat of the station wagon behind Eli, who was sitting up front in the passenger seat. It didn't take long before Mom and Eli were at it again. They weren't screaming at each other; that would come later. Fighting? Maybe. A disagreement? Absolutely. But not a healthy one.

"But I want to play with my friends."

Eli was a born athlete. Blessed with extraordinary eye-hand coordination, he made fielding a grounder and throwing on the run look as natural as a bird in flight. At the plate, Eli didn't hit for power but could see any pitch

19

and carved up the field, roping line drives wherever he pleased. He had a gift and loved the game.

"You're too good for that team. We're moving you up to the fifteen- and sixteen-year-olds, and you'll be on the Blue Herons, playing for Coach Largess."

"But everybody hates him. It won't be any fun."

Rose Atkins yanked the car to the right and pulled off the road, spraying gravel as she threw the car into park. Eli and Walker, thrown forward and then falling violently back into their seats, were paralyzed with fear as their mother, left hand gripping the steering wheel, knuckles white and bloodless, jabbed her right index finger at Eli like a crooked scalpel just inches from his face.

"You're just like your father, selfish and lazy, hoping to get by on talent alone. Well, I won't stand for it. You will not embarrass me. Your grades are poor, so if you're going to college—and you will go to college—it will be because I pushed you. Why can't you be more like Walker? He never disappoints me."

Walker winced, closed his eyes, and curled up as if punched in the gut. Every time their mother compared them, he wanted to disappear or disappoint her, so Eli wouldn't blame him. But he knew that his mother's sting was far worse than any condemnation Eli could muster, so he remained a silent witness to Eli's humiliation, loathing his own cowardice.

She jerked the car back onto the road, and they drove silently for the next ten minutes until they reached the ballpark. Rose walked with a determined stride past where Eli's friends were practicing and toward the field for the older players. Eli, head slumped and dejectedly dangling his glove off his left hand, walked several steps behind. Rose introduced herself and Eli to Coach Largess, and then Rose and Coach moved a few steps away and spoke just out of earshot of Eli. The decision was made.

"Eli, I'm Coach Largess. I've heard a lot about you. Join the other boys in the field and shag a few grounders."

Eli shuffled aimlessly onto the field, and Rose made a mental note to chastise him later for not sprinting.

*   *   *

It wasn't until later that summer that Rose told Walker that Eli had a different father. Rose was driving Walker to a friend's house. Eli was not along for the ride, so Walker got to sit in the front seat. Then, out of the blue and without any prompting or context, Rose told Walker a stunning truth while simultaneously trying to bury it.

"Walker, there's something I need to tell you," said Rose.

"What is it, Mom?"

"I was married to another man a long time ago, before I met your father. That man was your brother's father," said Rose.

Walker didn't know what to say. He just stared at his mother, waiting for an explanation, but nothing more was said. When Walker asked his mother questions about Eli's dad, she refused to answer him.

Silence filled the car. As they pulled up to the house where Walker's friend lived, Walker asked one last question.

"Does Eli know?"

"Yes, of course," said his mother. "But your father adopted Eli. Now don't ever ask me about it again."

For an eight-year-old, this was very confusing because it raised so many questions about his mother. Who had she married before Monty? Why wasn't she still married to him? What else was she keeping from him? And what did his dad think? From watching Monty with the boys, you would never know that Eli had a different biological father. Monty loved them both, played with each of them in the backyard, and treated them the same.

*   *   *

The paternal bond Monty felt toward Walker did not diminish his feelings for Eli in any way. Monty knew Eli needed a father, and he was determined to be that father.

Nevertheless, despite Monty's best efforts, he could never permanently erase Eli's lurking sadness or feelings of not belonging. In family pictures of the four of them, because of their age difference, Eli loomed so much larger than Walker. And he did so in an odd, misplaced fashion, making it appear that Eli's presence required explanation as if the camera had captured Eli's feelings of isolation.

CHAPTER 5

Hope

"Momma, where's Daddy? Is he gonna make it here to see me?" asked Rose, her eyes filled with equal parts hope and sadness, knowing what the answer would be. Rose and her mother, Beulah, had arrived at the Miss Junior Alabama pageant in which Rose was a contestant.

"No, darlin'," answered Beulah. "But don't you fret. Stand up there proud and bring home that crown, and he'll show you how proud he is. He loves you—he just don't know how to show it, that's all. It's what I been tellin' you all along now."

Beulah squeezed Rose's hand and the two of them leaned into each other before Rose stood and took to the stage with the other finalists.

Rose was born on October 1, 1935, into abject poverty. She was the only daughter of Cleotus Barstol and Beulah Rose Barstol, Depression-era farmers living in a shack outside of Muscle Shoals, Alabama; Rose never knew indoor plumbing until she began school.

School was Rose's sanctuary. She was a voracious reader of anything and everything that gave her hope—hope of living someplace other than where she lived, hope of being someone other than who she was, or more accurately, who she saw herself as.

Beulah had begged Cleo to come to Birmingham and see his only daughter compete for Miss Junior Alabama. First-place money would be enough to pay for two years of college at the University of Alabama. Rose was a beautiful young woman. Attending college was Rose's dream, and it was Beulah's dream for Rose.

Cleo told Rose he'd try to make it, but there was work on the farm, and someone had to make sure it was done. He said you couldn't trust a negra to put in an honest day's work if a white man wasn't around to see to it.

Cleo was an alcoholic and a racist. One could excuse many white Southerners of the day for their attitudes because that's the way it had always been. Over time, though, through living, working, and dying together, attitudes were changing, and racism was fading as more folks, and not just the young, called for an end to segregation. But for Rose's father, Cleo, it was different. His racism was ingrained, and it ran deep; it was a mean, bitter hatred that ate at him. He was, as the apostle Paul described, apostate, beyond redemption. Rose's mother, on the other hand, was a saint, but one stifled by the times. Her life was resigned to tending to her garden, her children, and her husband.

*   *   *

The governor of Alabama took the stage and was asked to read off the names of the finalists and the winner. Rose could hardly focus on what he was saying, she was so nervous. Winning was her only way out. She had dreamed of nothing else for over a year. She was in a fog and only vaguely heard the words she had imagined hearing since the day she learned of the prize money. And then, while not quite comprehending what was happening, the other girls were crowding around and congratulating her.

"And the winner, and this year's Miss Junior Alabama, from Muscle Shoals, is Miss Rose Barstol."

She saw her mother in the audience, and they both began to cry. This was her chance, her chance to escape, her opportunity to escape the nightmare. They both knew it.

*   *   *

The first time Rose's older brother Hank raped her she hid in the barn. Ashamed to show her face, she stayed through the night. Her mother was worried sick when she wasn't at the breakfast table the next morning, but her father showed no concern. Later that morning, he saw Hank passed out in his car parked behind the small shack he lived in on the back end of Cleo's farm. Shortly thereafter, he saw Rose lying behind a bale of hay, sobbing. Rose tried to tell her father what had happened. That was the first but not the last time he struck her. Never in the face, where it might be visible to others; always to the body.

Cleo didn't understand why a woman wanted to attend college. He made no secret of the fact that he had wanted another son, and he never once expressed any love for Rose. It'd be hard to know what left the deeper scars, the beatings or her father's total disinterest in her as a person. Rose wanted to get as far away as possible, and for the time being, going to college in Tuscaloosa was it.

CHAPTER 6

Storm Clouds Gathering

THE UNIVERSITY OF ALABAMA; AUGUST 1953

It was a bright, clear day, a day full of promise, just five months after Rose had won the Miss Junior Alabama pageant. Despite the heat and the season, a slight breeze kept the weight of the humidity at bay. Rose, standing at the bottom of the stairs leading up to the women's dormitory, imagined all that awaited her. Rose had received mail earlier that summer from the university describing freshman orientation, and she had counted the days until it was time to leave home.

At the breakfast table earlier that day, she wept along with her mother. Her father, to the surprise of neither, left before sunup. Her older brother Hank, to her great relief, had not been around for some time, so Beulah and Rose sat across from each other at the kitchen table and laughed and cried.

Beulah was a strong woman of above-average height. She had long brown hair that she kept in a bun, but this morning it was still hanging down past her shoulders. Her soft smile emanated more from the crinkle in her eyes and tilt of her head than from the upturned corners of her mouth. It was easy to see that as a younger woman she had been quite beautiful. The many hours outdoors, stooped low and tilling the soil, however, had aged her. She did not complain, though. She enjoyed the work and felt most alive in her garden.

Beulah was the daughter of a circuit pastor who preached at several Methodist churches in Colbert County, along the Tennessee River. Her father was a humble man who preached the gospel, but a gospel filled with a healthy dose of fire and brimstone. She was taught to read sheet music and play the piano by her mother, who traveled with her father, providing the music for church services and tent revivals.

Beulah was a faithful member of the First Baptist Church down the road and had taught Sunday school to most of the children in the area for as long as anyone could remember.

Though times were hard, she provided a few creature comforts for herself and her daughter. Nevertheless, she knew there were only two things in this world she could give her children. She could bring them into the world, and she could tell them about Jesus. Beyond that, she relied upon prayer and the Lord's good graces.

That morning she had given her daughter a Bible and a purse filled with cosmetics and some hard-earned money.

"Mother, I couldn't! Where did you get it?" asked Rose. "Momma, if you took that money from Daddy's desk, you know he'll miss it."

"Don't you worry about that. I know where he keeps a stash of money. By the time he misses it, you'll be long gone. He won't be able to put two and two together, and he'll likely think one of the help stole from him."

Rose and her mother sat together that morning until it was time for her to leave for the bus. Beulah cried tears of joy as her only daughter walked out of the house, carrying both of their hopes and dreams with her.

* * *

"Ma'am, may I help you with your bag?"

In front of Rose stood a young man with his hands in his back pockets and his right foot resting on the first step of the dormitory entrance. The sun was at his back, and with a bag in each hand, Rose couldn't guard her eyes but instead just squinted. "Excuse me?"

"Your bags, ma'am. We're here to help with orientation. It's the only day men are allowed in the women's dorm, to help with move-in, or at least that's what they'll tell ya tonight when you meet your RA," he said with a roguish smile.

"RA?"

"Your resident advisor. Don't worry, it seems a bit overwhelming at first, but you'll do fine."

Rose stared at the man, seeing in him something dark but strangely familiar. Breaking the silence, he announced, "My name is Rath."

"Rath? That's a peculiar name. I don't think I've ever heard it before."

"It's short for Rathbone, my granddaddy's name, but everybody just calls me Rath." Then Rath slid closer and took the bags from her hands. "And what should I call you?"

He was standing close, too close, and she smelled alcohol on his breath, yet she was taken by his dark eyes and calm southern swagger. He was tall and lean, sinewy even. His forearms rippled as his large hands gripped the handles of her suitcases. She quietly answered. "My name is Rose. I'm from Muscle Shoals."

"Well, 'Rose from Muscle Shoals,' let's get you moved in."

The two of them started up the stairs, and Rose noticed the weather was changing as a dark cloud moved across the sun. A storm was coming.

*   *   *

At first, college was everything Rose had hoped for, and she had never been happier. When she wasn't in the classroom, she could be found in the library where she took a job earning extra money to pay for textbooks and the last two years of college. The time she spent didn't seem like work, though, for she simply loved books.

As a young girl, she rarely had been without a book in her hands. At the age of ten, she read Margaret Mitchell's *Gone with the Wind* in a single weekend and since then had read it countless times over. Southern literature was her favorite, and while she was familiar with the works of William Faulkner and Tennessee Williams, she was growing more excited about a new batch of southern writers like Truman Capote and Flannery O'Connor. She dreamed of becoming an English professor and maybe a writer herself.

But books were her crutch, and by keeping her nose buried in one, she avoided contact with others. She joined a sorority, and for the first time in her life, enjoyed the company of girls her own age. But Rose was uncomfortable at large social gatherings. Despite her beauty, she was embarrassed in sorority settings because her clothes were shabby and plain at best. Ashamed of the extreme poverty she came from, she feared attracting any attention.

When it came to boys, she was utterly out of sorts, not knowing what to do or say. She attracted more than her share of attention, however, and her sorority sisters were jealous. Whenever she was in the room, the boys were drawn to her. But Rose was envious of her sisters because they were comfortable around boys, and she was not.

She certainly liked boys and very much wanted a beau, someone who would pick her up at the sorority house and take her out. Someone who would court her and make her feel special. Someone who would love her and protect her. But deep inside, she did not feel special or worthy of such attention, of being loved. She'd see a boy's eyes linger on her, and she'd remember her brother's hot, stale, alcohol-tinged breath burning her neck. She'd imagine a boy wanting to talk to her, and then Rose remembered her father's loathing and wonder why any boy would spend time with her.

When she closed her eyes, she recalled his words she had overheard.

"Woman, is she stupid or somethin'? She just sits off by herself with her ugly face shoved in a book."

"Now, Cleo, don't say such things. She's not stupid. No, not at all. She's very bright, and she loves to read. Reading gives her hope, hope of a better life," said Beulah.

"Better life! What's wrong with what we got? I work my fingers to the bone, and I only got Hank to help on the farm. You can handle the gardening on your own, so what good is she?"

"Cleo, stop it. She's your daughter."

"Beulah, she's your daughter. I got no time for her."

One night at a sorority open house, Rose stood in the corner, speaking with a girl from one of her classes, when the other girl remarked that a handsome young man was coming their way. Rose looked up and smiled nervously as the boy approached.

"Hello, 'Rose from Muscle Shoals.' How ya been?"

"It's Rathbone, isn't it?" asked Rose nervously. The other girl, seeing that Rose knew the handsome young man, quietly slipped away.

"Rath, if you don't mind."

"Oh, that's right. Rathbone is your father's name, right?"

"Close enough. I see you're drinking the punch they serve here. How would you like something a little stronger?"

The smell of alcohol seeped from his pores like steam from a carcass and awakened dark memories she'd tried to put down.

"I don't think so," she said as she ducked under his arm and stepped away.

"Now that's no way to treat a man that's courtin' ya," he said as he grabbed her shoulder and spun her around.

When Rose's glare met his, she didn't see a gentleman caller but Hank. Fear and feelings of helplessness rose up, overwhelming her. Stifling a scream, she freed herself from his grip and ran from the house.

The other girls stared in mock disbelief, laughing behind their hands as they whispered about the poor little girl from the backwoods. Rose felt their stares and condemnation as she fled, vowing never to return.

So Rose withdrew, and over time she was spoken of mockingly as the shy girl from the sticks who could be seen wandering through the rows of library bookshelves. She committed herself to her studies and grew more determined each day to rise up from her impoverished beginnings, finish college, make something of herself, and prove to everyone that she was better than her upbringing, better than them.

CHAPTER 7

Storm Clouds Open

THE UNIVERSITY OF ALABAMA; FALL 1953

A dark cloud had settled over the campus. The body of a young girl last seen leaving a party two weeks prior had washed up three miles down the river adjacent to campus. Everyone was on high alert, and the men on campus, boys really, were stationed across the grounds escorting girls on their way home from nights at the library, late classes, and Greek functions.

"Rosebud, you know you shouldn't be walking home alone," Rath said. "Let me escort you back to your dorm."

He was patient. He was drawn to Rose. She had something he wanted. Rath went out of his way to speak to her. When she had her library hours, he would stop in and pretend he was there to study. Following their encounter at the sorority house, Rath was on his best behavior whenever he was around Rose. His persistence won out, and he began walking her home on a nightly basis.

Rose looked forward to his library visits. She heard the rumors and had seen him talking with plenty of other girls. Still, when he asked her to a fraternity social, she was over the moon and dismissed the stories as the idle gossip of jealous girls.

He was the perfect gentleman that evening, and from then on, they were a couple. The shy girl from the backwoods had a beau and a handsome one at that. She hoped her sorority sisters noticed and were jealous. Inside, though, she wondered how long it would last. She couldn't shake the feeling that one day he would cease to find her desirable, that one day he would abandon her.

Rath came from money, and this impressed Rose. He drove a convertible and always had cash in his pocket as he played the part of the big spender. Rath invited Rose to Mobile for a weekend with a few of his buddies and their girlfriends. The other girls were seniors from wealthy Birmingham families. Rose wanted to make a good impression; she felt these were the sort of people she should associate with. Rath offered to pay for the weekend, and she was thrilled; she had never seen the ocean. But when Rath refused to pay for a second room, Rose wavered. Rath pressed for an answer, the weekend was nearing, and Rose, knowing she couldn't afford the trip on her own, held out hope he would pay for a second room.

Rose wasn't ready. She knew other girls were having sex with their boyfriends, but they were typically seniors and engaged to be married. Rose wasn't a virgin and was ashamed. She harbored guilt, believing she was at fault. She felt dirty. Unlike most of the girls she met, she didn't even like talking about sex. She had never told anyone what her brother had done and didn't know how she could. She figured that on her honeymoon, if her husband questioned whether she was a virgin, she'd tell him that the damage had been done while she was horseback riding.

Rose desperately wanted to wait for marriage, though. But at the risk of losing her boyfriend? She liked having a boyfriend. Having a "steady" made her feel older, more worldly. It made Rose feel valued.

It was a Friday night in early November, and the weather had turned cold. Rath took Rose to dinner and a movie in town. At dinner, he talked about the upcoming weekend in Mobile and all the great places he knew to go, but Rose kept changing the subject. On the way back to her dorm after the movie, instead of stopping off at his favorite pool hall, Rath led Rose on a detour along the Black Warrior River, where earlier in the day he had hidden a sleeping bag. Now that they were alone, he pressed his case.

"You want your own room? But Rosebud, the others are all game. What gives?"

"Rath, you know how much I like you, but I keep telling you it's not the right time," said Rose.

"Not the right time? Well, if it ain't the right time, when will the right time be?"

Knowing what he had to do, he looked at Rose and uttered the words she had convinced herself were all she needed to hear.

"Rose, I love you. You know you're the girl for me."

"You love me?" pleaded Rose.

"Yes. So why won't you let me show you how much I love you?"

Rose wanted nothing more than to believe that a man could love her, could really and truly love her, and here was a man professing what she had longed to hear. How could she say no? How could she risk losing him? She was sure that with this man loving her, she would appear to all as valuable and worthy.

So she closed her eyes and tried to push away the demons; she tried to forget and give herself over. But forgetting who you are—or rather who you've been told you are for all these years—takes more than a night of sex in a sleeping bag under the stars with a gambling drunk who had just won a bet with the other guys heading to Mobile for a weekend.

*   *   *

Rose accompanied Rath as his girlfriend on the weekend trip to Mobile. She shared a bed with Rath but her inexperience made it difficult for her to process his actions. Did all men seem so self-absorbed during sex? She tried to enjoy it and managed to convince herself that she did even if she felt strangely detached throughout.

But she was genuinely thrilled to be accepted by the older girls, girls from wealthy, prominent families. Upon their return to campus, Rose clung to Rath for dear life. As long as they were a couple, she could keep her thoughts and fears at bay. He said he loved her, and she believed him. She had to— believing anything else was too painful.

At first, all was good. Rose excelled in school and had a date for football games and sorority functions. But cracks appeared when Rose pressed Rath on his post-graduation plans. She would ask Rath about his classes, and he'd laugh it off and joke about how he was breezing through. As his number of unexplained absences grew, Rose's suspicions mounted. She often smelled alcohol on his breath in the middle of the day, in the middle of the week. Over time, Rath lost his patience when Rose pressed him to explain his whereabouts.

"Who the hell do you think you are?" he'd yell. "I already got me a daddy. I don't need you harpin' on me too."

"But Rath, what are we going to do when we graduate? You're a junior. Graduation will be here before you know it. Have you thought about a job or a career?" she would ask.

"Plans! Rosebud, wait till you hear my latest idea. I'm gonna be a millionaire by the time I'm thirty."

Rose was beginning to see his talk as more delusional than realistic and would try to bring him back around to a more sensible plan.

"What about the job your older brother offered you?"

"FUCK HIM," screamed Rath.

Rath's older brother was the apple of his father's eye and doing exceptionally well.

"What, ain't I good enough for ya? What about my dreams? Daddy's money will set us up just fine until I get going."

"Of course you're good enough, Rath. Of course you are," pleaded Rose.

Rose came to notice in Rath a temper lurking beneath the surface. With his fuse as dry as kindling, the slightest insult could ignite it. And then there was the drinking. Because Rath and all his friends drank, Rose drank. Not much at first, just enough to fit in. But then she found it was easier to be with Rath if she drank more. The sex was not as gentle as the first time, and he was more and more demanding.

Fearful of losing her boyfriend and the association with the Birmingham families, she drank more, not just to fit in but also to dull the pain. She'd seen Rath with other women and knew of the rumors about his gambling debts. She pushed them aside, choosing to believe the version of Rath that set her free from her demons. But she did so at great personal cost.

Her grades slipped, and as her first year of college was ending, she weighed the social advantages of Rath as a boyfriend against the risks and began to doubt the wisdom of staying with Rath.

But then everything changed.

"Rath, I have to speak to you."

"Can't it wait, Rosebud? I'm late for an important meeting."

"Don't tell me about some meeting. I know you spend your time at the pool hall."

"So what if I do? You're smart enough for the both of us," said Rath, wearing his roguish smile, a smile Rose had grown weary of. "Look, if this is about me coming home with you this summer and working for your daddy, I already told ya, I have a job in Mobile. We'll just have to write. Don't you worry, though—I'll be here when the next semester starts."

"Rath, I'm pregnant."

CHAPTER 8

The Sun Breaks Through

Rose and Rath married quickly. Rath's parents were mortified, but being good Methodists, they would never encourage Rath to shirk his responsibilities. Rath, however, took some persuading. Rath's father did the persuading when he threatened to cut Rath off financially if he did not walk Rose down the aisle.

It wasn't the storybook wedding Rose had imagined as a young girl, but it was a wedding, nonetheless. Cleo and Beulah, as poor as they were, had no visible means of footing the bill. Actually, Cleo had more than enough cash hidden away, but once Rath's father had offered to pay for the wedding and the reception, Cleo kept his mouth shut. There would be no honeymoon. No one knew what Beulah threatened Cleo with, but he played his part and dutifully walked Rose down the aisle.

When Rose and Rath returned to the University of Alabama in the fall, she was four months pregnant. Although married, Rose's condition, in the minds of her sorority sisters, disqualified her from sorority membership, and she was told to leave. That was just as well since the dues hardly fit their budget.

Rath and Rose moved into an apartment that Rath's parents agreed to pay for as long as they were in school. Rose needed no such incentive to stay in school but was happy for the help. The baby was due in March. She would finish her fall classes but completing the spring semester was out of the question. On top of that, her mother asked how she planned to care for a baby and attend classes come next fall. Rose didn't have the answers, but she was determined to not only stay in school but also graduate with honors.

Rose returned to the University of Alabama as Mrs. Rathbone Cummings, fully committed to the classroom and her job at the library. Rath, however, committed himself fully to the pool hall.

For most men, becoming a husband and father so quickly would have a sobering effect, but not for Rath. Life had been too easy. He had been admitted to college on a baseball scholarship, but he squandered that opportunity when he continually mouthed off to the coach. Rath was a natural at all sports, but he was not good enough to get by on talent alone. He'd have to work at it, but Rath was averse to work.

He had grown up fed by a silver spoon but owing to his father's long absences from the home, he grew up without discipline. His mother hadn't known what to do with him. As he did with most women he encountered, he charmed her too. So he limped by on talent, good looks, charm, and his family's money. But in his gut, comparisons to his father and older brother ate at him and served as a continual reminder that he just wasn't good enough.

The love of a strong mother would have helped bolster his self-confidence, but Rath was raised by the help. Some said it was for the best since, by early afternoon, his mother was typically on her third cocktail.

At first, Rath tried to be a good husband and even attended his college classes, but it didn't take. Rath had a wild streak, and Rose's efforts to keep him close to home backfired. He stayed away from the apartment more and more, and when he was home, he was aloof and usually had a drink in his hand. They spent Thanksgiving with Rath's family, and Rath's father let it be known that he expected Rath to clean up his act and prepare to step into the family business.

Recrimination from his father pushed him over the edge, and not too long after their return from the Thanksgiving break, he disappeared. Rose's desperate phone calls to Rath's friends turned him up in a jail in Mobile. His arrest had broken up a barroom fight and likely saved his life. It seems that Rath owed the wrong sort of people a substantial gambling debt, and if they couldn't extract the money they were owed, then they'd exact retribution some other way.

*   *   *

Rose didn't know what to do. She had no money and couldn't face her father were she to run home. She drove to Mobile and retrieved Rath. He promised to change. A week later, he stumbled home after midnight and found her waiting up for him, and he hit her. She was gone the next morning.

Desperate and not knowing what to do, she remembered the words to the first song her mother had taught her to sing. "Jesus loves me, this I know, for the Bible tells me so." Rose drove to a church not knowing if anyone would be there so early on a Thursday morning, and was comforted to find the chapel open. The weather was crisp, and the sky was blue. She was scared and lonely and stood outside for several minutes before entering the church.

She sat toward the back and wept. Her mother had told her since she was a young girl that the Lord loved her; but with a father who made it clear he did not, Rose wondered how any man could love her. And since God was a man in her understanding of the Bible, well then, where did that leave her? She was sure she was being punished for something, so she wept, and prayed, and wept some more. Not knowing what to ask for, other than forgiveness, and not understanding God's capacity for forgiveness, Rose bargained for it and promised to do better.

Rose sat in the pew for quite some time, though she would have been hard-pressed to tell you how long. No one else had entered since she arrived, and then she heard a noise coming from the back of the chapel. A young man entered, not expecting to see anyone. Rose looked up over her shoulder and saw a man about her age. The first thing she noticed about him was his eyes; they were kind.

"Oh, excuse me, ma'am. I'm sorry to disturb you." The young man, a student at the university, attended the church and volunteered his time cutting the grass once a week. Glancing at him, you wouldn't notice anything special about his appearance. Of average height and build, clean-cut and with dark hair, the young man was handsome in a comforting way.

Red-faced from crying and a bit embarrassed, Rose responded, "Oh, that's quite all right. I'm about to leave."

"Well, please don't leave on my account." The young man took a step closer, and that's when he noticed she had been crying.

"Ma'am, are you all right?"

He took another step and saw the bruise on her face. "Who did this to you?" he asked with quiet determination.

Rose, embarrassed, turned her head to the side and tried to cover her face.

Visibly concerned, the young man took a seat beside her and repeated, "Who did this to you?"

"It's no one. I'm okay. But thank you for your kindness. I'll be leaving now." Rose stood, exited the pew, and started down the center aisle.

"Can I drive you somewhere?"

"No, thank you," said Rose. "That won't be necessary."

And then she hesitated and looked back at the young man with the kind eyes. "May I ask your name?" she asked.

"Of course. My name is Montgomery Atkins, but everyone just calls me Monty."

CHAPTER 9

Choices

Rose attended church the following Sunday, her first Sunday services in over a year. Earlier that week, she had moved into a hotel with what little money she had, intent on finishing the semester before heading home for Christmas break. She returned to the church in search of what she had found on her previous visit, a calming of her spirit, and Monty. She slid into one of the back pews as the service was beginning. It didn't take her long to find Monty. He was singing in the choir.

After services ended, the two of them met on the patio, where the rest of the congregation was sharing coffee and donuts. As the crowd dwindled and most folks set off to have lunch with their families, Monty and Rose, with no place to go, spent another two hours together at a local diner. Rose told Monty her story, and Monty listened. She walked out of the restaurant that day knowing that this was the first time any man had ever listened to her. Rose was married and certainly in no condition to start up with a new boyfriend, but she was smitten. And Monty? Well, he was too.

They saw each other as much as possible, but final exams were only two weeks away, and then they would break for Christmas. While at home, she thought long and hard about what lay ahead. She was six months pregnant, married to a drunk who hadn't contacted her since she had left their apartment in the middle of the night, and with no visible means of support short of returning home and admitting defeat to her father. There were two bright spots, however. First, the classroom. One of her professors was encouraging her to pursue a teaching career and said he saw her as a college professor one day. Second, Monty.

She returned to school, still lacking the means to pay for two more years of college but not ready to give up. She approached the university and asked if she could take the spring semester off and apply the balance of her scholarship to the upcoming fall semester. She hoped to make enough money in the spring and summer to pay for another year of college. The school obliged. A family at the church let her stay in their spare room in exchange for tutoring their children. A member of the choir, who was a friend of Monty's, was a lawyer, and he helped her file for a divorce. Rath did not contest.

Things were looking up. She was a soon-to-be-single mother, but her dream of graduating from college was still alive, even if only by a thread.

*   *   *

The last six weeks of her pregnancy had been difficult, and she was placed on bed rest. Rose gave birth to a healthy baby boy on March 17, 1955. She named her son Elijah Mitchell, Elijah, after her grandfather on her mother's side, and Mitchell after Margaret Mitchell, the author of her favorite book, *Gone with the Wind*.

Monty visited her regularly and was sitting in the waiting room with the other expectant fathers when Eli entered the world. Rose was flattered but couldn't understand it. Why would any twenty-two-year-old man with plenty of prospects pay so much attention to a single mother? But he did, and when Monty first set eyes on baby Eli, they both just beamed, and mother gently cried tears of joy.

Monty talked to Rose about his plans for after college, and he was curious about hers. He saw her as part of his future and hoped she felt the same way about him. Finally, one night, Monty got down on one knee. "Rose, I love you. Will you marry me?"

Rose was not surprised by the question.

"Oh, Monty. You are the best thing to have happened to me, I want you to know that. But no, I won't marry you. I want to finish college and become a professor. You're looking for a wife, and you're going to be busy putting yourself through law school. Now how is that going to work?"

"But who will take care of little Eli when you return to school?"

Rose explained that by the time fall classes began, Eli would be old enough to be left in the daily church nursery.

Monty spent the rest of the evening trying to talk sense into Rose, as he saw it. She wouldn't budge.

Monty was hurt and didn't know where to go from there. He loved her but understood she needed to love him and not marry him as a solution to her problems. They saw less and less of each other. Rose attended his graduation, and they said goodbye to each other.

Rose loved Monty, or at least she thought she did, but in the wake of Rath, Rose was gun-shy on the topic of marriage. She knew one thing, though. She wasn't going to let a man hold her back again.

CHAPTER 10

Doors Shutting, Windows Opening

ATLANTA, GEORGIA; NOVEMBER 1957

In the fall of 1955 when Rose returned to Tuscaloosa, she had counted on her scholarship to cover the cost of the new semester. Despite assurances from the university that she could resume classes in the fall, it didn't work out. The state of Alabama learned of her divorce and her child and felt that funding her education was not in keeping with the ideals of the Miss Junior Alabama Pageant. They rescinded the scholarship. The University of Alabama said she could attend all the classes she wanted but not as an enrolled student.

Her situation appeared hopeless. Unless enrolled, she couldn't accumulate credits and graduate. She had saved, but not enough. Her father refused to help. She couldn't go home. Not again.

Job prospects in Tuscaloosa were few, and Birmingham was not far enough away from home. An older woman at the church in Tuscaloosa where Rose and Monty first met, one of several who had befriended her, said she had a cousin in Atlanta who would take her in until she got on her feet.

So in the fall of 1955, instead of returning to school, Rose, with Eli in tow, moved to Atlanta. She found a job with Coca-Cola. The woman she moved in with took her to church, and as in Tuscaloosa, the Lord provided. A network of grandmothers from the church helped with Eli, and after a year, she had saved enough money to start night classes at Emory University in Atlanta.

But Rose was exhausted, sick more often than not, poor, destitute, and with few prospects. Her two years in Atlanta had been difficult. Nevertheless, she pressed on, determined to better herself and prove to her father and to everyone back home that she was worthy, better than them. But then there was Eli, angry all the time. Rose saw little of him, and he was passed continuously from one babysitter to another. He misbehaved, screamed ceaselessly from his crib, and was developing a horrible temper. At night, she would hold him while he wailed and slammed his fists into her until he wore himself out, eventually falling asleep in her arms.

Rose was scared for Eli, and if truth be told, she was scared for herself. She'd changed. She was not the same person who'd left Tuscaloosa two years earlier. When she looked in the mirror, she did not see the young, vibrant winner of Miss Junior Alabama, the young girl full of hope. No, she saw a prematurely aged woman burdened by a fatherless child and dwindling expectations. She'd grown bitter, and her heart was hardening. She was short with people, especially those lending her a hand.

One night when she was picking Eli up from the house of one of the church grandmothers, the woman asked her inside for a moment. Rose resisted, insisting that she was tired and needed to get Eli to bed.

"Now child, you need to set with me a spell because I have some questions you need asking."

The woman, named Odell, was small in stature but considerable in influence and was loved and respected by all. She hadn't changed her hairstyle since her late husband died twenty years earlier. She was barely over five-foot-five inches tall and shrinking by the day. Quiet and humble by nature, she did boast that she still sewed her own clothes, but arthritis in her hands was taking its toll. The pastor defined her as wisdom itself, and she was willing to help everyone who crossed her path but rarely pushed herself on anyone. She made an exception, though, and pushed herself on Rose for as she saw it, not only had Rose come across her path, but she'd stayed.

"Rose, my dear, you look like you could use some unburdening. Why do you put on airs so?"

"Put on airs? I don't know what you're talking about," replied Rose, taken aback by Odell's forwardness.

"Honey, you need help, and you sure do take it, but you won't get down off that ladder you've climbed to truly thank anyone."

"Is that it? I haven't said thank you enough? Well, excuse me, but between my job at Coca-Cola, attending college, and raising a boy by myself, I guess sometimes I'm too tired to bow down and say thank you enough for your liking." Rose's voice was rising and sharp as it oozed condemnation.

"Rose, us ladies down at the church know all about your job at Coca-Cola and you attending college. How could we not? You like to remind everybody whenever you can. We just didn't know you was tryin' to raise a child too." From anyone else, Odell's challenge would have been dismissed as the sarcastic backtalk of an old woman, but coming from her, it cut to the marrow, as the truth often does.

Rose was stunned and did not know what to say. Tears welled up and slowly streamed down her face. Months of exhaustion burst through. "I'm just so scared. I don't know what to do."

Odell stood from her rocking chair, sat down next to Rose, and gently drew Rose's head onto her shoulder. "Now, child, don't you forget. Jesus loves you, and so do I."

Rose cried even harder. She recalled her own mother saying the same thing. Rose missed her mother terribly but could only afford one phone call a month, and even then, for only a few minutes.

"Odell, no, I don't think He does. He's forgotten me. He ignores me."

"So, you believe the good Lord has forgotten you?"

"Yes. Every time I think I see the Lord answering my prayers, every time I think I see the Lord providing, it all falls apart."

"Well, maybe He's providing what *you* want, but not what you need. Maybe the fruit you want isn't what you need, and He's allowing you to taste it for yourself. Maybe He's waiting for you to come around and start praying that He would show you *His* way."

Rose sobbed even harder as Odell's words took hold, and then after a few minutes, a calm descended over her and the room.

"Sounds to me like the good Lord is actually quite involved in your life. Now, why else would He go to all this trouble?" asked Odell, her arms tight around Rose.

"Because He loves me?"

"That's right, child, because He loves you."

*   *   *

COLUMBIA, SOUTH CAROLINA; NOVEMBER 1957

After graduating from the University of Alabama, Monty moved back to Columbia and began law school at the University of South Carolina. He took a part-time job with a contractor to help pay his expenses and taught himself how to read blueprints and prepare material and labor estimates.

He hadn't forgotten Rose and heard from friends at the church in Tuscaloosa that she had moved to Atlanta. He wrote to her twice. She answered the first letter.

Monty, how wonderful to receive your letter. I'm so happy for you that law school is going well. As you now know, I left Alabama, but I am delighted to be here in Atlanta. I have a wonderful job at Coca-Cola that pays well. I am saving enough money to start college classes at Emory next year. Eli is a joy and has adapted very well. I have help watching him during the day, and he just loves everyone. Please take care. Fondly, Rose.

His second letter went unanswered.

Monty was planning a road trip to Atlanta with some fellow Alabama alums with whom he attended law school. Alabama was playing Georgia Tech in football. Georgia Tech was coached by the legendary Bobby Dodd, who had last led Tech to a national championship in 1952. Of all of Alabama's Southeastern Conference foes, Georgia Tech was the team Monty most wanted to beat. But Alabama was struggling under Head Coach Jennings Whitworth, and while it was only his third season, rumor had it that it would be his last. There was a young coach at Texas A&M with ties to Alabama whom the school had its sights on.

As the weekend trip approached, Monty decided he'd take a chance and write Rose one more time.

*   *   *

Rose and Eli slept over at Odell's house that night, and the two women talked late into the evening. The next day was Saturday, and Rose was planning a morning at the park with Eli before dropping him off with one of the church grandmothers while she spent the afternoon and evening at the library. She decided instead to accept Odell's invitation to dinner Saturday night.

The day at the park with Eli was terrific. It was a beautiful fall day. The leaves had changed, and the air was crisp and clean. Eli had slept the night before better than he had in weeks. Her time with Odell had been extraordinary. She felt charged and alive, but calm just the same. She was still poor, but for the first time in a long time, when she woke up, she wasn't angry.

Upon returning home from the park that afternoon, she retrieved the mail. Her heart fluttered as she held in her hand a letter from Monty.

"Rose, I hope this letter finds you well. I certainly enjoyed hearing from you last fall when I wrote. I must tell you, I was disappointed when my second letter went unanswered. Maybe you have a boyfriend! I wouldn't be surprised. I know you must be busy working and attending school and, of course, raising Eli. How is Eli? Well, the reason I'm writing is that I'm coming to Atlanta in a few weeks for the Alabama vs. Tech football game, and I'd love to see you. Your friend always, Monty."

Rose could hardly believe it. Maybe Odell was right. The Lord truly worked in mysterious ways. She couldn't wait to share the news with Odell.

*   *   *

Rose wrote Monty back and told him she would love to get together. But she was embarrassed about her living conditions, so meeting at her apartment was out of the question. She suggested they meet at the Varsity. The Varsity was a favorite hangout for Tech students, but since kickoff wasn't until 6:00, Rose wrote that they could have lunch and avoid the large crowds of Tech fans who would show up before game time.

Rose took the bus to midtown and was let off just a few blocks away. She was almost ten minutes late. She wanted to be a few minutes late, not wanting to look too eager, but ten minutes late scared her. What if he had arrived and left? She quickened her pace.

Rose walked into the Varsity, looked around, but didn't see him. Momentary panic. Then remembering that the Varsity was famous for its carhop service, she stepped outside and scanned the parking lot. She saw him standing next to his car, three rows back, shielding his eyes from the sun and scanning the parking lot. Their eyes met, and he broke into a big smile. He approached her, slowly at first and then more quickly, arms outstretched, and he took her hands in his. They just stood there for a moment. She remembered his kind eyes, and right then she couldn't imagine why she had said no to his marriage proposal.

They were sitting in his car, each not knowing quite what to say when they were interrupted by a carhop.

"What'll ya have?"

Three hours later, they were still seated in Monty's car. They spoke unhurriedly, but the time flew by. The parking lot was filling up with game-time traffic. Rose didn't want the day to end. Monty suggested that they meet in the morning before he drove back to Columbia. He wanted to see Eli. There'd be no hiding it. Rose was proud and didn't want Monty to see where she lived, but she was too tired to care anymore.

"Yes, Monty. I'd like that."

Georgia Tech won 10-7 on a late field goal. Another disappointing season was shaping up for Alabama, but Monty's disappointment was tempered with thoughts of Rose. He knew he was still in love with her.

*　　*　　*

Rose tried her best to spiff the place up, but there was only so much she could do. Eli wasn't making things any easier. He was cranky and wouldn't stop crying. She almost broke into tears but held herself together; she wanted to look her best, and red-faced and puffy-eyed wasn't her best.

Monty arrived right on time. He wasn't sure he had the right address as he approached the apartment complex. Monty sat in his car for a few minutes, double-checking his bearings. Well, either he'd written the address down incorrectly or he'd better brace himself. The stench of urine followed him as he passed through the stairwell on his way to the second floor.

He slumped against the railing with his back to the parking lot and stared at the door marked B-216, wondering if he'd made a mistake in coming, when he heard a baby crying inside. It was Eli. He raised himself off the railing, stood tall, and knocked on the door.

She opened the door slowly with Eli on her hip and stepped aside so he could enter. Eli was still crying. Monty reached out and gently but firmly took the boy from Rose. Eli stared into Monty's eyes and stopped crying; there was a small, barely perceptible smile on his face. Rose couldn't hold the tears back any longer.

*　　*　　*

Monty visited Rose the next two weekends, making the drive down from

Columbia after his last Friday class. He invited Rose and Eli to spend Thanksgiving with his family. She happily accepted. Monty pressed her to move to Columbia while he finished law school, but Rose wanted to finish the semester at Emory. She was protective of every college credit she had earned, for they had come at such an extraordinary personal cost.

So it was agreed. Rose and Eli would return to Atlanta, and when she finished the semester, she would move to Columbia in time to spend Christmas with Monty and his family. Rose wrote to her mother about the news.

Dear Mother,

I'm writing to tell you that I am moving to Columbia, South Carolina. My move to Atlanta has not worked out the way I had hoped. I have no money and live in horrible conditions. I can't finish school, keep a job, and continue to raise Eli. It hasn't been well with Eli. He cries all the time. I'm afraid that passing him from sitter to sitter all this time and the absence of a father have permanently affected him. I feel at such a loss and like such a failure. I was so hoping to make you proud by graduating from college and becoming a professor.

I met a man, a kind man. Actually, I met him while I was in Tuscaloosa shortly after I left Rath. I may have mentioned him to you the last time I was home. His name is Monty. Well, Monty has reappeared. He loves me, Momma, and I may love him too. I'll be moving in with his parents until I find a job and can afford a place of my own. I'll write when I get settled. I have enclosed a picture of Monty and Eli together. It will be nice for Eli to have a man around.

Your loving daughter,

Rose

Rose packed up and boarded a bus to Columbia on December 18, 1957. She was excited about her future; it certainly appeared more promising than what lay in store if she stayed in Atlanta. But despite it all, Rose couldn't shake the feeling that she had failed. She couldn't let go of those haunting words: "Beulah, she's your daughter. I got no time for her."

*   *   *

Monty and Rose were married on June 9, 1958, in Columbia, South Carolina in the small church Monty grew up attending. Monty adopted Eli immediately. A year later, after Monty graduated from law school, he took a job as an associate attorney in Charleston, South Carolina. Rose found herself moving again. She'd kept busy while in Columbia, working various part-time jobs and raising Eli, but she was no closer to a college degree. In her mind, Monty just didn't understand why it was so important to her. Monty felt Eli needed his mother, and he believed that raising children was the noblest calling in the world. Rose verbally agreed with Monty, and she could see the positive changes in Eli since moving to Columbia. While he still possessed a powerful temper, it flared far less often.

But Rose hadn't forgotten her dreams. Of graduating from college. Of proving herself better than her upbringing. No, she hadn't forgotten, and she never forgave. In her heart, she harbored extreme disappointment over never finishing college and it was a disappointment that would fester and become bitterness and resentment. And if asked what kept her from obtaining her dreams, what was the wellspring of Rose's pain, the answer was easy. Her father. Rath. But with her father out of the picture and Rath gone, Eli.

CHAPTER 11

Kiawah Summer Rental

KIAWAH ISLAND, SOUTH CAROLINA; LATE JULY 1969

"An extra week at Kiawah," exclaimed Monty to his empty office. "Hot diggity!"

The rental agent explained that the July renters had suffered a death in their extended family and would leave early, so Monty could take the place beginning the last week of July. The owner of the cottage would even discount the rate if he said yes on the phone. Monty said yes.

This summer, their third at Kiawah, Monty had signed on for the entire month of August, their longest stay to date. Monty felt like a kid, he was so excited. He called Rose and told her to put Eli and Walker to work packing the car. They were headed to the Island.

Kiawah Island was a short forty-five-minute drive from their home, but it seemed like another world. The change of scenery would do the Atkins family good. June had been a tough month at home. Eli was miserable playing baseball with the older boys on the Blue Herons, and his mood soured relations with his little brother, Walker. Eli could compete at the higher level—that wasn't the problem—but he missed his friends. The other boys on the team didn't help matters much. They had never fully embraced him as a teammate, most likely due to jealousy. Eli could hit and field better than anyone else on the team. It came so easily for him.

And Eli loved to play baseball. He looked as if he were born to play America's game. Blond-haired and blue-eyed. Broad-shouldered and taller than most his age, he moved gracefully across the field. And he had great hands, large and powerful, yet capable of subtle dexterity. Nature had smiled on Eli.

Yes, Eli loved baseball, and for him it was a game, pure and simple. Which is why he never understood it when his coach yelled at the players to work harder. Work? Baseball was fun. It wasn't work. But at Eli's age, much of what made the game fun was the time with his friends. Absent this connection, and since the coach had said it was work, he didn't play with the same abandon. Coach Largess told Rose that Eli had natural God-given talent but that he was lazy and content just to get by.

Eli wasn't lazy; he just missed his friends. But for Rose, the coach's words unlocked painful memories.

"After all I did to get you on this team, and this is how you repay me? By loafing? And I did it for you. Ugh. You remind me so much of your father. Lazy. Not caring. Not trying. Just look how you've let me down. I hope the coaches in the league don't think Walker is like you."

To make matters worse for Eli, in the last game of the season, the league championship game, Eli went four-for-four with two home runs and owned center field. His teammates carried him around the bases in celebration of his game-winning line drive in the bottom of the ninth. Monty and Walker met him in the parking lot with high-fives when Eli ran to the car, the trophy held high.

Standing next to the car, stone-faced and arms crossed, Rose snapped, "Why can't you do that every game?" She turned toward the car and waited for Monty to open the door. No one said a word on the ride home.

*   *   *

Walker worshipped his brother Eli. Nearly six years older, Eli—always the best player regardless of the season—took on the stature of a Greek god. Walker reveled in Eli's on-field triumphs, attending every practice and every game. Eli's teammates adopted Walker as their unofficial mascot and welcomed and encouraged him to hang around the practices. When possible, the team would order an extra jersey for eight-year-old Walker, who could be seen wearing the jersey at every game, running up and down the sidelines.

When Walker was old enough to play team sports himself, he set matching Eli's heroics as his goal. There was only one problem; he lacked Eli's natural ability. But Walker was determined to stand out somehow, so he did the one thing his dad told him every coach loved; he became the hardest working player on every team. He arrived early for practice, stayed late, and worked harder than anyone else. He never quit.

This summer, though, marked a turning point for the boys. They were growing apart and Walker couldn't understand why. The first signs of trouble between the boys appeared when Eli was moved up to play with the Blue Herons. As usual, Walker wanted to attend every practice and hang out with Eli and the other boys on the team, but Eli wouldn't have it. He didn't feel welcome on the team and was self-conscious about being both the youngest and best player, so he told Walker to stay away.

Mom's constant praise for Walker was taking its toll as well. Walker won the Hustle Award on his team, and Rose didn't let a day go by without mentioning it. Eli began to resent Walker. Eli grew more isolated, aloof, and sullen, all of which reinforced Rose's conviction that he was lazy, definitely his father's son.

So, with this drama serving as the summer's backdrop, Monty breathed a sigh of relief when they pulled into the driveway of their summer rental. The boys bolted out of the car straight for the beach.

"Dinner's at seven," shouted Dad. "We're cookin' steaks so don't be late."

"We won't," cried Walker as he struggled to keep up with Eli.

"Now look, you can't hang out with me anymore," said Eli.

"Why not?"

"Because."

"Because why?" pleaded Walker.

"Just because. I'm older now. I'm heading into the ninth grade, and I'm too old to be playing pirates and other dumb games."

Walker was staring up at Eli with one hand shielding his eyes from the sun. "But what am I gonna do all summer?"

Eli looked past Walker and made a quick wave to someone down the beach. Walker turned and saw a girl waving back at Eli.

"You'll figure it out. Don't worry. We'll go fishin' later this week, but I gotta run. I may not make dinner, but act like you don't know nothin'. Okay?"

"Okay," said Walker dejectedly.

And with that, Eli took off down the beach and caught up with the girl and a larger group of older kids. As he watched Eli jog down the beach toward the bikini-clad girl, he instinctively knew things would never be the same.

That night at dinner, under the glare of his mother's watchful eye, he swore he did not know where Eli had gone off to.

"I swear, I don't know," pleaded Walker.

"Don't swear, young man. Do you understand me?"

"Yes, Mom. But I still don't know where he is."

"Honey, it's okay." Monty said. "I'm sure he's fine. Probably ran into friends and lost track of the time. Now let's not let it ruin our dinner. I'm starved." Monty cut into his steak and savored the first bite, thinking that everything tasted better at the beach.

"Hey, Son, we've still got some daylight left. Do you want to play catch after dinner and then watch the Braves game?"

"Sure, Dad." Walker worshipped his father and loved it when they played catch. He figured he was getting too old for it but didn't care.

And then his mother took all the joy away. "You are such a wonderful son, Walker. You make your father and me so proud."

Suddenly, he wanted to break something, anything. Every compliment from her was laced with expectations and what he perceived as an unfair comparison to Eli—unfair to Eli, that is.

He still played catch after dinner, but it wasn't the same, and he insisted they move away from the kitchen window so Mom couldn't watch.

Eli didn't come home till after midnight. Walker heard the squeaky back door slowly open, its noise amplified by the lateness of the hour. Rose was waiting in the living room ready to pounce, and even with their hushed tones, Walker knew they were fighting.

*   *   *

The next morning Dad and Eli were sitting at the kitchen table. Walker snuck down the hallway so he could listen in.

"Look, Eli, I understand, believe me, I do."

"No, Dad, really, you don't. She hates me. I don't want to hang out at home or be anywhere around her."

"Son, she loves you. She just doesn't do the best job of showing it. She pushes you because she wants the best for you."

"No. I embarrass her. It doesn't matter what I do. It will never be good enough. Why should I even try?'

"Now, Eli, please..."

"Come on, Dad. Look, I have to go. I'm meeting some friends."

"Okay. Okay. Go. Have fun. I mean it. I'll take care of your mom. You're growing up. I get it. But don't let your mother smell cigarette smoke on you again. Okay? Look, chew some gum, run sunscreen through your hair, and carry a clean shirt in your backpack to change into before coming home. That's what I did when I was your age."

Eli smiled and laughed. "Really? You smoked growing up?"

"Son, you have no idea. Now get out of here."

"Love ya, Dad," shouted Eli as he ran out the side door.

"Love you too, Son."

Walker climbed back into bed, placed his hands behind his head, and broke into a big grin.

CHAPTER 12

Friends, Summer at the Beach & a Naked Girl

Mom and Dad were quiet at breakfast. Walker knew they'd been arguing about Eli. With most of his friends not arriving on Kiawah Island until August, Walker didn't know what to do, but he wasn't going to hang around the house. So with no particular place to go, he headed to the beach with his ball and glove.

Walker was walking down the middle of the road tossing the ball in the air and catching it when he heard a voice yell out.

"Hey, ya wanna play catch?"

Walker looked in the direction of the voice and saw a boy his age running down the front stairs of a cottage two at a time. The house wasn't large, but it looked like a picture—pastel-colored with a hammock on the front porch and a bicycle leaning against the handrail alongside the steps.

"My name is Toby. Toby Robertson. What's your name?"

"Walker," and then because of the boy's formality, he added, "Walker Atkins."

"So, do ya wanna play catch?"

"Sure."

And just like that, Walker and Toby became fast friends the way children do, unencumbered by the fears and expectations that plague adults. That night at dinner, Walker excitedly told everyone about his new friend. Eli had made it for dinner, so Dad was in a great mood.

"He's from New York City. And last summer his whole family went to England. They're moving to Charleston. His dad heard about Kiawah Island, so while he's buying a house in Charleston, they rented a cottage for all of July and August. Mom, you'd love it. It looks like the cover of one of your magazines."

Walker was excited about Toby. He had lived someplace else, and to Walker, a young boy who had never been farther than Atlanta, someplace else, and in particular New York City and England, sounded pretty grand.

"We'd love to meet him. Why don't you have him for dinner one night?" asked Monty.

Rose knew the house they were renting and was instantly curious about the family from New York and quickly embraced the idea. "Why, of course. In fact, why don't we invite the entire family?" asked Rose expectantly.

"Aw, Mom, that'll ruin everything." Why couldn't she just let things be?

The next night, the Robertson clan came to dinner.

*   *   *

Walker, all arms and legs, and Toby, still hanging on to his baby fat, were inseparable. Two eight-year-old boys, shirtless and barefoot, running loose from dawn till dusk. They explored the island from one end to the other on their bikes. Kiawah was still largely undeveloped, and on their daily bike rides, they came across deer, pigs, and the occasional alligator. But the most memorable ride of all occurred late one Friday afternoon.

It was approaching dusk, and Toby, Walker, and a passel of other boys were riding their bikes along a wooded path far away from any homes or streets. They stopped to take a swig from their canteens when the boy at the front of the pack motioned for them to join him. The boys, crouched like he was, moved toward him and, hiding behind bushes, looked in the direction he was pointing.

And there she was, the first naked girl any of them had ever seen, straddling Beau Eastley no less, the star quarterback. His hands were grabbing her breasts, which were more beautiful than anything the boys had imagined, capped with dark brown nipples and swaying in rhythm to her gently rocking hips. Her moaning was intoxicating, and they were mesmerized, speechless. In their excitement, they moved too close and gave themselves away.

"Sweetheart, I think we have company."

Beau saw the boys and yelled at them to scram. He lifted her off him, grabbed a towel, and gestured angrily at them. The boys ran, but Walker stayed. Hiding behind the tree, he gazed at Ella Gaston, the prettiest girl in town, letting his eyes fall, hypnotized by the soft brown tuft of hair at the top of her legs. When Beau and Ella were confident that they were alone again, they resumed. Walker watched until they finished and then snuck away when he was sure he would not be noticed.

The boys returned to that place in the woods throughout the summer but never saw them again. The memory, though, they would carry with them forever.

*   *   *

The days ticked by as the summer advanced, and Eli spent less and less time with the family, routinely skipping dinner. Monty tried to walk an impossible line between siding with both his teenage son and his demanding wife but succeeded only at alienating each of them.

Occasionally, Eli would take Walker and Toby fishing, but Eli had gravitated toward an older crowd. When Walker ran into Eli and his new friends, they'd be drinking, and Eli would shoo Walker away, making him swear not to tell Mom and Dad. Walker would beg Eli to let him have a beer.

"No way, man. Mom would kill us both. She's grooming you to be president. Don't you know that?" Eli's friends would laugh, and Walker, humiliated, would slink away.

The centrical force of Eli's life carried him farther and farther away from the family. Monty wanted nothing more than a cohesive unit, a family who ate dinner together, vacationed together, and did so joyfully. But Eli's life continually collided with Rose's demands. Monty was determined to hold them together, but his efforts succeeded only in pushing each farther away from him and no closer to the other.

From Eli: "Dad, she hates me. Why can't you take my side for once?"

From Rose: "Oh, Monty, if only you knew how your betrayal hurts me so."

And Walker? He observed from the sidelines and committed himself to do what was expected of him, with no expectation that he could ever do what he wanted.

CHAPTER 13

Church, Brunch & Debutantes

JAMES ISLAND, SOUTH CAROLINA; OCTOBER 1972

"Reverend, that was a fine sermon. This church is blessed to have you shepherding us through these difficult times. Not enough churches speak the hard truth these days." Rose enjoyed a sermon steeped in theology, and today Reverend Coker sermonized on Romans 8:28-30, proclaiming with certainty that the fate of our souls and our life's direction were predestined by God, before time.

"Why thank you, Rose. The Lord has laid it on my heart to call it as I see it."

Turning to Monty, Reverend Coker said, "Now, Monty, speaking of calling it as you see it, how do you see the game going today?"

Game seven of the World Series would be played between the Cincinnati Reds and the Oakland A's, and the Reds, playing at home, were favored to win. Billed as "the Hairs against the Squares," the series was turning out to be one for the ages. Even though the A's were without their superstar Reggie Jackson, who had badly pulled a hamstring stealing home in the final

65

game of the American League Championship Series, their pitching—from Catfish Hunter and Vida Blue to relief ace Rollie Fingers—kept them in every game.

The matchup between the Reds and the A's was not just a matchup of the National and American League champions, but it carried with it the undertones of a cultural battle between the liberal West Coast and the traditions of the South. While Cincinnati wasn't in the Bible Belt, its fans certainly reflected the same values. The Reds' management did not allow facial hair whereas the A's stars sported beards, mustaches, and audacious sideburns.

"Reverend, the Reds are gonna win," Monty replied. "Their bats finally came alive in game six. Besides, there's no way the good Lord is gonna let a bunch of hippies win the World Series. Why, I believe tonight's outcome is predestined!"

"Monty! That's blasphemous," Rose said.

Monty ignored Rose, knowing she could do self-righteous better than most anyone.

"Now, Rose," said the reverend, chuckling, "on matters of the Good Book, I'll profess my standing, but when it comes to baseball, I'll happily defer to Monty here. Y'all enjoy the rest of your Sunday and enjoy the game, Monty. And you too, Walker."

After Rose made the rounds in the courtyard behind the chapel, saying hello to all the right people, she joined Monty and Walker, already in the parking lot waiting by the car. The three of them were headed to the club for brunch. Monty and Rose didn't ask Eli to join them for church or brunch anymore—or for much of anything, for that matter.

*   *   *

Monty had joined Wappoo Country Club the year before at Rose's insistence. She had craved membership in a private country club for as long as Monty could remember, and whenever the subject came up, it had to be Wappoo Country Club. He'd beaten back her arguments in the past for why they should join with the simple truth: he couldn't afford it. But that was no longer the case. His law practice had grown, and business was good. Rose insisted that joining the club would help them meet the right sort of people and would be good for Walker. Monty sarcastically asked Rose what sort of people they'd been meeting up till then. Rose didn't do sarcasm. Shame and guilt? You betcha, but not sarcasm. Monty's remark was met with silence and a sideways glance. And when would he have time to enjoy a country club, he'd reply, since he would work nonstop to afford it?

So, Monty joined the club reluctantly, but much to his surprise, he enjoyed it. Wappoo Country Club was situated south of Charleston just across the Ashley River on the Wappoo Creek. The golf course, designed by Seth Raynor in 1922, was reminiscent of a traditional Scottish layout. The course's primary defenses were the large undulating greens, the wind off the marsh, and in the summer, the mosquitoes.

Monty had played golf a few times over the years but had never devoted the effort the game demands. Well, after he broke ninety for the first time, everything changed. The golf bug bit him hard, and he played every Saturday and regularly stopped at the driving range after work during the long summer days.

Brunch at the club, however, was another matter. Monty hated brunch. Everyone felt compelled to stop and say hello to everyone, although they saw each other all the time already—at school, at church, and of course at the club. The women dressed up for each other, and while Rose would blanch at the mere suggestion, Monty was sure she was as determined to be seen at the club as she was at church.

The buffet was the same every week, only changing to accommodate the seasons. Still, everyone gushed over it as if the food served at their club was the most sumptuous food served on the planet. No, brunch Monty could do without. Besides, the baseball game, a game seven for Pete's sakes, was on TV at 1:00. Monty was looking forward to kicking back in his recliner and watching the game with Walker. Was there anything better than a game seven?

Earlier that year, Monty had finally convinced Rose to drop the subject of Eli attending church. It led to nothing but fights.

"How does it look to others when you don't attend?" Rose would ask. "I teach the adult Sunday school classes, and your father is a deacon. What will people say?"

"I don't give a damn what people say. Don't you get that?" Eli would demand.

It would go downhill from there.

Walker didn't much care for church or brunch either and didn't understand why Eli never had to go. Walker felt that Eli was rewarded for his rebellious behavior. He didn't attend church or brunch, while Walker was punished for doing what his parents demanded, and he had to go to both.

So you could have knocked Monty and Rose over with a feather when they looked across the room and saw Eli brunching with Stephen and Gloria Prestwick, denizens of all things proper in Charleston society. Sitting straight and tall with her hands folded delicately in her lap and beaming from ear to ear was their beautiful daughter, Kimberly.

*   *   *

Eli and Kimberly had been secret high school sweethearts since the previous spring, the second semester of their junior year. She knew who he was; he was a jock. But she didn't know much else since they didn't share any classes. She thought he was cute—all the girls did—but he didn't stand out in her mind. He held back, unsure of whether he belonged. Possibly he just felt awkward or embarrassed by his mother's constant presence on campus. Rose Atkins was president of the PTA and had her hands in every aspect of school life. She hovered over Eli's little brother Walker, but Kimberly had noticed that she hardly acknowledged Eli's presence.

For Kimberly, everything changed the day she was assigned to cover the baseball game for the school newspaper. The boy she saw on the field was nothing like the shy boy at school. Eli was the team's vocal leader, and my, oh my, could he play. He went four-for-five that day, stole two bases, and played center field with a reckless abandon, launching himself for two diving grabs that robbed the opposing team of run-scoring hits. Kimberly was hooked.

After the game, she hung around the dugout so she could get a quote from a few of the players—well actually, only one. When the other players saw her approach Eli, they let him have it, hurling good-natured barbs his way. He threw them a quick glance, and they retreated. Standing before Kimberly was a born leader. His smile was natural and evidenced a love for where he was and what he was doing. This was not the same aloof boy she saw at school trying to avoid being noticed. Standing so close, she felt an electric charge and struggled to find the words for the question she wanted to ask. She was falling for him and falling hard.

Eli was at ease when he was away from school, out from under his mother's shadow, and most certainly on the diamond. He had a way about him that cut across social and racial lines. He was as comfortable hanging out with the black kids as he was with the South of Broad crowd. The black kids never saw him as a white kid they should be suspicious of. Many in the South of Broad crowd actually felt uneasy around him because his presence was a challenge to their worldview. He had no desire to be one of them, was jealous of no part of their lives, and harbored no ill will toward them. For most of the SOB kids, they just assumed everyone fell into one or more of these categories. Kimberly was an SOB gal.

She held up her writing pad in her left hand to shield her eyes from the sun setting over Eli's right shoulder. He removed his baseball cap and placed it on her head and pulled it down snuggly over her ponytail. She smiled and cast her eyes down shyly.

"Would you like to go somewhere and talk about the story you need to write?" he asked.

Kimberly hesitated, but only for a moment.

"My mother wouldn't approve of me leaving with you," she answered.

"That's okay. My mother wouldn't approve of you leaving with me either."

CHAPTER 14

Worlds Clashing

SATURDAY NIGHT; MAY 19, 1973

Rose was alone in the family room, knitting and watching a PBS special on TV. Monty and Walker were away on a father-son camping trip, so for at least for a couple of nights, she'd get a break from watching the Braves.

The headlights splashed across the living room window before she heard the car coming up the driveway. Not expecting anyone, she went to the window and pulled back the lace curtains. As the car came into focus, her eyes narrowed, and the hatred and fear inside crept forward, furrowing her brow. She walked to the front door and opened it as two uniformed police officers climbed the stairs.

"What has he done now?" she asked.

THE NIGHT BEFORE

Eli and Kimberly were seated at a table in the back of Bowens, a popular hangout for the young crowd. The band hadn't taken the stage yet, so they ordered a meal to share: a dozen oysters, a bucket of cold shrimp, crab cakes, some fried okra, a small basket of hush puppies, and a pitcher of beer.

Eli and Kimberly were inseparable and had been since the previous spring. It was bad enough that most boys at school envied Eli's athletic prowess, but now he was dating the beautiful Kimberly Prestwick, the oldest daughter of one of the wealthier and more prominent families in town. Kimberly had girl-next-door looks. The kind of girl every boy's mother dreamed of for their son—wholesome, natural, vibrant. Kimberly was taller than most and had long blonde hair that fell down past her shoulders. Her smile screamed popularity and sweetness. But despite her looks, she did not intend to rest on them. No, she was smart, attentive in the classroom, and determined to go to college and have a career.

Early on, they hid their relationship from all but their closest friends. Eli hid Kimberly from his parents out of habit. Kimberly kept Eli from hers not because of who Eli was, but because of who he was not. He was not one of them.

When Kimberly and Eli first started dating, she was busy with a full slate of debutante activities. The St. Catherine Society was the oldest, most exclusive and prestigious debutante society in all the land, according to Kimberly's mother, and the St. Catherine debutante ball was the highlight of the social calendar.

Kimberly's father, Stephen Prestwick, was a fourth-generation Charlestonian and, along with his wife, Gloria, formed a couple of high standing. Stephen was determined to see his only daughter marry a young man whose father was also a St. Catherine member. It was the only way she could remain in proper Charleston society.

Membership passed from the father to the son, and thus a young girl could only attend events as her father's daughter or as the date or wife of a member or a member's son. However, if the daughter of a member married someone whose father was not a member, then she was forever barred from attending future St. Catherine's events, even if she subsequently divorced her first (and unworthy) husband and later married the son of a member.

Stephen and Gloria regularly preached this message to their daughter. They thus believed that second only in importance to selecting the dress for the debutante ball was choosing the escort. Stephen and Gloria had their heart set on Randolph Middleton IV, the progeny of fellow St. Catherine member Randolph Middleton III.

Kimberly knew she'd never convince her parents to let Eli be her escort, which was just fine with Eli, but she was tired of pretending that Randy was anything other than her escort. She had told her parents about Eli the summer before their senior year. They were disappointed but kept hope alive that she'd come around and see the wisdom of their plans for her.

Randy, a charming young man, knew all about Eli and understood he had no chance with Kimberly. He was an excellent escort nonetheless, and they had a grand time at the debutante ball. But once it was over, Kimberly told her parents that Randy, a lifelong friend for sure, would never be Mr. Right. She was in love with Eli.

The waitress brought the pitcher of beer and the oysters. Kimberly was twirling her hair. She did this when she was nervous. Eli knew something was wrong. It wasn't long before Kimberly started up about college.

"You just can't play baseball your whole life," she said.

"Why not? I'm good at it. It's what I love."

"But how will you support yourself? Do you want to be poor your whole life?"

"Who says I'd be poor, and so what if I was? I know a lot of unhappy rich people, a lot of happy rich people, and a lot of happy and unhappy poor people, and everything in between. If you ask me, having or not having money has nothing to do with happiness."

"Well, it helps—having money, that is. At least that's how I see it. That's how my momma and daddy see it."

"Not in my book, honey. Besides, do you know that Hank Aaron makes over $200,000 a year? There's also something now called free agency in baseball that lets a player change teams more easily and play for whoever will pay him the most. Kimby, I'm gonna be the best center fielder of all time. Better than Willie Mays."

"But won't you even consider college?" she pleaded.

It had been this way since spring break. Kimberly's parents had hoped Eli was just a fling, a fling that would play itself out. But now their greatest fear was that their little girl would end up in the family way, so they brought more pressure to break things off with Eli, and Kimberly, in turn, pressured Eli to attend college. If only he were college-bound, she was sure her parents would see things differently.

Stephen Prestwick was the president of First National Bank and knew Eli's father, Monty, both professionally and from around the club. Stephen was taller than most and prematurely gray. He possessed a deep, resonant voice, and when he spoke, he took on an authoritative aura. When standing, he'd pace about with his hands behind his back, lecturing the room. If seated, he'd lean forward with his elbows on the table or desk and his hands and fingers interlocked as if he might be leading the group in prayer.

"Kimberly, Eli's father is a fine attorney," he'd say. "I've hired his firm to do some work for the bank, and he is the head of a fine family, but you can do better. I know Eli has his heart set on the major leagues, but he'll likely end up right back here coaching high school baseball. Now is that the kind of future you want? Besides, haven't you noticed how much time Eli spends with the colored boys?"

"Daddy, how can you say such a thing!"

"Kimberly, don't talk back to your father that way." Gloria was bound and determined to see her daughter marry well and obtain proper standing in the community, and it all started, in her mind, with obeying one's parents. Why until Gloria met Stephen, she had hardly ever had a thought that her mother hadn't had for her. As a young girl, Gloria had been a debutante as well. Stephen had been her escort all those years before, and she was still best friends with the girls who were part of her homecoming court her senior year in high school. Gloria wanted everything to stay as it always had been and that included her weight. She credited her trim figure to the Slender Bender, the latest exercise equipment fad, where she could keep those unwanted pounds off in the comfort of her own home. Stephen credited the diet pills that he knew his wife swallowed like Pez candy.

"It's okay, honey," said Stephen. "This whole race thing is being shoved in these kids' faces. Now, Kimberly, I have nothing against black folk. I'm not a racist like those backwoods Klansmen. I just think it's best if people keep to their own kind, that's all. I don't expect them to like George Jones or Johnny Cash, so why should I have to like their music? That's all I'm saying."

It was the same conversation every week. "If only you'd give him a chance," she'd plead. But that was something her parents had no intention of doing.

*　　*　　*

The man lived in his truck, sleeping where he could, spending most nights under a blanket in the bed of the truck. With summer coming, he was heading north toward cooler temperatures. He figured Canada, and then head west.

He'd spotted them a few weeks earlier. They'd show up with friends sometimes, and other times, just the two of them. Normal high school kids sneaking off to get drunk, fool around, and maybe smoke a little dope. She never smoked, though, and seemed a bit self-conscious with this group. This was a curious crowd; this was the boy's crowd, a mix of kids from all walks who together were entirely at ease. But when they were with the clique they had been assigned at birth, they seemed out of sorts. Kimberly, though, was at ease with her assigned clique, the South of Broad crowd, and the only other girl here from Kimberly's neighborhood was the girl rumored to have had an abortion the summer before.

From his car, he watched as the girls slipped their dresses over their heads, revealing beautiful, young bikini-clad bodies. The boys, typically shirtless, when they weren't leaning on the hood of their cars, were throwing a football or a Frisbee. The boom box played the soundtrack of their youth, and as the night rolled in, they started a campfire, and a couple or two slipped away to find a place for themselves. The boys without girlfriends kept drinking. The girls without boyfriends laughed too loudly and told dirty jokes.

Early on, the man set his sights on her. She had an air about herself, an air that said she thought she was better than the others. She would decline a joint handed to her and sit up a bit straighter when the other girls scoffed at her for passing. She never drank too much. She was there because of him. That they were a couple made it all the better. An unexpected surprise. The boy was at ease with this group. Relaxed. In control. Comfortable in this setting. This group, they weren't outcasts, but they weren't the in crowd, and they were satisfied with their anonymity.

But the man knew she was no saint. With the binoculars he kept in his glove compartment, he'd seen them fucking in the woods. The boy kept a sleeping bag behind the driver's side of his truck. The evenings were warm, so they lay on top of the sleeping bag, her on her back, legs up high, and the boy, his hands clenching the soil on each side of her, gently rising and falling, her hands grasping his strong shoulders, her ankles interlocked, eyes shut and mouth slightly open in ecstasy, as her head rolled back and forth, matching his rhythm.

It would be different with him.

* * *

In the end, Kimberly's talk of college drove them to fight. Tonight was no different, and now neither of them knew where to go from there. Eli was frustrated. He didn't handle confrontation well. Every obstacle was evidence he didn't fit in. Eli had a short fuse, an anger that could surface quickly and violently, an anger that emanated from fear, a deep-seated fear, a fear of rejection. He knew from his days as a child that he had to suppress his temper. When the monster got ahold of him as a young boy, he'd wrap his arms around himself and rock back and forth until he was no longer angry, until he was no longer scared.

"But your SAT scores are so good! You could still go to college. Make better grades and transfer," Kimberly would plead. "I don't understand why you try so little in school."

"It will never be good enough."

"For who? Your mom?"

"Both of them, Mom and Dad, but mostly Mom. She hates me."

"That's not true. They love you. All moms and dads love their kids. They just don't get us, that's all."

"No. My mom hates me. I remind her of her first husband and the mistake their marriage was. The marriage was a mistake, so I must be a mistake too."

"Then show them. Show them how smart you are. Show them by making it to UVA with me."

"Kimberly, you don't get it. They have Walker. That's where her attention is. Even my dad, not my real dad, but Monty—even he sides with her. I heard them one night, my parents, fighting. He took my side and defended me, and she told him that I would bring Walker down and she wouldn't have it. Mom told Dad that he had to decide between her or me. She said that if he didn't take her side, it meant he didn't love her.

"Once, after Dad had been in Atlanta for several weeks for a big trial, when he got home, she told him she was leaving and taking Walker with her. She left. Dad didn't know what to do. He was so scared, so upset. I saw him at the kitchen table late one night, just sitting there, crying. He saw me standing around the corner and motioned for me to come to him. His shoulders were shaking, and he couldn't get the words out. He put his arms around me and squeezed me tight. I felt his tears on my face. It was the happiest moment I have ever known with either of my parents, because for that moment, right then, I felt loved, I felt needed, I felt loved for just being his son.

"But then she came back the next day, and everything returned to normal. To the best of my knowledge, Dad never defended me in front of her again. My grades were never good enough. I could always try harder. I'd be sent to detention after school and she'd tell me I was an embarrassment to the family, and I was holding Walker back. I'd break curfew, come home drunk, and she'd tell me she expected nothing more from me. At some point, you know that whatever you do will never be enough. Eventually, you just quit. You see, Kimby, in her mind, I will never stop being who I am, a reminder of her first husband."

"Oh, Eli. Please don't talk that way. It scares me."

*　*　*

He was growing impatient and impatience bred sloppiness. The pain, though, was piercing and unrelenting. There was only one way to gain relief. He made a decision; it had to be tonight. He had followed them, staying a few cars back, and turned into the parking lot of the popular Charleston nightspot. He waited in his car until it was safe to enter. He slid to the end of the bar, far from the crowds, but where he could keep an eye on them, and he ordered a beer. He was careful not to order anything the bartender might remember. He would be careful now. He was on the hunt, locked in, focused, fueled by hatred as much as by need. Watching them suffer, that was his tonic. It made him feel powerful, invincible. He'd been watching her, bringing himself close to climax, but always stopping, choosing to wait. Yes, tonight. It had to be tonight.

*　*　*

The band was preparing to play, and the locals were pouring in. From the looks of the newcomers scurrying into the bar, it had begun to rain. *Perfect*, he thought, as he kept an eye on the two young, quarreling lovebirds and witnessed it all.

She sat back in her chair. Eli's head dropped, and he reached out to grab her hand as she stood to leave. She yanked her hand free, and Eli jumped up, knocking the table over in the process. Heads turned; it was no secret they were fighting. She ran out. He stood there alone, feeling every eye in the bar. He knew what they were thinking. "You don't belong with her. You're not good enough for her, and now she knows it too."

Eli lifted the table and set it right side up, then slumped back into his chair. The commotion delayed the band's opening song, and Eli, unable to shake the unwanted attention and prying eyes, grew angrier by the minute. He stood, and with a determined look on his face, walked out of the bar, turning in the direction she had gone.

Huge drops pelted the gravel parking lot and Eli ran to his pickup, dodging puddles along the way, and quickly hopped in. He saw Kimberly sitting in her car, her shoulders shaking. He got out of his truck and approached her, rapping his fingers on the passenger side window and pleading with his body language for her to let him in. She looked his way and shook her head no; she started the car and pulled away, leaving Eli standing in the rain.

Eli walked back to his pickup, oblivious of the Ford truck pulling out behind Kimberly. Eli got into his pickup and pulled out onto the road heading in the opposite direction, with no place to go. The band had just started and wouldn't take its first break until 10:30. The clock on his dashboard read just a few minutes past 9:00.

*   *   *

The storm was fierce but over quickly, and since Rose enjoyed the night air after a storm, she was sitting in her rocking chair on the front porch when Eli pulled up the driveway. He parked as far from the house as possible and walked up to his room above the garage. Rose glanced at her watch—9:35—and thought it early for him to be coming home on a Friday night. Eli stood momentarily at the top of the stairs, and as Rose looked up from her needlepoint, they locked eyes, if only for a moment. Nothing was said, and Eli went inside, the screen door bouncing shut behind him.

He was awake early the next morning and left before dawn. He was meeting friends for a day of fishing and had no plans to return home anytime soon.

CHAPTER 15

Worlds Broken

Kimberly's mother rolled over and sensed her house was emptier than it should be. Stephen was gone, but that was no surprise. It was Saturday morning, and Stephen had a standing 8:00 tee time. He worked hard during the week and looked forward to his Saturdays. Golf, followed by lunch, and then the afternoon in the Men's Grill watching the game on TV. The "Men's Grill" annoyed some women, but not Gloria. She thought men and women, mind you, needed time together, away from their spouses. If her husband wanted to spend all afternoon in the Men's Grill watching whatever game was on TV and smoking cigars, she was fine with that. It also made her girls' trips to New York City easier to sell.

Stephen's absence was expected, but this feeling of hers was something else, something lonely and foreboding. She rose from the bed, put on her housecoat, swallowed a diet pill, and set off for the kitchen. No sign of Kimberly. She looked out on the porch. Nothing. She quietly walked down the hall, hoping to find her still asleep. She slowly opened the door and looked inside. The bed had not been slept in. She walked hurriedly toward the garage, already knowing what she wouldn't find, her car.

It was probably nothing. Kimberly did not have a curfew. She was a senior and would be heading to the University of Virginia in the fall. At Stephen's insistence, Kimberly was to be treated like an adult, and that meant no curfew. At first, Gloria had struggled to fall asleep until she heard the garage door open and close, but as her husband insisted, they had nothing to worry about with Kimberly. Kimberly was smart and made the right decisions; her life was charmed. Over time, Gloria was able to fall asleep before the garage door signaled Kimberly's arrival. The bottle of wine at dinner always helped.

Gloria wondered whom she should call. She had been seeing that boy Eli, but she couldn't call the Atkinses, not yet. Calling them shouted that they did not have control over their oldest daughter, and how would that look? Besides, what would she say? Anything she asked could be taken as an admission that their daughter was not a virgin, and that couldn't be. No, she would wait. She was sure Kimberly was sleeping over at a girlfriend's house.

*   *   *

Stephen walked off the course in a damn good mood. The up-and-down on the eighteenth hole had secured the win in their weekly Nassau match. He'd pocket twenty bucks for his efforts. Stephen wasn't a big gambler, but a little money on the game focused his efforts, and besides, it was more about friendly camaraderie and bragging rights than about the money.

"Mr. Prestwick, may I have a moment?" The club's general manager was coming his way.

"Of course, Charles, what's on your mind, and can it wait till our meeting Tuesday? I have to collect twenty dollars from Fred and David before they forget they pressed on the last hole," said Stephen with a good-natured chuckle.

"No, sir, it's not club business. Your wife has been calling—she says it's urgent. You can use the phone in my office."

Stephen hesitated and wondered what it could be. Gloria would never call unless there was trouble. His thoughts ran to his daughter, his pride and joy.

"Guys, order me a beer, I'll be there in a moment," said Stephen over his shoulder to his playing companions.

*　　*　　*

"Just press nine to get out. I'll be in the main dining room helping the staff," Charles said. "We have the Johnston wedding tonight. They're expecting over three hundred people."

"Yep, should be something. We'll be here. Now, Charles, could you shut the door on your way out? This should just take a minute."

"Of course, Mr. Prestwick, and if there is anything you need, please let me know."

"Thank you, Charles."

Gloria picked up on the first ring.

"Stephen, she's missing. No one knows where she is, and I've called everyone."

Gloria was panicked. Stephen tried to remain calm.

"Now, Gloria, just slow down. I'm sure everything is all right. Who have you spoken to?"

Gloria recounted everything. She had waited until 10:00 a.m., and with no sign of Kimberly, began calling her girlfriends. No one had seen her since she left Bowens last night.

Stephen told his golfing buddies that he needed to skip lunch. He collected his winnings and told the bartender to put a round of drinks on his tab.

"Will we see you tonight at the Johnston wedding?" asked Fred.

"Absolutely. Just need to take care of a few honey-dos around the house. I promised Gloria and plain forgot. Sorry I'm missing lunch. See y'all tonight."

*　　*　　*

The two black and whites parked in the driveway looked foreign and out of place on this cul-de-sac. Stephen pulled into the garage and shut the electric overhead door behind him, a desperate act to restore, if only as a mirage, the serene isolation from the world of police cars.

His wife was sitting in the living room with a policewoman. A second policeman was on his radio and a third was paying an inordinate amount of attention to the framed family pictures around the room. Stephen recoiled at the familiar way he had made himself at home.

Gloria ran to Stephen and folded herself into his arms, sobbing, unable to speak. The officer on the radio turned to him. "Mr. Prestwick, I'm Officer

Pearlman. We understand from speaking to your wife that your daughter Kimberly has gone missing."

"That's right. But she's only been missing for a short while. Why all the police cars in the driveway? Is all this necessary?"

Gloria sobbed more loudly.

"Mr. Prestwick, could you please come with us? Mrs. Prestwick, I'd prefer it if you would stay here. Officer Cairns will stay with you."

As the men left the house, Stephen again tried to exert control over the situation. "Now officers, tell me what's going on. I have a right to know."

Officer Pearlman spoke in a commanding voice he hoped Mr. Prestwick would associate with authority, but in a tone he hoped would also convey concern and empathy. "Mr. Prestwick, I just spoke with a state highway patrolman. The body of a young woman was found over off the Savannah Highway. I'm afraid the patrolman's description matches that of your daughter. Could you come with us, please?"

Stephen heard words he thought were only ever spoken on TV or in the movies. This wasn't real. It couldn't be. An hour earlier, he'd been playing golf at the club. This wasn't happening. Not to Kimberly, not to them. Kimberly was young and beautiful. They lived in a grandiose home; they had a perfect life. It was all laid out for Kimberly. Happiness was a given.

Thirty minutes later, Stephen walked into a wooded area at the side of a road he'd driven countless times. He put plastic booties on his shoes at the police officers' direction. He never did things like this. This would all be over soon. There had been a horrible mistake. Yes, a father and a mother had lost a child today, but not them. Yes, it was all some sort of terrible mistake, but no, it was not Kimberly. It couldn't be.

He approached the yellow tape, tape that screamed "murder," and the coroner pulled back the blanket. Stephen stood motionless in his bootie-covered shoes, not daring to breathe. Sprawled before him was an empty shell, a spirit-drained body, a body that resembled Kimberly, but wasn't. Kimberly was gone, never to return, and in her place lay a lifeless form, a corpse, for death begets a stillness this world does not know.

The walk to and from the car was surreal. Each step felt like ten steps away from his old life. Nothing would ever be the same. He had entered a world for which he had no reference point, a world of sorrow and incalculable loss, a world without Kimberly, a world that possessed a monster that had murdered his little girl.

CHAPTER 16

Worlds Under Attack

THAT EVENING

"Mrs. Atkins, my name is Officer Pearlman, and this is my partner, Officer Tyrell. May we have a few words with you?"

"Of course. Please, come in."

Officers Pearlman and Tyrell, by all appearances, were exact opposites. Officer Pearlman was a string bean and Officer Tyrell was short and squat. Officer Pearlman, a white man with the complexion of chalk, and Officer Tyrell, skin black as coal, had been partners for going on four years; away from the office, they were best friends.

Rose was uncomfortable having a black man in her house, even a policeman. The city had taken to pairing white and black officers together as part of a community outreach program. Rose may have disowned her father but was like him in more ways than she would ever admit. When you have lived your life full of self-loathing, what better way to soothe your pain than to look down on others?

The officers entered the Atkins home, removed their hats, and took a seat across from the sofa where Rose was seated, her needlepoint work spread about her.

"You have a lovely home, Mrs. Atkins," commented Officer Tyrell.

"Why, thank you. Now how can I help? Is Eli in some sort of trouble?"

"What makes you ask?" inquired Officer Pearlman.

"Well, this couldn't be about my son Walker; getting into trouble is not his nature. Besides, he's away camping with his father this weekend. I know no one died because you didn't bring any clergy with you. So that leaves Eli, not that I'm surprised."

"Is your son Eli here?" Officer Pearlman led with the questions.

"No, and before you go asking, I don't know where he is. He doesn't confide in me. Maybe Officer Tyrell could be of help. His son and Eli are on the same baseball team. Maybe Eli is off with...what's your son's name again? I know he's one of the pitchers."

"His name is Leroy, ma'am."

Rose nodded and waited.

"Well, what on earth is all the mystery about?" asked Rose. "Can't you just get to the point? I'd like to get to bed early. I'm teaching Sunday school in the morning, and I still have some scripture work to do."

"Mrs. Atkins, can you tell us where your son Eli was last night?"

"I don't know. I already told you...he doesn't confide in me."

"Did he go out?"

"Yes."

"Do you know when he got home?"

Rose hesitated before answering. She didn't know why she didn't come forward with the truth, but she sensed that the answer to this question could be critical. She decided to keep it to herself.

"No, I don't," she lied. "I went to bed very early last night, about 8:15 or so. I had a migraine. My doctor says the changing weather brings them on. The pressure dropped, usually does before a summer storm, and if you remember, it rained last night. So I took a pill and got in bed."

"What kind of pill, ma'am?" asked Officer Tyrell.

"That is none of your business! Now again, and for the last time, what is this about?"

"Mrs. Atkins, Kimberly Prestwick's body was found earlier today. She's been murdered. She was seen at Bowens earlier Friday night with Eli. Witnesses say they'd been fighting, and then Kimberly ran out of the bar.

Eli left a few minutes later, visibly upset. That was the last time anyone has seen either of them."

*   *   *

The reception following the Johnston wedding was in full swing. With over three hundred people in attendance, the Prestwicks' absence had hardly been noticed—that is, until word began to spread. First, from a corner occupied by the high school kids in attendance, a late arrival, in a conspiratorial voice, whispered to a small group what she had heard. Kimberly Prestwick was dead. She'd been murdered, and yes, she'd been raped. The story spread like a brushfire in a drought, as a deafening hush fell across the room. Speculation as to who did it jumped from the mouths of a jury of her peers and filled the room with mumbled verdicts announcing she'd last been seen the night before at Bowens, fighting with Eli.

*   *   *

SATURDAY NIGHT, AT THE ATKINSES' HOME

"Mrs. Atkins, are you okay? Can we get you anything?"

Rose barely heard the officers. What were they saying? Were they accusing Eli of killing that girl? No, it couldn't be. He wouldn't! He couldn't! But she knew of his temper, of his father's rage. Did the police know? Did they know of her first marriage? Did anyone know? She had worked so hard to bury it. That all happened back in Tuscaloosa. No one could know. What was to happen? How would this look? Where was Eli? She had to protect Walker.

"Mrs. Atkins?"

"Yes, Officer. I'm fine. Why wouldn't I be?" she asked.

"We'd like to speak with Eli. We believe he may have been the last of her friends to see her."

"Yes, you said that. Well, as I told you, I don't know where he is," said Rose.

"When he gets home, will you give us a call?" asked Officer Pearlman.

"Yes. I'll tell Eli to call you."

"Thank you, Mrs. Atkins. Here's my card. The number for the police station is on the back. Please call just as soon as he comes home. We'll show ourselves out."

Rose remained seated as the officers left. She heard the car doors slam, first one and then the other. She stood and approached the window and watched as the police car drove away.

"Oh, Eli, what have you done to me?"

*   *   *

"Identification, please." The border agent announced more than asked.

He wordlessly handed over his driver's license.

"State your business."

"Pleasure."

"That's a nasty cut you got there. Everything okay?"

"Yep. No problem."

The border agent turned the driver's license over in his hand as he eyed the American visitor.

"Okay, then. How long will you be staying?"

"Just a couple of weeks."

"Welcome to Canada."

*   *   *

She heard Eli pull up the driveway close to 2:30 Sunday morning, long after decent folk had gone to bed. Rose didn't call the police station right away. She needed time to think. There was nothing unusual about the hour for Eli. Neither Rose nor Monty knew much about his friends or what he did when he wasn't playing baseball. Rose just knew he spent his time with the wrong sort of people, but then again, he was his father's boy. When Rose saw Eli, she saw him. And she saw her brother. She felt their hands on her, and their vile penises against her flesh, invading her, punishing her for being white trash. She heard her father's words all over again. But she was not trash. She shook her head in defiance. She saw her ugly past returning to hold her back, and she would not allow it. She had worked too hard. She had come too far, and she had so much farther to go. Her house was under attack. She was under attack. She would do what had to be done.

CHAPTER 17

Chester

Rose called the church office first thing Sunday morning and asked if they could find someone to teach her class.

"I'm not feeling my best," Rose told the church secretary. "A migraine kept me up all night."

She was in the kitchen having her coffee when Eli walked in and headed toward the refrigerator without saying a word.

"Eli." Rose, turning her coffee cup absentmindedly in her hand, spoke without looking at him. "The police were here last night. I guess you know why."

"No, Mom, I don't." Eli shut the fridge dispassionately and turned to look at her between swigs from the bottle of orange juice.

Staring back, she tried to read what was behind those eyes, his father's eyes. She'd fallen for them once before. She would not make the same mistake twice.

"Where were you Friday night?" asked Rose.

Eli took a seat at the kitchen table. "What do you mean 'Where was I Friday night?' You sound like a damn cop."

"Well, you'd better get used to it, mister. The police were here, and they're going to be back. In fact, I was supposed to call them when you got home last night, but your father really should be the one. He should be home soon from his weekend with Walker. Oh, how this is going to upset him so."

"Mom, what are you talking about?"

"Eli, Kimberly is dead. She's been murdered."

Silence. Rose gauged him for a reaction. Eli just stood there, not reacting, not knowing how to.

"What?"

"You heard me. She's been murdered. Kimberly. Your girlfriend. Eli, are you listening to me?"

The room fell from beneath him. Stumbling backward as he tried to stand, the chair fell over. Catching his balance, he grabbed the counter for support. What was his mother saying? And why was she staring at him that way? He bolted from the house.

"Eli, where are you going? You get back here."

He didn't know where he was going, but he had to leave. Kimberly, dead? But Eli couldn't lean on his mother. He couldn't seek solace. He couldn't show weakness in front of her, knowing she'd use it against him. No, he had to get out of there.

* * *

"Good morning. May I speak to Officer Pearlman, please? This is Mrs. Rose Atkins. Yes, I'll hold," she said.

"Mrs. Atkins, Officer Pearlman here. How can I help you?"

"You asked me to call when he came home. Well, he got home this morning."

"You mean Eli?" asked Officer Pearlman.

"Of course, I mean Eli. He came home about 2:00 a.m.," she answered. "No, I didn't call right away. His father should be the one. Besides, I didn't see the need at such an hour.... No, he's not here. I told him the police had been by, and when I told him that Kimberly was dead, he ran to his truck and took off.... Yes, of course. If he turns up again, I'll be sure to call right away."

Rose hung up the phone and returned to her needlepoint. Monty and Walker wouldn't be home for a couple more hours.

* * *

Eli took off for Kimberly's house. He didn't know why, but it felt like the only place to go. He pulled into a driveway full of cars and pickups and ran up the front stairs. The door was open, and family and friends were gathered in the entrance and spilling out onto the porch. The crowd grew still as everyone stared at him in disbelief until a grief-stricken scream shattered the eerie silence that had descended upon the home with the arrival of the day's first mourners.

"Get out! Get out! You killed her."

Gloria was coming toward him. The mix of rage and anguish on her face froze Eli in his tracks. He turned to see Kimberly's father emerging from the kitchen. Everything around him slowed down. He reacted. He ran and pushed his way through the crowd as a few attempted to slow his escape. He made it to his truck before Stephen Prestwick could close the gap. Eli's truck tore the bumper off a car at the edge of the driveway as he sped away.

A few miles down the road, the lights of several police cars appeared in his rearview mirror, and then he saw them up ahead approaching in the oncoming lanes. He veered off the road and bolted from his truck. In a flash, they were on him, guns pulled, and he was facedown, his hands cuffed behind his back.

*　　*　　*

Walker and Monty returned from their camping trip early Sunday afternoon. "We're home, and you won't believe how many fish we caught," announced Walker as they stepped through the front door. Met with silence, they entered tentatively, both sensing something was amiss.

Monty lowered his backpack and fishing pole to the floor and set off for their room where he found Rose under the covers, lights out, and a cold towel on her head. The room felt ten degrees colder than the rest of the house. She'd heard them pulling up the driveway. They were still laughing, coming up the front stairs as she crawled into bed.

"Rose, are you okay?"

"Oh, Monty. Thank God you're home."

Twenty minutes later, Monty came out of their bedroom. Walker was worried. It was never good when Mom took to bed in the middle of the day.

"Is everything okay, Dad?"

"Yes, Son. Don't you worry. Now why don't you put the fish in the freezer, and we'll talk soon. But leave your mother alone. She's not feeling well."

"Okay, Dad." Walker was worried, and he wondered where Eli was.

* * *

The Prestwicks were already at the police station meeting with the chief of police when Rose and Monty arrived. The Atkinses were waiting in the front room when Stephen and Gloria Prestwick exited the chief of police's office, their lawyer in tow. A few members of the press, huddled together in the corner of the front lobby, saw the developing confrontation and quickly manned their cameras.

Rose lifted Monty's hand from hers and walked slowly toward the Prestwicks, removing a white lace handkerchief from her purse as she approached. She walked up to Mrs. Prestwick, took her hands into hers, looked into her eyes, and with her head slightly nodding as proof of her sincerity, spoke: "Mrs. Prestwick, my heart is so heavy for your loss. As only another mother can understand, the pain you must be going through is unimaginable. My women's prayer group will pay special attention to you and your family's needs this week and every week. If there's anything I can do..."

Cameras whirred and clicked, and tomorrow's front page of the local *Post and Courier* was captured. And just like that, Rose had both granted Gloria Prestwick victim status and stolen some for herself. Gloria was silenced, too stunned to respond. How could this woman, the mother of her daughter's killer, speak to her as if she wasn't in some way responsible? But of course, in Rose's mind, she too was a victim, as all mothers were, all mothers with children living in a world filled with violence.

Mr. Prestwick, with one hand on his wife's shoulder and his other on her waist, guided her past Rose Atkins and out the door. Rose stood, motionless, in the center of the room, casting a gaze in the direction of Kimberly's mother, a gaze brimming with sympathy and shared purpose, tears gently rolling down her cheeks, all for the camera to see.

Monty witnessed it all, wondering: *Who is this woman?*

* * *

After Rose told Monty about the visit from the police, he called Chester Baslin, a fellow lawyer and member of the criminal defense bar. Chester and Monty had met several years earlier at a local bar association meeting. They were drawn together by their mutual love for shrimp 'n' grits. They were partial to hole-in-the-wall diners and got a kick out of sharing with the other any new establishments they'd stumbled on. While their paths didn't often cross, when they did, the two clicked as if they'd been close friends for years.

When Monty had a client in need of a criminal defense attorney, he referred them to Chester. Monty's friends, associates, and typical clients detested criminal defense attorneys—that is, until they needed one. Then they would gladly pay any amount to quickly and quietly put matters to rest. Chester understood the dynamic and made the conscious decision to neither join their private clubs nor put himself into the same social circles as his potentially wealthy clients. As for his clients of lower economic status, they could not afford to carry airs of superiority and were more lavish in their genuine appreciation of anyone who would help.

At six feet six inches and over 250 pounds, Chester was an imposing figure. He was a local football legend, having dominated both in high school and in college playing for the Gamecocks. Upon graduation, he shocked everyone by entering law school instead of the NFL. When asked about forgoing a promising career, he would chuckle and tell them to wait a few years, and they'd see a Baslin playing pro football. Chester and his wife Leigh were raising three boys who each looked like future first-round draft picks.

Chester walked into the police station and up to the window. The attending officer, knowing why he was there, told him where he could find his clients. Although police officers openly viewed criminal defense attorneys as the enemy, Chester's reputation in the police department as tough and thorough, but honest and a straight shooter, served Chester and his clients well.

Chester found Monty, Rose, and Eli sitting together in a private room set aside for their use.

"Ches, thanks for coming out on a Sunday. We're a little lost here."

Chester, despite his size and reputation in the courtroom, in his personal affairs was a humble, gentle man with a genuine heart for others.

"Don't mention it. I'm here to help. It's what I do. Mrs. Atkins, it's a pleasure."

"How do you do? My husband has spoken of you often. I'm sorry we're meeting under these circumstances."

Chester's antennae went up. He was picking up on an interesting family dynamic. In Chester's experience, when a son was accused of a crime, the mother typically sat between her son and the father. Not here, though; in fact, just the opposite. Monty was seated between Rose and Eli.

Rose's attitude screamed, *I don't belong here, in a police station.* Her son had embarrassed her and the family by bringing them here. Such behavior was standard if the offense in question was a drunken barroom fight, for instance, but they were talking about murder, and in a state that administered the death penalty, no less. Chester quickly concluded that Monty was walking a fine line between protecting their son and standing by his wife and that doing so placed him with one foot on each side of the line.

Chester began to explain what would happen next. "Now, I've spoken to the judge, and Eli, even though you are only seventeen, the judge said he was not inclined to offer bail. I explained your family's standing in the community and I chastised the police for rushing to judgment and bringing you in cuffed. When I talked about filing a motion for a venue change because of the cops' rash conduct, he said he'd think on the matter of your bail. I believe he'll come around. Neither the judge nor the police want this case tried anywhere but here."

"How can they be talking about trying a case?!" Monty asked. "They haven't even investigated the crime. Why do they simply assume it was Eli?"

Chester understood Monty's anger and frustration, but he wanted to establish a relationship with Eli early on, so he refrained from speaking about him as if he weren't in the room.

"Eli, your father is a good attorney, and he's right. However, the police do have a case, and barring the appearance of evidence over the next twenty-four hours that clears you, they will charge you with murder. Once they file, they will have to share their evidence with us. We'll collect our own evidence and hire a private investigator. Still, I believe we should prepare as if this case is going to trial."

"Now, Rose and Monty, I know we have some business to work out, but if the three of you are comfortable with me representing Eli, then I'd like some time alone to speak with my client. And then, Monty and Rose, the three of us can talk."

Monty nodded in agreement.

Eli spoke for the first time. "I didn't kill Kimberly."

Chester responded, "Son, it's not important what I think; what's important is what the jury thinks. But know this: I will represent you before the court and the jury to the best of my ability." Chester turned to Rose and Monty. "You have my word on it."

Chester developed an opinion about a client's guilt quickly. He believed Eli was innocent, and he believed him because Eli used Kimberly's name when he proclaimed his innocence. He didn't say, "I didn't kill *her*." He said, "I didn't kill *Kimberly*." In Chester's experience, that subtle difference spoke volumes.

The tears Monty was barely holding back as he reached across the table and shook Chester's hand spoke volumes too, as did Rose's quiet detachment. She had uttered barely a word the entire time they were together.

*   *   *

Eli would spend the night in jail. It was Sunday, and the earliest a bail hearing could be scheduled was the next day. Chester left the three of them alone in the witness room. Eli and Monty hugged as father and son do when a handshake isn't enough, and Monty assured his son that everything was going to be okay. Eli swore again and again that he didn't kill Kimberly, that he loved Kimberly, that he would never hurt her.

"I know, Son. I know. It's going to be okay. Chester Baslin is a fine lawyer. It's all going to be okay. You'll be back out on the diamond before you know it, and all this will be behind you."

"Dad?"

"Yes, Son."

"I love you."

"I love you too, Son." Monty didn't hold back the tears this time.

With nothing left to say, Rose and Monty started toward the door, but then Rose turned and walked up to her firstborn and kissed him on the forehead.

*   *   *

Monty and Rose agreed to meet Chester in his office later that afternoon. They wanted to check on Walker and explain what was happening. Frankly, as Monty saw it, Rose seemed more concerned with Walker than with Eli.

"Oh, my poor baby. My poor Walker. He idolizes Eli so. This is going to devastate him. And how will others see Walker? Are they going to see him as no different than Eli? They just can't! They just can't. Walker is different. He is. He was born different."

Rose kept on about Walker, and Monty couldn't take it anymore. He slammed the brakes and pulled the car off the road onto a dirt shoulder, narrowly missing a sign that warned of a sharp curve ahead.

"Listen to yourself! Your son, OUR SON, was arrested today for killing a girl I believe he loved very much, as much as a seventeen-year-old can. Have you thought for one moment what he must be going through? No, you haven't. You're so caught up in how you will appear in the eyes of others that you can't see the anguish your son Eli is suffering."

Rose stared straight ahead, looking into the distance, not focused on anything. For a moment, she said nothing, and then she lowered her head and gazed into her hands, folded together in her lap. "You're not a mother. You'll never understand what it's like. What it's like to have your own flesh and blood turn on you. To have a child that you carry for nine months, that you sacrifice so much for, lash out and try to destroy everything you have done for them, and that is what Eli has done to us, to Walker, to me."

Monty, both hands on the steering wheel, looked at the woman he loved, a woman he had promised to stay with "until death do us part." At that instant, he feared his wife had vanished, finally swallowed up by the shame and guilt that had consumed her all these years. Should he ask her if she believed her son had killed Kimberly, whether he was capable of such a thing? In the end, he was afraid to.

He put the car into drive, pulled back onto the road, and headed home, wondering whether the life he had when he woke that morning would ever return.

*   *   *

Walker ran down the front steps screaming hysterically and met Monty and Rose coming up the driveway, blocking them from pulling into the garage. They could barely make out the words, he was sobbing so uncontrollably. Rose climbed from the car and threw her arms around Walker, but Walker wouldn't have it and stepped back defiantly.

"Why didn't you take me with you? He's my brother. He didn't do it. Why didn't you tell me what was happening?"

When Monty and Rose had left for the police station, they told him Eli was in trouble, but they hadn't told him the gravity of the situation. How do you tell a child their sibling had been arrested for suspicion of murder? Monty had wanted to take Walker with them. He was afraid Walker would hear about Kimberly's murder and his brother's arrest from someone other than him. Rose prevailed on Monty to leave Walker in the dark, convincing him that in the time they'd be gone, Walker wouldn't hear a thing. Rose didn't want Walker associated with Eli if she could help it.

Monty stepped forward. "Walker, I'm sorry. You're right. I should have told you what was happening. Of course, Eli is innocent. He'll be home tomorrow night. I promise."

*   *   *

"Ches, thank you again for giving up your Sunday and helping us on such short notice." Monty was truly thankful. Though he suspected weekend interruptions were standard fare for criminal defense attorneys, he wanted Chester to know he did not take his representation for granted.

"Monty, enough. This is what I do. My wife understands as do our boys. Besides, they won't miss me a bit. They all have their own lives. As much as I'd like to think their worlds revolved around mine, I know better," remarked Chester as he softly chuckled.

Chester led Monty and Rose over to a small seating area in the corner of his office. The conference room afforded more room to pace, and Chester could see Monty was a pacer, but he needed Monty to sit and relax and cede control of the situation to him. Having a lawyer as a client was tough enough, but a client accused of murder with a father who was an attorney? Well, that was something else entirely, uncharted territory for Chester.

Chester offered tea and coffee, and then the three of them took their seats. Chester went into greater detail than he had earlier that day, reviewing procedures the police had to follow, explaining the purpose of an arraignment, and outlining what a murder prosecution and defense entailed.

"Now Monty and Rose, as much as I believe in the necessity of a criminal bar to hold authorities accountable and guard against abuse, I don't do this as a hobby. This case, a case in which the district attorney may seek the death penalty, will take up most of my time. My associates will pick up the slack on our firm's other cases and your son's defense will be my primary responsibility."

Monty interrupted before Chester could continue. "Chester, we know you are paid to do what you do and we are prepared to do what it takes. Just please tell me. What are we talking about?"

"Well, first, you'll need to post bail. For a murder case, and one that will draw lots of attention from the local media, expect bail of up to $75,000. Now, Monty, as I know you know, you don't need to come up with the full

$75,000. You'll need cash for 10 percent of the bail, but you'll post collateral for the balance. I'm hoping you have some equity in your home and business. I contacted a bail bondsman I've worked with in the past, and if y'all are all right with that, he can be here tomorrow morning at 8:00. You can use my conference room. The banks open at 9:00 a.m. That'll give you enough time to sort matters out before our hearing in front of the judge tomorrow afternoon."

Monty was a man in control—or at least he felt he was in control. But he was most certainly a man who grasped onto the illusion of being in control. But here he was, standing on shifting sand, accepting a helping hand extended graciously by a peer.

"Thank you, Ches."

Chester then explained the fee arrangement and the necessity of a retainer. Monty nodded and quickly agreed. He saw their college savings vanish and wondered how they would manage, but he never questioned whether they would.

Finally, Chester turned to the day-to-day reality that would set in and warned them of what they could expect. Their circle of friends would shrink. It might be tough on Walker, as kids, we all knew, could be cruel. As difficult as it might be, Chester encouraged them to draw together as a family and carry on as if nothing had changed.

Chester explained. "If you go to church on Sundays, keep going. If you head to the club after church, then keep it up. Monty, if you play golf on Saturdays, keep playing."

Rose spoke for the first time. "Mr. Baslin, shouldn't we respect the sensibilities of others and keep to ourselves if our presence in polite society makes others feel uncomfortable?"

"Well, I can't tell you how to live your lives, but it is my experience that the more folks see you as a family, the less likely they'll see Eli as a murderer."

"You mean, by Eli's association with us?"

"Yes, Mrs. Atkins. By reinforcing in the minds of potential jurors that you are family."

Rose sat quietly for the remainder of their time, trying to appear attentive, but her mind was elsewhere. Graduation ceremonies were planned for the following Saturday. Walker would graduate from the sixth grade in the morning, and Eli's graduation ceremonies would be held in the afternoon. He was a senior with no concrete plans for his future. With the last name Atkins, Eli would be one of the first names called. At least he wouldn't be the first name called. Thank heavens for the Adams family. What would everyone say? What would they think? Walker would begin the seventh grade at Porter-Gaud come September. Attending Porter-Gaud had been Rose's idea.

*   *   *

Walker had complained loudly at dinner the night Rose told him she had turned in his application at Porter-Gaud. "But Mom, I don't want to change schools. I like my friends."

"Walker, after all we've done for you. Your father works so hard so you can attend the very best schools. And you know, I didn't have to be a stay-at-home mom—I could have gone to work. I wanted to be a teacher or maybe even a college professor, but being a mother is the noblest and most thankless job in the world. So I do it without complaining. Now, not another word about this. You'll need to pass the entrance exam. The next test date is this Saturday."

"But Mom, I have a game this Saturday!"

"Don't disappoint me. I don't know if I can take it. Eli won't go to college, says he's going to be a baseball player, of all things. I don't know what I'm going to say when people ask me where he's going next year. Oh, the looks I'll get. So I will not hear another word about it. Do you understand me?"

"Honey, maybe we should talk about this a little? This is the first time Walker has heard anything about changing schools." Monty walked a fine line. He wouldn't force Walker to attend Porter-Gaud if he really didn't want to, but he hoped Walker would change his mind. If only Walker would visit the school, then maybe the idea would become his own.

Rose looked at Monty and began to weep. "I'm just trying to do what is best for my son, for our son, and this is the thanks I get, the two of you ganging up on me. Never mind—if you want to be a nobody and just stay with your friends, then you go ahead. I've certainly done all I can."

Walker succumbed. "Okay, Mom, I'll go."

And now the carrot, as she reached over and patted Walker's left hand. "You make me so proud. Do you know that?"

*   *   *

There was no joy at dinnertime that evening for the Atkins family. Eli sat alone in a jail cell Chester had arranged. At the dinner table, Rose talked and talked as if nothing had happened. The harder she tried to convince Monty and Walker that nothing had, the more agonizing became the silence when she paused.

*   *   *

Monty was out the door early the next morning. He stopped by his office on his way to his appointment with the bail bondsman to meet with Jonathan Davis, his most senior associate. After briefing Jonathan on his clients' most pressing matters for the upcoming week, he hopped in his car for the short drive to downtown Charleston. Chester's law offices were on Broad Street. Broad Street was home for many of the city's law firms, its youngest and oldest, its largest and smallest.

Monty concluded the morning's business with Chester, the bail bondsman, and the bank by 1:00. The bank gave Monty a $200,000 line of credit secured by his law practice and a second lien on his home. The bail hearing was scheduled for that afternoon. That left Monty with enough time to have lunch at Henry's over on Market Street. Chester promised to pick up the tab and said the shrimp 'n' grits were some of the best in town. All things considered, the day had been a success with the unknown outcome of the bail hearing the elephant in the room.

*   *   *

The hearing proceeded as Chester had said it would. Monty and Rose sat on the front row just behind the defendant's table, where Chester was seated with Eli. Monty wanted Walker seated with them, but Rose wouldn't have it.

"Please, Monty, let's not direct more attention to this sordid matter than we have to," implored Rose.

The judge didn't take long to render a decision. With a bang of his gavel, Eli was released on bail and free to go home. Eli walked tall through the gate in the wood railing separating the front of the courtroom from the public seating area and tried his best to hold back the tears. But when he saw his father's open arms, he fell into them, pressed his head into his father's shoulder, and shook. Rose stood dispassionately to the side. Monty released one arm from Eli and gestured toward Rose to join them. She reluctantly joined her husband and oldest son's embrace.

That night Monty dined with Walker and Eli. Rose went to bed early, complaining of a migraine. The weather was as clear as a bell. It wasn't long before Monty and the boys were relaxed and laughing at the table, having a great time. After dinner, they retired to the living room to watch the Braves game.

Rose lay in bed, lamenting her lot in life. She saw men as the careless gender. It had fallen to the women in the world, as she saw it, to see that life progressed, that duty was honored. Men were selfish, and all too often, brutish. She loved Monty but couldn't understand why he let the boys slide. Well, she wouldn't have it, not with Walker anyway. She saw no hope for Eli, given who his rightful father was. Those genes were inferior. Monty was a good man, though, and she'd see to it that Walker showed the world that Rose Atkins was not white trash, not at all.

*   *   *

Walker slept in Eli's room that night. They hadn't shared a room since they moved to James Island.

"Eli, what's gonna happen?"

"I don't know, but Mr. Baslin told me that everything was gonna be all right and that he'd tell my story so the jury could learn the truth."

"But since you didn't do it, that means the real killer is still out there."

"Yep. And the police better catch him before I do. I swear on my life if I ever get my hands on that bastard, I'll kill him sure as I breathe."

Eli and Walker talked late into the night. After a while, they stopped talking about the murder, the trial, and Kimberly and talked instead about the coming summer, fishing, and whether the Braves had a chance. Walker wished the night would go on forever. Eli did too.

CHAPTER 18

Lord, Help Her

Monday night, while the boys were at baseball practice, the parents voted to kick Eli off the team. Neither Monty nor Rose had received a phone call about the impromptu team meeting. Standing in the parking lot, they elected the team mother's husband to tell the coach after practice, which he reluctantly did as the other parents huddled together a few feet back. The fathers were not in favor of the decision. Eli was their best player, but they were afraid to publicly voice their opinions, fearing the women's wrath. Alone with their wives, they defended Eli as innocent until proven guilty, and alone with their husbands the wives were reluctant to push the matter, but bound together, the wives' voices would not be silenced.

The coach told the parents the boys would be devastated. The parents were united in their decision, though, and it was agreed that the team mother's husband would call Monty that night and deliver the news.

A bunker mentality set in at the Atkins household. That Eli was told to leave the team, while not entirely unexpected, was bad enough, but when Walker's team took the same path, that was one too many blows. The news drove Eli, Walker, and Monty closer together but also isolated Rose from the men in her house and further divided Rose and Monty. Rose wanted to fight for Walker's spot on the team but Monty furiously proclaimed, "If they don't want one boy, then they can't have either!"

Rose cried, "Oh, Monty, if you only knew how much it hurts me when you take sides against me."

"What are you talking about, Rose? I'm not taking sides against you."

"But you are. Look at you with Walker and Eli. It's as if you don't want Walker playing ball this summer. You and your stubborn pride. Why won't you help him? It would bring a little joy to my life right now to see him playing with his friends. But no, your stubborn pride in announcing, 'If they don't want one boy, then they can't have either.'"

Rose raised her voice and shook her fist like a revival tent pastor in mock condemnation of her husband.

"I'll bet Eli put you up to it. He has you wrapped around his little finger," said Rose. "Oh, Monty, you can be so naïve."

"Rose, the boys need each other right now, and Walker doesn't want to play if Eli can't. They're together on this. I don't know why you can't be."

"Walker's too young to know what's best for him. He'll listen to his mother, though. Trust me, he wants to play—he's just afraid to stand against Eli and his own father. I'm surprised you can't see that."

"All right, all right. I'll talk to Walker and see about getting him back on the team."

*　　*　　*

Graduation ceremonies were less than a week away. The school principal phoned Monty at work Tuesday and complained about the pressure he was under to bar the Atkins family from the commencement ceremonies. Monty wanted to crawl through the phone and strangle the man, but he kept his cool. He knew the principal was hoping they would voluntarily stay away so he could dodge making a decision. Kimberly's parents had paid the principal a visit the day before. They opposed the Atkinses' presence at graduation, and they were considering a sizeable donation to the school's booster club if the gym were renamed in honor of their daughter. Principal Edgers thought that was a fine idea.

After dinner that night, the boys retreated to the driveway to shoot hoops while Monty told Rose about the conversation with Principal Edgars. Rose said nothing while Monty vented and declared adamantly that they would not cower but would attend both ceremonies, Eli's and Walker's, and do so proudly as a family.

When he finished, Rose spoke in a flat, resolute voice. "Monty, you're so stupid. You don't get it, do you? What you see as a family *isn't*. He's not *ours*. Walker is *ours*. I'm not going to let you destroy what we have over some romantic notion of what you think you have." Rose then complained of a migraine and went to bed.

Monty, staggered by her blows, grabbed a beer and retreated to his home office. Sitting alone in his recliner, he remembered when he had first met Rose and how thunderstruck he was. Cupid had hit him hard. Rose was beautiful, smart, funny, and knew what she wanted. But even then, he sensed she was wearing a mask and carrying a brokenness inside, pain and fear that handicapped her ability to trust. He knew some of what she had suffered growing up, but not everything. She was still holding back, hiding, even from him. Whatever the reason for her anger, the damage was done, and the person sitting across from him he did not know.

Something evil had a toehold in Rose and was turning her. At times like this, Monty believed he'd be happier single or with someone else, but he took his vows seriously. "Till death do us part," he'd promised before God. He would keep the promise; besides it was best for the boys. How could he ever look at them again if he divorced their mother? So Monty, not knowing how he'd walk the tightrope Rose had laid before him, did what he did in these situations. He prayed.

"Lord Jesus, I need help. I try so hard to please you, to be a good husband and a good father, and sometimes it seems I can't do one without failing at the other. Please forgive me, Lord. And Lord, I pray for Rose. Help her, please. I don't know what ails her, but it's like she's sick in her mind sometimes. She's so angry at Eli, and it seems she's angry at him just for being alive. Please help her love him."

CHAPTER 19

Choices Made

Late the next day, Monty phoned home and Walker answered.
"Walker, is your brother home yet?" Eli was to meet Mr. Baslin after school.

"No, not yet. I haven't seen him all day. He must have left early this morning."

"Okay, tell him I'd like to talk with him tonight when I get home. I want to hear about his meeting with Mr. Baslin."

"Okay, Dad."

"And tell your mom I'm working late and for y'all to eat without me."

"Okay, Dad."

When Walker told Mom that Dad wouldn't be home for dinner, she told him he should go to the Robertsons' house if he wanted any dinner. Toby Robertson was Walker's best friend. His parents told Rose and Monty they thought it was terrible about Walker being kicked off the team and that he was always welcome in their home.

"In fact, Walker, why don't you sleep over at the Robertsons'?"

"Mom, I don't want to. I want to see Eli when he gets home."

"Now, Walker, don't argue with me. I don't want you talking with Eli about such things."

Walker said nothing. He knew it was useless. Rose called Mrs. Robertson and sent Walker on his way. It was a short bicycle ride.

Rose sat on the sofa and stewed over all she'd been through, where she'd come from. She was bound and determined that proper society accept her, and that Walker have everything he deserved, everything she deserved. She called Monty and encouraged him to stay as late as necessary. He apologized for the long hours and hung up grateful for the long hours.

*   *   *

Rose was sitting on the sofa when she heard Eli pull up the driveway. Rose liked the crunching sound of an automobile rolling to a stop on a worn, tabby driveway. She associated it with the comfort and stability of a home. The sound tonight, though, seemed hollow and distant.

Eli took the back stairs to his room above the garage. The summer before, he'd asked if he could turn the room above the garage into his bedroom. Monty was in favor, wanting to show Eli he trusted him, and Monty wanted to treat Eli "like the man he was becoming." Rose saw it all as sentimental baloney but put up no fight.

"If you ask me, you coddle him too much, but I certainly won't object, not that anyone would listen to what I have to say. I'm only his mother." It was hard to hear the sarcasm through the drip, drip, drip of her self-pity.

Eli came downstairs and tiptoed into the living room where his mother sat with her needlepoint.

"Mom?"

"Yes, Eli."

"I had a good meeting with Mr. Baslin today."

"That's nice. I'm glad you think so."

"Mom, I didn't do it. You believe me, don't you?"

Rose didn't look up from her needlepoint but kept stitching and hesitated just long enough before answering.

"Of course, I do. I'm your mother."

"I talked with Mr. Baslin all about where I was when Kimberly was murdered, and he believes that when we tell the jury I was home, that there's no way they will believe I killed her. I told him you saw me come home early that night, and even though you're my mom and the jury might think you'd say anything to help your son, Mr. Baslin thinks people will have a hard time not believing you."

This time Rose put her needlepoint down, raised her eyes to meet Eli's, and spoke in a condescending voice of ultimate power.

"But Eli, I didn't see you come home that night. Remember? I told the police Saturday night when they came to the house that I hadn't seen you come home Friday night."

Eli trembled with fear, not fear of the trial or of a guilty verdict, but of the woman who sat before him. He knew she'd seen him come home because their eyes had met as he started up the stairs. They both knew!

Rose continued. "Now how is it going to look to folks if I'm caught in a lie on the stand? Surely Officer Pearlman will testify that I had told him I went to bed early that night and didn't hear you come home. I'm not going to let anyone show me to be a liar, and certainly not that uppity nigger."

Rose's voice grew louder and louder with each word. She began to shake, her anger pouring forth from a deep-seated fear, her fear of being found out. She got ahold of herself, casually picked up her needlepoint, and resumed her sewing.

"But I'm not concerned about me. Goodness no. A mother's first job is always her children. I'm just so worried about how all this is affecting Walker. Eli, have you thought for one minute how all this is affecting our son, Walker?"

Eli had never felt so alone, so isolated as when she uttered those words "our son, Walker." Wasn't he their son too?

"Eli, if you love Walker, if you love your father and me, then you'll make all this go away. Only you can make it go away. You heard Mr. Baslin say the trial may not be held till late this year. Now how can you let this hang over this family for that long? Don't you feel selfish? Doesn't it make you feel awful knowing what you are doing to Walker? What you're doing to this family? What you're doing to me? To my family?"

Silence filled the room, and it felt as if time stopped. Eli stood there, and tears streamed down his face. Emotions poured out of him he'd tried so hard to bury. Eli was alone and scared. But worse, he was unloved, he was unlovable.

"Eli, in the closet in your father's office, you'll find a safe where he keeps emergency money. The combination is our wedding anniversary. Now I'm going to bed. I feel a migraine coming on."

Rose stood from the sofa, bent over to pick up her needlepoint, and headed toward her bedroom. She stopped at the bottom of the stairs, and with one hand on the railing and her left foot on the first step, she turned and stared at Eli. "I'm hopeful that tomorrow when I wake, my pain will be gone."

And with that, she strode slowly, purposefully up the stairs.

*   *   *

The noise didn't startle her. On any other night, it would have. A crashing noise, a door broken down. And then silence. Ten minutes later, the sound of the tabby driveway being crushed under car tires. She always found that noise so comforting, the sound of a happy, stable family.

Rose rolled over and closed her eyes.

*   *   *

Monty pulled into the driveway just past midnight. All the lights were out, and Eli's car was gone. Monty was too tired to worry as he entered his home.

Monty quietly climbed into bed so as not to wake Rose, but she came to him and pressed her body against his, and she slid her hand across his body, gently grazing his nipples, and down into his boxers. This was unexpected, but welcome, and he was too tired to question this gift from her.

*   *   *

By late the next day, it could no longer be denied that no one knew where Eli was. Walker had not seen him at school. He had missed his meeting with Chester, and he was not at the dinner table. Under normal circumstances, they would have called friends to ask about him. But for this situation, they had no playbook. Shortly after 10:00 p.m., Monty went upstairs to his office to call Ches at home, and that's when he saw it—the recliner in the corner had been moved.

He walked over to the chair and saw why; it had been moved to hide the damaged closet door. Monty entered the closet and looked at the safe in the corner. The door to it was ajar and the full-length London Fog hanging in front of it had been moved to one side. His heart raced. "Oh, Eli. What have you done? Please, Eli. Please don't be true."

Monty opened the safe. The cash was gone. Ten thousand dollars. Eli was on the lam.

PART TWO

You thought God was an architect, now you know
He's something like a pipe bomb ready to blow
And everything you built that's all for show goes up in flames
In twenty-four frames.

TWENTY-FOUR FLAMES
BY JASON ISBELL

Many are the plans in the mind of a man,
but it is the purpose of the Lord that will stand.

PROVERBS 19:21

CHAPTER 20

Now What?

"Are my clients under arrest?"

Chester Basil's question was met with silence. "I repeat: Are my clients under arrest?"

Shortly after Eli fled, the rest of the Atkins family came under suspicion. Most folks figured they had helped Eli run or at least knew where he was. Monty convinced Chester to take them on as clients. Chester explained that he likely had a conflict of interest, but Monty argued persuasively that no such issue would arise if Eli returned, at which point Monty and Rose would not need an attorney. In the end, Chester agreed to represent them.

"No, Chester, they're not," answered a frustrated chief of police.

"Then they're free to go."

"Yes, but if I was you, I'd advise your clients to stay in town. Fleeing the scene may run in their family, and we're likely to have more questions for them."

"We'll give your advice the weight it's due," said Chester.

111

And with that, Chester nodded at Rose and Monty, who were seated quietly in Chief Riddle's office like back-row church folks arriving late and hoping not to be noticed.

Five minutes later, Chester, Monty, and Rose were standing in the parking lot outside the Charleston police department. It had been a hellish three weeks since Eli had disappeared. Graduation ceremonies had come and gone. The Atkinses, of their own volition, had stayed away with Walker while his friends and classmates matriculated.

The police had conducted a manhunt for Eli in Charleston, throughout the surrounding areas, and across the low country. Police departments in the states of Georgia and North Carolina, as well as the FBI, were alerted given the capital nature of Eli's alleged crime.

There was absolutely no sign of Eli, and after three weeks, the search was abandoned. Rumors ran rampant. It was no secret that Eli was an accomplished outdoorsman. The police received tips that he'd been seen in the Blue Ridge Mountains and the low country swamps. The most outrageous rumor had it that he'd made it to Cuba and was playing semi-pro baseball.

The police questioned Rose and Monty extensively. Most everyone presumed they knew where Eli was and had helped him escape. It was the logical conclusion. How else could an eighteen-year-old just vanish? The police, though, lacked any proof of their cooperation, and of course, there wouldn't be any such evidence because they hadn't cooperated.

Monty was a wreck. He couldn't sleep wondering where Eli had run off to. He told the police about the missing money and showed them the busted doorframe. This served to convince some but not all within the police department that Rose and Monty were not involved.

Among the police, several quietly celebrated Eli's vanishing act. Officers Pearlman and Tyrell never believed Eli was guilty in the first place. When he ran from the gathering at the Prestwick house, their training kicked in, and they had chased him down. They regretted bringing him into the police station for booking in handcuffs, but that was the procedure.

*　　*　　*

Monty was growing impatient. He was ready to hit the road so he busied himself organizing the AAA road maps in the car's glove compartment as Rose continued talking with Chester Baslin. "Chester, we don't know how to thank you for all you've done for our family," said Rose. "We wouldn't have survived this ordeal without you."

"I appreciate your kind words, and thank you, but no more mention of it is necessary. This is what I do," explained Chester.

"Well, you're awfully good at it," remarked Rose.

Chester had noticed that Monty and Rose seemed closer. Rose was certainly warmer and more supportive of Monty. Monty had seen it too. The change had occurred after Eli left. Chester smiled, nodded humbly, and said thank you.

"So now what?" asked Chester.

"We're packing up the car and taking Walker to Atlanta for a few days. The Braves have a three-game series with the Dodgers next week. After that, we may drive to Florida for a week. Hilton Head and Kiawah are off-limits," said Monty.

"Yes, I'm afraid so," added Rose. "The chances of running into someone from Charleston at either place are just too great. We need some time alone and away from all this."

"Chester, do you think we need to take Chief Riddle's warnings seriously? You know, about not leaving town?" asked Monty.

"No. Not at all. Just call me once a week. If the chief needs to speak with you, he knows to call me first. If I can tell him where you are and that you're staying in touch, all will be fine."

"That's a relief. Rose is right. We need to get away in the worst way. We just need things around here to settle down. We need a chance at a normal life," said Monty.

Monty started to well up. He could pretend all he wanted, but Eli's absence was killing him. Walker too. Monty knew he was innocent, but then why did he run? Rose stood closer by his side and gave him a reassuring hug. He turned and smiled at her.

"Okay then. I guess it's time to hit the road," announced Monty as he gave Rose a quick peck on the lips.

They all shook hands and promised to stay in touch. Chester held Rose's door as she got into the passenger side of the car and he watched them drive away. He said a silent prayer for them, and for Eli, and for the Prestwick family too. Chester didn't share Monty's optimism about life returning to normal around here. Not by a long shot.

*   *   *

Chief Riddle sat in his office and watched the three of them through his window, looking for signs of collusion. He didn't believe for one minute their claims of ignorance as to Eli's whereabouts. Parents would do anything to protect their children. Hell, he knew he would. He knew Monty would. He wasn't so sure about Mrs. Atkins, though. She was a cold one.

After Eli ran, the police had continued to work the case. The evidence from the crime scene was carefully bagged and stored. The new police-woman they had hired earlier in the year was determined to employ a new evidence-gathering procedure that was being called a "rape kit." The rape kit outlined a protocol for taking and storing samples from a rape victim that might assist in obtaining a guilty verdict. She took samples from the victim, Kimberly Prestwick, and carefully stored them. When quizzed about the usefulness of such evidence, she said that breakthroughs in forensics would someday make it possible to identify whether a semen sample taken from a crime scene belonged to a particular defendant. Chief Riddle was skeptical. But, since there would not be a trial, he didn't have to share any evidence with the defense because without a defendant, there would be no trial, and without a trial, there would be no deadlines for the prosecution to turn over evidence.

"Mrs. Babcock, can you step in here, please?"

Mrs. Babcock was a fixture in the Charleston Police Department. She had been working for the department for fifty-five years. Her first husband, a police officer with the department, was killed in action trying to apprehend an armed bank robber. They'd only been married a little over a year at the time. The police department rallied around the young Mrs. Babcock and had all but guaranteed her lifetime employment. She married again, and they raised a large family. Her usefulness around the office, however, had waned with each passing year, but what were you going to do? No one had the heart to fire her.

"Yes, Chief Riddle." Mrs. Babcock scooted into his office with a pen and pad in her hand, ready to be useful. She stood barely five feet five inches tall. Her employment file, opened fifty-five years earlier, listed her at five feet eight inches.

"Did the report come back from the hospital yet?" asked Chief Riddle.

"Yes, Officer Tyrell has it. Would you like me to get him for you?"

Chief Riddle could have rung him from his desk phone, but he got a kick out of Mrs. Babcock's always helpful attitude. "Yes, would you please?"

"Right away, Chief," said Mrs. Babcock with a quick salute as she scooted back out the door and down the hallway, choosing not to call him from the phone on her desk.

Five minutes later, a distraught Officer Tyrell was leaning against the door frame of the chief's office with a yellow evidence folder under his arm.

"Well, Officer Tyrell, what's the verdict?" asked Chief Riddle.

Officer Tyrell waddled into the office and sat in the chair across the desk from the chief. "The hospital reported that the blood sample is human and not from an animal," answered Officer Tyrell as he leaned across the desk to pass the file folder to the chief.

"Anything else? Is the blood A negative? O positive? Anything like that? If we knew that, then we could compare it to Kimberly Prestwick's and see if we got a match," said the chief as he thumbed through the file.

"No, sir. The blood sample was dry. The hospital only has equipment for running those types of tests on wet samples. The technician I spoke with said there are new test methods under development that allow more extensive testing on dry samples. She suggested we contact the FBI for further help."

"I don't think that will be necessary," said the chief. "We have a hot-headed boyfriend seen fighting with his girlfriend in a bar right before the girlfriend storms out, leaving him alone, embarrassed, and angry. That girl turns up dead a few hours later with injuries caused by a serrated hunting knife. The boyfriend runs from the police to avoid arrest. His family hires a high-powered attorney, but he skips bail anyway, and now we learn that the hunting knife with the serrated edge found in the bed of his truck has dried human blood on the blade. Seems open and shut to me. Wouldn't you agree, Officer Tyrell?"

Officer Tyrell shifted his large frame in the chair before answering. "Chief Riddle, with all due respect, I do not. Anyone could have put the knife in his truck," said Officer Tyrell.

"Now that's a stretch. Eli had motive. Your mystery killer, what's his motive? You can only guess. Your theory is just that, a theory and a theory that rests on nothing more than your desire for him to be innocent. You're too close to this. I'm aware that your son, Leroy, and Eli were friends, quite close actually. But sometimes, the most obvious answer is the answer. Most of the time, in fact," replied Chief Riddle.

"Then why were fingerprints wiped from the knife handle, but the blood-stain wasn't?" asked Officer Tyrell.

Chief Riddle stared curiously at the officer in front of him, not searching for an answer to the question but wondering how he was going to put this matter to rest. He had a perfect record of solved cases, and he wasn't going to sacrifice that because a perp had fled the scene.

"Well, we would have found out on cross-examination if the defendant hadn't run. Officer Tyrell, the case is closed. Please box up the contents and place the evidence box in storage. Mark it for disposal in seven years. If Eli doesn't show up in seven years, we'll presume him dead."

CHAPTER 21

The Prestwicks

THE PRESTWICKS

Burying Kimberly had upset the natural order of things for Stephen and Gloria Prestwick. Children are supposed to bury their parents, not the other way around. Young couples fall in love, have children, build careers, and nurture families. On the horizon lie the anticipated joys of retirement: a slower pace and, of course, grandchildren. For the Prestwicks, when they lost their oldest child to violence, those dreams, once propelled forward by a seeming inevitability, came crashing down around them suddenly and without warning.

As couples start a family, a husband and wife's focus often turns from the other and toward the child. Parents are encouraged to elevate the child's needs above all else. "It's for the children!" Spouses may begin to view their mate more as a partner in child-rearing than as a partner in this life together. This re-shifting in focus can leave a void in the life of either a husband or wife, who, to fill that void, may turn to what elevates their self-worth. For a man that can be his work; for a woman it can be work as well but more often her relationships with others, with the community, and, of course, with a child.

As Stephen and Gloria became partners in child-rearing, the fact that they were partners during their time on earth together fell out of focus, and when Kimberly was ripped from their life, the resulting chasm, not just between them, but within each of them, had to be filled. Stephen filled it with work.

It was an exciting time in the banking industry as it had recently been deregulated, thus allowing banks to compete nationally for loans and deposits. Banks, large and small, competed for clients and their deposits by paying higher interest rates. Smaller regional and local banks, savings and loan institutions, as well as thrift banks and credit unions, were no longer content to originate conservative business loans and home mortgages but began speculating on ever riskier and more lucrative real estate-backed deals. Banks earned higher fees, and interest rate spreads grew. A bank president who wasn't generating the same profits as other bank presidents was a future ex-president.

Stephen oversaw tremendous growth for his bank as he pushed it to become a leading real estate lender in the Carolinas. It seemed as if his distinguished face appeared in every local newspaper and magazine. Under his direction, the bank also purchased numerous smaller banks. Stephen was the darling of the local business community and both Stephen and his bank attracted outside attention. There was talk that the bank was a takeover target. Positioning the bank for just such a takeover had been his plan all along, and as an owner of bank stock and stock options, he stood to become a very wealthy man.

Stephen was never able to soothe the pain of losing Kimberly. The long hours at the office helped him forget a bit, and it was easier to ignore his perceived failings as a father—his failure to protect his daughter—when he saw his success in the boardroom. But Stephen paid too much attention to his press clippings. He began to see himself not merely as a successful bank president but as the reason for the bank's success. He felt that others must or should see him the same way, and most certainly his wife.

Gloria, however, didn't celebrate his professional successes. She complained about the long hours. She complained when he played golf. She complained when he went to dinner with clients. She tried to busy herself with charity work, at church, and at school. She would go to lunch, but her friends didn't know what to say. At these lunches, they would typically talk about their children and their families. Gloria's family was fractured, and in her mind, so was she. Slowly, Gloria withdrew, losing the battle for her sanity, and then she retreated to the bottle and pills.

Their loss drove them apart. In the immediate aftermath of Kimberly's death, they clung to each other like two people abandoned to the cold. But over time, every moment with the other was a reminder of what they had made and what they had lost. Unsaid, but felt by both though irrational on every level, each in some way blamed themselves but also the other.

They stopped having sex. For Gloria, there was simply no desire and what desire she might have conjured, the pills crushed. While merely symptomatic of the gulf that now separated them, for Stephen, the lack of sex was rejection. He was hurt. Why couldn't she be more supportive of him and his work? Why didn't she want to have sex? He missed Kimberly as much as she did. They needed each other now more than ever.

Stephen saw his needs as unmet. He was a successful and important man in town, and he had needs, like any man. Stephen soon found that Daphny, his young executive secretary, was able to meet those needs. His secretary knew how hard he worked. Unlike his wife, she appreciated him for all his talents. She sat in awe of him. She made him feel like the important man he saw himself to be, the important man he needed to believe he was.

Gloria learned of the affair from a group of her girlfriends who had each received an envelope in their mailbox with no return address, envelopes filled with pictures of Stephen and the young, long-legged, big-breasted Daphny, executive secretary extraordinaire. The caring girlfriends came with the news and to talk to her about her 10:00 a.m. cocktails.

Her humiliation was complete. She didn't want the divorce to be quiet; he did. She had her own family money to pay any attorney, but the pills kept her in bed most of the day. It became easier to surrender to the inevitable and just sign the papers and leave. Which is what she did. In the summer of 1975, a little over two years after Kimberly had been ripped from their lives, Gloria took their other two children, Kimberly's two younger brothers, and returned to her childhood home of Richmond, Virginia.

Stephen was now free to marry his secretary. Daphny was thrilled; no longer having to sneak around, she became the new Mrs. Stephen Prestwick, influential and socially prominent. Stephen, however, found that he liked the idea of a mistress more than the idea of a new wife.

Chapter 22

The Atkinses

The Atkinses

The Atkins family kept a low profile in the summer of 1973. They didn't attend church. They didn't rent at Kiawah. Monty went to the office and worked his caseload but didn't seek new clients. His practice suffered as his billings declined. A promising young associate left for greener pastures. Rose tended her garden but grew bored with it and took up tennis. She and Monty didn't know the tennis crowd at the club, so she hoped to slide in unnoticed and make new friends. But they knew her and stayed away. She would hit balls against the machine and took a few lessons, but her enthusiasm waned and she gave it up.

Walker was a hermit that summer. He didn't see his friends, didn't want to. He was confused, scared. Why did Eli run? Walker knew his brother wasn't a killer. But he didn't understand why he ran. Was Eli scared? What was he scared of? Who was he scared of? None of it made sense. But Walker missed Eli just the same.

Monty, Rose, and Walker made a few more short trips that summer, always someplace out of the way where they wouldn't be recognized. As the new school year approached, Rose grew impatient. She was determined to no longer live her life this way. In her mind, she'd given the town enough time to grieve; it was time to move on. She encouraged Monty and Walker to do the same.

"Walker, honey. Aren't you excited for the new school year? For a new school? You're going to love Porter-Gaud. You'll get to start over," exclaimed Rose.

Walker wasn't excited, but he was hopeful. Hopeful he could attend school unnoticed. Hopeful his mother would let him be.

"Monty, snap out of it," she'd say. "You're just going through the motions. Your law practice was successful before this mess, and we were making money. Don't let your hard work go to waste. Don't lie down."

Monty knew she was right, but he had a hard time finding any fight in him.

Rose, though, had enemies, real and imagined—enemies from her past that drove her to succeed. Nothing was going to keep her from showing everyone in town that she wasn't white trash, that she wasn't as her father saw her, that she was, in fact, better than them.

Monty, on the other hand, was struggling in part because he couldn't define what ailed him. His battle was with himself. He battled lethargy. His practice was off, but they were still very comfortable. He was carrying more debt than was prudent, but he could service it.

His problem was that he just didn't give a damn. Before Kimberly was murdered, before Eli vanished, they were doing well. Life was understandable, predictable. He was making money and belonged to a prominent private club. He had purchased the Kiawah beach house they had been renting. Eli had a real shot at a pro baseball career, Walker was a savant in school, his law practice was thriving, and Rose was content as a mother and in her role with her myriad clubs and associations. Sure, Rose and Eli fought all the time, but outwardly they were a happy family, and he knew what was important. At least he thought he did.

And then, everything had changed. Monty no longer had any fight in him. Even if he'd had any fight in him, he didn't know what to fight for because he didn't comprehend what he had lost. Yes, he'd lost Eli, but it was more than that. He'd lost a reason to strive. He'd lost any hope for joy. His faith in God was rocked. Rose barked that he should just "snap out of it." If only it were that easy.

Monty was adrift. He knew Eli wasn't a killer. He knew there was no way he could have committed the crime. But why then did Eli run? This was the question that haunted him. To deal with the doubts, he did the only two things he knew to do. He worked, and he prayed.

Monty turned to his legal practice and applied a disciplined focus that helped him get through the days. There was also the matter of the fee he'd paid Chester, and more importantly, the bail money Monty had to turn over to the bail bondsman after Eli skipped town. Monty used the bank loan he had arranged the day of Eli's arraignment to pay the bail bondsman, but now he owed the bank plus interest that was accruing. Quite simply, cash was tight. He couldn't afford another downturn in his business.

Monty focused on growing his client base. He attended bar meetings, spoke at conferences, wrote guest articles for journals, and generally did whatever he needed to do to grow his business. Folks were reluctant to warm up to him, and even some longstanding clients were leery of the association with the father of Kimberly Prestwick's suspected killer. But Monty was persistent. He refused to quit. If someone turned him away, he'd politely thank them for their time and move on to the next prospect.

But the long hours ground him up. His health was suffering. He had no real appetite and barely slept anymore. And then he had to quit the church choir, the one remaining joy in his life. His voice was growing weaker. At times, he'd lose his voice entirely for days on end, and then it would reappear. Rose begged him to see a doctor. He did. They had no explanation.

*   *   *

WALKER

Walker had moved to Porter-Gaud at the beginning of seventh grade. This transfer had been set in motion by Rose long before Kimberly was murdered and Eli had vanished. It was assumed by most that the move had been engineered in haste by Rose and Monty the summer following Kimberly's murder and done to protect Walker. Rose would have been fine with folks believing either the fact or the fiction just so long as they saw Walker as different from Eli.

The change provided what Walker initially hoped for—anonymity. Physically, he didn't stand out. As a younger boy, he'd been taller than most his age, but he hadn't had his growth spurt yet and the others had, so they were catching up. Furthermore, he was content to go along and attract as little attention as possible. During his seventh- and eighth-grade years, he succeeded. Hardly anyone could have said they knew him. If his classmates had been asked about him, they would have described him as the new kid, kind of quiet. Never the first to enter or leave the classroom. He didn't go out for sports, and he kept to himself. His grades were excellent, but he could apply himself in the classroom without attracting attention. He was miserable, lonely, adrift, and wondering if he'd ever feel comfortable around people again. Worst of all, he was growing comfortable with feeling this way. The other kids weren't mean to him, but they let him remain aloof; it was easier for them that way too.

Rose and Monty were worried. Rose was relentless, encouraging him to become involved.

"You know, Walker, laziness is a sin, and when you succeed, I succeed. I celebrate your every success. Why, in the adult Sunday school class I taught last week, I spoke on that very subject."

Of course, what Walker actually heard was what Rose didn't say but what Walker was quite sure she actually meant: "And when you fail, I fail, and how do you think that makes me look?"

Monty was a bit more understanding but no less concerned and no less demanding. Monty saw the world in simple terms. If you wanted something, you had to go get it, and if someone else had it, then you had to take it from them.

"Son, you know I love you, so I'm saying this for your own good. Don't be a quitter. You have to fight and work hard in this world. Son, you're special. You can do anything you set your mind to. I've seen it. Now get back out there and show them what you're made of."

Walker had heard so many versions of these speeches, he could give them himself. He witnessed his mother pushing herself back into society without a care for what others thought, determined as she was to show them she belonged, and it was painfully obvious she was going to employ Walker to fulfill her dreams of acceptance. Walker must succeed if she was ultimately going to be seen as a success.

Walker witnessed his father's relentless drive at the office. It was as if he never rested. Even when he was watching the Braves on TV, he read legal journals and briefs. The golf course provided him his only respite, but he hardly made time for golf anymore.

But lurking inside was the nagging feeling that his parents were right. He didn't want to disappoint his mother, and he tried to make his father proud, but most of all, he didn't want to disappoint Eli.

He'd never forget the sound of his father crying out that night, the night Eli left. He ran up the stairs, not knowing what he'd find. His father was sitting in his chair with his head in his hands. He looked up at Walker as he stood in the doorway to Monty's home office. Tears streamed down, and Walker saw a look of utter fear on his face.

*   *   *

Walker crawled into bed that night sobbing. He was so confused. Eli couldn't have done anything wrong. But why did he run away? Why didn't Eli say something to him? Walker wondered all these things and more. Walker wanted to run too, but he didn't know where to run or how to. Walker picked up his outfielder's glove and absentmindedly put it on. He wanted to play center field because Eli had. When Walker put his hand in the glove, he felt a piece of paper. He pulled it out and sat up. He turned on the bedside lamp and read:

"Walker, I didn't do it. Now go out into the world and make your big brother proud!"

The note Eli had left Walker in his baseball glove that night burned unrelentingly, and the more he tried to ignore it, the hotter it burned. What was he supposed to do? He was just a kid. He didn't know, but he couldn't shake the feeling that Eli was depending on him too.

"Walker, I didn't do it. Now go out into the world and make your big brother proud."

*   *   *

As the ninth grade approached, Walker was coming out of his funk. Central to his awakening was the return of his good friend from a few summers before at Kiawah, Toby Robertson. Toby had attended boarding school in the Northeast the last few years. Instead of returning to Kiawah for the summers, his family had spent their summers in a place called Nantucket, a place Walker had never heard of.

This summer, Toby's family was renting the same house at Kiawah they had the summer Toby and Walker first met. They were each so excited when they saw each other, and they picked up right where they had left off. Toby's family was making a permanent move to Charleston, and Toby would be attending Porter-Gaud the next year with Walker.

Toby had lost his baby fat since two summers before. He was shorter than Walker but more than compensated for his stature with a very outgoing, some would say precocious attitude. He wore glasses and his brown hair a little long. Walker told him he'd have to cut it before he could attend school. Toby knew all about dress codes, having attended a prep school in Connecticut. He said his parents let him grow it out all summer.

Toby knew nothing of the Kimberly-Eli episode. But after a few days, Toby sensed that something had changed with Walker since they had last seen each other. Toby asked about Eli and Walker would change the subject. Toby persisted.

"Walker, something's wrong. I can tell. Every time I ask about Eli, you get all weird and try to change the subject. What's eatin' you? What's goin' on?"

Walker told Toby everything, even about the note Eli left. Toby just sat there and didn't say a word. An adult would have butted in and tried to help Walker, but somehow Toby knew better; he knew that just sitting with his friend and listening to him was the right thing. Walker cried in front of his friend. It was the first time he'd cried since the night Eli left. They sat on the beach for hours, and Walker just let it all out.

When it looked as if Walker was done, Toby said: "So then what are you gonna do?"

"What do you mean?" asked Walker.

"You know. How are you going to make him proud?"

"You mean Eli?"

"Yeah, I mean Eli!"

"I don't know. That's the problem. I don't know what to do."

"Well, I know that sittin' here crying like a girl ain't gonna help. But I can help you."

"How?" asked Walker.

"Well, I don't know exactly, but we're gonna start by gettin' you off your lazy ass for one. Tomorrow morning we're going for a run."

"A run? Why?"

"Because I was on the JV cross-country team at my school last year, and I intend to make the Porter-Gaud team this fall, and you're going out for the team too."

"Okay," said Walker, not really knowing why he agreed to but not being able to think of a reason not to.

And that's how it started. Toby and Walker were inseparable. They ran almost every day. Within a couple of weeks, Walker was keeping up with

Toby, and by the time the fall cross-country tryouts were announced, Toby couldn't keep up with Walker. Walker was a natural. Running became his outlet. He found that he could run and run and that he grew stronger as the run progressed. He could run alone or with a group, but running on a team gave him a way back in, a way back into hanging out with other kids. Running saved his life, and he had Toby to thank.

*   *   *

Monty and Rose attended the same church as did the Prestwick family. Monty and Rose could always be seen ten or eleven rows from the front—never too close to the front to draw attention and never too close to the back for the same reason. Monty had resigned as a deacon in the church to save the other parishioners the embarrassment of having to ask him to step down. Rose was not so accommodating when it came to teaching Sunday school. Not only did she continue to teach, but she volunteered for even more service around the church. By her presence, Rose dared people to ask her to leave. She was the picture of piety and humility, though, and over time she wrestled the mantle of victimhood away from Gloria Prestwick.

Not that Gloria put up much of a fight. Before news of Stephen's affair became public, Gloria and Stephen had stopped going to church altogether. Stephen was never much for church to begin with. He saw religion as a crutch for weak people who needed help, and since he was very successful and not in need of help, he reasoned there was no reason to attend church just so folks could feel sorry for him. He saw Gloria, however, as needing help in light of her growing drinking problem, but the last thing Stephen wanted was for more people to know about it so he never encouraged her to attend one of the prayer groups or social service organizations the church offered.

Gloria was in no mood to attend any church-based services anyway for the simple reason that she couldn't see room for God in her life. All she'd been taught growing up about God was proven a lie by what happened to her daughter Kimberly. Gloria had been raised to believe that if you went to church, tithed, and believed in Jesus, then your sins were forgiven, and God would take care of you. She'd done all those things, and God had failed her. So either it was all a lie or Gloria wasn't actually a Christian, and God was punishing her. Rather than seek the answer to this question or others, she anesthetized herself—better not to feel at all than to feel pain.

The tragedy that had befallen Monty's family and the Prestwicks also gave

Monty reason to doubt, but never about whether God was real, or about whether God was active in the world, or about the promise of salvation. No, Monty never doubted the fundamental elements of what he'd been raised to believe; to conclude otherwise would have required a tectonic shift of his worldview that he knew he couldn't survive. No, what Monty concluded was that God was testing him, and he was failing.

Monty tried to snap out of it and push forward, but the passion never stuck, and he'd slip back. He hadn't picked up a Bible in months and had attended church only once since Kimberly's murder. He felt guilty for not going. Maybe this was the problem? Perhaps he wasn't a good Christian? Maybe he needed to pray more, read the Bible more, serve on a few church committees? Perhaps then the Lord would answer his prayers? Was that how it worked? He didn't know and frankly didn't like the idea of the extra burdens, but it was how he'd been raised. The Lord had given him talents, and if he didn't use them, then the Lord would take them away.

He found inspiration in his son Walker. One night at the dinner table, Walker told Rose and him about his goal to become the fastest high school distance runner in South Carolina. Embracing this goal focused Walker and launched a turnaround in his attitude. Monty decided that he too needed a challenge. He also needed goals.

Yep, that was it. Monty was sure of it. Simply stated, God expected more from him. He concluded that he wasn't performing in the manner Jesus expected of him. The Lord was testing him. Well, he was up to the challenge. It took a while, but Monty was starting to feel it. Monty was back. He recommitted himself to the Lord, to work, to the job of being a good husband and a good father, to everything. He vowed to God and in private moments with the church pastor that he would honor his wife even more.

Despite the difficult financial times he was facing, he committed to tithing 20 percent and not just the 10 percent the Bible required. Monty was a humble man and did not boast of his religiosity; he just did it. In time, he was asked to serve as a deacon again. He took this as a sign that the Lord was pleased with him. So he worked even harder. He knew he'd be back on top in no time. The Lord would see to it. The Lord would bless his plans. He was on the right track. He just knew it.

What Monty didn't know was that a freight train was barreling down the track, determined to destroy him and what remained of his family.

CHAPTER 23

The Freight Train

The freight train's name? Stephen Prestwick.

Stephen refilled his drink and took a walk down to the end of the dock. Stephen had recently purchased a home on James Island with a deepwater dock. It was a gift to himself; he knew his wife preferred their downtown home, south of Broad.

It had been a perfect day. His wife, Daphny, was away in NYC shopping with girlfriends. He played golf in the morning with the husbands, and they had the course to themselves. Lunch after the round of golf was followed by an afternoon watching the Masters. Tom Watson won with a birdie on the seventeenth hole. Stephen thought that Jack Nicklaus would birdie the eighteenth for sure and send the tournament into extra holes, but Jack bogeyed the eighteenth instead. Looked like a passing of the torch. There was talk Jack would never win another major.

The setting sun was a beautiful sight. The wind was down and the water calm. Yes, a perfect day, but all was not right with Stephen. He had

129

everything—everything, that is, but peace. And why not? Because in a month, he would mark the fourth anniversary of Kimberly's brutal murder, and still, no one had paid. There had been no justice. The police hadn't turned up a thing. The private detectives he hired had similarly come up empty. There was no sign of Eli.

The worst part was that the community's attitude toward the Atkins family, what was left of it, was changing. In the immediate aftermath, most folks kept their distance from Rose and Monty Atkins. Monty couldn't get a golf game at the club and spent most of his time on the range or sneaking in a quick nine holes late in the day by himself. But lately, Stephen noticed that people were warming up to him.

This wouldn't stand. Despite Stephen's business success and his stunning new and very attentive wife, Stephen wasn't happy. Frankly, his wife had become a pest. She was spending money like water and had taken to her lofty position in society a bit too easily. The root of his anger, though, was not just his loss—Kimberly and his former life—but it was that no one had paid for her murder.

He heard the voices of some in town lament, those who believed Eli was innocent, that the Atkins family had suffered too. They had lost a son, after all, when Eli fled. Stephen seethed when he heard this talk.

No, in Stephen's mind, they had not suffered. Not at all. And someone had to pay. That someone would be Monty Atkins. Stephen vowed that he would ruin Monty if it was the last thing he did. Stephen finished his drink and walked back inside as a plan began to hatch.

*   *   *

April 11, 1977

"Good morning, Mr. Prestwick. Did you have a good Easter?" asked Becky, Stephen's new executive assistant.

"Easter? Oh, yeah. Sure. How about you?"

"I sure did."

Becky took a step into Stephen's office and stood with her hands clasped behind her back and turned slowly side to side. Stephen noticed her blouse and how it accented two of the reasons he was so quick to hire her.

"Well, that's great," replied Stephen. "Look, I'm going to need some quiet time this morning with my door shut, but then what do you say we have lunch together? Let's go over a few action items for the second quarter."

"A business lunch! That sounds wonderful. Should I reserve your favorite table at Henry's?" she asked.

"No, I think I'll mix it up. I know a little out-of-the-way place. Just a short drive from here. It'll be perfect."

Becky beamed and bounced a bit on her toes as she turned and sashayed out the door.

Stephen took a seat behind his desk and found the number in his Rolodex he was looking for. He picked up the phone, dialed the number, and propped his feet up on the desk as he waited for the man to answer. Panja always answered his own phone. Having no associates came with the territory.

"Private investigations. Louie Panja speaking."

"Panja. Stephen Prestwick here. I require your services again."

"If it's about finding that kid Eli, save your money. He vanished like a fart in the wind."

"No. It's not about that piece of shit. But how would you like to help me ruin his dad?"

"I'm listening."

*　　*　　*

Stephen was in an excellent mood at lunch. In his phone call with Louie Panja, he had explained that he wanted to know everything concerning Monty. His finances, personal life, upbringing, parents, legal practice, etc.... a complete dossier. He was after information. Everyone had a weakness. He would learn it and exploit it. Louie told him it would take about a month.

Over lunch, he feigned business talk with Becky and complimented her on her performance in the office. "You could go far with us," he said. "It's all about who you tie your wagon to." She nodded her pretty little head like she understood perfectly. Stephen doubted she understood much of anything.

After her second glass of wine, she excused herself. Stephen admired the view as she walked toward the ladies' room. The joke in the men's room was that you could rest a beer mug on her ass. Stephen decided it was time to find out.

*　　*　　*

To Stephen's way of thinking, hiring Louie Panja to help him bury Monty had been a brilliant decision. Knowing he had a top man on the job allowed him to focus on work—growing the bank's profits and enhancing the bank's profile in the community. The previous year he had taken real strides forward when he completely revamped the loan committee. For too long, the committee had been manned by old, stodgy, overly conservative local businessmen with no real vision. It was as if they took pride in saying "No." They were continually voting him down. He was the president, dammit!

He knew he needed new people on the loan committee, but even though Stephen was the bank president, he couldn't just replace them. The board of directors had a say in the matter. A few men would be stepping down from the board because their term would end. He needed two others to retire early, and he'd be able to swing the committee.

That was about the time he had first met Louie Panja. Stephen met Louie at a two-day conference in Savannah. Sitting at the hotel bar late one night, Stephen got trapped in a conversation with a drunk at the bar who couldn't stop complaining about some asshole private dick who had ruined his life. The man was a peer in the banking world who Stephen knew, even if only superficially, so Stephen didn't immediately remove himself from the conversation. But as the man described how the private detective his ex-wife had hired was able to learn things about him which he'd forgotten himself, Stephen became more interested.

"Resourceful, you say?" asked Stephen.

"More like a ruthless son of a bitch if you ask me," cried the drunk.

"And he lives here in Savannah?" asked Stephen. "A guy like that could come in handy," joked Stephen.

"Yeah, if you needed a stand-in while you were shedding your own skin."

Yep, everyone had secrets; secrets they were willing to do almost anything to keep secret, including accepting early retirement from the board of directors. Secrets Louie turned up.

Louie Panja wasn't a private detective, not anymore. Private detectives were licensed, and Louie lost his license when one of his associates was caught suspending a man by his feet off the edge of a bridge. Louie felt that "the strictures of state licensing requirements frustrated his efforts to serve his clientele." Louie was thin, with a gaunt face made more the so by a permanent five o'clock shadow. His hair was long and greasy on the sides and bald on top. He sported unruly sideburns, and for reasons no one could fathom, he felt he was attractive to every woman he encountered. He wore brown or pea-green leisure suits exclusively, except on hot days when he'd wear the pants but replace the shirt and jacket with a sleeveless T-shirt.

When five vacancies opened up, Stephen stacked the bank's board and loan committee with golfing buddies, many of whom knew nothing about sound lending practices but enjoyed the prestige of their positions and the power to grant "bold, business-minded loans to a new generation of entrepreneurs," as the local newspapers and business periodicals were fond of saying. These larger loans meant fatter bank fees. Larger loans also meant larger clients who would then bring the bank all their banking business, including their deposit accounts. Bank deposits meant more money to lend, making Stephen's bank, First National Bank, an attractive takeover target for a national bank.

*   *   *

MAY 1977

A month later he was sitting in the corner of a hole-in-the-wall bar with Louie Panja. Louie lived and worked in Savannah, so it was doubtful anyone in Charleston would know him, but Stephen wasn't taking any chances by meeting him in a more popular setting.

Panja handed Stephen a thick folder. "There you go. Everything you need to know about one Montgomery Atkins," said Louie.

"Excellent. Give me the short version. What do we have on him?" asked Stephen.

"This guy's a real choirboy. I got nuttin' on him personally. And his wife? She's wound so tight you could shove a piece of coal up her ass and have a diamond in a week."

Stephen looked pissed. "And this took you a month? To find out nuttin'?!" announced Stephen sarcastically. Stephen was not happy.

"Settle down. Settle down. I didn't say it was hopeless."

"Go on."

"He's got debts."

"Something we can work with?"

"You still buyin' banks?" asked Louie.

"Yes, but what does that have to do with anything?"

"Ever think of buying Low Country Savings & Loan?" asked Louie.

"Why would I buy that piece-of-shit little S&L?"

"Because Monty Atkins owes that little piece-of-shit S&L over $100,000, and he's behind on his payments."

Stephen broke into a grinch-like smile and asked, "Louie, anyone ever tell you that you're a beautiful human being?"

"You'd be the first."

And the two of them clinked their glasses in a toast to the day when Stephen Prestwick would bankrupt Monty Atkins.

*　　*　　*

Louie finished his drink and made his way back to his car, declining another drink on account of the drive back to Savannah he had ahead of him. Stephen, though, instead of going home to wife number two, formerly mistress number one, headed downtown to a finer establishment and saddled up to the bar for another drink.

Stephen met a man at the bar that night who described himself as a private lender and an experienced real estate investor. He was from Phoenix, Arizona, and his company was looking to expand its business operations in the Southeast. He explained that he was in Charleston to scout out the area and hopefully establish mutually beneficial relationships with a quality bank dialed into the local economy.

After listening to Stephen expound on himself and his bank, the private lender named Stan Moore told Stephen that he was very excited to have met him, for Stephen appeared to be precisely the sort of intelligent, forward-thinking businessman his company, Cutthroat Capital, was hoping to find. Stephen expressed dismay at the company name, suggesting that inclusion of the word *cutthroat* wasn't the smartest PR move for a lender.

Stan laughed. Stan had an infectious laugh, and when you spoke to him his eyes never left yours. Stan made you feel like the most important person in the room when you were speaking. Tan from living in the desert, Stan looked healthy. He had a hearty handshake, the kind that pulled you toward him as he pumped his hand. The slight scar over his left eye gave him character and made him look rugged and handsome. A real man's man. "We get it all the time. Kind of a private joke amongst us. My partners and I all love fly fishing. We have an annual corporate retreat every summer in Colorado at this great little fishing lodge where the trout, Cutthroat trout that is, just about leap out of the water and onto your fly. It's amazing. We'll have to have you out there sometime. So hey, do you fly fish, Stephen?"

"No, purely spinning reel, but frankly, I'm more of a golfer."

"Well, we play a lot of golf out in the desert too. Got a game we like to play called Wolf. You a gambler, Stephen?"

"Sure, Stan, I like a little action."

"Excellent. We're going to get along great."

Stan and Stephen shook hands, exchanged business cards, and promised to follow up the next week with a meeting. On the back of Stan's business card for Cutthroat Capital was an image of a fly fisherman with a fish on, and the rod bowed. Stephen smiled to himself and walked down the street to an apartment he had recently purchased through a shell corporation Louie had set up for him. Becky would be waiting for him. Stephen looked forward to telling Becky about his meeting with this new business acquaintance, Stan Moore. He knew she loved hearing him talk about himself and his work. Yep, she'd hitched her wagon to the right horse.

CHAPTER 24

Leaving the Station

JUNE 1977

Stephen was sitting in the board room surrounded by lawyers and consultants charging him by the hour. God, how he hated lawyers.

"Stephen, you asked me to prepare a list of possible takeover targets for you, and that's what I've done. Today we'd like to review each bank and discuss the merits of each as an acquisition. How does that sound?" asked the bank's chief counsel. "I've brought in outside counsel as well as the bank consultant we keep on retainer to supplement my work," explained the chief counsel.

More like do *your work*, thought Stephen.

"Well, that's what I asked you to do, so yes, that sounds like a good idea," said Stephen.

Stephen was anxious to move forward. He already knew which bank he would move on, but for appearances, he took his time. Stephen couldn't make it look like he was purchasing Low Country Savings & Loan for the sole purpose of fucking over Monty Atkins. The bank had procedures to

137

follow, and if presented with a list of candidates, it wouldn't appear quite so obvious when he selected the bank holding the mortgage on Monty's home. He'd choose three banks from the list to further conceal his intentions.

The presentations took over two hours, during which time Stephen asked questions about every candidate. It was evident to all that he was engaged. A genuine captain of industry.

"Men, I think that will do. I'm going to study these documents and make a decision over the weekend. Bob, as the bank's chief counsel, you'll run point on any acquisitions and keep these sharks circling the table here from overbilling us."

Nervous laughter all around.

"And this goes for everyone in the room: I demand absolute silence as to our intentions. No one is to know what we're doing until it's done. Is that clear?" asked Stephen.

"Of course, Stephen. Just like on previous acquisitions."

"No! Not like on previous acquisitions when everyone knew we were buying the bank before the ink on our letter of intent was even dry. I demand absolute confidentiality. When we announce the takeover, I want that to be the first anyone without a need to know has heard about it. So one more time: Is. That. Clear?" demanded Stephen.

"Yes, sir," replied Bob the chief counsel. All the other bobbleheads around the table nodded in agreement.

The last thing Stephen wanted was for Monty to hear about the impending takeover and refinance with another bank. Paranoia was not Stephen's modus operandi. He doubted Monty knew the degree to which he loathed him. How could he? Stephen was always professional and cordial toward Monty when their paths crossed. Still, it was better to be safe than sorry.

"Very well. This meeting is over. You guys can turn off your meters now," said Stephen.

Nervous laughter all around. God, how these lawyers hated bankers.

CHAPTER 25

Monty is Torn but Young Love is Born

The storm from the previous evening had never materialized, draping the morning with an oppressive humidity worn like a wet shawl. Monty and Rose were finishing their coffee and preparing for church. Walker was, as usual, waiting till the last minute to join them in the kitchen.

"Why do I have to wear a tie?" complained Walker.

"Because it's a sign of respect and honor for God," explained Rose. "And after all Christ has done for you! Really now, Walker."

"Dad, do I really have to wear a tie?"

"Do what your mother says."

"Besides," said Rose, "we're going to brunch at the club after church."

"Ah, Mom. I don't want to go."

Rose stared at Walker over her glasses. Monty objected as well but fared no better. He did persuade Rose to take two cars so he could stay and hit balls on the range. Walker said he wanted to go to the range too, but Rose objected.

"Walker, how will it look if I have to drive myself home? You're becoming such a fine young man. I think it would be wonderful if you would sit with me a little longer at the club while your father hits those ridiculous little golf balls. Won't you do this for me? And then you can drive me home. Besides, you could use the practice, what with you getting your driver's license in August."

"I can practice driving home with Dad."

"Oh, Walker." Rose's head dropped, and she peered into her knitted hands.

Walker's insides knotted up tightly, and he flinched as the pain rippled through his gut. He'd disappointed her, and Rose played the role of victim of his assault flawlessly. But lurking behind the victim's façade was menacing anger that scared Walker.

Complicating his feelings further was the growing frustration of helplessness. He was not able to think for himself. Any action lacking his mother's approval was forbidden. Maybe he would have offered to drive his mom home, but not now, knowing it wasn't his idea and that he didn't have a say. If he said no, she'd sit through lunch cool, pouting, not saying a word, and if he said yes, then he'd have to withstand her praise for being such a fine young man, and the thought of that was stomach-turning.

Whenever she praised him, he heard her silently comparing him to Eli. He missed Eli. He'd always looked up to Eli, and her comparisons made him feel guilty for not defending him when he had been at home. Where was Eli? This thought was never too far away.

It was such a small matter, whether he drove her home or stayed at the club, but it ate at him so. It ate at him because it was so much like every other exchange they had. It was her way or the highway, and she got her way not through persuasion or advocacy but through cold-blooded manipulation.

"For Pete's sake, Rose, let the boy hang out at the club this afternoon."

"Walker, would you like to hit balls with me?" said Monty. "Maybe we can find another twosome and play this afternoon. Even if we only play nine holes. Would you like that?"

"Sure, Dad. Thanks."

"I guess I'm supposed to just go home and wait for the two of you to come home. I guess I'm just supposed to go home and fix the two of you dinner. Is that it?"

"Now Rose," pled Monty.

"Don't you 'Now Rose' me." She was veering away from the edge of tears, as anger and righteous indignation took center stage.

"I'm taken for granted, and now you're trying to drive a wedge between my son and me. All a mother has is her family, her children. You have your job; that's what makes you happy. And now you want to take my son from me. He'll be heading to college soon enough. Can't you let me have some joy while he's still at home?" The anger recedes; self-pity returns.

Monty didn't know what to say. These roller-coaster mood swings caught him so off guard, and they were happening with increasing frequency as her world seemed to rotate more and more tightly around Walker. Always in the back of his mind, competing for attention, were two conflicting thoughts: "I'd be happier with someone else" and "till death do us part."

He looked at Walker and Walker looked back, and they both knew what the other was going to do. "Walker, maybe we can hit the ball together next weekend."

"Sure, Dad."

They were silent partners.

*   *   *

By the time they reached the club for Sunday brunch, Rose had rebounded. There would be no mention of the kitchen table dispute that morning. It had never happened. Walker and Monty played along, leery of saying the wrong thing.

As they entered the main dining room, Rose scanned the crowd, her eyes coming to rest at the table in the center of the room. She broke into a practiced smile as she waved, in an exaggerated manner, at Constance Beauchamp.

Rose quickly weaved through the tables and made a beeline for Constance. "Why, Constance, what a delight it is to see you."

Constance and Connelly Beauchamp, seated at the best table in the room, were surrounded by five beaming and beautiful children, Connie, Catherine, Carl, Corinne, and Curt. The Southern Baptists' answer to the Osmonds.

"Hello, Constance," said Rose. "How *are* you?" The accent on the word *are* was pronounced and drawn out.

Constance remained seated as did her daughters, but Connelly, Carl, and Curt stood and remained standing while Rose and Constance made chitchat. It's a wonder any southern gentlemen ever finished a meal in these settings, what with the comings and goings of all the fine families.

"Monty, tell the maître d' we want this table," said Rose, pointing to the table next to the Beauchamps'.

Rose stood impatiently until Walker realized she was waiting for him to hold her chair while Monty asked Russell, the head waiter, or as Rose liked to call him, the maître d', to seat the three of them next to the Beauchamps although it was a table set for a party of six.

Back at the table as Walker was holding her chair, Rose asked: "Now, Walker, you know Connie, don't you? Aren't you two in several AP classes together?"

"Yes, Mom."

"Hi, Connie"

"Hi, Walker."

"Walker, would you like to sit with the Beauchamps?"

Rose had been trying to fix up Walker with Connie since she first saw a picture of Connie in the society pages, with her mother being honored by the Daughters of the American Revolution. The awkward silence from the Beauchamp table would have signaled a lesser climber to drop the subject, but Rose persisted until Walker announced, "Mom, I'm fine sitting with you and Dad."

Monty returned in time to change the subject as Walker and Monty took their seats, one on each side of Rose. Rose continued to talk up Constance and was trying to draw Walker in when Walker's attention was drawn to the beautiful young girl filling his water glass. Walker was captivated. She smiled shyly at him as she put down the water pitcher while holding the menus under her left arm.

"Oh, let me help you...," exclaimed Walker as he half stood and thrust his hand out to take the menus, upsetting the table and knocking over the water pitcher in the same motion.

The noise from the clattering glassware and the suppressed laughter from the Beauchamp Five attracted the attention of every eye in the room, but none more piercing than Rose's. Walker could read her inner monologue, sure of what she was thinking about him: *How dare you embarrass me!*

She recovered quickly, though, and lashed out at the young girl, instead.

"You clumsy little girl! Look what you've done," said Rose.

"Oh, I'm so sorry," pled the young girl.

Russell hurried over. "Is everything all right?"

"No, everything is not all right. This *waitress*," said Rose, pronouncing the word in disgust, "just spilled an entire pitcher of water across our table. What are you going to do about it?" demanded Rose.

"Mom, it was my fault."

"It was nothing of the sort. Oh, Walker, you are such a fine young man, but there's no reason to protect the help that way."

The tears trickled down the girl's face, and she quickly left the room. Walker shot his mother a look that could kill.

"Mrs. Atkins, we'll have a word with her later, but in the meantime, let's move you to a new table."

Monty spoke up. "Walker is right. He caused the accident, and that's all it was. An accident. Russell, there's no reason to take any action; she seems like a delightful young girl. Rose, there's no reason to make a scene. Let's just move to a new table and enjoy our lunch."

They ate their lunch in virtual silence. Monty finished his meal and turned to Walker. "Son, let's go hit the ball."

Monty stood, folded his napkin, placed it in his chair, and said, "Rose, you can drive yourself home. I'm going to go play golf with one of my boys."

*   *   *

After a few holes, Walker was able to relax and find his swing. Monty, on the other hand, was striking the ball as well as he could remember from the very first tee. There was hardly anyone out that afternoon, so they had the course to themselves. They talked about the Braves' chances of making the playoffs and of a fishing trip they were planning for the fall. Neither could remember the last time they had such a relaxed, wonderful time together. Just laughing and enjoying each other's company.

Monty loved his son more than words could describe. He had such hopes and aspirations for the boy. Monty wanted nothing more than for Walker to return home after college and maybe go to work with him. But lately, he'd begun to doubt the wisdom of his dreams. The pressure from Rose was smothering. He could see his boy cower and bend to her will. It wasn't good; worse, it was destructive.

But Monty felt trapped. He knew he was supposed to side with his wife, but didn't the Bible admonish parents not to test their children? At times Monty was ashamed for not standing up on Walker's behalf in the face of one of Rose's withering guilt trips. He was thinking it might be best for Walker to settle someplace other than Charleston after college. But not too far. Maybe Atlanta.

As they were walking out of the men's locker room after their round, Monty turned to Walker and tossed him the car keys and said, "Why don't you drive the car around to the front and pick me up? I saw my friend

Steve head into the clubhouse, and I want to talk to him about playing next Saturday."

"Okay, Dad."

A few minutes later, Monty strolled out of the clubhouse and got into the front passenger side seat.

"Her name is Isabelle."

"What? What are you talking about?"

Monty was smiling. "I just spoke with the head waiter and asked for the name of the young girl. Don't act like you don't know who I'm talking about. Her name is Isabelle Dawson. I know her father. He's a good man."

Walker began to blush. Monty kept smiling.

"She's a knockout."

"Dad!"

"And don't worry, she's not in any trouble."

"Good."

Walker pulled away from the curb and headed home. After a few minutes, he simply said, "Thanks, Dad."

"No problem, Son. No problem."

Monty was beaming inside. So was Walker.

*　　*　　*

Walker spent more and more time at the club playing golf and tennis and hanging out at the pool. He'd use any excuse to walk through the main club-house in the hopes of crossing paths with Isabelle Dawson, the girl with the beautiful smile he couldn't stop dreaming of. His efforts paid off, and before long, the two of them were sneaking off together.

He spent his summer training for the upcoming cross-country season and hanging out with Isabelle. He would begin his junior year in just a couple of months and was expected to compete as one of the top distance runners in the state. The Kiawah Cup would be the first big meet of the season and he was determined to win it this year. While Walker was training, he noticed that Eddie was playing golf. Walker would have no excuses. It would be his year. It had to be.

Isabelle transferred to Porter-Gaud that fall for the beginning of her junior year. Walker was ecstatic. Isabelle hit it off with Toby, still Walker's best friend, and the three of them, along with Toby's girlfriend, Ella, were inseparable. They were all active in school sports, did well in the classroom, and made it to their fair share of house parties when parents were out of town or to the beach parties in coves the police weren't likely to patrol.

All seemed good with these kids. Isabelle, though, saw a side of Walker that no one else did, and she worried for him. Walker appeared happy to those around him, but Isabelle knew better. Walker would talk to her about Eli and the burdens he carried. The pressure to succeed, to perform, to uphold the family name. The pressure was from every direction, and it came hard, unrelenting.

From his father, who encouraged Walker to work and work, assuring him that if he did, the Lord's blessings would be his reward.

"Remember, Son, 'I can do all things through Christ Jesus who strengthens me'; it's right there in the Bible and I'm living proof of that."

"Yes, Dad," Walker would reply.

Another favorite of his father was Isaiah 40. "Son, when you're in a race or just competing in life, always remember what the Lord tells us in verse 31: 'They shall run and not be weary; they shall walk and not faint.'"

"Yes, Dad, I'll remember."

He loved his father and craved his approval, wanting his father to be proud of him. But he didn't know how to talk to him, and it seemed his father had the same problem. He didn't know what to say to his son. Most every conversation, every interaction, centered on how well Walker was or was not doing. Would this action or that decision help or hurt his chances for the right college, for success? Fishing and talk of the Braves provided the only break.

And from his mother, the toxic mix of shame and guilt, holding her approval out like a carrot.

"Oh, Walker. You make me so proud. Do you know that?" Or, "Oh, Walker, after all I've done for you, and this is how you disappoint me."

And from himself. His own drive to succeed, wherever it came from, fueled by the Protestant work ethic drilled into him every Sunday. Or was it a fear of failure? From his earliest days of attending Sunday school, he'd heard the parable of the talents more times than he could remember. How many times had he been lectured that hard work was rewarded by God with more talents, whereas slothfulness was damned by the very same God?

And finally, from Eli. "Walker, I didn't do it. Now go out into the world and make your big brother proud!" It was up to Walker to redeem Eli, at least that's how Walker saw it.

CHAPTER 26

Debts, Prayers & Laz

Monty sat impatiently in the lobby of Low Country Savings & Loan; his right foot was tapping nervously. Once he noticed it, he stood up and approached the receptionist.

"It's such a nice day," he said, "I think I'll just wait outside for Mr. Bowrey. Can you let me know when he's ready to meet?"

"Yes, Mr. Atkins," answered the receptionist.

"Thank you."

Monty stepped outdoors and took a deep breath, trying to calm himself. It was, indeed, a beautiful day. Fall had arrived—the temperature in the low sixties, the sky blue, and nature in full bloom. Crepe myrtle trees lined the streets, and the honeysuckle aroma of the bougainvilleas drifted in intoxicating fashion throughout each day.

Was this really the first day of fall? he wondered. Monty loved that Charleston had four distinct seasons, and fall was his favorite. Had he missed the changing of the seasons? Had he been so preoccupied with, well, everything, days coming and going, that he hadn't noticed? So it seemed.

Monty was at the bank to ask for a larger line of credit. His billings had picked up. The practice was growing again, but cash was tight. As he read in the business journals to which he subscribed, the number one killer of a growing business was choking on that growth and not being able to fund it.

His persistent head-down approach to the day-to-day running of a law firm was finally paying off. He'd landed a few new clients, and the new associates were working out. The real surprise was the renewal of work from First National Bank. After Eli ran, work from the bank ceased overnight. He wasn't surprised. Stephen Prestwick was the bank president, after all. Stephen took his time approving Monty's outstanding bills, but the bank paid.

So you could have knocked Monty over with a feather when he received a call from the bank's chief counsel asking him if he could handle the work. Monty asked the chief counsel, Bob Driscall, if Stephen Prestwick was aware of the phone call. Bob assured Monty that Stephen was a professional and was committed to the best interests of the bank and its shareholders, and spreading around the bank's legal work to qualified firms around town was in the bank's best interest regardless of what personal issues might exist between himself and any particular attorney.

Monty thanked him for the call and told him that yes, he could take on the extra work. Monty didn't want to jinx things, but it appeared that the fallout from Eli's vanishing act was starting to lift.

"Mr. Atkins? Mr. Atkins?"

The receptionist's voice brought Monty back.

"I'm sorry. I was lost in my thoughts," explained Monty.

Smiling, she responded, "Mr. Bowrey will you see you now."

"Thank you," replied Monty as he picked up his briefcase and held the door for her and then followed her back into the bank.

* * *

DINNER THAT NIGHT

Monty and Rose were alone and seated at the dinner table. Monty said grace, and they began their meal. Walker was out with the cross-country team. On Thursdays after practice, they'd go out for pizza and talk about the upcoming Saturday meet.

"Rose, I met with the bank today, and they approved lending us more money and extending maturity. They were impressed with the steady growth in my billings and in my firm's growth. Bringing on the additional associate certainly helped," explained Monty.

When Rose didn't respond, Monty continued.

"There is one thing. The bank insists on additional collateral. We need to give them a lien on the beach house, and so they need your signature on the loan docs."

"Rose, cat got your tongue? Did you hear what I said? Great news, isn't it?"

"So they'll have a lien on your business, on this home, and if you get your way, the bank will have a lien on our beach home too. Do I have this right, Monty?"

Good grief, this drilling was more onerous than what the loan officer had put him through. "That's right, Rose. It's just business."

"Monty, if your business is doing so well, why do you need to borrow more money?"

"Well, honey, we've gone over that. A growing business requires money to grow. I pay my associates and the staff and the rent long before I'm paid by the clients. I'm making money, but I'm cash poor right now. And I'm still carrying the loan the bank gave us to help pay Eli's bail and legal costs."

"And where did that get you?" Rose cut her chicken slowly, deliberately, never looking up from her plate.

Monty felt the temperature in the room drop.

"What are you saying, Rose?"

"And as for our expenses, I know one you could cut. You're still paying that private detective to find Eli, aren't you? What's that costing us? And what if you find him? Surely, you're not suggesting that he come home! What then? So he can stand trial? So he can embarrass us all over again? No, Monty, no. I won't go through it. I won't put Walker through it. If you want to borrow more money from the bank, that's fine. I'll sign the papers, but only if you agree to stop paying that damn detective to find Eli."

Monty sat speechless, not having a clue what to say or who he was having dinner with.

"So, Monty, it's your call."

*   *   *

Monty returned to his office without finishing his meal. As he walked out the door, Rose told him she'd keep his plate warm, but he didn't hear her over the sound of the clanging screen door behind him.

The same fight, all over again. Neither Monty nor Walker ever gave up hope that someday they would be reunited with Eli. They both believed he was innocent. But if he was innocent, why did he run? Since they were convinced of his innocence, they concluded something, or someone, must have spooked him. But what? But who?

Rose, on the other hand, would have none of it. She was adamant. "If we are to stay together as a family, we must put this behind us and move on," she'd proclaim.

"But Rose, honey, he's out there somewhere. How can you so quickly just move on as you say? He's innocent. I just know he is."

Rose would remain silent and then simply repeat some version of the same admonishment that they "just had to move on."

Monty had waged a fight for over four years now–fighting for his law practice, for a relationship with Walker, and for his marriage. He was tired. He worried about Walker. Walker drove himself so hard but never seemed to have any fun. There was no passion in Walker, and he rarely smiled unless he was with Isabelle. And then there was Rose and his marriage.

Back at his office, he sat in near darkness with only a single desk lamp to illuminate the room. He kept a bottle of bourbon at his office. Monty wasn't a big drinker, but tonight he felt like getting drunk. The first sip burned. By the third sip, the bourbon's warm spicy flavor coated his throat, making the second and third drink go down smoothly. Confusion turned to anger, which eroded into fear and feelings of hopelessness and helplessness.

Sitting at the desk, holding the shot glass between his two hands with his head bowed in resignation, Monty cried out quietly.

"Oh, Lord, what am I to do? I promised to stay married to her through thick and through thin. But I just don't know anymore. I love her. I truly do, but it's as if she's making me choose between her and Eli. How can I be a good husband and a good father? What have I done wrong? Why are you punishing me? What more can I do? Just tell me. Show me, and I'll do it. I know, just as you tell us, that I can do all things through Christ Jesus who strengthens me. Lord, I feel so alone."

Monty waited and waited on the Lord, but he felt as if his prayers went unanswered that night. He put the bottle down while he could still drive. After another hour alone in his office, he drove home.

*   *   *

The next day Monty was up and out of the house before dawn. Despite the early hour, Monty was not the first to arrive at the office. *You have to love young associates*, he thought as he walked back to his office. They arrived early, stayed late, billing hours the entire day, and they made the coffee. Monty stopped by each associate's office briefly with a nod and a quick hello. He entered his office, hooked his jacket on the back of the door, and took a seat at his desk. Sometime over the course of the evening a plan had begun to formulate. It was time to act.

Monty had met Lazare Fontenot at a bar meeting in Atlanta shortly after Eli had run. Chester Baslin had made the introduction. Monty remembered Chester telling him, "Laz is the best. I wouldn't put you in touch with him if I couldn't vouch for him."

Lazare Fontenot was fourth-generation Cajun. He bled purple and gold and spoke with an accent so thick it was if he permanently had a mouth full of mashed potatoes. Laz's special gift as an investigator was his ability to blend. He had a keen insight into human nature, was a diligent researcher, and seemed to approach virtually every challenge with a similar refrain.

"Well, I may not know who to talk to, but I have a cousin who lives in that neck of the woods, and if anyone knows, he knows."

Laz seemed to have an endless network of cousins. Monty voiced some concern at the outset about Laz's fee, and Laz remarked, "I got a lot of cousins to feed."

Laz was an early riser as well. He picked up on the second ring.

"Fontenot Investigations. How can I help?"

"Laz, good mornin'. Monty Atkins here."

"My bon ami! And how is life in Charleston?"

"Can't complain. And you? Is all well?" asked Monty.

"Mighty fine. You wouldn't be callin' to back out of our bet this weekend, would ya? The Tigers are gonna roll your Tide, bon ami," exclaimed Laz.

"No sir, Laz. Not at all. In fact, care to raise the stakes? Say, make it an even twenty dollars?"

"You still givin' me ten points, right? You know I gotta lot of cousins to feed."

"Listen to you. Crowin' out of one side of your mouth and beggin' out of the other. Yeah, I'm still givin' you ten points."

Monty could hear Laz smiling through the phone.

"Good man, Monty. Now I don't think you called this early to jaw about football, so what can I do fer ya?"

"Well, Laz, it's about Eli."

CHAPTER 27

He's the Boss

Stephen and Louie Panja had a standing call every Monday and Thursday. Stephen insisted that he initiate the call. Becky, his career-minded executive assistant, kept a record of every incoming call but kept no such record of outgoing calls. If Louie needed to speak sooner, he'd leave a message stating he was from a janitorial firm in Savannah looking to earn their business; the callback number was always to a disconnected line.

"What d' ya have?" asked Stephen.

"What? No 'Hello, how are you?'" replied Louie. "I got feelings, ya know."

"So do piranhas."

The two chuckled at their own wit.

"I just thought you'd like to know that your pal Monty visited our favorite S&L the other day and received an advance on a larger line of credit *and* he had to give the bank a lien on his beach home in Kiawah as extra collateral."

"Really. How very interesting."

"It gets better. My guy inside says that he had to pledge his Kiawah beach home as extra collateral and that Mrs. Atkins had to cosign and was none too happy about it."

"Just wait till I buy that S&L and put the squeeze on them."

"I was wondering about that. If he don't miss no payments, how can you foreclose?" asked Louie.

"He'll miss payments. I instructed my legal department to send work to Monty's firm, enough to bury them. They'll have more work than they can handle; he'll have to turn away other work or hire more associates."

"I don't get it. Sounds like you're helping the guy."

"Well, when we buy the S&L we'll stop sending his firm the work on the grounds that we can't send work to an attorney when the bank holds his lawfirm's line of credit. That would be a conflict of interest."

"Okay, that'll hurt him, but he'll just go get the old clients back, won't he?"

"Not as easy as it sounds. It'll take time, and Monty won't win them all back. But the real blow will come when we, or I should say the bank and the S&L we're buying, refuse payment on the invoices for all the work he's already done for us—the bank and the S&L, that is."

"Yeah, but can't he sue for payment?"

"Sure he can, but that takes time. Meanwhile, as he's trying to collect from First National Bank, my bank, the bills he owes will keep rolling in. The cash crunch will kill him. But the real blow will come in the form of a bar action he'll be too busy defending.

"You see, in our due diligence, we discovered a conflict of interest between Monty and Low Country Savings & Loan. He does legal work for them and has a business loan and a mortgage with the S&L. Now they could have papered over the conflict with a few simple waivers and other documents, but they didn't.

"A story or two will leak to the papers about the bar action, a few clients will leave, and no other bank in town will touch him. Finally, I have it on good authority that another firm in town will happily hire away his associates if it means they'll get my bank's work. Oh, yeah—he'll miss a few payments."

"Sounds like you've thought of everything," said Louie.

"Yes, I have. Now, gotta go. Meeting with a new client who's bringing in some fantastic deals."

"That guy from Arizona you was tellin' me about?"

"Yeah, Stan Moore. You'd like him."

"You want me to check him out for you? You know, to be safe?" asked Louie.

"No. That won't be necessary. I'm a good judge of character."

"Whatever you say. You the boss."

Smiling, Stephen said a quick goodbye, hung up the phone, and paged Becky.

"Becky, please send in Mr. Moore."

"Yes, I am. I'm the boss," said Stephen to himself.

*   *   *

Stan and Stephen had much to talk about. Since their fateful meeting in the bar earlier that year, Stan had uncovered some fascinating real estate projects. He'd package deals by bringing together landowners and developers. Sometimes he'd participate, and other times he'd assemble the players and move the deal along for a fee. Stephen asked Becky to order lunch in for the two of them as they sat down to review the projects under consideration.

The business relationship between Stan and Stephen was proving to be very profitable for the bank. Stan would always tell Stephen over drinks that it was a shame how little a man of his talents made working for the bank, even as the bank president.

Stan wanted to help, and he told Stephen he'd let him invest with his partners back in Phoenix. Usually, the boys in Phoenix wouldn't take in a new partner for less than a $250,000 minimum investment, but because Stan had vouched for Stephen, they were willing to let him in for $100,000. They'd pay interest monthly on the hundred grand at the annual rate of 20 percent, no questions asked, all invested in Arizona projects.

Stephen knew to be suspicious of anyone promising 20 percent, but he felt Stan was right—he was underpaid. He should make more money given how smart he was. Just look at what he was doing for the bank. As a bank stock owner, he knew that someday his hard work would pay off, but many of his golfing buddies were getting rich now. Only problem—he didn't have $100,000. Stan said he'd take care of that too. He would personally lend Stephen the $100,000 at a meager rate. Why, the interest spread alone would earn Stephen enough money to pay back the principal in six years. All Stephen had to do was pledge his bank stock to Stan.

CHAPTER 28

The Trap is Set

Monty was hurrying out of the office; Walker had a track-and-field meet that afternoon.

"Monty, I know you want to cut out early today, but we need to talk," said Abigail.

Abigail Baker had been Monty's secretary since he first opened his practice. She was fresh out of college when she answered Monty's ad in the local paper. A Charleston native, like her mother before her, Abigail had attended Ole Miss. Her folks were surprised when she took the job. They figured she'd be married by now and spittin' out kids.

Abigail was single by choice and not because of any apparent shortcomings. She didn't want to marry right away, as did the majority of her sorority sisters. Abigail had her share of suitors. She was bright, blessed with a quick wit, and easy on the eyes. She had long, wavy brown hair that danced across her shoulders, green eyes, and a figure that both men and women noticed. She loved college football, and while her knowledge of the game was off-putting to most women, for the guys it was both confusing and a real turn-on. When she predicted that Ole Miss would beat Notre Dame in football the prior year, Notre Dame's sole loss on their way to winning the national championship, she had been dismissed as a silly girl—that is, until the last whistle blew and the Rebels—the "giant killers," she liked to call them—celebrated their 20-13 victory over the Fighting Irish.

Abigail wanted to be a lawyer, though, and was attending law school at night. In her mind, there was plenty of time to wed and raise kids. Her parents were resigned to waiting a bit longer for grandchildren. Her mother reasoned she might meet a nice young man at law school.

Monty asked, "About what? Can't it wait till Monday?"

"Monday you'll come in with a long list of things you hope to accomplish next week, and you'll ask me if it can wait till Friday. No, you need to think over the weekend about what I have to say."

Abigail had his attention. "Okay, let's talk."

Abigail shut the door and sat down across the desk from Monty.

"It's about the firm's finances," said Abigail.

"Billings are up. What's the problem?" asked Monty.

"Yes, billings are up, but that is the problem. We're running out of money again."

"Look, I know what I'm doing. We're growing. That's all. The bank extended my line of credit. I'm sorry I hadn't told you. I'll draw on it next week. You'll see the money in the bank. There. Does that fix things?" asked Monty.

"Monty, don't condescend. Hear me out."

Monty sat quietly, fuming as he stared at his bookcase. He hated being told what to do. This was his business, and he knew how to run it. But he'd been raised right, and Abigail knew this about him. She'd wait him out.

After a moment, Monty regained his composure, looked at her, and spoke humbly: "Abigail, I'm sorry. You know how much I value you and what you do. Please, go on."

"Yes, your billings are up, but look at them. Over half are with First National Bank. I'm taking a class this semester on the economics of the legal practice. This firm looks like a classic case study. Yes, your billings are growing, but you cut your rate to get the bank's work. So you're working harder but at a lower margin, and your concentration is overly weighted with one client. What happens if you lose the bank's work?" asked Abigail.

Monty barely heard the second half of what she said. He was formulating his reply before she finished.

"Abigail, you make a good point. But First National Bank is growing. Stephen Prestwick is a real mover and shaker in this town. They are acquiring other smaller banks and are talked about as a takeover target as well. I can grow my practice as his bank grows. I know the work is less profitable, but we still bill our other work at higher rates."

"Monty, we're going to lose that work," said Abigail.

"Nonsense," Monty said, a bit too loudly. Calming himself, he continued: "We'll hire more associates. I can work more hours. Abigail, thank you for bringing this to my attention. Sometimes it's good to be refocused. Next week I'll call our other clients and touch base, so they'll know we haven't forgotten them."

This meeting wasn't going as Abigail had hoped.

"Monty, I worry about you. You look terrible. You're losing your voice."

"Look. I'm doing what has to be done. I'm in control. I have big plans for this firm," Monty said adamantly.

"You can't be all things to all people. You never say no to anything but help. You can't keep working these hours. The pace will kill you."

Monty was growing impatient, his heart racing and his neck turning red. Clenching his fists, he refrained from saying what he would no doubt later regret.

"I know that you are regularly approached by managing partners at other firms about merging. I wish you'd at least consider it," said Abigail.

"Abigail, do you see the name on the front door when you come to work each morning?"

"Yes," Abigail said, sighing.

"That's my name. I built this. I came from nothing. My father was a door-to-door insurance salesman. He never rose any higher. He never saved a dime. We took a one-week vacation every summer in a neighbor's beat-up camper they let us use for free."

Monty paused and thought about stopping but decided to go on.

"Five years ago, I almost lost everything. When Eli ran, life changed overnight. My name in this town was mud. People wouldn't look me in the eye."

Monty was fighting back tears.

"Abigail, you were one of the few who stuck with me. And here I am. I survived. I'm back. I'm still married. My business is growing. And I know this may sound strange, but when Stephen Prestwick, Kimberly's farther, started sending work to the man whose son he believed killed his oldest daughter, well, that was validation. In fact, I believe he will send us more work. Stephen is the keynote speaker at the state bar association luncheon next week. He invited me and included a personal note. He said First National Bank would be making some big moves and that these moves would propel the growth of one or more law firms in town. Abigail, he thanked me for our work and said he wanted me to be there when he made the announcements."

Monty paused and wiped a small tear away. "I've won back the respect of my peers. I can go to church now and not have to pretend I'm invisible. I go to the club, and I can find a game. Abigail, I feel worthy and valuable again."

Abigail made no effort to hide her tears. They stood and met at the side of the desk in a hug.

Monty gently broke the embrace and said, "I'm going to see Walker run this afternoon."

"Good. You deserve a break."

"Thanks, Abigail."

She just nodded and decided not to ask the last question on her mind: "But can you trust Stephen Prestwick?"

PART THREE

There's a man going around taking names
And he decides who to free and who to blame.
Everybody won't be treated all the same.
There will be a golden ladder reaching down
When the man comes around.

THE MAN COMES AROUND
BY JOHNNY CASH

Come to me, all who labor and are heavy laden, and I will
give you rest. Take my yoke upon you, and learn from me, for
I am gentle and lowly in heart, and you will find rest for
your souls. For my yoke is easy, and my burden is light.

MATTHEW 11:28-30

CHAPTER 29

The Trap is Sprung

MONDAY, MARCH 27, 1978

The attorneys for both banks gathered around the table—the buyer's attorneys on one side, the seller's attorneys on the other. Absent from the room was any representative from either bank. Consequently, without anyone to preen for or impress, the meeting proceeded smoothly.

The lead attorney for Low Country S&L took charge of the meeting.

"So, are we ready to close?"

Positioned at the center of the other side of the table sat Randolph Graves, the lead outside counsel for First National Bank. Randolph—no one dared call him Randy—was fifty years old but wouldn't live to see sixty. Horribly out of shape, a pack-a-day smoker, and overweight, he had long since given up wearing a jacket or any pretense of style, suspenders being his lone sartorial vice.

"Yes, we are," he boomed triumphantly.

"And we're still set to close this Friday?"

"Absolutely. And that'll be perfect, the last day of the month, the last day of the quarter. The pointy-headed bean counters will love it," he joked.

Every lawyer in the room laughed. On the verge of finalizing the deal, they could now joke together. While fights and disagreements had occurred along the way—hell, there had to be, otherwise, how could lawyers demonstrate their irreplaceable value?—this would be an easy transaction.

"Okay. Then as agreed, all bank activity at the window will go on without a hitch, but there will be no loan activity of any sort this Friday except for loan payoffs or paydowns. That means no draws on lines of credit or loan proceed disbursements. This comes straight from the top. From Stephen Prestwick himself. Are we clear?" asked Randolph.

Everyone agreed.

"Excellent. Then let's go over these final documents and assemble the closing packages," boomed Randolph.

*   *   *

Friday mid-morning, March 31, 1978

Monty sat in Abigail's office, staring at the accounts receivable report, not wanting to believe what was right in front of him. The largest outstanding balances, for work performed for First National Bank, were over sixty days old.

"I don't understand. What did they say when you called them?" asked Monty.

"They won't return my calls," answered Abigail. "And look at this, the billings report. We haven't done any work for Low Country S&L in over a month. And they pay on time. We miss that work."

"Well, everyone else pays well," said Monty.

"True. But look in the thirty-day column. Not much there because we're doing less and less work for our smaller clients, clients who pay on time and who pay the higher hourly rates."

Abigail said nothing more, hoping this time Monty would take things more seriously. He flipped the pages back and forth in the hope that he had missed something, that she had missed something. He tossed the report back on her desk and stood up.

"Look. I'm sure there's nothing to worry about. I'll see Stephen Prestwick today at the bar association luncheon and ask him about it. I'm sure there's been a simple misunderstanding."

"Let's hope so. Payroll is due next Friday and I'm expecting a slow collections week," said Abigail as she waved the accounts receivable report above her head.

"I'll call the bank as soon as I get back this afternoon and draw on the line. We'll have the money Monday."

Abigail smiled. "Okay. Enjoy your lunch."

"Will do. See you this afternoon."

*   *   *

Monty walked into the lobby of the Francis Marion Hotel and picked up a program for the day's festivities. Stephen's presentation was entitled "Navigating the Banking Industry in these Changing Times." The program also announced that Obadiah Johnson was finally stepping down as the president of the South Carolina chapter of the American Bar Association. The newly elected president, Winston Spiel, would be introduced immediately following lunch.

That name sounded familiar. Where had he heard it? Winston would say a few words about Obadiah, thank him for his years of service, and then introduce Stephen Prestwick. Monty chuckled when he noticed that Obadiah had not been granted a speaking spot. Everyone knew you couldn't get him off the stage.

Monty was directed to the ballroom and found his table, where he was seated with representatives from the press and the state bank examiner's office. Stephen came over and shook everyone's hand and made a few jokes about this being the one table that could sink him.

"Except for my friend Monty here. You wouldn't hurt me, would you, Monty?" asked Stephen as he put his arm around Monty's shoulders.

The newspaper reporters and bank examiners laughed at Stephen's good-natured ribbing, as did Monty.

Monty turned to whisper to Stephen. "Stephen, I know you're busy, but I was wondering if I could have a word with you after lunch?"

"Right you are. I'm very busy today. Afraid I won't have time here. But I tell you what, I'll call you at your office this afternoon. Will you be there, say about 3:00?"

"Yes, that's perfect. Thanks, Stephen," replied Monty. "And thanks for the invite today and, of course, congratulations on all your success."

Stephen shook Monty's hand firmly, not letting go, leaned in, staring directly into Monty's eyes, and said: "I can't tell you how much that means to me coming from you. I'm so glad you're here. Give my best to your wife."

Stephen turned and walked toward the head table, stopping along the way to glad-hand with friends and suck-ups. Standing with his napkin in his hand, Monty stared at Prestwick as he walked away. He couldn't put his finger on it, but something wasn't right.

*   *   *

1:30 p.m., Monty's office

"Excuse me? You're demanding what?" asked an incredulous Abigail Baker.

"I'm here to collect all files on any open matters this firm is working on for First National Bank," said Bob Driscall.

"What are you talking about? On whose authority? You can't do this," pleaded Abigail.

Abigail was incensed. Standing behind the bank's chief counsel were two young men hiding behind their boss, trying to look tough and confident. Standing behind them was a bored-looking private security guard.

"Oh, but I can. I'm the bank's chief counsel . . ."

"I know who you are," Abigail interrupted. "But what the hell is going on?"

"We are pulling our work from your firm," he said.

"But why? There haven't been any complaints."

"Complaints? Funny you should ask. Here is a copy of the complaint being served this afternoon on your boss Monty Atkins and this firm. It's all in there. Now if you'll please gather the files, my assistants will take them off your hands."

*   *   *

A few minutes after 1:40 p.m. at the Francis Marion Hotel

Monty kept looking at his watch. He was growing anxious. He wanted to get back to the office. Stephen was fifteen minutes into his speech about changes in the banking industry and the important partnership the banking and legal community needed to forge if South Carolina was going to be a player in the national banking and finance industries.

"At First National Bank, we are committed to Charleston and the surrounding low country. We want to partner with businesses, large and small, and encourage and support growth and entrepreneurship in our community. As part of our business plan we are actively acquiring banks that bring strategic strengths to our portfolio. Furthermore, for us to achieve our goals, we need good partners and that means we need good lawyers. So, I'm pleased to make two announcements today. First, as of the close of business today, we will have purchased Low Country Savings & Loan. The president of this fine institution is here today. Philip, could you please stand?"

Philip Wright, sitting at the head table, rose and waved at the crowd.

Monty began to sweat a little. Stephen was buying the bank that held the mortgage on his home, his beach home, and a lien on all the assets of his firm, including his accounts receivable. Something was definitely wrong.

"Thank you, Philip. Philip has built a great bank and we look forward to him staying on with us. Now this brings me to my second announcement. Our bank will be opening additional branches, not just in South Carolina but in North Carolina and Georgia as well."

The room applauded. Stephen stood tall with both hands grasping the top of the lectern and waited for the applause to subside.

"To navigate these waters, we need strong legal counsel. I'm pleased to announce that we have hired the firm of Jenkins, Jones & Daye to help us with this growth. Bill Jenkins is with us. Bill, take a bow."

Monty didn't see Bill, also sitting at the head table, take his bow. No, his vision was caught by Stephen Prestwick looking straight at him with a devilish grin. Monty had to get out of there. As he stood to leave, however, he was approached by a man and a large uniformed guard.

"Are you Montgomery Atkins?" the man asked, speaking loudly enough to be heard over the noise in the room.

"Yes, but you'll have to excuse me."

Monty moved quickly toward the back of the room, hoping he wouldn't be noticed, but he was stopped by the uniformed guard. The commotion drew the attention of the press members sitting at his table and the tables nearby.

"What's going on?" he asked.

"Montgomery Atkins, you are hereby served with this complaint and notified that you have thirty days to respond in Superior Court."

Cameras flashed and captured the image of the process server serving Monty, who had a look of total bewilderment on his face.

*   *   *

Speeding back to his office, Monty braced himself for the worst. Abigail was in the lobby when he pulled up and she ran out to meet him as he exited his car. She was talking so fast and his mind was racing that he hardly heard what she was saying, something about the files and the lawsuit being bullshit. He walked into an office in chaos. Waving everyone off, he pleaded for a few minutes to sort things out.

"Look, I'll be back in a few moments. I need a few minutes and I'll explain everything," he yelled. Only one problem. He didn't know what was going on himself.

He fled to his office, shut the door behind him, and picked up the phone. The first order of business—draw on the line of credit. After sitting on hold for ten minutes, he was finally put through to his account manager.

"Mr. Atkins, thank you for your patience. It's a busy day here. I'm sure you heard the big news."

"Yeah. I heard. Look, I need to draw on the line and I need to do it now. All of it. I need the full $50,000 left on the line," demanded Monty.

"Well, that's going to be a problem."

"What! Why? I negotiated the loan, so that money is rightfully mine. Move it into my account *now*."

"Mr. Atkins, there's no reason to raise your voice. It's out of my control. We're closing the sale today and we've been told that for accounting purposes we cannot distribute any loan proceeds today, the last day of the month and the quarter. I'm sure you understand. It's for accounting purposes. The lawyers and accountants want a clean cutoff. Call back Monday. We'll take care of it then."

Monty wasn't so sure but was powerless to do anything. He apologized for losing his temper, thanked the man, and told him to expect a call first thing Monday. Now, time to face the troops. First stop, Abigail's office.

Abigail explained that she had done all she could, but Bob Driscall had threatened her with criminal action if she stood in the way of the bank taking their files back. Monty was surprisingly calm. What could he do? He told her about the call with the bank and assured her everything would be fine.

"Monty, the lawsuit is bullshit. I read it. It's all lies. I don't understand. What's going on?"

"I don't know, but don't worry. Everything will be fine. Why don't you take off early today? There's nothing more to do this afternoon. But first, before I walk back out there into the lion's den, what do they know?"

"Hard to say. I do know one thing."

"What?"

"Most of them have already received phone calls from Jenkins, Jones & Daye. Job offers."

"You're kidding."

"No. Seems that firm picked up Prestwick's bank as a client and wants to hire our associates since they've been doing all the work anyway," explained Abigail.

Monty called everyone into the conference room and tried to look as cool and confident as possible.

"I know that some of you have already received job offers at Jenkins, Jones & Daye. I'm asking that you don't decide just yet. Give me some time."

"But they said we had till Monday to decide or else they'd offer the job to someone else," said one of the associates.

"Then take the weekend, for Pete's sake. Give me till the end of Monday. That's all I'm asking."

The assembled crowd shuffled their feet, looked about the room, and either avoided Monty's gaze or glanced his way with a noncommittal nod of agreement. Monty wished everyone a good weekend and retreated to his office. Abigail came by and dropped the mail on his desk.

"I'm sorry, but in the day's confusion I didn't have time to sort through it," she said as she gave him a reassuring hug and then left his office, closing the door behind her.

Within five minutes everyone else had left. He sat in his office and replayed the day's events. It was approaching 3:00. Would Stephen call? Not knowing what to do and with ten minutes to kill, Monty haphazardly picked up the mail.

As he flipped through the Wappoo Country Club newsletter, his eyes scanned the list of newly admitted members. There it was, the name Winston Spiel. He knew he recognized it. The name of the new president of the South Carolina chapter of the American Bar Association. He'd seen the name posted on the bulletin board in the Men's Grill as a proposed new member. And now in the newsletter, Winston Spiel was on the list of newly admitted members. And his sponsor's name? None other than Stephen Prestwick.

The phone rang. He hit the speaker button and answered. "Monty Atkins here."

"Monty, Stephen Prestwick. How has your day gone? As well as mine?"

"Stephen, I don't understand this lawsuit. It's baseless, and you know it."

"Do I? Maybe, maybe not. You know how these lawsuits go. Months and months of discovery, interrogatories, depositions, and mounting legal bills. Baseless? Maybe. Who knows?"

"Stephen, please tell me. What's going on? My office is in chaos."

"Chaos? You wanna know what chaos is? Try losing a daughter to a sick bastard. Then you'll know what chaos is, Monty. And as for what's going on? I'll tell you. It's payback time. You were down. But then this town let you get back up off the ground after your pathetic murderous, piece-of-shit son killed Kimberly. That's a tragedy, an incomprehensible tragedy and that won't stand.

"Monty, I own you. I bought the bank that has a lien on your home, your beach house, and your firm. I know about your phone call to the Low Country Savings & Loan this afternoon. Buying that piddly-ass S&L was too good to pass up once I learned where you banked. No need calling back Monday; there will be no further disbursements on your loan. You see, I'm calling your loan."

"You can't do that. I'm current with the payments," said Monty as firmly as possible.

"Oh, but I can. Yes, you're current with the payments, for now. But you've breached several non-monetary provisions in the loan documents—provisions requiring that you stay in compliance with all regulatory requirements and that there be no outstanding bar actions against you."

"There aren't any," declared Monty.

"Check your mail yet?" asked Stephen.

Monty flipped through the mail and at the bottom was a legal-size envelope from the state bar association. He opened it and scanned the contents as Stephen kept talking.

"When I spoke to the newly elected president of the state bar, Winston Spiel, and explained the clear conflict of interest we discovered conducting our due diligence on the Low Country acquisition, he was truly alarmed. I then asked the attorneys at Jenkins, Jones & Daye to review some of the work you've done for us and they were shocked at what they found."

"Lies! *All lies!*" screamed Monty.

Stephen chuckled. "Maybe. It's all in the bar complaint."

Monty was staring at a bar complaint signed by the newly elected president of the bar association and Wappoo Country Club's newest member. "Son of a biscuit!" muttered Monty.

"Yes, you're current now, but for how long? I own the mortgage on your home, on your beach home, on your firm. What's going to happen when I don't pay your invoices to my bank? Excuse me, I mean your invoices to my *banks*? What's going to happen when I foreclose and take your home? Your beach home? Your law practice? What then, Monty old boy? How long will your wife stand by you?"

Stephen said nothing. Nor did Monty. Monty felt himself falling into a bottomless pit.

"You see, Monty, your son took my Kimberly from me, and now I'm going to take everything from you."

When Stephen hung up, the disconnect tone played ominously through Monty's speakerphone like an eerie revelry marking not the just the end of the day, but for Monty, the end.

CHAPTER 30

The Voice

Monty slammed down the receiver, silencing the infernal drone of the disconnect tone. He was alone in his office, screaming at the top of his lungs, incomprehensible guttural wallowing. Monty didn't pace his office; he lunged, lurched chaotically as if moved by an exterior force, head in his hands, hyperventilating, his heart racing. Was he having a nervous breakdown? Is this what it felt like? Feeling faint, he slumped down to the floor before he fell.

Trying desperately to get a grip on himself, he slowed his breathing by force of will, but then the tears came, fast and furious, followed by erratic breathing all over again. He rolled onto his side, curled into a ball, lying defeated on the floor for how long he knew not, until the tears ran dry, and the rise and fall of his chest slowed. He sat up and leaned against the wall of his office behind his desk.

Monty was afraid, and the fear was what kept a red-hot anger from rising up and consuming him. Alone in his office, Monty felt alone in the world. God had abandoned him. Rose would too. Eli was gone, and his relationship with Walker would never survive this. The shame. The ruin. The public humiliation.

Monty was drowning. His belief that God would take care of him, protect him, and bless his actions had anchored his worldview for as long as he could remember, and for the last five years had been his life preserver. So how could this happen? How could God turn his back on him?

"Damn it," Monty screamed. "You promised. I believed you. 'I can do all things through Christ Jesus who strengthens me.' I believed that. I lived it. It's right there in your Bible. I believed you. I've done everything you asked of me. I work hard. I go to church. I tithe. I go to that boring men's prayer breakfast with all those pompous posers. Hell, I'm no different than them. I'm a joke. You abandoned me."

Silence.

"Maybe you were never there."

Monty was broken. Truly and utterly broken. Five years of nonstop planning and working and striving had led him right here. He was physically ill. The stress had taken its toll. Monty had no appetite and had struggled to keep a meal down while his voice had grown weaker every day. Broke, out of ideas, and exhausted beyond all comprehension, he knew the fight was over.

He was still sitting on the floor when the tears returned, and he cried out in utter anguish: "Oh, Lord, help me. Please help me. I don't know what to do. I'm hopeless. I can't go on. I need help. I need everything. I can't do anything on my own. I've tried and failed. Oh, Lord, I'm sorry. Please show me the way. Please, Lord. Please. I beg you. I've done everything you ever asked."

Monty was still, very still, when he heard a voice and felt a presence, a presence that for the rest of his time on earth would live in his memory as the most real and genuine experience of his life.

"And when did I ask you to do those things?"

CHAPTER 31

Doors Shut & Windows Open

The ringing phone brought him back. He stood and answered, somewhat in a daze.

"Atkins and Associates. Monty Atkins here."

"I wasn't expecting you to answer. Is Abigail off today?" asked Rose.

The exchange had a surreal quality.

"I let her go early. She had some personal thing to take care of," Monty lied. What would he tell Rose? The truth, he knew. But how? When?

"Well, I need you to pick up Walker after practice today. I have to run to church. An emergency meeting of our women's prayer group. Dottie Scanlon was diagnosed with cancer."

"Oh, I'm sorry. No problem, but why isn't Walker driving himself? That's why we bought him his own car."

"He's grounded, Monty. Again. If you were more involved with your family, you'd know these things."

"I'm involved, Rose. I just forgot. Yes, of course, I'll pick him up."

Monty straightened up and left the office, still trying to understand all that had happened and the warm embrace of the last few minutes of solitude before the phone rang.

*   *   *

Monty pulled into the parking lot behind the stadium where the track-and-field team was finishing practice. He entered the gate alongside the concession stand and saw a few dads leaning against the low fence separating the bleachers from the oval track that circled the football field. A few fathers, separated by their accustomed personal space, were lined up against the fence, unlike the mothers sitting close to each other in the stands, locked in deep conspiratorial conversation.

"Monty, how are you?" asked Mitchell Robertson as Monty walked up to the fence. Mitchell was still wearing his suit but had loosened his tie and was casually reading the business section of the local paper and keeping an eye on the boys on the track when Monty walked up.

"Good. How 'bout you?" replied Monty as the two men turned and shook hands.

"I think we're both here for the same reason," remarked Mitchell. Monty was remembering—both their boys were grounded. They had lied to their respective parents, claiming that they were each spending the night at the other's house as cover for not coming home. From two of the brightest boys in the class, Monty expected a better story.

Monty laughed and shook his head in bemusement. "So I guess Toby lost his driving privileges too. Hey, did you ever figure out where the boys were?" he asked.

"No, but I have a pretty good idea," said Mitchell as he nodded toward a gaggle of girls sitting in the third row of the bleachers. Monty recognized Isabelle Quaid, Walker's girlfriend, in the group.

"Were we any different?" asked Monty.

It was Mitchell's turn to laugh. "Don't think so."

Mitchell turned toward Monty and, in an apparent effort to not be overheard, tilted his head slightly as he began to speak. Monty panicked, fearing that Mitchell knew about the suit filed against his firm or possibly even the bar complaint.

"Monty, your name came up this morning in a breakfast meeting, and I was elected to speak with you," explained Mitchell.

"Oh, really?" Monty trod lightly, not knowing where this was going.

"Yes. You know Thomas Wentworth, right?"

"Of course. Eddie's dad."

"That's right. Well, Thomas and I are putting together a business venture, and we would like to discuss it with you."

Though everything in his life was spiraling out of control, elaborating on his dire straits made no sense, so he played along.

"What kind of venture?" asked Monty.

"We want to start an investment firm. Some private equity, some distressed debt. Concerning private equity, we'll invest in small to mid-sized companies and take active roles on the boards. As for distressed debt, we'll buy nonperforming bank debt at steep discounts and either receive repayment in full of the original loan amount or foreclose on the collateral," explained Mitchell.

"I thought you and Tom were already busy buying distressed debt?" asked Monty.

"We are. The 1973 recession was good to us. We purchased a fair amount of bad debt that banks were in a hurry to unload, and now we have a few things going on. Some of the loans paid off, leaving us with cash to reinvest. On the loans that didn't pay off, well, we foreclosed and now we own real estate. Some of the real estate we'll manage, some we'll sell. Finally, we're looking to expand. Till now, we've invested our own cash and the cash of a silent partner—you know him, but I'm not at liberty to reveal his identity. But we think it's time to raise additional outside capital."

Monty knew the silent partner was Quaid Dawson, Isabelle's father. That the three of them were business partners was the worst-kept secret in Charleston.

"That sounds exciting. I'm wondering how my name came up," remarked Monty.

"We want a fourth partner, someone with a legal background."

"So you're looking for in-house counsel," stated Monty.

"Not exactly. Acting in that capacity will certainly be one of the job duties, but we're looking for someone who also has business skills and judgment. Frankly, real estate attorneys are a dime a dozen. We're looking for a true business partner."

Monty was looking over Mitchell's shoulder into the distance, not believing what he was hearing.

Mitchell continued: "We've been mulling this matter for a while. Last week we decided to each compile a list of three names we believed were right for the position."

"And my name was on one of the lists?" Monty asked.

"Yep."

"Well, Mitchell, I'm flattered, but you know I have a law practice. I'm fully employed."

"Monty, don't say 'no,' not yet, not without talking to the team, not without thinking about it."

Monty couldn't believe what was happening. Was this good news? Was this an answer to prayer, or was this a further complication? What would Mitchell and the rest of his team say when they learned of the bar action alleging violations of the ethical code of conduct and the lawsuit, etc.?

"Okay. I won't say 'no' right away. Mitchell, thank you."

"Monty, that's good to hear. Please take this opportunity seriously. Talk to Rose about it and get back to me. I have a good feeling about you."

The two men shook hands and were saved by the awkwardness of what to say next by the appearance of Mitchell's son, Toby.

"Hi, Mr. Atkins."

"Hello, Toby. You guys are looking strong out there."

"Thanks. We're all just trying to keep up with Walker and Eddie," said Toby as Walker walked up.

Walker smiled and looked at his shoes in genuine embarrassment. Walker was a bit cocky around most runners but not Toby. Toby was the reason he was running and was still Walker's best friend.

"Hi, Mr. Robertson," said Walker.

Monty beamed inside. He was so proud of his son.

"Hello, Walker. Good luck tomorrow. Are you running the mile tomorrow?" asked Mitchell.

"Yeah, all three of us are. Me, Walker, and Eddie," Toby blurted out. "Going for a clean sweep."

"That's great," remarked Mitchell. "I bet y'all pull it off."

"And Toby made the 4 x 440 relay team," said Walker.

Mitchell high-fived his son. "Well done."

The four of them said goodbye. Monty and Mitchell shook hands, and Monty promised to get back to him. Mitchell and Toby headed toward their car.

"Okay, Son. Let's get going. I'm sure Mom has dinner waiting."

"Hey, Dad?"

"Yeah?" Monty, fishing the keys out of his pocket, stopped and turned back toward Walker, still standing by the fence. "What's up?"

"Isabelle asked if I could go to their house for dinner."

Isabelle had been talking to her girlfriends and was now walking this way. "Hi, Mr. Atkins."

Monty could certainly see why his son was so taken with Isabelle.

"Hello, Isabelle. How are you?"

"Just fine, Mr. Atkins. Can Walker come over for dinner? My mom is preparing a big pasta meal. Walker says that the carbs are good the night before a big meet," she explained.

Monty chuckled slightly. "That would be fine, Isabelle. And can you give him a ride home?"

"Dad, I thought I'd spend the night at Toby's house tonight. Can Isabelle just give me a ride to Toby's?" asked Walker.

"Sure, Son."

Walker broke into a big smile. "Thanks, Dad. I'm sorry you had to come out here for nothing."

"Oh, that's all right, Son," replied Monty, thinking that it wasn't for nothing at all.

As he walked back to the car, he knew he'd be having a long talk with Rose. Best that Walker was out of the house. As he put the car into drive and pulled out of the parking lot, Monty asked out loud: "Lord, what on earth is going on?"

CHAPTER 32

A New Partnership

On the drive home, Monty wondered what he would tell Rose. Lying was out of the question. But could he justify a lack of full honesty? He'd been rationalizing similar behavior since the night Rose told him to "stop paying that private detective to find Eli." Her exact wording was his amnesty. Monty had promised to stop paying the private detective to look for Eli and kept his word. But Monty didn't fire Laz. No, if anything his expenses for Laz's services had risen. Monty figured that if Eli was innocent, then the real killer was still on the loose. So Monty started paying Laz to find the real killer.

But hiding the news of this day from Rose was a different kettle of fish. It would be impossible. She'd hear about it for sure, probably come this Sunday at church. No doubt, some well-meaning gossip would gleefully express false sentiments for our well-being and promise to keep us in their prayers. No, he had to tell Rose, and it had to be tonight.

Monty pulled into the driveway, sat in his car a little longer, and feeling at peace, asked the Lord for the words when he sat with his wife. He'd been walking on eggshells around his wife long enough, pretending that everything was just fine. Time to come clean.

He walked through the front door, placed his briefcase at the bottom of the stairs, and set off for the kitchen where Rose was busy setting the table for three.

"Honey, Walker is having dinner at the Quaid house tonight and then he's sleeping over at Toby's house. It'll just be the two of us."

"But I made his favorite. He never asked me or even mentioned it."

"Rose, it's for the best. We need to talk."

Monty walked into the living room, took a seat on the sofa, and motioned for Rose to sit next to him. Rose took a seat on the other end of the sofa and eyed him coolly. For Monty, the distance between them was real and foreboding.

Monty told her about their finances, about the lawsuit, the bar complaint, the threatened foreclosure, Stephen Prestwick's backstabbing, everything, everything but what Laz was up to. He told her about the job offer from Mitchell Robertson, and he told her about the voice he had heard. God speaking to him. He was sure of it.

Rose never interrupted, never said a word. She sat on the sofa, cool as dry ice.

"You're such a fool, Monty. I feel a migraine coming on, so I'm going to bed. You can sleep above the garage tonight."

Rose started up the stairs, stopped, and turned her head slightly to speak down to Monty. "You will fix this. Neither Walker nor I will suffer for your failures."

* * *

Monty ate dinner at a Waffle House that night, enjoying the company of others, not knowing anyone's name nor speaking to a soul. Upon his return home, he climbed the back steps to Eli's old room and fell into bed, grateful Walker was spending the night at Toby's house

But sleep eluded him despite his exhaustion. Sometime around 2:00 a.m., Monty stepped out onto the small deck he had built with Eli. He opened his Bible to Philippians 4:13 and read, for the millionth time, the verse he'd relied upon: "I can do all things through Christ Jesus who strengthens me."

Lord, what happened? I don't understand. Why have I failed? And what did you mean this afternoon?

Monty sat quietly and then was moved to read a little more of Paul's letter. His eyes drifted up the page, and he read the two preceding verses and then, with a proper context suddenly revealed to him, reread his personal mantra:

"Not that I am speaking of being in need, for I have learned in whatever situation I am to be content. I know how to be brought low, and I know how to abound. In any and every circumstance, I have learned the secret of facing plenty and hunger, abundance and need. I can do all things through Christ Jesus who strengthens me."

Oh, good grief, thought Monty. I had it all wrong. All these years, I've recited this verse and never knew what it meant. Within five minutes, Monty was fast asleep.

* * *

Monty woke the next morning, having slept more soundly than he could remember. He called Mitchell at home, and they agreed to meet that afternoon. Now what to do with the rest of the day? There was plenty to do at the office. That was his natural inclination, but going made no sense. No, he'd go see Walker run.

Forty minutes later, not in the mood to mix with the other parents, he took a seat in the stands on the top row. He expected to see both Toby and Eddie's fathers but was hoping to hold off a conversation with these gentlemen until later that afternoon. It wasn't too long before Mitchell spied Monty but seemed to understand and gave him his space.

Monty nodded at Mitchell and then turned his attention back to the track, spying Walker on the ground, stretching. Monty knew Walker only had two races today, the 4 x 400 relay and the mile. They were expected to win the relay running away. The mile, that was Walker's focus.

Monty didn't have to wait long. Ten minutes later, the boys were lining up for the mile. Monty watched with such pride, taking joy in his son's speed and competitiveness. The outcome, though, was the same, second. Eddie Wentworth had a stronger kick. End of story. It appeared as if Walker was destined to finish second as long as Eddie was competing. The boys shook hands at the end of the race. A clean sweep, first, second, and Toby coming in third. Grounds for celebration, but Monty knew there'd be no joy in his household that night.

Monty didn't know what to say to his son. He was so proud of him, but it seemed as if everything he said came off sounding condescending or demanding. Walker seemed likewise to be without words around his dad. Monty snuck out of the stands as quietly as he had snuck in. Walker noticed and drew his own conclusions.

* * *

"Dammit! Dammit! Goddammit!"

"Walker, that's enough," said Isabelle. Isabelle was sitting on a bench between the park alongside the track and field stadium. She was wearing blue jeans and a light cotton sweater. Her long, black hair was swept over one shoulder, and she was looking at Walker with a mixture of impatience and genuine concern.

"Goddammit! I lost again." Walker was still wearing his track shorts but had changed into a clean shirt. He was wearing flip-flops, and his running shoes were lying half in and half out of the athletic bag sitting on the ground. Walker was pacing nervously back and forth in front of Isabelle.

"You didn't lose. You ran a good race. My word, that was your best time ever. You came in second. You didn't lose."

"It's losing to me."

"Well, just who do you think you are? You can get off that high horse right now if you ever want to kiss me again."

Walker sighed heavily and sat down on the bench next to her. The race in which he had just placed second was a popular invitational that attracted competition from across the Carolinas and Georgia. The day was a great success for their school's track-and-field team. But of course, for Walker, losing, and losing to Eddie, were what hurt.

"Izzy, what am I going to do? I can't beat him."

"So?"

"What do you mean 'so?' You of all people know how hard I'm working."

"And maybe that's the problem."

"What do you mean?"

"Walker, when was the last time you had fun running?"

"Fun? What are you talking about?"

"Have you ever watched Eddie run?"

"Of course I have. Every day in practice and passing me in every race," said Walker sarcastically.

"No, Walker, you haven't. Because if you had, then you'd see what I see."

"And what do you see, Miss Smarty Pants?"

"Eddie, having fun. He likes to run. Yes, I know he's fast, but as competitive as you both are, he runs because he loves it. You, though, you run like you're trying to prove something or exorcise demons or some God-awful thing. I don't see you having any fun. And if you're not having any fun, then why do you put yourself through it?"

Walker sat quietly. He didn't know what to say. Isabelle was the only person who would talk to him this way. His father could, and if he did, Walker would certainly listen. But would his father ever talk to him the way Isabelle did? Walker knew the answer to that question, and the answer was no, he would not. No, his father would say something like, "Son, God gave you a talent for running, and you glorify Him when you run and train your hardest. Now get back to it. Don't waste this talent."

Walker didn't know God, really. He knew a lot about God, but he didn't know God, and there's a difference. For Walker, the closest representation was his father. He loved his father, and he knew his father loved him, but he also knew his father expected a lot from him. He couldn't help but think at times that the two were linked—his father's love and meeting his father's expectations—and so he grew up thinking that they must be linked for God too.

"No, Izzy, it may not be all that much fun, but I am fast."

"Oh, Walker, you are so fast, and I would love nothing more than for you to win. But actually, there is one thing I would love more."

"What's that?"

"Go for a run with him, not against him, but with him."

"I don't get it. What are you talking about?"

"Just do it. Please," Izzy said softly in an encouraging yet slightly pleading tone. "Just run with him, and ask him why he runs."

"You want me to run with Eddie and ask him why he runs?" asked Walker in a tone of bewilderment.

"Yes, Walkie Talkie. I do."

"I'll think about it."

*   *   *

Quaid Dawson, the silent partner in the business proposal Mitchell had made to Monty, was waiting on the front porch of his modest home when Monty drove up. "Monty, thank you for coming," said Quaid.

"Well, thank you for meeting me on such short notice, and thank you for having Walker over for dinner last night."

"Our pleasure. You and Rose can be very proud of your son. He's a fine young man. We couldn't be happier with Isabelle's choice of boyfriends. Now let's head upstairs. I have a small office here at home, and Mitchell and Thomas are waiting for us."

*   *   *

Mitchell and Thomas spoke for thirty minutes about the business plan. It was simple and straightforward. Monty asked a few questions. The four men developed an easy rapport, but Monty knew they had no future as a partnership if he wasn't honest with them right now.

"Gentlemen, this is exciting, but there's something you must know," explained Monty. He looked at the men for a sign they already knew. He couldn't get a read and decided he shouldn't play poker with these men.

"I'm in a bit of trouble."

Quaid spoke for the first time. "We know."

"Does it bother you?" asked Monty.

"No," answered Quaid. The other two men shook their heads in agreement.

"Stephen Prestwick is cruisin' for a fall. The loans his bank is making are ridiculous. He's overpaying. Never works out. I know. I'm holding a seller carryback lien on several properties, and the owners are close to defaulting on the primary loans held by First National. I figure I'll get the properties back in foreclosure," explained Quaid.

"Won't the bank defend their first mortgage position and bid up at the auction?" asked Monty.

"Doubtful. The projects are upside down. There's no equity left," explained Quaid. "They'd be throwing good money after bad."

"But what about you? Wouldn't you be throwing good money after bad? You'd have to pay off the first mortgage," said Monty.

"You'd be right if the first liens were valid," said Mitchell. "But the First National Bank loans will likely be declared predatory or invalid when it surfaces that Stephen Prestwick invested in hard money loans that those same borrowers received from an outfit in Phoenix, the very loans that pushed the borrowers into default."

"I'm not following," said Monty.

"A crooked operation out of Phoenix, Arizona—they call themselves Cutthroat Capital—is running a scam. They brokered a lot of real estate deals between buyers and sellers. Stephen's bank loaned money to the buyers to help them purchase the real estate but did so based on phony appraisals prepared by companies Cutthroat Capital controls. These appraisals pumped up the value of the projects. Cutthroat Capital then made additional loans to the borrowers to help them with the projects but did so at absurdly high interest rates. It's only a matter of time until the borrowers will default on their monthly payments to Cutthroat Capital. At that point, everything will begin to unravel, including First National Bank."

"How do you know all this?" asked Monty.

"A friend of mine in Phoenix filled me in on the Phoenix group," said Quaid.

Stunned, Monty couldn't help but chuckle.

"It's his arrogance, Monty. Stephen Prestwick's arrogance will be his undoing," said Quaid.

"And you're sure about all this? That Stephen Prestwick and First National Bank are in trouble?" asked Monty.

"No one can predict the future, Monty, but if you understand human nature, you can be sure of its direction," answered Quaid.

"So Monty, what do you say? Are you on board?" asked Mitchell.

"I can't believe this is happening. I want to say yes, but I'm struggling with the reality that I have debts and a law firm to run. And then there's my son, Eli. Things may be heating up on that front; I'm still hopeful we can clear his name and bring him home."

"Monty, how do you expect to clear his name?" asked Quaid.

"By finding the real killer, or at least convincing the Charleston PD that arresting Eli was premature," answered Monty.

"And do you think your chances are good?" asked Quaid.

"Yes, I do. Things are happening," said Monty.

"How much time do you need?" asked Quaid.

"I don't need to spend every minute on it. I just need to focus from time to time on the matter. Lately, I've been so busy keeping my head above water that I can't do anything well," said Monty.

"So if your workload was more manageable, you could catch the real killer?" asked Thomas.

"Or as I said, convince the police they rushed to judgment when they arrested Eli," answered Monty.

"Then what?" asked Mitchell. "What do you hope to come from it?"

Monty cast his eyes downward to fight back the tears. "I hope and pray Eli will hear of what I've done and that he'll come home, safe in the knowledge he will not be tried for Kimberly's murder."

Quaid stared intently at Monty and leaned forward a bit. "Monty, I have a good feeling he will. Take the time you need," he said and then sat back in his chair and cast a nod Mitchell's way, yielding the floor to him.

"Monty, I believe we can help on all fronts. We want to put your firm on retainer. That'll get you some money to help you through a tough spell," said Mitchell. "We'll lend you the money to pay off your loans with Low Country S&L. You'll still owe the money, but you'll owe it to us."

"Yes, but let's not do that right away," said Thomas. "We may be able to buy those loans at a discount when the shit hits the fan at Stephen's banks."

Monty couldn't help but smile at the thought.

"Monty, let go of the attorneys in your firm that Jenkins, Jones & Daye offered to hire. They handle all your regulatory banking work, right?" asked Mitchell.

"Yes, but I hired those guys. I feel a sense of loyalty to them."

"Did you sense them reciprocating that loyalty Friday afternoon when they pressed you for an answer?" asked Thomas.

Monty shook his head and answered regretfully, "No."

"Monty, you and I have talked before about your practice. I know what you enjoy—the tax and estate work, financial engineering, the deal-making. You hate the mundane, the regulatory work. Go back to a solo practice, doing what you love. Clean up a few items and then partner with us. You can continue serving those clients whose work you truly enjoy. You'll be content," said Quaid.

There was that word again, *content*. Monty sat up in his chair and looked at each of the men in the room. "I'd be honored to partner with you."

The four men smiled, stood, and shook hands.

"We'll draw up the documents and send them over pronto," said Mitchell.

Monty couldn't believe his good fortune. Just yesterday, he'd seen all his plans, dreams, and hard work come crashing down. And now, barely twenty-four hours later, he was saying yes to an opportunity he could never have engineered.

"How long have y'all been thinking of me for this position?" asked Monty.

"Your name was the only one on all three lists when we met last week," answered Mitchell.

Monty smiled and thought that some would call it fate, but he knew it was an answer to prayer, a prayer he hadn't even prayed yet.

"Now, don't get all high and mighty about yourself," said Quaid with a slight glint in his eye. "Remember, I like to buy distressed assets. You're an asset all right, but you sure as hell are distressed."

The four men laughed and cemented their new partnership with a drink from Quaid's liquor cabinet, a shot of Old Rip Van Winkle.

CHAPTER 33

Front Page News

Monty was up early, sitting on the front porch waiting on the weekend edition of the *Post and Courier*. The overnight thunderstorm had cleared out the humidity, delivering a temporary break from the heat.

Monty was in a fantastic mood as he thought back over what the summer had brought. It had been three months since the Friday afternoon Stephen Prestwick called and gloated about what he saw as Monty's inevitable implosion. The following Monday, after he had struck a deal with Mitchell, Tom, and Quaid, he let everyone in his office go—everyone, that is, except Abigail. She could have taken a job with any firm in town, but she stuck with Monty, his new partners having assured him she'd have a job.

The firm of Jenkins, Jones & Day hired every lawyer Monty laid off, gutting any claims of mis-, mal-, or nonfeasance concerning the work his firm had performed for First National Bank. The bank couldn't assert wrongdoing by the attorneys who had worked for Monty's firm when it turned right around and gave the work to the exact same attorneys working for a different firm. The bar complaint was dropped three weeks later.

That same first week of April, Monty moved his checking accounts to a new bank, one in which Quaid Dawson was a shareholder. The promised retainer gave Monty the breathing room to ride out the storm, but as Quaid had predicted, the storm didn't last long. Stephen's pride and arrogance indeed preceded his fall. True to Mitchell's word, it wasn't long before they bought Monty's loans from Low Country Savings & Loan, and did so at a discount, passing some of the savings on to Monty.

Stephen's shenanigans had been grist for club and church pew rumor mills for the last several months. One reason Monty was anxious for the delivery of this morning's paper was that it would put an end to the rumors, or at least some of them, with a front-page, above-the-fold exposé. The truth would come out for all to see! Monty knew that to enjoy Stephen's demise was small and petty, but he couldn't help it. He walked back inside to refill his coffee and heard the newspaper skid across the driveway. He retrieved the paper, returned to the porch, and sat down to read about the rise and fall of one Stephen Prestwick.

Yes, it had been an extraordinary summer for Monty and Stephen, the lives of each man following a trajectory that a few months earlier seemed wholly implausible, if not impossible. And all the while, Monty was an observer, and a recipient of blessings.

But there was a second story that would run in today's Sunday edition. Now the second story, that was where his hope lay.

But first, the exquisite details of Stephen's demise.

*   *   *

Early in their relationship, Stan Moore, the private lender from Cutthroat Capital, had introduced Stephen to three appraisers from Phoenix looking to expand operations. These appraisers came to town with aggressive pricing and quick turnaround, music to a lender's ears. In no time, these three appraisers secured the lion's share of the bank's business. Typically, banks work with several appraisers and employ a random method of appraiser selection, thus making it harder for a borrower or loan officer to influence the appraiser since they would not know which appraiser would be assigned to a loan file.

What Stephen didn't know was that these three supposed independent appraisers were controlled by the same group of men from Phoenix working with Stan. Stephen was also unaware of Stan's behind-the-scenes role in many of the real estate transactions the borrowers were bringing to the bank. For instance, Stan's Arizona partners would make private loans through Cutthroat Capital to potential bank borrowers if they could not come up with the down payment necessary to purchase the real estate.

Other times, Stan extended private lines of credit to help borrowers make the monthly interest payments. The line of credit allowed borrowers to claim that 100 percent of bank loan proceeds would "go into the ground" and not be used to pay loan interest. Stephen's handpicked loan committee would then boast that they drove hard bargains by insisting that no loan would be made unless borrowers demonstrated the ability to make interest payments without dipping into loan proceeds.

Invariably, Stan's money arrived at the eleventh hour as the deadline for the real estate developer to close on a critical acquisition was fast approaching. By this point, the real estate developer feared losing the deal and the confidence of the investors backing him and was thus desperate for a savior. The private lender's terms were surprisingly reasonable for those of a last-minute lender, but Stan would always say that a "good loan was a loan that got a good deal done!"

What no one noticed, or what everyone ignored, was the fine print in the loan documents prepared by Cutthroat Capital. Extraordinarily high interest rates and penalties kicked in if a borrower defaulted. Neither the real estate developers nor the loan committee at Stephen's bank was overly concerned. They were confident the underlying real estate projects would be a huge success. Why shouldn't they be? They were all smart, successful businessmen who knew what they were doing. Besides, they had appraisals to back them up.

*   *   *

The trouble began the first Monday of April 1978. The Monday that followed the Friday Stephen lowered the boom. The Monday that marked the beginning of Monty's new professional career. A borrower, who had taken out a loan to develop a second home community on Daufuskie Island, called with the news that they would miss the monthly interest payment. Daufuskie Island is located between Hilton Head, South Carolina, and Savannah, Georgia. The only means of transportation to the island was by ferry. The loan was structured as an interest-only loan, making it possible for the developer to borrow more money. With the extra money, the developer dreamed big and built a runway on the island in the hopes of attracting the super-rich or possibly a small commuter airline.

The borrower pleaded for more time, and yes, more money, but primarily more time. Due to difficulties transporting labor and materials to the island via the unreliable ferry system, they had fallen behind the construction schedule published in their loan submittal package.

Two months earlier, a private lender from which they had taken a line of credit and a smaller short-term loan had informed them that missing these construction benchmarks constituted material breaches under the terms of both loans. Consequently, the interest rate for both loans jumped to an egregious annual rate of 30 percent. The borrower made the payments for two months, but no more. Interest and penalties were now accruing daily, and the private lender had called the loan. Stephen asked who this private lender was. The borrower answered that it was the lender Stephen had introduced them to, Cutthroat Capital.

At first, Stephen was not concerned. Every banker wanted performing loans, and no banker wanted to foreclose. But every banker understood that they could foreclose and that the ability to do so and thereby force the sale of the real estate serving as collateral was critical to the lending process. No lender would ever lend money without assurance that they would either be repaid or have the ability to force the sale of the property in order to recover the money they loaned.

However, since the loan was an interest-only loan, the borrower had not paid down the principal. Stephen was a little more concerned, but again he knew they could take back the property, sell it, and use the proceeds to offset the loan amount on the balance sheet. He reviewed the loan file and saw they had loaned an amount equal to 75 percent of the appraised value. A bit aggressive, but they'd be okay. He relayed the phone call to the legal department, and they took over.

Thirty days later, Stephen was in an emergency meeting with bank lawyers, the foreclosure trustee, the loan officer on the Daufuskie loan, and two senior loan committee members. The bank had received an unsolicited offer to buy the Daufuskie loan from the bank. Under bank rules, they were obligated to consider any written offers before proceeding with a statutory foreclosure sale. The proposal was ridiculously low—$2.5 million for a loan that the bank was still owed $12 million on. The bank would lose $9.5 million and the outfit offering to purchase the loan stood to either collect the $12 million outstanding loan balance or foreclose on the loan and potentially own the real estate for $2.5 million. A steal!

The bank lawyers termed the meeting an "emergency" because of what else they had learned. The bank's outside counsel had ordered an appraisal of the island property so they could best advise their client. They used an appraiser with twenty-five years of experience in South Carolina. This appraiser visited the island—something the original appraiser hadn't done but had claimed to on page one of their appraisal—and reported that the property was now worth less than when the project began. Anyone who purchased the development would be taking over an ill-conceived, partially built community. The appraiser opined that the property was worth $5 million at most.

Stephen, in a voice he hoped concealed his state of shock, asked who had made the offer to buy the loan. The loan officer said the offer came from a group out of the Cayman Islands, a group he had never heard of, and that it wasn't the only loan they had offered to buy. The group had made offers on two dozen other loans. If they had low-balled the Daufuskie loan, had they done so on the others? What did they know? Who was this group? The magnitude of the bank's exposure dawned on Stephen and everyone around the table, as fear of the answers to these questions and others swept through the room.

The lawyers finished auditing the other two dozen loan files by the end of the week. In every case, the same three appraisers had been used, and in every case, Stan's company had lent money to the borrowers to help get the deal done. Stephen personally called the presidents at each company, and they all had a similar story. They were paying exorbitant default interest rates and penalties to Cutthroat Capital due to minor breaches, though breaches defined as material in the loan docs provided by Cutthroat Capital. And yes, they would be defaulting on the bank loan as well.

Stephen panicked. He called the appraiser who had done the most work on the identified loans. No one answered the phone; it just rang. He called the other two appraisers, and again the phone just rang. He bolted from his office and drove to the address on record for each appraiser only to find they had all closed up shop.

Stephen didn't come back to the office that afternoon until a few minutes before closing time. Becky thought he'd been drinking. She told Stephen that Stan Moore and another gentleman were waiting in his office and had been all afternoon. Stephen stared at her blankly, walked into his office, and shut his door.

Yep, he's been drinking, thought Becky.

"Stephen, you don't look so good," said Stan. "Is something wrong?"

Stan was sitting in the chair across from Stephen's desk. Seated on the sofa against the wall and holding a framed picture of Stephen's children was the largest man Stephen had ever seen. Every feature was comically over-sized. His neck was so wide it made his bulbous bald head seem as if it were attached directly to his shoulders. And his hands! Each one was the size of a Honey Baked Ham. Stan made no effort to introduce the man, and the sofa sagged under his weight as he stared dispassionately at Stephen.

"What are you doing here?" slurred Stephen.

"I'm starting to hear things, Stephen," Stan said.

"What have you heard?" asked Stephen.

"Well, for one, you don't return phone calls."

"What are you talking about, Stan?"

"The group from the Caymans that made those generous offers on all your defaulting loans—they tell me they can't get an answer back from your bank."

"How do you know about their offers?" asked Stephen, and then it hit him like a two-by-four across his back. Of course. Stan was behind it all. The phony appraisals from his friends in Phoenix looking to expand to the Southeast. The generous loans at the last minute to get the deals done. And now the group from the Cayman Islands there to rob them blind by low-balling every defaulting loan. Stan was behind it all.

Stephen felt like he was having some sort of out-of-body experience while he watched a mobster movie. This sort of thing just didn't happen in real life. Not in Charleston, anyway.

"You'll never get away with it. The bank will never agree to sell the loans at those prices."

"But Stephen, my boy, that's where you come in. You're the president; you can get them to approve the sale of the loans."

"No, I could never persuade them."

"Well, let me see if I can persuade you to be more persuasive," said Stan. And then he nodded toward the silent giant sitting on the sofa.

And with that, the human eclipse stood and approached the desk, blocking out everything else in Stephen's view. He dropped an envelope on Stephen's lap. Inside the envelope, Stephen found pictures of him with his former mistress and now wife, the very same pictures that had been placed in the mailboxes of his former wife's friends. The same pictures Gloria had thrown in his face the night she demanded a divorce.

"You'll also find in the envelope proof that the $100,000 you invested with my partners in Phoenix was not invested in Arizona deals but instead was bundled with the money Cutthroat Capital lent to your bank's clients, clients that have now defaulted on loans from your bank because they first defaulted under loans from me and my pals, loans you profited from. Now how will it look when it comes out that you made the very loans that pushed your bank clients into insolvency?"

"So you see, Stephen, it's in everyone's best interest for your bank to approve the sale of those loans. Take the weekend to think about it."

Stan rose from the chair and started toward the door. As he opened the door to leave, he turned back and said, "Oh, and Stephen, lay off the booze. It doesn't become the office of a bank president."

*　　*　　*

The following week, the loan committee reviewed the offers to purchase the numerous loans in default. Stephen pushed hard for the bank to approve the sales, arguing that the quicker this was behind them, the faster they could limit the losses and recapitalize. As it turned out, his job was not as tricky as anticipated. Stephen wasn't the only board member who had invested with Stan.

The bank teetered on bankruptcy, and Stan encouraged Stephen to cook the books. As Stan explained, he worried about the value of Stephen's stock ownership in the bank, stock Stephen had pledged to Stan as security for the $100,000 personal loan.

But no amount of book cooking could paper over the bank's dwindling cash reserves. Once the auditors grasped the big picture, they called in the FBI. The FBI's case against Stephen was strong, made all the stronger by the testimony Daphny, his soon-to-be ex-wife number two, was willing to provide. But the FBI wanted Stan and his network, and for that, they would need Stephen's testimony. Stan's operation was an indecipherable maze; every company, partnership, and legal entity through which he operated was concealed by a veil of secrecy afforded by incorporating and banking offshore.

The FBI promised Stephen immunity for his testimony. He said no.

Sensing that Stephen feared for his life, the FBI offered him a place in the federal witness protection program. He said no. What the FBI didn't realize was that Stephen's two children, living in Richmond with his ex-wife Gloria, were being held by the same giant of a man who, along with Stan, had earlier paid him an office visit. When Stephen spoke with Gloria, she was beyond consolable. The message was clear; their children would be released once he'd accepted a prison term.

Without Stephen's cooperation, the case against Stan and his cohorts crumbled like a cheap taco. Meanwhile, the bank folded. The Cayman Islands outfit, one of Stan's many front groups, purchased the loans at ridiculously low prices, foreclosed, and used every legal maneuver available to clear title and place ownership of the property into the hands of benignly named corporate entities, all with no visible connection to each other, but each one controlled by Cutthroat Capital. Some of the properties were developed and others were quickly flipped. Stan and the boys from Phoenix and the Caymans, whoever they were, made small fortunes.

Stephen agreed to seven years in a minimum-security prison. His children were returned to Gloria, unharmed.

CHAPTER 34

Stirring the Pot

Monty, on his second cup of coffee while enjoying the Sunday paper, had moved on to the sports page when he heard Rose descend the stairs. A few minutes later, she walked out onto the porch.

"There you are," she said. "What are you doing out here?"

"It's a fine morning, Rose. The paper brought good news for once. Take a look at this story about Stephen Prestwick," said Monty as he held up the paper.

"I know all about it," she said. "Trudy Weathers' husband avoided jail when he spilled his guts to the FBI. He was on the bank's board, you know. I guess he was up to no good as well. Somehow Trudy has it in her head that her husband is a hero now. She just won't stop talking about it. Some people . . .," Rose said in exasperation.

Rose smiled and leaned over and gave her husband a kiss. "That Stephen Prestwick deserves everything he gets," she said. "Monty, I'm proud of you. You landed on your feet."

197

Monty smiled and let the paper fall into his lap.

"Now hurry up. Your breakfast is on the table. Let's not be late for church. I don't want to get stuck in the back row."

Monty turned the paper over and looked one last time at the second story that had captured his attention that morning, the story on page one below the fold. A story that carried the power to upset the calm that had recently descended on the Atkins household.

*   *   *

The service ran long. They always did. Monty wondered why they bothered printing a program. Every week it was the same thing, the preacher droning on, right past a half a dozen perfect ends to his sermon.

The congregation filed outside and broke up into small predictable groups, the older folks gathered around the donut table talking about what they talked about last week, children tugging on their mothers' dresses and fathers' trousers pleading to go, and the teenagers off to themselves, the girls looking bored and the boys looking awkward.

Rose was holding court about an upcoming fall trip for the garden club. She was president and protected her reign like a third world tenpenny dictator. While speaking to the preacher's wife, Rose, out of the corner of her eye, observed an animated Monty and the newly appointed chief of police in deep conversation.

*   *   *

"Monty, I saw you speaking to the new chief of police. What's his name?" Rose asked.

"Chief Crandall."

"What were you two talking about? You were very excited about something."

"Rose, there's been a break in the case."

"What case? What are you talking about?"

"What do you mean, 'What am I talking about?' I'm talking about the case against Eli. I'm talking about finding the real killer."

Rose remained stone-faced.

"Did you see the story in the paper this morning? The story about the serial killer?" asked Monty.

"I saw it, but I don't read such things."

"Well, you should."

Rose turned her head and stared out the window.

"Rose, I know you want to forget and move on, that you're afraid of a trial, but if they catch the real killer, then they can drop the charges against Eli. If news of his innocence were circulated widely enough, he might hear it and come home. The investigative journalist who wrote the story is tracking a serial killer. According to the story, this killer was in the Southeast when Kimberly was killed."

Monty turned toward Rose, looking for some recognition on her part.

"Rose, honey, don't you see this could be the break we need?"

"Monty, what if Eli is the killer the journalist is looking for? Have you thought of that?"

They drove to the club in silence as Sunday brunch awaited, each lost in their own thoughts.

*   *   *

When Monty commissioned Laz to look for the real killer instead of Eli, he told him that Rose must never hear a word about it.

"So, Monty, you want me to show up in Charleston as a private detective and investigate the murder of Kimberly Prestwick without asking the kind of questions that will get folks to talkin'?"

"That's right."

"Well now, that's quite a challenge," said Laz. "I'll have to study on it a bit, but I expect it will cost more than the usual."

"I know, Laz. I know. You got a lot of cousins to feed."

*   *   *

Laz first met Edmond Locard while working a case on behalf of an old-moneyed family from Baton Rouge. The family's youngest son, Francis, a bit of a wild one, had run off with a great deal of his father's money and taken up with a young girl from the wrong side of the tracks. The family had hired Laz to both find their son and bring their money home safely. It didn't take Laz long to find the boy; he'd left a string of unpaid bills across the French Quarter. Matters grew more complicated, though, when the young girl turned up dead and dismembered. The boy's parents knew their son was a reprobate. But a killer? No. The police saw things differently, however, arrested Francis, and held him without bail. The family then hired Laz to prove their son's innocence.

As it turned out, the arrest was the boy's saving grace, for while he was in jail, another young girl turned up dead and dismembered. The police were reluctant to release Francis, though, for he'd been a thorough pain in the ass while in custody, but they had no choice but to let him go after a young brash college graduate who was consulting for the FBI explained the psychosis of a serial killer. "You need to be on the lookout for a predator, not a drunken playboy," pronounced Edmond Locard.

Edmond was in New Orleans consulting with the FBI on a multi-state manhunt for a suspected killer of a half a dozen or more young women. After Edmond's brutally honest assessment of the crime scene facts and Francis' unlikely culpability led to Francis' release from jail, Laz took Edmond out for a celebratory dinner.

"The fee the boy's family paid me to free their son was the easiest money I ever made," said Laz. "Thanks to you. Let me buy you dinner at Arnoud's. The food there will make you believe in God."

"Well, I'd like that. Thank you," said Edmond.

"You was mighty impressive today, Eddie. You sure you're not Cajun? What with the name 'Locard,' you might as well be," said Laz.

"No, not Cajun. Third-generation American. My family came over from France in the late 1800s. Got off the boat at Ellis Island. I'm the first of our family even to leave New York."

"Well, you could have fooled me."

"Oh, and the name is 'Edmond.'"

Laz and Edmond struck up a professional relationship that week but also became friends along the way. When Monty called Laz and told him about his new plan, Laz thought Edmond would be the perfect addition to his team. Laz explained the situation with Monty and Monty's hopes for his son Eli.

"Laz, did you ever meet Eli?" asked Edmond.

"No."

"So you can't tell me anything about him?"

"'Fraid not," replied Laz.

"Well, that leaves me a bit in the dark," said Edmond. "You see, it could be that Eli killed his girlfriend out of passion and would never kill again. Or it could be that she was killed by a predator, what we call a serial killer, and then it could be that this boy Eli is a predator. If I knew more about him, I could rule out a few scenarios."

"So where do we go from here?" asked Laz.

"I'll need to investigate the murder of Kimberly Prestwick and determine whether she was the victim of a serial killer or not. And then I'll need to get a read on this young man, Eli, and assess whether he's a potential killer, and if so, what kind."

"Well now, that presents us with a bit of a problem. Monty's quite particular about his wife not finding out what we're up to."

"That doesn't make any sense," replied Edmond.

"It's a long story, but trust me, you'll need to be discreet."

"Not a problem," said Edmond. "They'll never know my true intentions."

*　　*　　*

Monty was in the chief of police's office early the next day. Randolph Crandall had been appointed chief of police the prior year. A career lawman, he'd risen through the ranks of the Washington DC, Metropolitan Police Department.

Early in his career, Officer Randolph Crandall would have taken down anyone who dared call him Randall. He'd been given the nickname "Randall" as a kid and he hated it. Randall Crandall. Over the years, though, he'd learned that being able to laugh at yourself improved community relations, and now he regularly invited people to call him Chief Randall Crandall.

"So, Mr. Atkins, how was the rest of your Sunday?"

"Please, call me Monty. Oh, just fine, thank you. Managed to squeeze in eighteen holes after Sunday brunch. And you?"

"Quite nice, thank you. Me and the missus visited with a few couples from a new-members Sunday school class we're attending."

"Mrs. Mendlebright teaches that class, doesn't she? I hear she's excellent."

"Yes, she is. The church is blessed to have her. Now let's get back to what we were talking about Sunday. I read the article in the paper you mentioned."

"Chief Crandall—"

Chief Crandall held up his hand. "Monty, when it's just the two of us, and there are no junior officers around, please call me Randall."

Monty nodded slightly as if to say okay.

"Randall, are you familiar with the murder of a young girl named Kimberly Prestwick that occurred in these parts about five years ago?"

"Yes, I've heard mention of it."

"Well, then, you probably know that our son Eli was arrested on charges that he raped and killed the girl."

"I didn't until this morning, but Mrs. Babcock saw your name in my appointment book and the Sunday paper on my desk, asked a few questions, and put two and two together. She then enlightened me as to the facts surrounding the entire 'sordid affair,' as she called it."

"Oh dear. I was hoping my visit would remain confidential. You realize that Mrs. Babcock has better circulation than the local paper. I can't believe she still sits at that desk out front. I bet you're the fifth chief of police she's worked for. How old is she anyway? She has to be pushin' eighty."

Officer Crandall smiled. "Turns eighty-one next month. And I'm the sixth chief of police who has worked for her."

It was Monty's turn to smile.

"Monty, I'll have a word with her about the importance of confidentiality. Now what is it I can do for you?"

"Reopen the case."

CHAPTER 35

Rumors

R ose was seated in the drawing room of Constance Beauchamp's home on Church Street for the quarterly meeting of the Society for the Preservation and Beautification of South of Broad. It was assumed one had to live south of Broad Street to be a member of the society, but Rose was nothing if not persistent. She had worked hard and managed to not only worm her way onto the committee but be elected secretary as well.

Rose was enjoying a cup of coffee when Trudy Weathers barged in, nearly tripping over her tongue.

"Rose, is it true?"

Rose stiffened ever so slightly, her eyes glancing quickly from side to side, assessing who may have overheard. "Is what true, Trudy?"

"That the police are going to reopen the Kimberly Prestwick case."

*   *   *

As soon as the quarterly meeting for the society had adjourned, Rose made as quick and graceful an exit as possible. If she left too soon, the others would stay and gossip about her. But the sooner she could confront Monty, the sooner she'd know what that fool of a husband had gone and done.

*   *   *

Monty saw Rose hurrying down the hallway toward his office. This couldn't be good. She never came to the office.

She strode into his office, closing the door behind her.

"What have you done?"

"It's good to see you too, Rose. Are you here to join me for lunch?"

He immediately regretted his sarcasm.

Rising from his desk, he approached her, arms extended, and took her two hands in his. "Rose, tell me what you've heard."

"Oh, Monty. That horrible Trudy Weathers knew before I did. You got the police to reopen the case, didn't you? That's what you were talking to him about Sunday, wasn't it? Why couldn't you talk to me first?"

"Talk to you first?! Honey, I've been trying to talk to you about Eli and his innocence since the night he vanished, but you won't have it."

"You mean the night he ran."

"No, I mean the night he vanished. Because that's what he did. He vanished from the face of the earth. The private detective I hired could find neither hide nor hair of him. But I know he's out there, and I know he's innocent. Our son is innocent."

Monty then sighed deeply, and the two of them leaned forward and rested their foreheads against each other.

"Oh, Monty. I wish I was as confident. But he's not our son, is he? Yes, you were a father to him all those years and a wonderful father, but I knew his real father, and he was a monster. Now please, tell me. Are they reopening the case?"

Monty told Rose all about his meeting with the chief of police.

CHAPTER 36

Edmond Locard

In his office the previous Monday, Monty had told Rose about his meeting with the chief of police, but still, he had kept her in the dark about the work Laz was doing. He hated his deceit, but given her attitude toward Eli, he knew no other way. So this morning, lying again, Monty said he was headed to the office. Instead, he hopped on Interstate 17 and drove to Savannah.

He pulled into the parking lot by 9:00 a.m. The humidity was oppressive. Dark, heavy clouds, collapsing under their own weight, ripped open the sky and soaked Monty as he ran from his car into the hotel lobby.

"You almost made it," said the young woman behind the desk. "And welcome to the Rodeway Inn."

Monty shook the water from his hair. "Just about. Thank you. Say, where can I find the restaurant?" asked Monty.

"Across the lobby, around the corner to the left. You'll see the signs. Will you be staying with us?"

"No, ma'am. Just meeting folks for breakfast."

"Well, if there's anything I can do, don't hesitate to ask."

"Thank you, ma'am."

Monty walked into the restaurant, where he saw Laz sitting in the corner booth with another gentleman.

Laz stood, took a few steps toward Monty, and greeted him with a firm handshake and a conspiratorial slap on the back. "Monty, I'd like to introduce you to Edmond Locard."

Edmond Locard was a dapper dresser and wore horn-rimmed glasses. He looked "a bit bookish," is how Monty would describe him, and he looked young, too young in Monty's opinion.

"Excuse me, but if you don't mind me asking. How old are you?"

"I love it how you Southerners are so polite when you put someone down. I'm twenty-eight. I'm from New York, and I graduated with degrees in psychology and journalism from Emory University. That's in Atlanta."

"I know where Emory is," clipped Monty.

"Of course you do. No offense intended."

"I love it how you Northerners never intend to offend but just can't seem to help yourself."

"Whoa now, boys. Is there going to be a problem?" asked Laz.

Monty removed his glasses, pinched his nose, paused, gathered himself, and put his glasses back on.

"No, not at all. Mr. Locard, I apologize. I'm just a bit frazzled, is all. I've put a lot of hope in this scheme of ours, and I was expecting an older, more grizzled reporter. You know, like you see in the movies."

"Apology accepted. I assure you, Mr. Atkins, I'm up to the job. I graduated at the top of my class at Emory, and I also have a degree in criminology from George Washington University. I work extensively with the FBI and am an expert on the subject of serial killers."

"Well, your article on serial killers certainly stirred up my household," said Monty.

"Stirring things up was the idea, wasn't it?" asked Edmond. "Now, shall we get down to business?"

"Absolutely." Monty turned to Laz, smiled, and gave him a reassuring nod.

*   *   *

Gloria Prestwick heard the mail fall through the slot in the front door. It had been over five years. The first several years following Kimberly's murder were dark, marinated in pills and alcohol. When Stephen was thrown in prison for his financial shenanigans, the creditors came after her once they had exhausted the marital estate. Fortunately, her trusts, established by her parents and grandparents all those years ago, were shielded from creditors. She couldn't get to the corpus of the trust, so neither could they.

She had climbed out of her depression and was doing well in Richmond. Her other children had adjusted, and if they could, by God, so could she. She had a good job, and her trust income more than provided.

Gloria was in a good place but still not prepared for what the postman delivered.

In an envelope postmarked from Charleston but with no return address, was a one-line, typed, and unsigned message:

"They're going to reopen the case."

*   *   *

An hour later and you would have never known that Monty and Edmond had gotten off to a rocky start. It was clear that Edmond was an expert in his field. Monty took a liking to him and let Laz know it.

"Laz, thank you for putting all this together," said Monty.

"But of course, mon ami. Edmond says he ain't Cajun, but I believe he just might be."

"So, where do we go from here?" asked Monty.

"I need to investigate Kimberly Prestwick's murder," answered Edmond.

"How do you propose to do that?" asked Monty.

"I'll start by driving to Charleston and meeting with the detective in charge of cold cases," answered Edmond.

Monty looked at Laz. "Laz, have you told Edmond about the sensitive nature of this covert operation of ours?" asked Monty.

"No worries, my friend," said Laz.

"Monty, I understand that it's important to you that no one, and especially your wife, gets wind of what we're up to. Do I have that right?" asked Edmond.

"You got that right," said Monty.

"Not to worry," said Edmond. "I wrote the article that got all this started. I have reason to investigate unsolved murders. I'll tell them I'm on the trail of a serial killer, and I'll learn what I need to learn. Simple."

"How does that sound?" asked Laz.

"That sound's great," said a relieved Monty. Turning back to Edmond, "How much time do you need?" asked Monty.

"Shouldn't be more than a week if the folks in the Charleston PD cooperate," answered Edmond. "I should be able to meet next week. Does Thursday work for everyone?" asked Edmond.

"And what about this location? Work for everyone?" asked Laz.

They all nodded in agreement, shook hands, and parted. Until next Thursday.

*   *   *

"I'm here to see the chief of police," said the immaculately dressed man standing in front of her. Charlene tended the front desk, which meant she met everyone coming and going and routed every phone call. If your actions caught the attention of the police, Charlene knew about it.

"Do you have an appointment?" asked Charlene.

"No, ma'am, I don't, but it's important."

"Do you need to report a crime? If you do, one of our officers on duty can take your statement," replied Charlene.

"No, I don't need to report a crime. Just please tell Chief Crandall that I'm here to see him," said the man as he passed over his business card.

Charlene rang Mrs. Babcock, turned her chair, and explained quietly, with one hand covering her mouth, that a Mr. Holbrook from Washington DC, was here to see the chief but didn't have an appointment. Mr. Holbrook looked on as the young woman nodded into the phone and then hung up.

"Mrs. Babcock is the chief's secretary," announced Charlene. "She says that you can wait back at her desk, and she'll see if you can get a meeting with the chief. He's awfully busy, you know."

Mr. Holbrook thanked her and walked down the hall toward a woman waving at him from behind her desk, a woman who could only be Mrs. Babcock. Within five minutes, he was inside the chief's office.

*   *   *

The chief alternated his gaze from the business card he'd been handed to the man in a dark blue suit and freshly polished shoes who had just handed over the card. The chief could never understand how "nonprofits" could afford to pay so much.

"Says here you're an advocate. What does that mean? Mrs. Babcock said you were a lawyer."

Mr. Holbrook stood with his heels together, both hands gripping his briefcase, palms in as if protecting his knees.

"I'm a lawyer by training. Sometimes I fight for individual clients and sometimes for a cause. Hence, I'm an advocate."

"Whatever you say. Now, what or whom are you advocating for today, Mr. Holbrook?" asked Chief Crandall.

"I'm here to talk to you about Kimberly Prestwick. Word has reached us that you intend to reopen the case. Is this true?"

"Word has reached you, you say? And how did that come to pass?"

"I'm not at liberty to say."

"Uh-huh. Well, then I'm not at liberty to answer your question. What's your interest in Kimberly Prestwick anyway?"

"As you can no doubt understand, were this matter reopened, it would prove traumatic to Kimberly Prestwick's family. And to what end, sir? I read the story in your local paper about a supposed serial killer on the loose. Quite a leap, don't you think, to conclude that Eli Atkins, the jilted lover with the white-hot temper, is therefore not the killer?"

"Mr. Prestwick is in federal prison serving time for bank fraud, so I'm not sure how much more traumatic things can get for him. Washington DC, ain't too far from Richmond, so I'm starting to connect the dots. You can tell Mrs. Prestwick that I will not be railroaded. I have nothing more to say. Now good day."

*   *   *

"Mrs. Babcock's office," said Mrs. Babcock as she picked up the phone. "How can I help you?"

"I need to speak to the chief of police."

"I'm afraid he's not in. What is this about, ma'am? Maybe someone else can help you. The chief of police is awful busy."

"No. No one else can help me. When will he be back?"

"Well, I don't rightly know. Who may I say is calling?"

"Gloria Prestwick."

Her answer was met with silence and a pause.

"Mrs. Prestwick, I believe I see the chief of police coming down the hall now. May I put you on hold for a moment?"

"What fortunate timing for me. But of course."

Mrs. Babcock stuck her head into Chief Crandall's door—she never knocked—and told him he had a call.

"Mrs. Babcock, can it wait? As you know, I'm with someone. You let him in here, for Pete's sake," said an exasperated Chief Crandall as he gestured toward Mr. Holbrook.

"It's Mrs. Prestwick on the phone. That girl Kimberly's mother. She's calling long distance from Richmond," explained Mrs. Babcock.

Chief Crandall looked at Mr. Holbrook, then at Mrs. Babcock, and then back at Mr. Holbrook.

"I think you want to take this call, Chief Crandall," said Mr. Holbrook.

"Very well, put her through. And Mrs. Babcock?"

"Yes, boss?"

"Shut the door."

*   *   *

"Mrs. Prestwick, my name is Chief Crandall, and I'm the chief of police here in Charleston. How can I be of assistance?"

Those were close to the last words he spoke.

"Yes, Mrs. Prestwick. ... No, Mrs. Prestwick. ... No, we have not reopened the case. ... No, we have no intention to at this moment. ... Yes, of course. By all means. ... We would definitely call you before we took any such action. ... I'm very sorry, and I understand. ... No, I don't know how rumors like this get started. ... I'll be sure to. ... Goodbye."

Chief Crandall hung up the phone, wishing he'd never met with Monty Atkins.

Mrs. Babcock sat at her desk throughout the call, opening the mail, marveling at the wonderful new hearing aid her son had bought her.

CHAPTER 37

A Covert Investigation

The following Monday morning, Edmond was at the Charleston Police Department speaking with Charlene, the front desk clerk.

"My name is Edmond Locard. I'm here to see Officer Rawlings."

"Is he expecting you?" asked Charlene.

"Yes, I believe he is. I called last week and explained to the woman who answered the phone that I was working with the FBI on a project involving unsolved murders."

"Oh, that's you," she exclaimed. "I'm the desk clerk you spoke with."

"Nice to meet you. Is Officer Rawlings in?"

"Yes. Yes, he is. Just hold on a minute, and I'll call him for you."

The desk clerk picked up her phone, punched in a few numbers, and waited.

"Officer Rawlings, that man I told you about? The man who wants to look at our unsolved murders? Well, he's here."

Charlene hung up and directed Edmond to the conference room down the hall and told him to help himself to the coffee. Edmond didn't have to wait long. Officer Rawlings, straight out of central casting, sauntered in and took a seat. Bushy mustache, slightly overweight with a donut in one hand and a thirty-year-old coffee cup that said "World's Greatest Dad" in the other.

"So you're the young fella that wants to look at our cold cases."

"Yes. Specifically, any unsolved murders."

"Charlene out front says you're with the FBI. Can I see your badge?" asked Officer Rawlings.

"I don't work with the FBI, in that I'm not a federal agent. But I consult with the FBI. My area of expertise is serial killers. Profiling them. Tracking them. That sort of thing."

"Heh, you're the guy that wrote the article about serial killers, aren't you?" asked Officer Rawlings. "I read it in the Sunday paper last week."

"Yes, sir. That's me."

"Well, I'm afraid you've wasted a trip. Can't say we've ever had a serial killer in these parts."

"Well, it's possible you did and just didn't know it. If I study your files on any unsolved murders, then I'd have a better idea if you're looking for a serial killer as a likely suspect," said Edmond.

"You see, that's the problem. We don't have any unsolved murders. Charleston's a small town. We don't have many murders, to begin with."

Edmond proceeded carefully. He needed to jar the officer's memory, stirring his recall of the Prestwick case without appearing to know the answer to the question.

"Am I to understand that for every murder committed in this town over the last twenty years, the police made an arrest, and the district attorney got a guilty verdict?"

"That's right," said Officer Rawlings a bit proudly, as if he deserved the credit.

Edmond didn't reply but instead let the silence build.

"Now, hold on," said Rawlings. "There was one case about five or six years ago. We didn't actually convict anyone."

"But you closed the case anyway?" asked Edmond.

"That's right. See, the young man we arrested skipped town. Jumped bail. The manhunt went on for close to a month. Never found him. Yeah, I'm remembering now. Kimberly Prestwick."

"Excuse me?" remarked Edmond.

"The girl that was killed, her name was Kimberly Prestwick. We arrested her boyfriend. His name was Atkins. Eli Atkins. He had a fine attorney and came from a good family. No one could figure it out. Why he ran, that is. Unless, of course, he was guilty. Yep, everyone figured he was guilty, and the case was marked closed," explained Officer Rawlings.

"Would you happen to know who the detective on the case was?"

"No, but I can find out. Just sit tight."

Five minutes later, Officer Rawlings strolled back into the conference room. "You'll want to talk to Officer Pearlman."

"Thank you, Officer," said Edmond, as he stood to shake hands. "You've been a big help."

Edmond contacted Officer Pearlman, and they agreed to meet at the Waffle House on Savannah Highway at 10:30 that night after his shift ended. Edmond was staying at the Holiday Inn right next door to the Waffle House, so the location was fine, but he couldn't understand how Southerners ate that food and lived past forty.

*   *   *

Officer Pearlman took a seat at a table alongside the counter separating the kitchen from the dining area and unfurled a rolled copy of the afternoon edition of the local newspaper. A waitress approached him and placed a cup of coffee in front of him without him even asking.

"Just you tonight, Bruce?" she asked.

"No, Darla. I'm waitin' on someone," he answered. "In fact, I think this may be him." Officer Pearlman waved at a man entering the Waffle House who matched the description Edmond had given him over the phone earlier in the day.

"Edmond Locard?" asked Officer Pearlman as he raised himself up from his seat to shake the man's hand.

"Yes. And you must be Officer Pearlman," said Edmond.

They shook hands and took their seats. Darla appeared in no time.

"Coffee?"

"No, thank you," answered Edmond as he realized she must be speaking to him. "Do you have a Tab?"

The waitress stared blankly at the young man, walked away without answering, and returned with a coffee and two creams. She pulled a pencil from behind her right ear and removed a small pad pressed against her hip by her apron, and asked, "What'll y'all have?"

"Steak 'n' eggs, the eggs fried but a little runny, hash browns, smothered, covered, and topped, and a side of bacon, crispy." Officer Pearlman slid the menu back behind the napkin holder and took a sip from his coffee.

Edmond stared at the menu in disbelief.

"Do you have a bagel?" he asked.

"'Fraid not, honey, but what d' ya say I bring you two eggs scrambled and a side of toast?"

"Perfect. Thank you."

She slipped the pencil back behind her ear, shook her head in dismay, then shouted out what they'd be eating in a code decipherable by the short-order cook and possibly a few regulars.

"Officer Pearlman, thank you for meeting me on such short notice," said Edmond.

"No problem and please call me Bruce. When you told me what you wanted to meet about, well, I was a little curious. So you think Kimberly Prestwick was killed by a serial killer?"

"Well, I don't know. I'm investigating unsolved murders, looking for evidence that might indicate whether the murderer was a serial killer. If I can establish patterns and routines, not only will it help us solve some of these cases, but we'll do a better job profiling serial killers in the future."

"And you're working with the FBI on this?"

"I have worked with the FBI and continue to." Edmond hoped his non-answer was enough of an answer to keep Officer Pearlman talking.

"Very well. How can I help?" Officer Pearlman asked.

"Can you tell me about the crime scene?"

*   *   *

THURSDAY, AUGUST 17

"Are y'all ready to order?" asked the waitress.

They were, and they did. A little over a week later, Monty, Laz, and Edmond were sitting in the same Rodeway Inn restaurant.

"Edmond, how was your visit to the Charleston Police Department? Did you learn anything about Kimberly Prestwick's murder that'll help our cause?" asked Laz.

"Yes. Yes, I did," answered Edmond.

"Okay. Let's get right to it," said Monty. "What's it going to take to clear Eli's name?"

Edmond leaned forward, placed his arms on the table, one hand clasped in the other, and began. "What we need is physical evidence from the crime scene."

"What kind of evidence?" asked Monty.

"Blood and hair samples, for instance. I understand the girl was raped. In that case, semen samples."

"You've got to be kidding, right? Any blood or semen would be long gone by now," said Monty.

"Not necessarily. Dried blood and semen stains can be found on clothing, leaves, in soil samples, and on weapons, for instance."

"Okay, maybe so, but then what?" asked Monty. "We run tests or something to determine whose it is? The blood samples would have come from the girl who was murdered. Where does that get us?"

"I'll come back to that in a moment, but the semen stains would have been left by the killer, would they not?"

"Of course, but so what if we have semen stains? How do we prove the semen's not Eli's?"

"Okay. I understand your frustration, Monty. So let me explain," said Edmond. "Forensic science has come a long way since the old ABO blood group system was first developed. Under that system, blood was cataloged as A positive, B positive, etc. But since there are literally billions of people with the same blood type, identifying someone as belonging to one group or another rarely helped solve a crime. However, we've made great advances and are well on our way to meeting the goal of individualizing human blood."

"What do you mean 'individualizing human blood?'" asked Monty.

"Individualizing human blood rests on the idea that everyone's blood type is unique like their fingerprint. More specifically, forensic scientists believe we have genetic markers in our blood, detectable with reliable test procedures, that no one else in the world has. These genetic markers are made up of protein and enzyme systems."

"So everyone has a unique genetic profile—is what you're saying."

"That's right, Laz," said Edmond. "Armed with this knowledge, we can then run tests on two different blood samples, Sample A and Sample B for instance, and state with 100 percent confidence that Sample A came from Person A and Sample B came from Person B. Once this goal is achieved, the FBI can store the genetic profiles of convicted criminals in a national database."

"Like we do for fingerprints," stated Laz.

"That's right," said Edmond.

"So how are we doing?" asked Laz. "How close are we to individualizing human blood, as you say?"

"We're not there yet, but we're making huge strides."

"Edmond, this is great and all," said a frustrated Monty, "but help me here. If we're not there yet, how do these huge strides help Eli *right now*?"

"Well, we don't have a full understanding of the genetic markers necessary for complete individualization, but we have achieved partial individualization. This capability, combined with our knowledge of population genetics and the frequencies of genetic marker types across the population, allows us to often draw one of two conclusions in a trial. Either the defendant's genetic markers do not match those in samples taken from a crime scene, thus exonerating the defendant, or the defendant's genetic markers fall into the same population group of those found at the crime scene, a population group of no more than a thousand people in the entire world. This type of testimony can be very damning for a defendant," explained Edmond.

"Yes, I'm sure it can. If only Eli were here to give us some of his blood and semen, then we could clear this up and go home. This may come as a shock to you, Edmond, but while my wife and I kept extensive scrapbooks of the boys, we don't have any blood or semen samples!"

"Now calm down, Monty, and give Edmond a chance," said Laz.

"No, Monty, I don't expect you do. But let me tell you what I have. In conjunction with the FBI, we're building a database of samples taken from crime scenes of solved and unsolved murders and blood typing them. The database also includes information about the crime itself. Was a knife used? A gun? Some other weapon? Was sexual assault involved? Was the murder ritualistic in nature, etc.? We can then sort these crimes by various factors and look for patterns."

"But how does this database help Eli?" asked Monty.

"I believe we've found one," answered Edmond. "A pattern, that is. The pattern of a serial killer on the loose and working the southeastern part of the United States about the time Kimberly Prestwick was killed."

"You have my attention," said Monty. "Go on."

Edmond continued. "If evidence from the Prestwick crime scene has been preserved, and if there are any blood or semen stains on the evidence, then we can run tests and possibly determine the genetic profile of Kimberly's murderer."

"Fascinating, but since your serial killer is still on the loose, how do we get samples from him?" asked Monty.

"We can't. But we don't need them to clear Eli's name. If samples from Kimberly's crime scene match the genetic profile of samples from one or more unsolved murders I'm investigating, then the police can rule Eli out as a suspect, as long as Eli has an alibi for the other murders."

"Of course he would. He was in high school, for Pete's sake," said Monty.

Monty turned and looked out the window and said to no one in particular, "The first ray of hope in some time."

*　　*　　*

Darla leaned over the counter and passed the men their meals. "Can I get y'all anything else?" she asked.

"No thank you, Darla," said Officer Pearlman. "This looks perfect. But how about a refill on the coffee?"

Edmond lightly salted his eggs and watched Officer Pearlman tear into his meal. "Bruce, you were about to describe the crime scene," Edmond said.

Bruce waited for his coffee refill and then started back up. "I'm not likely to ever forget it," said Officer Pearlman. "I've been a cop for over thirty years now, and I thought I'd seen everything. Kimberly Prestwick's body was mutilated. The coroner said the killer used a large knife with a serrated edge. Most likely a hunting knife. But not until he'd beaten her first. Her head and face, though, were untouched, resting on a mound of dirt. It was like the killer was presenting her."

"The mutilation. Did anything else about it strike you?" asked Edmond.

"I'll say. From the neck down, she looked like a field-dressed deer."

"Well, Bruce, from your description, it sounds like the work of someone who had killed before."

"What makes you say that?" asked Bruce.

"The killer had a method. And you said she was also beaten. Do you know with what?" asked Edmond.

"A baseball bat."

*　　*　　*

The waitress approached the table with a handful of menus and asked, "Can I interest y'all in some dessert? We've had a long summer so we're still getting some nice peaches and our peach cobbler is the best in Savannah." Monty and Laz each ordered a piece. Edmond passed.

"So, Edmond, what is a serial killer?" asked Monty.

"Well first, a murderer won't fit into the category until they've killed at least three people. But even amongst those who have killed three or more, we exclude killers hired by the mob, for instance. Killers for hire are an entirely different animal."

"So Charles Manson is a serial killer," stated Monty.

"No. Remember, to the best of our knowledge, Manson didn't commit any murders. He directed others to. He was a cult leader, and as wicked as they come, but not what we're talking about here.

"The typical personality profile of a serial killer is of someone charming, a bit of a rogue in some cases, often a smooth talker, and extremely manipulative. They're egocentric and see themselves as the real victim. They're deceitful, impulsive, incapable of controlling their emotions, and totally lacking any empathy. And even more horrifying, beyond merely lacking empathy, they enjoy inflicting pain and suffering on others, often deriving sexual excitement and release from it," said Edmond.

"Well, that doesn't describe my Eli. Not by a long shot."

"Well, sadly, it does describe some people that are walking around amongst us," explained Edmond.

"And you believe the serial killer you're lookin' for was in the Charleston area around the time of May 1973?" asked Laz.

"I can't be certain the killer was in Charleston," said Edmond, "not until we get test results from the evidence taken from Kimberly's crime scene, but I can tell you this much. The details from the crime scene, as described to me by Officer Pearlman, are gruesomely similar to those of other crime scenes we're investigating."

"So we just have to get the Charleston PD to fear there may be a serial killer at large and give you the file," stated Monty.

"That's right," said Laz. "And the article in the paper last week was step one. We've stirred things up."

*   *   *

The waitress leaned over the counter and refilled their coffee mugs.

"Bruce, can you tell me about the investigation and the arrest?" asked Edmond.

"There's not much to tell. A state highway patrolman called it in. He saw vultures circling and car tracks leading on and off the road. Kimberly's car was hidden behind bushes and wasn't visible from the road. It had rained a bit the night before, I remember, but we could tell that there were two sets of tire tracks leading off the road, but only one coming back on to the road. Understand, it's been a while since I thought about all this; my recall may not be perfect. Anyway, the highway patrolman called the station, and I was dispatched along with my partner, Will Tyrel. Good man."

"What were your initial reactions and your first steps?" asked Edmond.

"After the shock of seeing the body, we gathered ourselves. Identification wasn't hard. We found her driver's license in the car. It's a small town as well, and Officer Tyrell recognized her. Once the crime scene was secured and the forensics team and coroner were on-site, Will and I plotted our investigation. We set about putting together her last known whereabouts and assembling a list of friends, acquaintances, etc. Standard investigative procedure. But first, we had to notify her parents. Most gut-wrenching day of my career."

*   *   *

Gloria was standing in her kitchen, staring out the window and trying not to imagine the worst. She had just called the club for the third time in search of her husband Stephen. She was told he was still on the course but that he should be done soon. After her third call, the club general manager called her back and told her that he would personally see to it that Stephen phoned home as soon as he walked off the course.

She was still standing, leaning against the counter, when the loud, unexpected knock on the door startled her. She opened the door, saw the police officers, took several steps back, and broke into tears.

"Mrs. Prestwick, I'm Officer Pearlman, and these are Officers Tyrell and Baker. May we come in?"

"What's happened to her? Is she okay? Where's my baby?" she cried, nearing hysteria.

"Mrs. Prestwick, is your husband home?"

"Nooo, please nooo." She knew instinctively. Something was wrong. Something was terribly wrong.

*   *   *

"Bruce, I'm fascinated by police work, by forensics, and yes, by the criminal mind," said Edmond. "But what you police officers do . . . it's incredible. That had to be a tough house call. You have nothing but my respect."

"Thank you," said Officer Pearlman.

"Can you tell me what happened next?" asked Edmond.

"Sure. Well, after Mr. Prestwick positively identified the body, we began to recreate her last twenty-four hours. Establishing the time of death was fairly easy. The initial interviews all pointed to one person, her boyfriend, Eli Atkins. Initially, he was just a person of interest."

"How seriously were you taking him as the possible killer?" asked Edmond.

"Hard to say. The investigation was over and closed before it really got going. Their friends all had a similar story to tell. Eli and Kimberly had been dating a while, but lately, they'd been fighting quite a bit. It was no secret her parents didn't approve. The two kids were headed in different directions. She was college-bound. The University of Virginia, I believe, but like I said, it's been a while, so I may be wrong about that. Eli, on the other hand, had his sights set on major league baseball."

"Was he good enough?" asked Edmond.

"Oh, yeah. If you grew up in these parts and played baseball, you knew who Eli Atkins was. Trouble was, he had a temper, and occasionally it showed up on the field. He put a boy in the hospital once for bringing the tag too hard when Eli was stealing second. I don't know the details, but it's said that his ensuing suspension cost his team the state championship. He was in tenth grade at the time.

"Well, anyway, he was the last person to be seen with her. They were together at Bowens, a popular beachside dive around here, and had been seen arguing about something. She ran out of the bar; he followed. Next morning, she's found dead in a wooded area a short ways from the state highway but not visible from off the road. One set of tire tracks belonged to her car, and the other set of tracks were of the same style as those on Eli's truck. Not a perfect match, mind you—the rain prevented us from getting better molds—but damning, nonetheless.

"But what sealed his fate was when he ran."

"But wasn't that after his arrest?" asked Edmond.

"Both, really. We went to Eli's home the next evening to question him. This part I remember clearly. His mother wasn't terribly surprised to see police officers at her door asking about Eli. She told us he wasn't home, and that she didn't know where he was or when he'd be back. We asked her if he'd come home the night before and she said yes, but she couldn't tell us when."

"Did you tell her about Kimberly's murder?" asked Edmond.

"Yes, but not before asking the other questions."

"Do you believe she already knew?"

"No. When we told her, she definitely registered alarm. Not shock or sadness, though."

"Odd."

"I'll say. We asked her to call us as soon as Eli came home, and then we left."

"And did she?" asked Edmond.

"No, she didn't. She called Sunday morning to let us know he'd come home around 2 a.m., but he was no longer there. She said he just sped off in his truck when she told him Kimberly was dead and the police were looking for him."

"Where did you find him?" asked Edmond.

"He turned up at the Prestwicks' house. Family and friends had descended on the Prestwicks earlier in the day, doing what they could to comfort them. I was there too. As you can imagine, Eli created quite a stir when he pulled up the driveway. The story of their fight at Bowens Friday night had spread like wildfire. Things got a little chaotic at this point. Mr. Prestwick tried to chase him down, and the crowd grew restless. He saw me, and before I had a chance to talk to him, he took off in his truck. We pursued him and finally had to call in a roadblock."

"Did you arrest him?" asked Edmond.

"Yes, we did."

"And he ran again, didn't he?"

"Yep. Skipped bail one night. Broke into his father's wall safe at home and made off with over $10,000."

"Was there any evidence to tie him to the crime scene?"

"The knife."

"The knife that was used to kill Kimberly?"

"Possibly. We found a large hunting knife with a serrated edge in the back of Eli's truck."

*   *   *

Laz finished his peach cobbler in record time, but Monty, focused like a laser on what Edmond was telling him, had barely picked at his.

"Monty, I have to warn you," said Edmond. "There's no guarantee that what we find in the evidence locker will exonerate Eli."

"Of course it will," replied Monty.

"I just don't want to get your hopes too high," said Edmond. "There's no guarantee Chief Crandall will give us access to the evidence locker, and we have no real leverage."

"Well, I don't see the problem," said Monty. "In your next article, talk about how Kimberly was killed in the same manner as other girls in the South. Write about the gruesome crime scene, the hunting knife. For God's sake, we have to get people in the area worried so they'll demand the case be reopened."

A few in the restaurant looked their way when Monty knocked over his coffee cup, slamming his fist against the table.

Laz and Edmond exchanged concerned looks.

"Monty, there's something you need to know," explained Laz.

"The detective, Officer Bruce Pearlman...he told Edmond that the police found a serrated hunting knife in Eli's truck," said Laz.

Monty looked unfazed. "So? That's no big deal. Eli had a truck full of gear. If he wasn't fishing, he was hunting. Lots of young boys his age own hunting knives."

Edmond looked at Laz, and Laz nodded slightly.

"There was blood on the knife, Monty."

*　　*　　*

It was after midnight and Officer Pearlman indicated he needed to head home. Edmond asked for the check.

"Bruce, I know it's late, and thank you for your time," said Edmond.

"No problem. I hope I've been able to help."

"You've been very helpful. I just have one more question. The knife. Was it tested? Were any tests run to determine whether the blood on the knife was Kimberly's?" asked Edmond.

"Like I said, we're a small department. We placed the knife in an evidence bag and sent it to the hospital. They confirmed for us that the blood was human. A few of us knew the Atkins family. My partner, Officer Tyrell, his son and Eli played ball together. We were all hoping it'd be deer blood or something. Hell, we'd arrest Eli for hunting out of season and let him off easy. But that wasn't the case."

"Bruce, does the evidence gathered at Kimberly's crime scene still exist? Can that knife be located?" asked Edmond.

Bruce fiddled with his spoon and said nothing.

"Bruce, is there a problem?" asked Edmond.

"No, there's no problem. But if you ask the front desk for the evidence locker, they'll tell you it was destroyed last summer," explained Officer Pearlman.

"Damn, well, that changes everything." Edmond suddenly looked very tired, as if he'd wasted a great deal of time on a fruitless journey.

"I said that's what the front desk will tell you. I didn't say it had been."

* * *

Monty asked for the check, and after nearly three hours together, the three men went their separate ways, each with his own to-do list. Monty pulled into his driveway that night at his usual time, and Rose was none the wiser.

Monty and Rose ate dinner alone, again. Walker was out, Rose explained, studying with Isabelle at the public library. Walker spent less and less time with them. Monty understood but didn't like it. Walker was headed to college in a year, and Monty would miss him. He already did. But he understood. Young love. He envied his son.

* * *

After dinner, Rose adjourned to prepare for a Bible study she was leading for a victims' rights group. Just a few months after Eli disappeared, Rose had joined a group for mothers who had lost children to violent criminals. The balls that woman had.

That was fine with Monty. He had work to do to. Edmond gave him the dates of the unsolved murders he was investigating. Monty set out to establish an alibi for Eli for each of the murders. But how do you prove someone wasn't at a site? Simple; show he was someplace else. That's what an alibi was.

But to do so, Monty needed an unbiased witness who would testify they'd seen Eli on such-and-such a date, the date of the other murders, and at such-and-such a location, a location far removed from the murder scenes. Armed with this testimony, and the similarities between the murder scenes,

Monty hoped that Chief Crandall would turn over the evidence locker so they could run Edmond's tests.

A long shot, but still, all they had to do was get the case reopened.

As for the knife in Eli's truck? Well, Monty knew that either the hospital was wrong or there was some other explanation. There had to be. They'd deal with it later.

Monty stared at the dates of the unsolved murders and checked them against his old calendars. A little after midnight, after one date in particular kept jumping out, he hit pay dirt.

Chapter 38

The Pot is Stirred

It had been a busy week, and Monty, exhausted, crawled into bed early Saturday night. To his relief, he fell asleep quickly and didn't budge until 5:00 the next morning, wide awake and rested. He made the coffee and tried reading to pass the time, but it was hard to concentrate with one ear trained on the anticipated sound of the Sunday paper hitting their front step.

Monty was out of his chair as quick as a flash when he heard the boy's tires roll across the tabby driveway. The story appeared above the fold and described in horrifying detail the work of a killer in the southeastern United States, skilled with a serrated hunting knife. The similarities between the murders were eerie and disturbing. Monty devoured every word.

Rose sat at the table, feigning interest in the paper's garden section as Monty read. She'd glimpsed the article earlier when Monty tossed the paper on the kitchen table on his way to refill his coffee. He finished the piece, folded the paper, and placed it on the table.

"I'll be ready to leave for church in ten," he announced as he pushed himself away from the table.

As he bounced up the stairs, Rose called after him.

"I guess Walker won't be joining us, will he?"

"Don't suspect so," he hollered back.

In the clear and with ten minutes on her side, Rose read the article. She'd read the first one too.

As she read the article, she felt the clinging weight of tentacles reaching out from her past, desperately trying to pull her back, back under a blanket of fear, a fear she'd been running from all her life, a fear now darkening her door. She stood in a desperate effort to shake the feelings as she looked out the window. Storm clouds were gathering.

*   *   *

"Irresponsible journalism. That's what it is. Hell, it ain't even journalism. Just damned sensationalism. Do you have any idea how many calls we've had here today? Do you?"

"No, I don't believe I do. Would you like me to guess? What do I win if I'm right?" asked Edmond Locard.

Chief Crandall would have thrown him out of his office—and not just his office, but through the front window—if he were the only journalist in the station at the time. The lobby was full of journalists, and there was a growing stack of messages on his desk from papers, news agencies, and television and radio stations, all wanting a comment on the serial killer. And a story had leaked that the Charleston Police Department was going to reopen the Kimberly Prestwick case. Through the fog of his anger, he could barely make out the back of Mrs. Babcock's head, as she calmly opened the day's mail.

Monty and Edmond sat across from Chief Crandall as he paced back and forth on his side of the desk. Edmond, Laz, and Monty had decided that Laz should skip the meeting lest his presence raise too many questions they didn't want to answer.

Randall Crandall glared at the two men sitting in his office. Edmond, relaxed and leaning back in his chair, legs extended and crossed at the ankle, looked a bit too self-satisfied for Chief Crandall's liking. And then there was Monty, perched on the front of his chair, hands resting on a briefcase sitting across his lap, ready to burst with some exciting news.

Monty broke the silence that followed Edmond's smart-ass question.

"Chief Crandall. We have reason to believe that the same man who committed the murders Edmond described in his article also killed Kimberly Prestwick."

"I don't get it. Are you saying your son Eli killed those other girls as well?" asked Chief Crandall.

"No, of course not. Not at all. What I'm saying is that Eli couldn't have killed Kimberly because he couldn't have killed those other girls."

Edmond spoke up. "Chief Crandall, based upon our knowledge of the Kimberly Prestwick case, the similarities between her murder and the three I described in my article are so strong that the chances of two or more people committing all four crimes are astronomically small."

"How can you be so sure? Maybe you've got one killer and one or more copycat killers. Have you thought of that?"

"Yes, I did," answered Edmond. "I ruled out a copycat killer because the murders I'm talking about are all unsolved, and prior to my article, had not been linked. Precious little had been written about the murders so a copycat killer would not have had enough to go on. Besides, we only find copycat killers when one or more murders get sensationalized by the press so that people start talking about them. Once the talk starts, a copycat may kill someone in the hopes of riding on another killer's coattails, so to speak," explained Edmond.

"When the press sensationalizes a story, you say? Kind of like what you've done here?"

Edmond didn't take the bait.

Chief Crandall continued. "You two keep saying things like 'we have reason to believe' and, 'based upon our knowledge of the case.' Who have you been talking to? Who the hell is my damned leak? And Monty, I guess you have an alibi for Eli for these other murders. Is that your game?"

Edmond broke the silence this time. "Chief Crandall, could Officers Pearlman and Tyrell join us?"

*　　*　　*

A cockroach crawled out of the grease-stained pizza box and scurried along the bed. He watched it pause and then propel itself across one wall and then the other, losing sight of it as it dropped down behind the TV bolted to the broken-down dresser.

He didn't know how long he'd been there. The empty bottles strewn across the floor would give some indication. Yesterday's paper lay at his feet opened to a story about an investigative journalist on the trail of a sick and depraved killer. He sat up at the end of the bed and stared at his blood-stained hands, grabbed his bat, and smashed the TV. It was time to move.

CHAPTER 39

An Alibi

Officers Tyrell and Pearlman were on duty when they received a call directing them to return to the office that afternoon. Monty and Edmond ran back to Monty's office and ordered in lunch while they watched the clock. Now, back at the police station, the two officers, Monty, and Edmond, convened in Chief Crandall's office.

Introductions were made all around, but as Chief Crandall observed, they didn't seem necessary.

"Gentlemen, we have a situation on our hands, and I'm none too happy about it," said Chief Crandall. "This morning, I asked Edmond and Monty what made them so sure the murders Mr. Locard here wrote about in the paper yesterday could have been committed by the same man that killed Kimberly Prestwick five years ago. Do you know what they said?"

Officers Pearlman and Tyrel squirmed a bit but kept quiet.

"They said the same thing you're saying right now. Nothin'. But then they specifically asked if you two could join us. Now why would that be?"

More silence.

"Well, I think I know why. Because you two fools are my office leak, that's what I think. And here I was ready to string up Mrs. Babcock by her blue hair. For the love of Pete, what the hell is going on?"

Officer Pearlman asked for permission to speak. "Chief Crandall, if there's an office leak, it's me." He then proceeded to tell the chief about his late-night meal at the Waffle House with Edmond Locard.

"So, you're tellin' me that when you were asked to destroy the Kimberly Prestwick evidence locker, instead of doing so, you in fact preserved it?" Chief Crandall was a kettle at full boil.

"That's right," answered Officer Pearlman.

"And Officer Tyrell, you were in on this?" asked Chief Crandall.

"No, Chief. He wasn't. It was all me," explained Officer Pearlman.

"Then what in tarnation are you doin' here?" asked Chief Crandall.

"I'd kind of like to know myself," said Officer Tyrell.

Monty raised his hand like a school kid in the front row. "Chief, I can help with that."

"All right, go ahead," said Chief Crandall. "And this better be good."

Monty stood like an attorney approaching a jury, pulled several stacks of paper from his briefcase, and handed one stack to each man in the room.

"What you have in front of you is a synopsis of each murder Edmond described in his article. The date each body was found, where each body was found, and the coroner's reports establishing the date and time of each murder. I have also included pictures of each victim. Pretty gruesome. Edmond can go into the specifics regarding the wounds, but I want to draw your attention to the dates each murder occurred. Now please look at each date and ask yourself if any of them are meaningful to you."

Edmond in his chair, and Monty on his feet, watched as the others stared at the dates. After a minute or so of silence, Chief Crandall spoke up.

"Monty, where are we going with this? If you know something, tell us."

Monty continued to survey the room and went on. "Do any of these dates mean anything to any of you? Officer Tyrell, what about you? Can you think of where you might have been on any of these dates?"

Monty was standing right in front of Officer Tyrell when it clicked, and Will Tyrell looked up at Monty with a huge smile on his face.

*   *   *

APRIL 18, 1973

It was a beautiful spring afternoon. The smell of freshly cut grass drifted across the diamond. The boys took the field for what would be the deciding game in the best-of-three playoff for the South Carolina High School Baseball Championship.

Monty and Walker had been in the stands for close to an hour. The opposing team's ace was on the mound, a young man who had been drafted right out of high school by the Chicago Cubs. Even at a young age, he had a rare combination of power and control. The game was expected to be a defensive gem, with hits and runs coming sparingly for both teams. Monty looked around for Rose and glanced at his watch again. The first pitch was just moments away, and she was still nowhere to be seen.

The coaches exchanged their lineups. Eli would lead off. While he could hit for power, what was more important in this game would be base runners. Once on base, Eli wreaked havoc on a pitcher's concentration.

Halfway through the national anthem, the crowd on its feet with hands over hearts, Rose climbed the stairs and stood next to Monty. Monty placed an arm around her, pulled her close, and gave her a quick peck on the cheek. The boys took the field, having secured the homefield advantage with their superior regular season record.

Eli trotted onto the field, casually throwing a grounder the third baseman's way. He turned, running backward toward center field, and looking into the stands, made eye contact with Walker, seated to Monty's right. Monty glanced at Walker, then back at Eli, and what he witnessed was mutual pure, unadulterated joy.

*　　*　　*

"Will, why don't you tell Chief Crandall where you were on April 18, 1973?" Monty asked.

"I was sitting one row in front of you watching our boys take it to the Pirates in the state championship. Your boy Eli went four-for-five and covered center field like a gazelle," answered Officer Tyrell.

"And your son Leroy pitched a no-hitter through seven innings that night, didn't he?'

"He sure did!"

Will Tyrell jumped from his seat and hugged Monty as if they had just watched their boys win again. Monty fought back the tears—both men did.

"Well, if that don't beat everything. So what do you say, Chief? Should we take another look at who might have killed Kimberly Prestwick?" asked Officer Tyrell.

Officer Pearlman, still standing, looked at Monty. "Now I don't want to be a killjoy here, but from what Officer Pearlman told us earlier today about the knife found in Eli's truck, you may not be out of the woods yet, Monty."

"I'm willing to take my chances, Chief. That's what a trial is for. Examine and cross-examine. He didn't do it, so that means there's a rational explanation. But what's important now is whether you have what you need to reopen the case." Monty, still on his feet, looked on expectantly.

"But without Eli, we can't have a trial, can we?" asked Chief Crandall.

"No, but a renewed investigation may clear his name," replied Monty. "And if he hears about it, well, then he can come home. He'll be free to," said Monty.

Chief Crandall took a seat and looked at Officer Pearlman. "So, Officer Pearlman, think you can find that evidence locker?"

"Should be right where I misfiled it," said a smiling Officer Pearlman.

CHAPTER 40

Evidence Locker

"Monty and Edmond, I'm going to ask you two to leave now. Monty, you're clearly an interested party, and I can't have you anywhere near the evidence. This is police business. I'm sure you understand," explained Chief Crandall.

"Absolutely. I wouldn't want to do anything to contaminate the process. But what about Edmond here? He's somewhat of an expert in the field of criminology."

"Is that so?"

"Yes, sir. In addition to the subject of serial killers, I am well versed in the field of . . ."

Chief Crandall held his right hand up as if directing traffic. "I know, I know. In the field of forensic serology. I made a few phone calls and read up on the subject. My friends at the FBI vouched for you. I tell you what I'm going to do. I'll send any evidence we have to the FBI for testing. If they wish to consult with you, I will advise against it."

Turning toward Monty, he continued: "I don't know everything you've been up to, Monty, but your association with Edmond may have disqualified him from working with the FBI on this case. But if this case goes to trial, the defendant, whether Eli or someone else, is always free to hire Mr. Locard. That's the best I can do."

The men shook hands, and the meeting broke up. Monty walked out of the office ten feet off the ground.

*　　*　　*

Chief Crandall and Officers Pearlman and Tyrell entered the evidence locker in the back of the police station. Chief Crandall waved off the clerk, Butch, when he stood. "That's okay, Butch. We got this."

Officer Pearlman went to the second row from the back, climbed a ladder, and reached behind several boxes. After rearranging the top shelf a bit, he found what he was looking for. A banker box marked "Kimberly Prestwick/ Murder Investigation/5-18-1973." And below that, in red stencil, the box was stamped CASE CLOSED.

Inside the box, the officers found the following evidence, all properly bagged, tagged, cataloged, and stored:

- Crime scene photos
- Investigator's log with full accounts of testimonies gathered
- The coroner's report
- The victim's clothing
- A paper bag containing wrappers and packaging from KFC
- Leaves soiled with what appeared to be dried blood
- A used condom found in a rolled-up beach blanket from the trunk of the victim's car
- A hairbrush, lipstick, hair barrette, and other similar personal effects
- Molds of the tire tracks
- A large serrated hunting knife
- A forty-inch Louisville Slugger bat

"Nice work, gentlemen. Everything is in order."

"Thank you, Chief. What do you want us to do with it now?" asked Officer Pearlman.

"I have an old friend from the police academy who works in the FBI. I'll give him a call and see what he thinks he can do. Until you hear back from me, not a word of this to anyone. Understood?"

Officers Tyrell and Pearlman nodded their understanding.

*   *   *

It was close to 5:00, and Mrs. Babcock would be leaving soon. It was Monday night, which meant she'd drive to her son's house for her weekly dinner with his family. Every weekend, she made him her "famous chocolate cream pie." He'd rave about how wonderful it was and beg her to share her special recipe with his wife. Mrs. Babcock would smile and say she'd write it down someday in her recipe folder and leave it to her when she passed on. The recipe was a premade pie crust, Jell-O brand chocolate pudding mix, and whipped cream from a can.

She kept the pie in the breakroom refrigerator next to the back door exit to the parking lot behind the station. She paused outside the evidence locker to fish her car keys out of her humongous purse. Not even the chief of police could persuade her to relinquish her driver's license.

"Hello, Butch. Are you still here?"

"Yes, Mrs. Babcock. Just straightening up a bit."

"Oh, really? A busy day?"

"Not busy, mind you, but curious. Say, is that one of your world-famous pies I've been hearing about?"

She blushed like a schoolgirl. "I don't know about world-famous, but yes, I baked it myself." She paused. "Say, I was going to give it to my son and his family, but he called this afternoon. He had to cancel our weekly dinner."

"Oh, I'm so sorry. We all know how much you look forward to your Monday nights," said Butch.

"Yes, I do. But what am I going to do with this pie? I certainly can't eat it all. Butch, how would you like to take home this pie to your missus?"

"Well, now, thank you. That's right nice of ya."

"Butch, you said your day was curious. How so?"

Butch, despite his better judgment, told her about Chief Crandall's trip to the evidence locker earlier that day.

Chapter 41

The Ball Was Rolling Now

The ball was rolling now.

Monty, Laz, and Edmond met for breakfast to debrief after yesterday's meetings with Chief Crandall. Monty convinced Edmond to try their shrimp 'n' grits. Laz took no convincing and gave Monty his seal of approval. Edmond tried them, smiled good-naturedly, and told Monty he still needed convincing.

Despite Chief Crandall's warning to stay out of matters or risk contaminating the process, Edmond had called a few friends at the bureau that morning and shared with Monty and Laz what he'd learned.

"My friends say that Chief Crandall has already spoken to the FBI lab. Yesterday, the police department sent Kimberly's clothing and the knife found in Eli's truck along with other evidence to the FBI in Langley, Virginia, where a battery of tests will be run. The first test will identify whether blood or semen can be detected. If detection is possible, then they will collect samples of the detected fluids in their dried state for testing."

237

"They run those tests to determine the genetic profile of whomever the samples came from, the victim or the perp. Is that right?" asked Laz.

"Correct. These lab results will be sent to the Charleston PD, and the FBI will keep a copy," explained Edmond.

"Then what?" asked Monty.

"Then we convince the police to share the data with me so I can compare the samples with samples collected in other murder investigations and look for a match."

"And if they won't?" asked Monty.

"Oh, I expect that after yesterday, Chief Crandall will share the results," said Edmond.

"And if they don't, then Edmond writes a story about the local police department's refusal to help catch a serial killer on the loose," said Laz.

After they said all there was to say about the case, they talked about the pennant races and the upcoming college football season. Though Edmond never took to southern food while attending Emory, he had come to appreciate Southerners' passion for college football. He had attended a few Georgia Tech games over the years and adopted them as his team. He had learned enough about the game to realize he could get Monty's goat, whatever the hell that meant, by bragging that Bear Bryant wasn't half the coach Bobby Dodd was.

As breakfast came to an end, they shook hands and parted ways. Edmond's FBI friends said it would take two to three weeks for the lab to complete the tests. Monty was hopeful things around the office and the home front would return to normal. All the talk of Eli and a possible serial killer on the loose had chilled relations with his wife, and lately, he'd hardly seen his son Walker at all.

Edmond would drive back to Atlanta, and Laz was going to stop in Birmingham on the way back to New Orleans to see a cousin.

*   *   *

After breakfast, Monty headed to his office, looking forward to the new-found tranquility of his day-to-day environs. Following the mass firing on that fateful Monday, Monty's professional life had changed dramatically. He had let go of eight associate attorneys and three paralegals. He asked Abigail how many months were left on the lease. Thirty-four. One call to Quaid resolved the matter. Quaid knew the building owner was in financial trouble. Quaid purchased the building for a song before the month was up and released Monty from the lease, explaining that he liked the space and felt it would serve nicely as the headquarters for their new venture.

Freed from the burdens of tight cash flow and meeting payroll, Monty enjoyed his work again, spending half his time on the new venture and the other half cultivating clients of his choosing.

Monty's health had also improved. His appetite returned and he was sleeping through the night—well, almost. He had never appreciated the pressure he was under nor the health ramifications of the resulting stress until after it had been lifted.

Monty walked down the hall and whistled happily as he passed Abigail's office. She followed him with a stack of files and phone messages. He plopped himself down behind his desk and sighed peacefully.

"Well, aren't we in a good mood this morning?" said Abigail.

"Yes, Abigail, we are in a good mood. So what do ya have for me?"

"Here are your phone messages in order of importance. You'll find the corresponding file in the stack. You have a court appearance Wednesday and a meeting tomorrow afternoon with Mr. and Mrs. Hancock. They're potential new clients, so be on your game."

Monty smiled as he flipped through the phone messages.

"I see Hank called a few times."

Henry "Hank" Barstow had been delivering mail for as long as anyone could remember. In fact, delivering the mail was the family business. Hank was known to ramble on for hours with stories of his grandfather, who rode the Pony Express. As Hank told it, when the telegraph put the Pony Express out of business in 1861, his grandfather found himself out of work and in California, three thousand miles from home. In a state of despair, he got drunk one night, met a young girl in a saloon, and nine months later, Hank's Pappy was born in a room above that same saloon.

According to Hank, his grandfather made and lost a fortune during the gold rush. When his creditors lost patience, the three thousand miles of separation seemed like a good idea. So in the dead of night, he packed up his wife and newborn son and headed back to the East Coast, where he took to delivering the mail again.

"Yes, it's about the mining rights he claims to own in California. It seems his grandfather may have purchased a gold mine, if you believe that."

"Yep, I remember. Thinks he may be a millionaire," said Monty.

"Do you think he'd give up delivering the mail if he becomes a million-aire?" asked Abigail.

"I suspect not. He loves it, and frankly, I can't imagine Hank not delivering the mail."

"Do you think there's anything to the mining rights?" asked Abigail.

"No. Hank wants to talk to me about his daughter. The gold mine story is his cover, I imagine. His daughter gives him fits. Can you please call him and schedule a time for me to drop by the post office?"

"Will do." As Abigail turned to head back to her desk, she asked, "Do you want your door open or closed?"

"Could you shut it, please? I've got some work to do."

Yes, it was good to be back at the office.

*   *   *

SEPTEMBER 7, 1978, A COUPLE OF WEEKS LATER

On Thursday, Monty woke in a fine mood. Sharp and rested. A couple of uninterrupted weeks in the office had relaxed him; feeling productive always did. The lighter, more manageable workload had also freed up time to focus on bringing Eli home, and in Monty's mind, they had turned a corner. He was sure of it.

He knew much depended upon the results of the FBI lab tests, but he was confident. If the FBI turned up ties to the other crimes, crimes Eli could not have committed, then Monty felt certain the chief of police would reopen the case and publicly state that Eli was no longer a suspect. How could he not? Justice demanded it.

But would Eli hear the news? And if he did, would he come home? A conviction would be better. Yes, they had to catch the real killer and put him behind bars. Then Monty would appear on every TV network and in every major newspaper office across the country, shouting from the mountaintop that Eli could come home. He wished he could share this news with Rose. Surely, once the real killer was found, she'd welcome Eli back.

But the ball was rolling, and that was what was important. Now, back to work.

Monty's meeting with Mr. and Mrs. Hancock, potential new clients for his firm, had gone well. The Hancocks had recently sold their family's North Carolina-based textile mill. Mr. Hancock, fearful of growing state-subsidized competition from the Far East, felt both the time and the price were right. But their sale to a New York-based holding company was treason in the minds of the other textile mill families, and the Hancocks were now persona non grata in North Carolina. So they were pulling up all roots in Charlotte and starting the second half of their lives in Charleston.

Having purchased homes on the Isle of Palm and in town south of Broad, they were busy establishing customary business relationships. Mr. Hancock talked about buying a small business or maybe starting a restaurant. Monty discussed tax and estate planning, his expertise in corporate governance and business contracts, and the local real estate market, and he promised to introduce them to one or more accountants, bankers, and financial advisers. Monty was drafting an engagement letter to the Hancocks when Abigail reminded him of his meeting with Mr. Barstow.

"For goodness sakes, I almost forgot. What would I do without you, Abigail?"

"The wheels of progress would grind to a halt, no doubt. Will you be coming back to the office after your meeting?"

"I was thinking of sneaking off to the driving range this afternoon, maybe playing a quick nine. Would I be missed?"

"In ways I can't explain, but we'll survive."

"Thanks, Abigail."

Monty grabbed his briefcase and car keys and headed toward the front door. Sometimes he couldn't tell when Abigail was pulling his leg.

*   *   *

Monty entered the post office around 11:30. There were a few people in line. Hank Barstow saw Monty enter and waved him around to the side. Hank bent over and spoke to a younger man sitting at the desk. The man took Hank's place at the counter, and Hank walked over to a swinging gate where Monty was waiting.

"Monty, thanks for dropping by. I'm sorry I couldn't see you in your office, but we're a little shorthanded right now. One of my men is out with bunion surgery, and the new guy got himself shot two weeks ago bird hunting."

"I heard something about that. Is he all right?"

"Yeah. His pride was hurt most of all. Should be back next week. Follow me. I have a little office down the hall where we'll have some privacy."

Monty stepped through the swinging gate and waited for Hank as he grabbed a stack of mail. Hank was flipping through the mail as he walked down the hall, commenting aimlessly about the weather, when he stopped and held a letter up to get a closer look.

"Well, I thought we'd seen the last of these," said Hank.

"What was that?" remarked Monty.

"The letters your wife asked me to return to sender. Just got another one."

Hank looked at Monty and Monty at Hank as each came to the realization that Monty had no idea what Hank was talking about.

"Can I see that letter?" asked Monty.

"Sure."

Monty took the letter and opened it. The penmanship was crude and menacing. As he read the letter, Monty's world was flipped upside down.

Rose, it's been awhile. But don't think I don't know you've been thinking about me. I've been in the news, and I suspect you put two and two together and figured it was me. I told you I wasn't going to stop. Kimberly was just the first, well the first I told you about, that is. And just think—you may have been able to put a stop to all of it. Many of those girls would be alive today, and who knows where I'd be . . . probably strapped to old sparky by now. But I knew you was proud . . . too proud to go to the police. And now you're knee-deep in pig shit. You got too much invested, don't you? And just think what people would say all these years later if you was to go to the police? Oh my. No sir, that ain't happenin', is it? Well, I'll be signing off now. Just remember—every time I rape and kill, you deserve some of the credit.

Monty didn't make it to the golf course that afternoon.

"Monty, you okay? Do you need to sit down?" asked Hank.

"Hank, when did you get the first letter?" asked Monty.

"Well, I don't remember exactly, but I'd say it was about five years ago."

"Oh, good Lord," muttered Monty. Monty did the math in his head and realized that the man who wrote the letter he was holding had first mailed his wife Rose a letter approximately six months after he had killed Kimberly Prestwick.

"And you say my wife asked you to return these letters to the sender?"

"That's right," said Hank.

"But there's no return address on this envelope. Did the others have a return address?" asked Monty.

"No. They didn't. I tried to explain that to your wife, but she was set on me not ever delivering these letters to her."

"But how would you know? How would you know if all the letters were all from the same person?"

"Well, it was rather easy to tell. The envelopes were all standard business envelopes for one, and the handwriting is somewhat identifiable. But the real tipoff was what he'd write on the back of the envelope; in the bottom of the right corner, he'd write something kind of curious like 'Miss me?' or 'Maybe I'll pay you a visit.'"

"If you couldn't return them, Hank, what did you do with them?"

Hank looked a bit sheepish and stared at the ground in the hope his shoes held the answer.

"Monty, I'm well aware it's against the law to tamper with the mail, but I know your wife and what she's been through. My wife, Ethel, goes on about what a wonderful Sunday school teacher your wife is, and Rose was so upset when I attempted delivery of the first few letters. Well, I didn't know what to do, so I just kept them. I put them in a place where no one would find them. I call it my private 'dead-letter drawer.' I didn't feel right throwing them away."

"Hank, are you telling me you still have them?"

"Yes, sir, that's what I'm saying."

"Hank, I'd be obliged if you'd give them to me."

"Well, I don't know. They're not addressed to you."

"No, but they are addressed to the home I own."

Hank paused for a moment before commenting. "Yes, sir, they are. Would you like me to run fetch them?"

"Yes, Hank, I would."

"All right, then. You know, I'll feel better having them out of the office. What should I do if I get more of them letters?"

"Just give them to me, Hank. Just give them to me."

Monty stared out the window as he waited for Hank to return with a stack of letters addressed to his wife by the man who had committed the crime their son Eli had been charged with.

Yes, indeed, the ball was rolling. But Monty now wondered if it would crush everything in its path.

CHAPTER 42

A Plan Takes Shape

Monty remembered neither the walk to his car nor the drive to his office. It wasn't until he pulled into the parking lot in front of his office that he realized he hadn't spoken to Hank about his legal matters, the supposed gold mine, or his daughter, the very reason he had stopped by the post office to visit Hank in the first place.

After leaving the post office with the stack of letters, Monty walked to a corner coffee shop and read every one. Each letter was a window into the mind of a deranged killer. So focused was his hatred of women that Monty couldn't fathom what had drawn Rose to him.

All those years ago, after Monty rescued Rose from the depths of her depression, Rath was a fixture in their lives, lingering on the periphery, always there, as Eli's father. Rose's insistence that Rath's name never be mentioned in their house failed to banish him from their lives. Rose demanded perfection from Eli as proof that she wasn't like the white trash that had fathered her or her firstborn. But the early years living in squalor and being passed from one caregiver to another, combined with Rose's unrelenting demands, took their toll on Eli. There was no way Eli could live up to Rose's expectations. Every cry, every lashing out on Eli's part, was proof to Rose that she'd never be free of Rath.

And now these letters. She'd read the first one, that much Monty knew. That was damning enough. Rath had clearly admitted to killing Kimberly and boasted he'd continue killing young girls. Did Rose know he had continued to send letters? Many of the letters detailed the time, place, and method of other gruesome crimes. What was he to do? If he took them to the police, they'd have to reopen the case and drop all charges against Eli. But then the truth of what Rose had done would come out. Everyone would know she had allowed her son to be convicted, for all practical purposes, for the crime of murder. And why? Because she was too proud. She couldn't stand the thought of people speaking ill of her. And this is the woman he'd vowed to stay married to, through thick and through thin.

Monty knew bits and pieces of Rose's childhood, of her upbringing. In a rare moment of complete honesty and humility early in their marriage, Rose told Monty what her brother had done, and that her father had laughed it off. She told him of the things her father had said. "Beulah, she's your daughter. I got no time for her."

Monty hadn't known what to say or do, so he had just held her, held her tight. He knew she carried baggage. To have been raped by her own brother. Horrifying. Monty was left with the distinct impression that it had happened more than once. And for her father to have known and done nothing? It explained so much.

And then she met Rath. For reasons Monty could not understand, Rose had been attracted to a man like her father, a man she hated with every fiber. Monty was no psychiatrist, but perversely, it made sense. Rose wanted her father's love, so she was attracted to a man just like him, seeking his approval, his love.

No, Monty hadn't known what to say to Rose that night, but he promised himself that he'd do everything he could to love her and to make her feel loved. Rose had never known a man who simply loved her. Well, Monty would be that man.

* * *

"What? No golf?" asked Abigail when Monty returned to the office.

"Monty? Monty? Hello, Monty." Abigail hurried after Monty, a step behind, trying in vain to get his attention as he walked toward his office.

He never said a word. Just kept walking, entered his office, turned and shut the door, not once looking at or acknowledging Abigail. Alone in his office, the weight of years of trying to hold his family together came crashing down. He fell to his knees and cried out silently. "Oh, Lord. Now what?"

* * *

Throughout his life, Monty took control by taking control. Action. That's what made him feel good, and that's what gave him the illusion of being in control. If there was a problem, then there had to be a solution. And since Monty hated entrusting others to do what he believed he could do best, he acted without the counsel of others. So what he was about to do was, to say the least, out of character.

Forty-five minutes later, Monty poked his head into Abigail's office and announced he'd be back tomorrow. Fifteen minutes later, he was sitting in Chester Baslin's office.

* * *

"Chester, I need to hire you as my attorney," stated Monty emphatically.

"As your attorney? Go on," said Chester.

"That's right. I need an attorney. I need someone to talk to. Someone to strategize with. I have a situation on my hands, you might call it, and I'm not sure what to do."

"Monty, always happy to talk, but are you sure a lawyer is what you need?" asked Chester.

"I believe I'm in need of the attorney-client privilege."

"Monty, happy to help, you know that. But you also know there are limitations to the privilege. I have a duty to the court as well," said Chester.

"So if you tell others what we discuss, then you violate the attorney-client privilege, a privilege either of us can invoke, except in those cases when you have a higher duty, to the court, for instance," said Monty.

"That's right."

"So if you and I don't have an attorney-client relationship, then there's no duty of confidentiality to violate, and maybe there's no higher duty to a court. Right?" asked Monty.

"Possibly," said Chester with a note of hesitation, "but then I can be compelled to give testimony, and I can't use the privilege as a defense against doing so."

"Seems complicated, doesn't it?" remarked Monty.

"Yes, it does. Why don't we start over? Monty, what's on your mind?" asked Chester.

"Chester, I need a friend."

"Then let's go get a drink because that's what friends do."

*   *   *

The Mills House Hotel dates back to 1853. Its décor and hospitality epitomize Charleston's ties to Old World Europe and its less pleasant but historical connection to the Caribbean slave trade. On the north side of the lobby, one will find a cozy bar, and every Friday at the back table, you'll find Chester Baslin and his wife enjoying a drink before dining in the Barbados room.

Chester had proposed to his wife at this restaurant some thirty years ago. They held their wedding reception at the hotel and spent their first married night together in the honeymoon suite upstairs. As Chester remembered, in those days, things were different. Women weren't as obliging with their favors as they were today. Chester couldn't wait for the reception to end so he could squire his bride up the stairs. Chester was, by his own admission, old-fashioned, and to this day he says he didn't mind the wait. But he did hate how long all the toasts at the reception went on.

So when Chester and Monty walked in on a Thursday, the bartender was somewhat surprised.

"Mr. Baslin, to what do we owe the pleasure?" asked Nigel. "Does this mean we won't be seeing you tomorrow night?"

"Of course not, Nigel. The missus and I will be here, as usual. I'm just enjoying a drink with a friend. We'll take the table in the back. I'd appreciate it if you wouldn't sit anyone at the tables around us. Could you see to that, Nigel?" asked Chester.

"But of course, Mr. Baslin. The usual?"

"Yes, please."

"Monty, what can Nigel get you?" asked Chester.

Monty ordered a draft beer, and the two men took seats at the back table. Monty still had his briefcase with him and was gripping it with both hands when Nigel set a cold beer down in front of him. Chester eyed the briefcase and raised his drink to toast. Monty hadn't budged, looking as if he'd been nailed to his chair.

"Monty, you're going to have to choose between your beer and your briefcase, unless you'd like Nigel to fetch you a straw."

Monty forced a smile, placed the briefcase at his feet, and ceremonially clinked his mug with Chester's.

"Now, Monty. What's on your mind?" asked Chester.

Monty told him everything. About the work he'd been doing with Laz and Edmond, about what he hoped the FBI lab would turn up. And then about the eighteen-wheeler barreling full speed directly at him—that is, about the letter Rose had received five years earlier from Rath, and the depraved mind evidenced in the other letters. And that Rath was Rose's first husband, and Eli's father, and Kimberly's killer.

Chester sat quietly as Monty unloaded. Monty opened up to Chester about the struggles in his marriage, even going so far as to tell him that Rose didn't want Eli returning. Chester was a good listener and he knew it. He wondered why others had such a hard time listening. Half the battle was just keeping your own mouth shut.

When it looked like Monty had come to the end, Chester ordered another round.

"Monty, you've been carrying this load for too long. Thank you for confiding in me."

Monty sat back in his chair, and a sense of relief washed over him. Chester was right, and Monty knew it. He'd been carrying the weight of everything far too long. He never spoke to Laz about his marriage. He was sure Laz suspected, but for the most part, his relationship with Laz was professional. They'd become friends for sure, but for the most part, Laz was there to facilitate Eli's return. No, it felt good to confide in Chester, but it felt foreign. Monty wasn't wired this way. Few men of his generation were.

Chester sat up and placed both hands flat on the table. "Now, Monty, I'm here as your friend, but your friend here is a lawyer, as are you, so let's take what God gave us and put our analytical minds to work and see if we can fashion a way out of this mess."

Chester continued. "I'm going to summarize what you've told me. See if I can break down all you said into some bite-sized nuggets. You see, Monty, I'm giving you the gift of listening. I should have put you on hold a few times as you were unloading. Then I could have summarized what you were saying along the way, and you would have known I was listening. But all that unloading was de-stressing you, something you sorely needed. So I just let you talk."

Monty nodded in agreement and appreciation.

"Summing up all your fears would go something like this: If you take the letters to the police, doing so clears Eli of all charges. But if you do, then Rose's role in hiding the identity of the real killer, her ex-husband and Eli's biological father, would come to light, destroy her, and likely end your marriage. Did I get that right?"

"Yes," said Monty.

"You went on to openly ask why you should even care about your marriage to Rose in light of what she has done, and as you said, of what she has become. But you feel duty-bound to keep your wedding vows, as well as the promise you made to yourself years ago to be the man who would love her. Do I have that right?" asked Chester.

"Yes."

"And Monty, you told me that the strangest thing of all is that despite it all, you still love her."

Tears welling up, Monty replied, "Yes, Chester, I do."

"Okay. On the other hand, keeping the letters a secret dooms Eli to a life in hiding. You'll never see him again. Now, there is a chance the FBI test results move the Charleston PD to reopen the case. But these tests are new and may not be the panacea you are hoping for. For instance, if Rath is responsible for the other murders, then there is a possibility the tests will tie Eli to other crime scenes since Rath and Eli have the same genetic makeup. Finally, there is the small matter of your role in concealing the identity of a lunatic who has killed and will keep killing until caught. Am I right?" asked Chester.

Monty grimaced and nodded curtly in agreement.

"The third scenario. Keep the letters a secret, and let events take their course. Possibly the FBI test results point the authorities in the right direction, Rath will be apprehended and convicted, and Eli exonerated. At that point, you use the media outlets to, as you say, shout from the mountaintop that Eli can come home. But there are risks to this approach. The FBI test results may be inconclusive. Rath may evade capture. He may kill again. And if arrested, what's to stop Rath from talking about the letters? In fact, as you stated, having read the letters, you believe he would take Rose down with him if he were going down. So in all likelihood, even under the third scenario, were Rath arrested and Eli exonerated, the secret of the letters would be revealed.

"Yep, that about sums it up," said Monty.

The two sat quietly and sipped their drinks.

"Chester, I want to thank you for listening tonight. I can't tell you what a help it's been."

"Happy to help a friend in need. I may ask you to return the favor someday," said Chester.

Monty nodded in agreement, and they quietly clinked glasses again.

"So where do you go from here, Monty?"

"There is an option we haven't discussed," said Monty. As Monty had listened to Chester summarize his options, a vision had crystallized, and he knew what he had to do.

"Oh? What option would that be?" asked Chester.

Monty didn't answer but thought to himself as he waved for the check: *Clear Eli's name and then kill Rath.*

CHAPTER 43

Satan Loses His Perch

Monty and Chester shook hands over their covert agreement. Chester agreed to hold onto the satchel, and they each pretended that Chester didn't know what was inside. Monty didn't want the letters in his house or office, at least not until he knew what his plan was.

By the time Monty rolled into his driveway, it was nearly 8:30. Rose knew her husband to be prompt and reliable and if he was going to be late, he'd call. This just wasn't like him. So when Monty walked into the kitchen, Rose was teetering somewhere between being worried and angry. When she saw that he was okay and then smelled alcohol on his breath, she was no longer worried.

"You can wipe that look off your face, Rose, and have a seat," demanded Monty in a cool, calm voice.

"Don't you talk to me that way. I was worried sick about you."

"Were you? Really, I don't have the patience for it."

Rose stood her ground with her hands firmly planted on her hips.

"I had an interesting meeting this afternoon with Hank Barstow. You know Hank, don't you, Rose? Our mailman?"

Rose turned her eyes away from Monty's.

"I know about the letters, Rose. He's been holding onto a slew of letters addressed to you, from Rath. I know Rath killed Kimberly, and I know you've known all along."

The dishrag in Rose's hand fell to the ground as she reached out to catch herself. Lowering herself into a chair, she mumbled to herself, "Everyone will find out."

"What? What did you say?" asked Monty.

Rose stared out the window. "What will people say about me?"

"You're worried about what people will say about *you*? Are you hearing yourself, Rose? You betrayed our son Eli."

"He's not our son," said Rose.

"Goddamn it, Rose! He *is* our son. I know I'm not the father, but I love him like he was my own flesh and blood. And for the love of Pete, you brought him into this world. How could you turn your back on him?"

"You love him?" said Rose. "You say that like he's still a part of our family. Like he's still with us. But he was never part of our family. He was always an outsider, his father's son. I saw it in him. He wasn't mine." She was screaming now. "I tried to fix him! I pushed him, but he wasn't fixable. He pushed back. He wouldn't do what I told him to do. He wouldn't be who I needed him to be!"

"You pushed him away, just like you're pushing Walker away."

"Don't you compare them. Walker is mine. He proves to everyone that I'm worthy. He shows everyone that I'm not white trash."

Rose was hysterical. Monty feared he was losing her. Satan had gained a perch, a foothold—Rose was slipping away, and someone or something else was quickly taking hold. Monty tried to catch his breath and lowered his voice, hoping he could reason with her.

"Rose, you're destroying whatever hope Walker has of becoming his own man. You're smothering him. We've lost Eli, maybe forever, and I will no longer stand by and watch you emasculate Walker."

"You don't know what the hell you're talking about. Just look at Walker. He excels at everything. I'm pushing him to be the man he can be, to be the man God expects him to be."

"He's miserable," screamed Monty. "He excels at nothing, for there is no joy in anything he does. You've killed it. He performs out of fear of disappointing you if he doesn't win, but he performs at the risk of losing and thus disappointing you still. And he's afraid of you."

Rose leaned in and hissed. "You're weak, like all men. You will not cross me. You will not take Walker from me."

A calm descended on Monty. A clarity was forming. He knew what his choices were, and he finally felt free to make them. He'd vowed to stay married to Rose, but she was gone. The person standing in front of him was demonic, and Monty did not think he could bring Rose back.

"I won't have to. I'm going to help give Walker the freedom to say no to you," explained Monty.

"What are you saying?" demanded Rose.

"I'm going to save this family the only way I know how. With the truth. I'm going to the police with the letters."

"Nooooo. You can't. You can't!" Rose cried. "Then everyone will know the truth about me."

Monty looked on in horror and sorrow. Rose sank to the floor and was clutching his legs, sobbing like a small child.

"Please don't. Please don't tell anyone. Please. Please. Please don't tell anyone. I'll be good. I promise."

Monty lowered himself to the floor and placed a hand on each side of her face. "Rose, it's me, Monty."

She looked at him, but Monty wasn't sure she recognized him.

Monty pulled her in tight and silently prayed, "Lord, help me. Just give me the words. I don't know what to do. I feel so helpless. Oh, Lord, please help me."

Monty drew Rose in and just held her. After a few minutes as her sobbing subsided, Monty opened his mouth and spoke the following.

"Rose, I love you. I have loved you from the day I met you. I don't know all the pain that you have suffered, but I know that the Lord put me here to do the best I could to help heal that pain. But I can't do it on my own. Only the Lord can mend your pain, and He wants to. I just know it."

"But I'm worthless," cried Rose.

"No. You're not. You're worthy, and I love you."

"How could you?"

"Because you are lovable. You are worthy because the Lord made you. You are precious in His eyes and in mine too. I want to spend each day with you, Rose. I love you."

"I've let everyone down," said Rose. "I've let you down. I was never good enough. Not for my father. God has no use for me. Now everyone will find out what a fraud I am."

Monty pulled back a bit from their embrace and looked Rose square in the eyes. He saw Rose again. She was there, inside, fighting for her soul.

"Fuck 'em!" Monty slammed his hand on the floor.

"Monty?"

"You heard me. Fuck 'em. I don't give a damn what others think. We're going to get through this."

Monty pulled Rose in. She seemed so small in his arms. They sat there together until Rose stopped crying, and then they sat a little longer and took joy in the intimacy of conversation. The first conversation in some time in which each felt at ease, perfectly aware, and at peace with the other's fears, pains, hopes, and dreams. And they dreamt, and they planned, and they stood up recommitted to each other and to doing whatever they had to do to save their family.

Chapter 44

Good News

The alarm surprised Monty. He was usually awake long before it sounded. This morning was different. Monty couldn't remember the last time he had slept through the night. Rose and Monty had fallen asleep in each other's arms the night before. It was nice. As he turned to get out of bed, Rose lazily stretched and placed an arm around Monty, urging him to roll back over. He did. It was very nice.

Monty strolled into the office later that morning. Abigail noticed a spring in his step and followed him into his office with a few phone messages and a stack of files.

"Good morning, Abigail, and how are you doing this fine day?"

"Well, aren't we in a good mood." Abigail smiled. When Monty fled the office late the day before, he looked to Abigail as if he'd seen a ghost.

"Yes, Abigail. Yes, we are," answered Monty. "Now what have we got going on today?"

"Here is a first draft of the Hancocks' new will and various trust documents. Once complete, I'll mail them a copy, and then we'll set the next meeting."

"Sounds good. Anything else?" asked Monty.

"A runner delivered a package this morning from Mr. Dawson. It's on your desk."

"Excellent. Our first deal," remarked Monty. "And I want you working it and learning as much as you can, right along with me, Abigail."

"Is this a deal you're doing with your new partnership with Messrs. Dawson, Roberts, and Wentworth?" asked Abigail.

"Yes. We're looking at buying a note held by an out-of-state bank that Quaid knows is in financial trouble. The note is secured by raw land. Eddie believes the property will be valuable in about five to ten years. The borrower and the bank each misjudged the local economy, thinking the land's value would have doubled by now. It didn't."

"And what's our job?" asked Abigail.

"Research the title, check the loan documents, the deed of trust, that kind of thing. We will only buy the note if we can foreclose in the event the borrower defaults and can do so without any problems."

"How much will we pay for the note?" asked Abigail.

"As little as possible and far less than the amount of the promissory note, what the bank loaned," answered Monty. "Once the four of us have all reviewed the opportunity, we'll meet and decide on a strategy."

"Sounds fun," said Abigail.

"Yeah, it is."

Abigail stood to leave Monty's office but then stopped and turned back toward Monty.

"Oh, there's one other thing. A man named Laz called this morning. He said you would know what it was about. Here's his number," said Abigail.

Monty maintained a poker face the best he could as he reached for the yellow message slip, trying not to look anxious or excited about what Laz would report.

"Very well. Could you shut the door on the way out, Abigail?"

*　　*　　*

"Laz, Monty here. Do we have news from Langley?" asked Monty, eager to get any updates from the FBI.

"We most certainly do, mon ami, and I do believe you will be pleased," said Laz.

"Hot diggity! Tell me more," demanded Monty.

"Our good friend Edmond just happened to be in Virginia and secured a meeting with the folks in the lab," explained Laz.

"Just happened to be in Virginia, you say?" commented Monty. "On my nickel, I suppose?"

"That be sure, but don't you fret. My bill will be easy to swallow. He stayed with a cousin of mine, so you just be payin' for gas."

Monty stood, and with the phone in his left hand and the receiver pressed to his right ear, he paced his office, the cord following him about. "Laz, if the news is as good as you say, I'll happily pay double. Now give me the details."

"The evidence from the crime scene was well preserved, and they were able to identify separate samples from two different people. Of course, we expected to find samples from Kimberly Prestwick, but they also found samples from another person," explained Laz.

"What kind of samples are we talking about here?" asked Monty.

"Hair, blood, that kind of thing. Look, Monty, this is all new to me, so I'm learning as well. Whoever was on the scene from the Charleston Police Department had the good sense to take samples from under Kimberly's fingernails. She fought back, and they ran tests on dead skin taken from under her fingernails. Markers identified in this sample match blood samples on her clothes. The lab techs believe Kimberly struck him in the face, probably the nose, and caused the attacker to bleed."

"Well, I'll be. Way to go, Kimberly, way to go," said Monty.

"I got more. Edmond persuaded the FBI to compare the genetic profile of the other person at Kimberly's crime scene with profiles ascertained from samples taken at other crime scenes in the southeastern United States, crime scenes for unsolved murders of young women. The samples match."

"Are you saying that the FBI believes that whoever killed Kimberly also killed the other girls?" asked Monty.

"Yes, Monty. That's exactly what I'm saying."

"Oh, Lord, thank you," muttered Monty.

"God is good, isn't he?" responded Laz.

"Yes, He is," said a beaming and slightly tearful Monty.

*　　*　　*

There was a buzz of energy within the Charleston Police Department. The weather was perfect, so people were outdoors. More specifically, young people. When summer ended and kids returned to school, life in the

Charleston Police Department slowed down—that is, until football season began. You could set your watch for an uptick in DUIs, drunk and disorderly offenses, and public nuisances by late in the third quarter of Friday night high school football games taking place across the country. But to the veteran cops in the department, it seemed that young folks today began their weekends on Thursday nights.

The phone rang, and the call was transferred to Mrs. Babcock.

"Mrs. Babcock's office. May I help you?" she asked.

The door to Chief Crandall's office was open and Chief Crandall shook his head in amused frustration. It didn't matter how many times he had asked her to answer the phone as "Chief Crandall's office."

"Yes, Chief Crandall is available. Who may I say is calling?"

Mrs. Babcock rose from her chair and grabbed a legal pad and a pen, walked into Chief Crandall's office, shut the door, took a seat, and told him that a man from the FBI was on the phone.

Chief Crandall picked up the phone and announced, "Chief Crandall here."

He listened to the man introduce himself as the Director of Special Investigations, calling with information about the murder of Kimberly Prestwick.

"Yes. Could you hold for a moment?" asked Chief Crandall. He placed his right hand over the mouthpiece and looked at Mrs. Babcock sitting upright in the chair with the legal pad in her lap, pen poised, and ready for action.

"Is there anything else, Mrs. Babcock?" asked Chief Crandall.

"No. I thought you might want someone to take notes."

"No, thank you. I can handle it."

Mrs. Babcock didn't move.

"That will be all, Mrs. Babcock. Could you shut the door on your way out? Thank you."

He waited until she gathered herself and walked out, in a bit of a huff, forgetting to close the door. Chief Crandall rose from his chair and shut the door as he resumed talking to the FBI man.

"So you have some test results I may find interesting," remarked Chief Crandall.

Mrs. Babcock busied herself at her desk until Chief Crandall finished his call.

*   *   *

After hanging up with the FBI, Chief Crandall reported the details of the call to Officers Pearlman and Tyrell. A man from the FBI would visit in a week and report in greater detail. In the meantime, Chief Crandall wanted Officers Pearlman and Tyrell to quietly reopen the case and formulate a plan of action pending a full briefing by the FBI.

"And most importantly, don't breathe a word of this to anyone," implored Chief Crandall. "Not until we know what we're dealing with."

Ah, the best laid plans.

*   *   *

Later that day, Friday afternoon, Monty Atkins and his wife, Rose, walked into the police department and asked to see Chief Crandall. As he was telling the front desk to inform Rose and Monty that he was unavailable, Mrs. Babcock, quick as a flash, was out of her chair and showing them into his office.

"Hello, Monty," said Chief Crandall.

"That will be all, Mrs. Babcock," said Chief Crandall with a slight bow.

Mrs. Babcock left the office, closing the door behind her.

"Randall, I don't believe you have formally met my wife, Rose."

"Mrs. Atkins, it's a pleasure," said Chief Crandall.

"Thank you. It's nice to meet you as well. My husband speaks very highly of you," replied Rose.

With a subtle smile and a nod of the head, Chief Crandall asked them to take a seat.

"How can I help you two this Friday afternoon?" he asked.

He spied Mrs. Babcock through the glass windowpane in the door sitting at her chair, opening the mail. Good God, it seemed as if that was all she ever did.

Monty sat up on the edge of his chair. He turned slightly and reached out his left hand, gently taking hold of Rose's right hand.

"Randall, it has come to our attention that the FBI has information that will exonerate our son Eli."

Rose squeezed his hand gently in a reassuring manner.

"It has come to your attention, you say?" replied Chief Crandall.

Randall fought back his anger and frustration over the constant leaking of sensitive information. He had just heard from the FBI that morning. *How did Monty and Rose know?* The folks in front of him were concerned for their son. He was a father and wondered if there was anything he wouldn't do if in their shoes. Still, he had a job to do.

"Monty, Mrs. Atkins. I don't know what you think you know or who told you, but I have my suspicions. And Monty, I know of your association with Mr. Edmond Locard and of his reputation with the FBI. But I encourage you to stay on the sidelines. If you want to help your son, then let us do our job. Anything you do could contaminate the integrity of the investigation."

"We understand. All we want is a press conference announcing that Eli is innocent."

"Oh, that's all?" said Chief Crandall in mock astonishment. "You know I can't do that! Police departments don't declare guilt and innocence. Juries do."

"You condemned him when you arrested him," said Rose.

"Mrs. Atkins, this department arrested him and released him on bail. Hardly a condemnation. And he condemned himself when he ran," replied Chief Crandall curtly.

Rose winced and slowly pulled her hand free from Monty's. Monty observed Rose's reaction but couldn't describe or explain it.

Turning back to Chief Crandall, Monty continued, "I know you don't declare that someone is innocent, but you can announce that he is no longer a suspect."

"Right now, Eli is still a suspect, and there are open warrants out for his arrest," said Chief Crandall. "Look, Monty, we are waiting on a full report from the FBI. I will not rush to judgment. I can't give you this press conference. Now if we are done, I'll ask you to leave."

Both Monty and Chief Crandall stood and waited for Rose to rise from her chair. Chief Crandall held the door for her, and she walked out of the police department with Monty close behind. As they exited the building, Monty fumed.

"Son of a biscuit! What are we gonna do now? We can't wait on the FBI. We need that press conference *now*. But Rose, don't you despair. Let's stick to the plan. I'll get him to hold that press conference if it's the last thing I ever do."

"Monty, leave this to me," said Rose.

"I don't follow. You heard what he said. How are you going to get him to change his mind?" asked Monty.

"Monty, there's more you don't know."

CHAPTER 45

Press Conference

Monty and Rose had agreed it was time to take Rath's letters to the police and let the chips fall where they may. As was often said, the truth will set you free. Goodness knows, Rose had lived long enough tied down by a web of lies—lies she believed about herself and the lies of omission—her failure to do all she could to bring Eli home. Though making this decision brought a sense of relief to Monty and Rose—they were taking the first step in putting it all behind them—neither was in denial about what Rose would suffer.

So when Laz had given Monty the good news from the FBI, Rose and Monty were overjoyed. Not just for Eli but for Rose and their family. It might be possible to save Rose from it all. It might be possible to bury the letters forever. They agreed to hold on to the letters a little longer and see if the FBI findings alone were enough to get the ball rolling.

Rose and Monty were back at home at the kitchen table.

"Monty, please sit down. I'm getting seasick watching you pace back and forth," said Rose.

Monty took a seat, but only for a moment, and then popped back up.

"Monty, please. Like I said outside the police station, there's more you don't know. Now, if you'll give me a moment and let me explain, I think you'll understand."

Monty took a seat, and Rose reached across the table and took both his hands in hers.

*   *   *

WEDNESDAY, SEPTEMBER 8

Monty and Rose were back at the police department standing side by side a few feet behind Chief Crandall as he addressed local and national media. Standing on Rose's other side was Gloria Prestwick, her two children, and the immaculately dressed Mr. Holbrook, who had appeared in Chief Crandall's office just a month earlier as Gloria Prestwick's advocate. Rose had told Monty to do what he could to attract national media attention. Monty called Laz and Edmond, and they went to work.

Earlier that morning, Gloria Prestwick and Mr. Holbrook had been escorted into Chief Crandall's office. Much to his surprise, instead of threatening the police department if they reopened the case, Gloria Prestwick encouraged Chief Crandall to find the real killer.

"So, Mrs. Prestwick . . . ," began Chief Crandall.

"Cunningham. I've gone back to my maiden name," explained the former Gloria Prestwick. "My children are still Prestwicks, but I've moved on."

"Of course. So, Ms. Cunningham, do I understand correctly—you now want me to reopen the investigation into your daughter's murder?" asked Chief Crandall.

"Yes, just I like I told Mr. Holbrook, I now believe the real killer is still on the loose. I can't stand the thought of anyone else suffering what I have. I read the stories about a possible serial killer on the loose."

"Now, Ms. Cunningham, we don't know that to be the case," said Chief Crandall.

She waved him off.

"To be honest, I never believed Eli killed Kimberly. But when he ran, well, it made my grieving easier when I had an object for my hatred. But given recent revelations," said Gloria as she glanced at Rose, "I've had to let go and acknowledge what I've always suspected—someone else killed her."

"Ms. Cunningham," said Chief Crandall, "you've driven all this way from Richmond, so I want to be respectful, but I can't hold a press conference at this point in time. We have an ongoing investigation, and we're working with the FBI. We'll hold a press conference when the time is right."

"Chief Crandall, if I may interject?"

"Yes, Mr. Holbrook, what do you want to interject?" asked a tired Chief Crandall.

"Just a question. When will the time be right?"

"Why is everyone so gall-danged anxious to have a press conference?"

When the chief's question went unanswered, he ventured a guess as to when he could hold a press conference. "In a month or so," answered Chief Crandall.

"I see. Well, that gives the press a full month to run with the story while you do what you do."

"Excuse me? The press? Really?" asked an exasperated Chief Crandall.

Mr. Holbrook and Gloria Cunningham stood, and Mr. Holbrook held the door as they exited the chief's office, leaving a bewildered chief alone, wishing all the more he had never taken a meeting with Monty Atkins.

*   *   *

LATER THAT DAY

Chief Crandall's press conference was short and to the point.

"Standing behind me today are two courageous women: Gloria Cunningham, the mother of Kimberly Prestwick, who was brutally murdered over five years ago, and Rose Atkins, the mother of Eli Atkins, the young man accused of the murder. I'm here today to announce that, in cooperation with the FBI, we are taking a fresh look at the case. New evidence has come to light that casts real doubt on whether Eli Atkins was the murderer. This new evidence also implicates a man at large who may be responsible for multiple murders in the southeastern United States. I want to thank Monty and Rose Atkins for their role in bringing this evidence to our attention and to Gloria Cunningham for her support. In my discussions with Ms. Cunningham, she was adamant that the true killer be found. Thank you for coming. That will be all."

Flashbulbs went off, and questions were shouted as Chief Crandall left the stage. Police officers escorted Rose, Monty, and Gloria through the crowd. Mr. Holbrook brought up the rear. Oh, how he wanted to answer their questions, but Gloria had threatened to withhold payment for services rendered if he did.

Chief Crandall headed home. Time for a cold beer. What a day. The damnedest thing of all was how adamant Monty and Rose were that he thank them at the press conference for their role in bringing the evidence to his attention. And they were precise about the wording. He could have fought them, kicked them out of his office once he'd agreed to the press conference. And he would have too, if it hadn't been for Mr. Holbrook's threats to go to the press. *What an asshole,* thought Crandall.

Well, they got their press conference. And now his department had a serial killer to catch.

CHAPTER 46

It's Time

The windows were open, and curtains danced in the warm ocean breeze that swept through the palm trees and into his bungalow. The surf, rolling and crashing in the background, played like the soundtrack to a favorite old movie.

He heard the screen door open and the sound of the mail falling to the floor. As he walked into the front room, he saw a large yellow envelope, picked it up, and smiled at the familiar return address. He opened the envelope and read the press clippings about Walker's latest accomplishments.

"Way to go, Walkie Talkie. Way to go."

Inside the large envelope was another smaller one containing a collection of newspaper stories of a decidedly different subject, and a short, simple handwritten note: "Eli, it's time to come home."

He placed the envelope in a drawer with the others and sat behind the small desk, staring out to sea before setting off for town, wondering if he really could.

CHAPTER 47

Louisville Slugger

He sat on a stool at the far end so he could watch folks enter and leave. What held his attention, though, was the black-and-white TV behind the bar.

"Hey, buddy, could you turn it up?"

The bartender barely glanced his way.

"The TV. Turn it up?" he demanded.

The bartender was drying a mug, trying to ignore the man. On his fifth beer, the man was lean and cut and wore a dirty tank top, two sizes too small. His worn blue jeans were pulled down over unpolished, pointed-toe cowboy boots. His long, sinewy arms were covered in tats, and he hadn't shaved or showered in days. Unkempt greasy hair, hidden by a baseball cap, hung over his collar. But his eyes were alert, moving from side to side, taking in his surroundings, not as someone curious about the world around him, but as a predator.

"Hey, did you hear me? I said, turn up the damn TV and bring me some more nuts."

The bartender returned the mug to the shelf below, reached for the TV, and turned up the volume before walking a fresh bowl of nuts down to the man. He then returned to the other end of the bar.

"Now was that so hard?" asked the man as he plunged his grimy fingers into the bowl, licking them clean before plunging them into the bowl again, never taking his eyes off the TV.

There were only a handful of sad souls in the bar, a dump really. Wednesday afternoon and no better place to be than a rundown bar with no kitchen.

He sat on his stool, enthralled by what he was hearing. *I'm a celebrity,* he thought as he watched the woman on the TV talk about him. *They're calling me the Louisville Slugger.* He looked around the bar to see if anyone else was paying attention. They were not. *Losers. All of them. Worthless losers,* he thought. *I'm a fucking god.*

His attention was drawn back to the television.

"And now we're going live to Charleston, South Carolina where the Chief of Police is holding a press conference," announced the local TV anchor.

Standing behind me today are two courageous women, Gloria Cunningham, the mother of Kimberly Prestwick who was brutally murdered over five years ago, and Rose Atkins, the mother of Eli Atkins, the young man accused of the murder. I'm here today to announce that, in cooperation with the FBI, we are taking a fresh look at the case. New evidence has come to light that casts real doubt on whether Eli Atkins was the murderer. This new evidence also implicates a man at large who may be responsible for multiple murders in the southeastern United States. I want to thank Monty and Rose Atkins for their role in bringing this evidence to our attention and to Gloria Cunningham for her support. In my discussions with Ms. Cunningham, she was adamant that the true killer be found. Thank you for coming. That will be all.

"What the fuck!" he muttered. "New evidence? What's that bitch up to?" he said to no one. The bartender registered alarm and moved further away.

He bowed his head in pain. Like nails piercing his temples, a blinding light burned the back of his sockets as he buried the heels of his hands into his shut eyelids. *She wouldn't dare,* he thought. *No, she's too fucking proud. The letters.*

He knew she'd never tell anyone. Too afraid folks would figure out she was nothing but trash. Fucked by her brother. Daddy too. So why now? After all these years?

"She thought she was too good for me. Ends up with that faggot of a husband. No one is too good for me," he pronounced to himself.

"I've let you alone long enough, Rose darlin'. I'm coming home. It's what you wanted, ain't it?"

He threw a few bills down on the bar, grabbed his jacket, and slinked out the front door like a cat, his head still pounding and only one way to ease the pain.

CHAPTER 48

Strikes Again

The young girl, a high school junior, had disappeared after the game Friday night. She was last seen shortly after midnight, leaving a 7-Eleven with friends on their way to the abandoned railroad switching station to drink and celebrate the team's win. The girl's parents reported her missing Saturday afternoon.

"Did she have a boyfriend?" the police asked. "Had you recently fought with your daughter?" they asked. "Had she disappeared before?" they wanted to know. "What about school? Was she a good student? Was she having trouble at school? Did she use drugs?"

"No. No." The parents answered every question the same way, increasingly frustrated, angry, and scared. "She's a good girl. She didn't get into trouble. She was on student council," they explained.

"Have you called her friends?" they asked.

"Of course! That was the first thing we did. Now what are you going to do?" demanded the parents.

The officers said that they couldn't officially report her as missing, but that they would alert everyone at the station. They asked for a recent picture of her. The girl's mother quickly produced a handful from her purse as if anticipating the request demonstrated that their daughter was responsible and not prone to trouble. The police wrote down a description of the clothes she wore out of the house the previous Friday and assured the girl's parents that they'd do all they could, but not to worry. In their experience, a lot of kids disappeared without explanation only to come home a few days later.

The police filed an official missing-person report Tuesday of the following week. By Friday, she was no longer missing. A body was found in a wooded area not far from a popular destination for high school kids, uncovered by animals digging in a shallow ditch, sparsely covered by dirt and fall leaves.

The first officers to the scene were the same two officers who had met the missing girl's parents a week earlier. They knew, instinctively. It was her. Cause of death, a single blow to the back of the head with a baseball bat. The officers hoped the parents never learned of the other atrocities reported by the coroner.

*　　*　　*

FBI, LANGLEY, VIRGINIA; THE FOLLOWING
MONDAY MORNING

It took a few minutes before the call was routed to the correct desk.

"Special Agent Morose. Can I help you?" The irony of the man's name was lost on no one.

"Possibly. My name is Officer Thomas. I'm calling from Vidalia, Georgia, about a murder I believe you folks may have an interest in."

Officer Thomas reported the details of the murder and the crime scene to Special Agent Morose. When Morose finished the call, he immediately called Edmond Locard.

"Edmond? Morose here."

"There's no reason to be. It's a beautiful fall morning," replied Edmond.

"Fuck off, Edmond. I'm not in the mood. Our Louisville Slugger may have surfaced."

*　　*　　*

Monty picked up the phone on the second ring. Calls to his direct line could only be from one of four people—Rose, Walker, Eli, and Laz.

"Monty here."

"Well, our plan is working, but maybe too well, mon ami."

"Good morning, Laz. I'm not following."

"This morning, Edmond received a phone call from one of his contacts inside the FBI. The press conference was aired on local TV stations around the Southeast. Well, we got a hit. A police officer from Vidalia, Georgia, reported a terrible, terrible thing."

"No," muttered Monty softly.

"I'm afraid so. A young girl was found murdered and raped, and Edmond believes the similarities with Kimberly Prestwick's demise point in the direction of our killer. The FBI is sending a man down to Vidalia tomorrow."

Rath, thought Monty. Monty hadn't told Laz yet about the letters.

"Monty, I was thinkin'. Vidalia, Georgia, ain't too far from Charleston."

"No, Laz, it's not."

Rath was on his way.

CHAPTER 49

Forces in Motion

Monty and Rose had finished an early dinner. Walker, though grounded for breaking curfew, was allowed out of the house to continue his cross-country training. He was on a long run. Monty and Rose had finished cleaning the kitchen and were sitting on the porch swing together.

When Monty and Chester shook hands outside the Mills House Hotel a little over three weeks ago—had it really been only three weeks? — Monty had pulled into his driveway later that night determined to kill Rath. He didn't know how but saw it as the only way out. He'd use Rose as bait to draw him in and then, somehow, kill him. Monty and Rose ended that evening together, on their knees in prayer, asking the Lord for wisdom and help. They each woke the next morning full of confidence and hope. But ever since the press conference on September 13, Rose's mood had grown dark.

Monty expected her to be overjoyed, anticipating Eli's return. He was working with Edmond on a plan to broadcast the news far and wide, hopeful that Eli would hear the story and come home. So Monty couldn't understand Rose's mood.

"Rose, honey. What's on your mind?"

"The letters, Monty. We should turn them over to the police," answered Rose. "Let them deal with Rath." This wasn't the first time Rose had suggested turning the letters over to the police. In fact, earlier they had agreed that was the best course of action, but then Laz called with the good news from the FBI, and Monty convinced Rose to keep the letters hidden a little longer.

"Maybe he'll slip up and get himself caught," Monty had suggested. "The letters are secure in Chester's office safe."

But with each passing day, Rose grew more insistent.

"No, Monty. It's time to turn the letters over. Let the police deal with him," she said. "He's evil. He'll kill you, and I can't go on living if I lose you too. I've already lost my firstborn."

"The Lord will deliver me, Rose. I just know it."

"It sounds like you're asking the Lord to trust your plans, instead of you trusting His," said Rose. "Monty, the truth is all we have. I'm ready to be free. Let's turn over the letters."

"But Rose, our plan is working," pleaded Monty.

"Is it, Monty? I'm afraid. I'm afraid we've set forces in motion we can't control."

"Rose, don't fret. I'm on it. Trust me."

"Monty, don't take this the wrong way, but I don't trust you. Oh, I trust your intentions. I trust your heart is in the right place. I don't doubt for a moment your honesty or integrity. And Lord knows, you love me. You've demonstrated that in both word and actions. I'm coming to terms with it, that someone can truly love me. And Monty, I don't know how to express my love and feelings for you. You stood by my side, and after what I've done."

"But what, Rose?"

"But I don't trust that you can deliver the outcome we want. We're playing with people's lives. Our plan's success depends on our actions. I've spent years trying to control the world around me, and I'm ready to quit. I'm ready to rest in the Lord. Monty, we need to tell the police about Rath."

Monty knew she was right, but he struggled with his need to be in control. He wanted to protect Rose as well, from the fallout over hiding Rath's letters.

"Monty, I'm afraid your passion for control is simply a way of masking your fear," said Rose.

Monty felt the earth move when she said that.

They reached a compromise. They would mail the police department an anonymous letter identifying Rath as the killer. They would include a picture of Rath in the envelope that Rose had cut from an album from her days at the University of Alabama. Fearful that a keen detective could probably link it all back to Rose, Monty suggested they mail the letter from a neighboring town. Rose agreed and they turned on the TV to watch some playoff major league baseball.

CHAPTER 50

Hell Comes to Town

MONDAY, OCTOBER 2

So the next morning, Monty was on his way to Savannah, Georgia, to mail the letter. He made good time and reached a mailbox outside a post office just off Highway 17 in a little over two hours. On the way back, he stopped for lunch at a Stuckey's and picked up two cans of Honey Roasted Pecans, one for the road and one for Rose. She loved them almost as much as he did. He'd be back home in time to hit the driving range before dinner.

*   *   *

"You'll get your driving privileges back at the end of this week," said Rose.

"Oh, Mom. Come on. I said I was sorry," pleaded Walker.

"I know, honey, but when you miss curfew, there are consequences. Now let's go. I need to stop at the market first, and then I'll drop you off at school.

I don't know why your coach couldn't schedule the practice debates right after school," said Rose.

"I told you, Mom. He's also the drama coach, and the state one-act play competition is this weekend, along with a debate tournament. They're both happening at the University of South Carolina campus, so he'll bounce back and forth between the two competitions. They need the extra rehearsals and they meet right after school."

"I know. I know. You told me. So Isabelle can give you a ride home?"

"Yes."

"Do you want me to keep a plate of food for you?"

"No, Mom. We'll stop at the Pizza Hut and get dinner."

"Pizza Hut? That's not healthy for a growing boy who's as active as you are. I'll keep a plate for you just in case."

"Mom!" complained Walker.

"Don't you 'Mom' me. Now get in the car and let's go."

*   *   *

He watched from around the bend, pulling out once she got into the car. The boy held her door. Good boy. "Think ya got him well trained, don't ya? What a pussy," he said to himself. He followed, but not too closely.

"Mom, slow down. Park over there."

"Walker, what is it?"

"Nothing, just park over there," said Walker, pointing to a spot around the corner and out of sight from the market entrance.

Rose saw a pack of boys on the other side of the parking lot closer to the entrance and recognized a few from Walker's class. Putting two and two together, she figured Walker was embarrassed to be seen riding in the passenger seat with his mom at the wheel. She obliged.

"All right, but it'll just be a longer walk for you carrying the groceries," she said with a slight smile.

Fifteen minutes later, they were walking back toward the car. To Walker's relief, the guys had left, but he hurried to the car just the same.

"Let's go, Mom, I'm gonna be late," said Walker.

"*Going* to be late, not 'gonna' be late," corrected his mother.

"Whatever. Can you open the trunk?"

Rose walked to the back of the car and popped the trunk so Walker could place the groceries inside. The back seat was full of trash bags with clothes for the Salvation Army. While Walker put the groceries in the trunk, Rose sat in the driver's seat, waiting for Walker to get in.

But then she smelled it, sensed it, the smell of death. But it was too late, and before she could react, Walker was seated in the car. He never saw it coming, the blow to the side of his head from Rath's brass-knuckled left hand.

"Drive, bitch," he hissed.

CHAPTER 51

The Stage is Set

Monty pulled into the driveway a little before 7:00, as the sun was setting. When he walked inside, he was struck by the silence. It was quiet. Too quiet. Not the quiet of a house when no one was home, but the kind of quiet when something was wrong.

"Rose? Walker? Anybody home?"

He checked the garage. Empty. He searched the kitchen for a note. Anything. Again, nothing. And then he saw it through the kitchen window. A cat nailed with a railroad spike to the post supporting a corner of the porch. He approached the cat, a wad of paper spilling out of its mouth. Removing the wad of paper, he read the note.

Monty, I'm looking forward to seeing you again. It's been too long. We have so much in common. For one, there's Rose. Two, she's the mother of our boys. Of course, mine was taken from me. And now, yours has been too.

I'll be in touch.

Call the cops, and I return them in little bitty pieces.

"What have I done?" said Monty to the empty porch.

*   *   *

They were on a boat. That much she knew, but little else. After leaving the Winn-Dixie parking lot, they'd driven north. The last turnoff she remembered was for Bull's Bay. He directed her to turn off the main highway, where they ended up on a dirt road. He dragged her from the car and told her to strip while he held a gun to Walker's head. He threw a pair of handcuffs at her feet and told her to put them on.

"You can run if you want. The highway ain't too far. I'm sure someone will stop for ya. You'd be abandoning your boy, though, but then you've done that before, haven't you, Rosebud?"

"Rath, let him go. He's just a boy. You have me. I'm who you want."

"Want you? Is that what you think? I don't want you. I don't need you. But I will take you, and I'll take everything important to you. Eli's gone. Walker's next, and then, of course, there's Monty. Dear sweet Monty. But you? Hell, I think I'll let you live. And do you know why, Rosebud?"

Rose wept uncontrollably.

"Answer me, bitch. Do. You. Know. Why?"

"No, Rath, I don't," she managed.

"Because you deserve a lifetime of suffering. Because you left me, thinkin' you was better than me. Because you took my boy from me. My seed. So then, I took him from you."

Rose turned toward him with a confused look on her face.

"That's right, Rosebud. I set your boy Eli up for that girl's murder. I followed them. I planned it carefully. The bloody knife in the back of Eli's truck. I placed it there. Even the baseball bat, my signature move, made folks think Eli had done it. But then again, I'm bettin' you had a part to play in it, didn't ya, Rosebud? You could have gone to the police with accounts of my wicked nature, but you didn't. Did ya?"

"Just kill me and be done with it," said Rose. "I'm ready to go home."

"Not yet, ya ain't." He reeled back and struck her with a fury born of a lifetime of self-loathing.

She woke on the floor of a small boat, head throbbing and now blindfolded. From the sound of the motor, she guessed it was an outboard and figured they were on a river or a swamp but not on the open sea. She heard Walker groan, and she called out his name.

"Walker. It's okay. I'm here."

A steel-toed boot crashed into her ribs. The pain was excruciating and would have doubled her over, but she was hogtied and could barely flinch.

"Speak again, and he'll feel the next one."

*   *   *

Panic-stricken, and not knowing what to do, Monty paced the house from one end to the other. Checked his guns. Monty hadn't hunted much since Eli had left. He was more of a fisherman but could still handle a gun. He surveyed his arsenal: a Browning 28-gauge over-under for bird hunting, a Remington .30-06 rifle for deer hunting, and a Smith & Wesson .38 revolver, just because. He loaded each weapon and laid them out on the kitchen table. Now what? He tried eating but had no appetite.

Rath said not to go to the police, he thought. *He said he'd be in touch. So I have to wait until I hear from him. But how long? What if they're dead already? Chester. I'll tell Chester, and he can go to the police. No, if Rath even sees cops, then Walker and Rose are dead. I'll give it a day. Two at most. But what will I tell people? Rose and Walker will be missed.*

Monty decided to tell folks, if they asked, that Rose and Walker had gone to visit her mother, that Rose's mother was ill. Of course, she'd passed away a few years ago, but who knew?

He tried to sleep. It never came.

*   *   *

TUESDAY, OCTOBER 3

Monty was at the office early the next morning.

"Monty, is everything okay?" asked Abigail. "You don't look so good."

"I didn't sleep last night. Bad oysters. Rose tried frying them. Bless her heart. I asked her to try some new things in the kitchen. She didn't take kindly to my suggestion, but she tried just the same. I think we'll be going back to Sunday leftovers for the Monday night meal next week, rump roast and vegetables. Anyway, I hardly slept a wink. Could you close the door on the way out, Abigail?"

"Sure thing, boss."

Tuesday was an eternity, a hellish eternity. The school called when they couldn't reach Rose at home. He told them the yarn about Rose's suddenly ill mother. The debate coach called that afternoon when he heard the news and wanted to know if Walker would be back for the tournament the upcoming weekend. Monty assured him he would.

Wednesday arrived. Another fitful night of sleep. He doubted Abigail would buy the "bad oysters" story two days in a row, so he minded his step and tried to look energetic.

His wait ended Wednesday. A letter arrived at the office addressed to him, marked confidential, and postmarked from Charleston. *He must have mailed it Monday,* Monty thought, *the day he kidnapped them.* The letter contained a single sentence.

Be patient now, Monty, and be on the lookout for a package.

CHAPTER 52

The Package

"Abigail, I'm headin' to lunch, then dropping by the post office. I need to follow up with Hank on a few matters," said Monty. Monty needed an excuse to pick up any package deliveries as soon as possible.

"Hank Barstow? We're working for him?" asked Abigail.

"Well, yes, Abigail. I thought you knew," replied Monty.

"It's just that you never recorded any time after your last meeting. I noticed when I prepared the bills."

"I haven't gotten around to it. And I may not. Hank's not well off. Thinks he is. Thinks he may own a gold mine," chuckled Monty. "Right now, I'm just helpin' out a little."

"You're the boss. What time should I expect you back? You know, in case any paying clients want to know," asked Abigail.

Monty collected a few things from his desk and reached for his jacket.

"Monty? Hello, Monty. What time should I say you'll be back?"

289

Heading out the door, his mind clearly elsewhere, he answered, "I don't know. Today. Tomorrow. Don't know."

Abigail, holding a stack of files, watched him walk down the hall. *Something's wrong,* she thought.

*   *   *

"Next," announced the man behind the post office counter.

"Is Hank Barstow in?" asked Monty.

"No. But he should be back soon if you want to take a seat over there," explained the young man.

"How long until he'll be back?"

"Ten minutes, maybe?"

"Okay. I'll wait."

"He usually comes through the back door. I'll put a note on his desk. Whom should I say is asking for him?"

"Monty Atkins."

"Mr. Atkins? I believe we have a package for you. Hold on a minute."

Monty rose from his chair and quickly approached the counter. The man disappeared into the back room, then returned shortly with a small package wrapped in brown kraft paper.

"If you want to sign right here," said the man as he presented Monty with a clipboard and a pen.

"Can you tell me where this package was mailed from?" asked Monty.

Leaning across the counter with his head turned, the young man examined the package and answered, "Looks like it came from the post office in Jamestown."

"Thanks," said Monty as he started toward the door.

"Hey, ain't you gonna wait for Mr. Barstow?"

*   *   *

Monty ripped the open package once in his car and found Rose's clothes and a note.

What do you say we have a little family reunion? Tonight. Drive north on Highway 17 past McClellanville until you come to the turnoff for the Santee Coastal Reserve. Go to the Anglers bait and tackle shop and rent a skiff. Head upstream on the Santee River. I'll find you. Come alone. Oh, and bring the letters. If you don't bring the letters, then bring their dental records—you'll need them.

So that was it, thought Monty. He doesn't want money. He wants the letters.

Monty was sitting in his car and he looked at his watch. Enough time to stop at Chester's office and then run by the house for a few things.

"Okay, Rath," said Monty to the inside of his car. "You want me? You want the letters? Fine, you can have me. You can have the letters. But Lord help you if you harm Rose or Walker. I'm prepared to die, Rath. Are you?"

CHAPTER 53

Evil Asserted

"Hello, Mr. Atkins. It's good to see you."

Brenda Wheeler had been Chester's secretary for as long as Monty could remember.

"Hi, Brenda. Is Chester in?"

"Yes, but he's with a client. How's Rose?"

"Uh, fine. Look, how long will he be?"

"It could be a while. Is there something I can help with?" asked Brenda.

Monty was at a loss and didn't know what to say. Stepping away from Brenda's desk, he looked around as if the answer lay somewhere in Brenda's office. That's when he saw Chester in the conference room with a young man and his parents. The sight refocused Monty.

"No thanks, Brenda. I got it."

He walked straight down the hall and barged into the conference room, Brenda struggling to keep up on high heels.

"I'm sorry, Mr. Baslin. I told him you were busy."

"That's okay, Brenda," said Chester.

"Monty, can't this wait?" asked Chester as he gestured toward his clients.

"No, Chester, it can't, but it will just take a minute."

Chester stood, apologized to his clients for the interruption, and said he'd be right back.

"Dammit, Monty. What do you think you're doing?"

They were standing in Chester's office. The first time he'd set foot in this office was with Rose and Eli.

"I need my briefcase," said Monty.

"What's going on, Monty?"

"You don't need to know. Just give me my briefcase, please. It's here, right? In a safe in your office, right? That's what you told me at the bar."

"Monty, is everything—"

"Just give me the damn briefcase," yelled Monty.

Silence. Monty stepped back and ran his right hand through his thinning hair.

"Chester, I'm sorry. You didn't deserve that. It's just—it's important. I need that briefcase," said Monty.

"He's here, isn't he? Rath's here. In Charleston," said Chester.

Monty nodded his head and looked away.

"You can't do this yourself, Monty. You need help."

"If he sees anyone but me, he'll kill Rose and Walker."

"And what makes you think he won't kill all three of you?"

"Nothing. Absolutely nothing. But I have to try."

*   *   *

Monty had his briefcase, and twenty minutes later, he was heading north on Highway 17 with the letters and his pistol by his side.

"Rose. Walker. Hang in there. I'm on my way."

*   *   *

Rose was still nude and sitting across from Walker, each tied to a chair. The day before, Rath had taken off for a while in the boat, leaving them alone in the cabin. Despite her humiliation at sitting naked before her teenage son, Rose held her head high and asked Walker to look her in the eye. She told him about Rath and their marriage. She told him that Rath had killed Kimberly and that they had just learned of it with help from the FBI. She did not tell him about the letters or of her betrayal of Eli. She knew she was lying to Walker by omission, but she trusted the Lord to work things out. And she told him that his father would send help. They prayed, and they prayed.

Rose expected to die in this shack and feared the same fate for Walker. Privately, she prayed that the Lord would spare him and take her. But she was at peace, knowing who waited for them on the other side, and this knowledge fueled her strength.

* * *

"Rath, I know I should pray for you, but I can't, and I'm okay with that," said Rose. Rath had returned to the cabin and now sat ten feet away from Rose and Walker, sneering at them.

"Pray for me? Bitch, you should be praying for yourself and your boy here," said Rath.

"You can't touch us. You can't take anything away from us because what we have has been paid for," said Rose.

"What do you have, Rosebud, that I can't take?" snarled Rath.

"Salvation and the knowledge that I'm loved, Rath."

The back of Rath's hand was a blur as it crashed into the side of her face, nearly knocking her over in the chair. Rose lifted her head high.

"You'll never get away with this," said Rose.

Rath paced the room furiously, snorting like a pig in heat. After a minute, his breathing slowed, and he tried to regain control of the situation.

"Walker, your momma here thinks I'm gonna get caught. What do you think, boy?" asked Rath.

"Leave him alone," she demanded.

"I'm talkin' to you, boy. Do you think I'll get away with it?"

"He doesn't know what you've done," said Rose. "How do you expect him to answer? Tell him. Tell him what you've done. Kimberly wasn't the first girl you killed, was she, Rath?"

"Nope. Not by a far stretch."

"You killed that girl back in college, didn't you? What was her name?" asked Rose.

"Louise Jones. She was the first."

"How many others were there?" asked Rose.

"Shut up, Rose. None of your Goddamned business," yelled Rath.

"Yeah, I thought so. There weren't any others, were there? You're all talk, Rath," said Rose mockingly.

Rath walked over to Rose and leaned down until they were eye to eye. "You want details, Rose? Will that get you off? Fine, details it is." And then, turning back to Walker, he named every victim over the last twenty years, providing gruesome descriptions of the murders and the location of their bodies.

"So Walker, my boy, what do you think now that you know a bit more about me? Hmm? Will I get away with it?" asked Rath.

"No," Walker answered. "You'll burn in hell."

Rath strutted around the shack like that was the funniest thing he'd ever heard.

"Well, on that, I do agree. Now say goodbye to your momma, 'cause you and I got a date with your dad."

"No, Rath, please. Take me. Leave Monty and Walker alone."

"Rose, honey, don't you worry. I'm gonna take you. But you'll have to wait 'cause Walker and I are off to rendezvous with the man you left me for."

Walker would never forget the sound of his mother screaming when Rath dragged him out of the shack, hands and feet tied behind his back.

CHAPTER 54

A Ghost

"So you think this man, this killer, is here in Charleston?" asked Chief Crandall. He addressed his question to the room, to all of them. Around the conference table sat Officers Pearlman and Tyrell, Edmond Locard, and FBI Special Agent Morose, who had arrived in town that morning.

"That's right," answered Morose. "There are striking similarities not just between Kimberly Prestwick's murder and others in the southeastern United States, as we have already identified, but also with the murder of the young girl in Vidalia, Georgia, that occurred last week."

"Okay, maybe so, but it's quite a stretch to conclude he drove *here*. He could have driven anywhere," replied Chief Crandall.

"Just yesterday, a call came in from a police officer in Albany, Georgia," explained Agent Morose. "He was hunting at a lodge that is opened at no charge a few times a year to local police officers. The officers get together, hunt, fish, swap stories, etc. Well, the officer who called was at the lodge last weekend talking to an officer from Vidalia, Georgia. As it turned out, the officer from Albany has an unsolved and equally gruesome murder on his hands. Based on the coroner's report, the girl found in Albany, Georgia, was killed less than a week before the girl in Vidalia."

"If you look at a map, it's a straight shot from Albany to Vidalia to Charleston," said Officer Tyrell.

Chief Crandall looked concerned but still not convinced.

"There's more," said Officer Pearlman. "Earlier this week, an abandoned car was called in. It had been spotted in the woods behind the Winn-Dixie. We had it towed. There was no license plate on the car, and the VIN had been scratched off. After Agent Morose briefed us this morning, we called the repo lot to check for any items found in the car."

"And?" asked Chief Crandall.

"A hotel key was found between the seats. For a Motel 6 in Albany, Georgia," explained Officer Pearlman.

*   *   *

"Monty Atkins' office. This is Abigail Baker. May I help you?"

The Porter-Gaud debate coach was on the line. The team was packing up the school station wagon, ready to leave for the tournament, and Walker was nowhere to be seen.

"I'm sorry, sir, but Walker and his mother are still visiting their sick grandmother," said Abigail. "No, Mr. Atkins is not in, but I'll tell him you called."

Abigail was trying to get off the phone because Hank Barstow was standing in the doorway, and the light on Monty's phone was blinking, indicating someone else was calling in.

"Yes, it is unusual. Walker is very responsible. I'm surprised too that he never called you," said Abigail.

She couldn't get off the phone. She smiled at Mr. Barstow and mouthed silently to him that she'd be with him soon.

"Yes, sir. Very well, sir. Yes, I will tell him," she said as she hung up.

"Mr. Barstow, just one minute, please. Let me pick up this line," said Abigail.

Hank nodded in assent.

"Monty Atkins' office, can you hold please?" said Abigail.

"Yes, but only for a moment. It's important," said Laz Fontenot.

"Mr. Barstow, thank you for your patience. But I didn't know you were coming in today," she said.

"So Monty told you that Walker and Rose were visiting Rose's mother," Hank said as much as asked.

"Yes, Monty said it came on suddenly, and that Rose and Walker left Monday after she picked him up from debate practice."

"Ms. Baker, Rose's mother died some time ago."

"Are you sure?" asked a stunned Abigail.

"Yes, ma'am. I deliver the mail in these parts. I know everything."

*   *   *

Mrs. Babcock entered the conference room without knocking and announced that a man on the phone needed to speak to Mr. Edmond Locard. Edmond stepped out and took the call in an office down the hall. Laz was on the line when Edmond picked up.

"Edmond, we got a problem," said Laz.

Laz told Edmond everything Abigail Baker had told him about the mysterious whereabouts of Rose, Walker, and now Monty.

"Edmond, you still there?" asked Laz.

"Yes."

"So you'll tell the FBI man and the chief of police?" asked Laz.

"Yes, and with everything else the chief has heard, he'll have no choice but to order a manhunt."

*   *   *

"A manhunt? You've got to be kidding," said Chief Crandall to the group in the conference room: Officers Pearlman and Tyrell, Edmond Locard, and Agent Morose.

Chief Crandall was frustrated, worried, and hungry. Edmond's news hadn't helped. The chief continued.

"Look, I'm worried. I am. But you watch too much TV. I don't have a SWAT team on call for manhunts. Besides, I wouldn't know where to look," said Chief Crandall.

"I do," said Chester Baslin, standing in the doorway, Mrs. Babcock right behind.

Chester told everyone in the room about Rath, who he was, and about the note nailed to Monty's porch Monday afternoon. Chester did not tell them about Rath's letters to Rose. Chester then asked Mrs. Babcock to tell everyone what she had learned.

"My son-in-law, Francesco, runs our family's bait and tackle stores," said

Mrs. Babcock. "He's from the Bahamas. Our daughter met him on a mission trip to the Caribbean. He took over running the business when my husband got sick."

Chester urged her to skip the formalities and get on with the story.

"Right, of course," she said. "Tuesday night, I had dinner with my daughter Amy, and Francesco told me that a skiff had gone missing overnight."

"Gone missing?" remarked Chief Crandall.

"Stolen," said Mrs. Babcock.

"A few minutes ago, Chester asked me to call Francesco and see if the skiff had turned up."

"Well, has it?" asked Chief Crandall.

"No," said Mrs. Babcock, "but Monty Atkins has. He rented a boat about thirty minutes ago. My son-in-law recognized him from the press conference. Said he seemed upset."

"You know what this means, don't you?" asked Chester of the room.

"I think we're putting it together," answered Chief Crandall. "It looks like Rath kidnapped Rose and Walker, and Monty set out on a fool's mission to rescue them."

"Yep, and now we know where to conduct our manhunt," replied Chester.

"That may be true, but I'm betting Rath has them hidden in the swamps somewhere," said Officer Pearlman.

"That's right," said Officer Tyrell. "They could be anywhere. There are dozens of fishing cabins, shacks really, in those swamps. And if you don't know where you're going, you're just as likely to get lost."

"What we need is someone who fishes those waters. Someone who can guide us in. We need a man who knows the area," said Chester.

"Maybe I can help."

And then a ghost walked in.

Eli Atkins.

CHAPTER 55

Evil Confronted

M onty was finally on the water. "Damn that press conference," he said. Monty feared that the man at the bait and tackle shop, Francesco he said his name was, had recognized him. Must have seen him on TV at the press conference. How else? Anyway, it had taken too long to rent the boat. The man at the counter had asked too many questions. "You goin' fishin'?" he had asked. "Crappie don't bite this time of year," he said. He suggested catfish, given the hotter water. "Do you need to rent any equipment?"

I should have brought equipment, thought Monty. *Looks suspicious, that's for sure.*

Monty sat with his left hand on the tiller and headed west on the Santee River toward Lake Marion. Despite the weight of his mission, he marveled at the beauty all around him. The sun would be setting in a few hours, bringing a kaleidoscope of colors reflecting off the water and the clumps of green algae scattered across the surface. The sky was alive with the sights and sounds of song sparrows and warblers. His skiff slipped past moss-covered trees rising up from the swamps and grass islands. Alligators slipped off the banks, eyes hovering above the water's edge.

"Lord, forgive me for taking so much of your creation for granted."

*   *   *

Fearful of crashing into a tree stump beneath the water's surface, Monty slowed his boat as the setting sun and growing density of the trees cast their shadows. His attention was caught by a flashing light. There it was again. Rath. It had to be. He hadn't seen another soul since he left the dock. Monty directed his boat toward the light. A few minutes later, out of the fog, another boat came into focus.

"Stop right there, Monty," the man cried out.

Monty lifted the motor out of the water.

"Okay, Rath, I'm here. I'm who you want. Just let them go."

"Shut the fuck up, Monty. Rose done told me the same thing. Said she was who I wanted and to let you and your boy go. Y'all don't get it. No one tells me what to do. I tell you what to do. You got that?"

"Yeah, Rath. Whatever you say."

"I figure you brought a gun, so throw it overboard."

Monty hadn't thought this through.

"Rath, I didn't bring a gun, and I didn't tell the cops. It's just me. Now let's talk."

"Okay, Monty. Come on over here closer, and I'll search you and your boat, and if I find a gun, I'll use it on Rose and the boy. Now do I have to tell you again? You don't want to piss me off."

Monty tossed the gun over.

"Now that wasn't so hard, was it, Monty? Now we're gonna motor upstream a bit. I got a surprise for ya," said Rath.

*   *   *

Officers Tyrell and Pearlman shook hands with Eli and then fell into a big group hug. Chester embraced Eli, fighting back the tears. Mrs. Babcock, Chief Crandall noticed, hung in the background, beaming from ear to ear like a proud grandmother. Chief Crandall couldn't put his finger on it, but he felt he knew less about the goings-on in the room than anyone else.

"Eli, I'm Chief Crandall. It's a pleasure to meet you."

"Are you going to arrest me, sir?" asked Eli.

"No, young man, I'm not. Now tell me how you can help."

As Monty had always said, if Eli wasn't playing ball, he was fishing or hunting. He was a natural, knew every inch of the low country, and felt at home, whether on the high seas or on the swamps of the Santee and Pee Dee rivers.

Chief Crandall said that he had access to a few powerboats that would help them catch up with Rath and Monty.

"You do that, you'll get us all killed," said Eli. "The swamps are littered with hidden tree stumps. And the duckweed will gum up the rotors of any inboard, so no boats with steering columns. You need flat-bottomed boats with tilled handles. No more than three men to a boat, one on the till, and the other two armed and at the bow. We'll need at least six boats," explained Eli.

"Excuse me, Eli. That sounds like a great plan, but if these waters are as harrowing as you say, where are we going to find more men to captain the boats who know the waters as well as you do?

"You got a phone I can use?" asked Eli.

*   *   *

Monty followed Rath deeper into the swamps for another twenty minutes. They approached land, and Rath hopped out and pulled up his boat. Monty saw an old shack on blocks some thirty yards away. Light from what he supposed was a lantern shone through the cracks in a boarded-up window. Monty hopped into shallow water and was pulling his boat onto dry land when Rath sucker-punched him in the gut, dropping Monty to his knees.

"That's to remind you who's in charge. Now get inside."

When Rath opened the door to the shack, Monty, doubled over and struggling to stand, saw Walker tied to a chair, and he summoned the strength to run to his son's side.

*   *   *

Forty minutes later, Officers Tyrell, Pearlman, and Crandall, Edmond Locard, and Special Agent Morose, along with eight Charleston policemen and FBI agents, were standing dockside. Francesco, Eli, Quaid Dawson, and five of his seven sons were busy outfitting six skiffs to Eli's specifications.

Eli had called Quaid Dawson from the police department and explained the situation. Quaid was not surprised to hear from Eli. Along with Mrs. Babcock, Quaid had helped Eli escape to the Bahamas. After Eli broke into his father's safe and took off, he fled to Mrs. Babcock's house. Eli was a regular at the Babcocks' bait and tackle shops and had come to know them over the years. When Mr. Babcock fell ill and was admitted to the Dignity Nursing Home, Eli had begun helping around the shop and Mrs. Babcock's home. So when Eli showed up at her back door, she welcomed him with open arms, never once believing he could have harmed Kimberly.

Eli had told Mrs. Babcock that his mother had threatened to withhold his alibi and deny seeing him come home early the night Kimberly was murdered. Mrs. Babcock, a devout and charismatic attendee of a Pentecostal church, was no stranger to spiritual warfare.

"Eli," she said, "it sounds like Satan has a perch on your momma's soul. Don't blame her, though, for the wickedness you've witnessed isn't her. But you should go," said Mrs. Babcock on that May night five years earlier.

Francesco said his family in Nassau could take Eli in until it was safe for him to move about on his own. It was just a matter of financing his escape. Mrs. Babcock knew what to do. The Dawsons attended the same church she did, and she felt Quaid would be sympathetic to their cause. Eli agreed. Though it wasn't until after Eli had vanished that Walker and Isabelle, Quaid's daughter, met and began to date. Eli was well acquainted with Mr. Dawson since he regularly fished and hunted with the man's sons.

Quaid paid a deep-sea fishing captain he worked with on his regular trips to the Bahamas to pick Eli up. Francesco drove Eli three miles out to sea, where Eli then climbed aboard the larger boat and headed to the Bahamas to start his new life. Quaid introduced Eli to a banker on the island that his family had been doing business with for years, and an account was opened in Eli's name. Quaid deposited money into the account until Eli could support himself. Quaid encouraged Eli to hold onto the money he had taken from his father's safe. "Eli, it's my hope you'll be able to hand that money back to your dad someday," he said.

Quaid and Mrs. Babcock hoped and prayed that Eli could return one day. Quaid routinely mailed packages to Eli by including them in larger packages he sent to his Bahamian banker. The banker would then courier the enclosed envelope to Eli. Whenever Mrs. Babcock needed to get information to Eli, she'd pass it on to Quaid at church.

When Eli had received the note a week earlier, stating it was time to come home, he approached the same charter captain who had picked him up five years earlier and reversed his route. Two days later, he climbed into a boat with a smiling Francesco waiting for him. He'd been staying with Mrs. Babcock since his return.

When the boats were ready, Eli and Quaid's five boys, ages eighteen to twenty-seven, each took command of a boat.

Chief Crandall pulled Eli and Quaid aside.

"Look, Mr. Dawson, I appreciate what you're doing here, but your boys, well, they're just boys. I can't have them leading my men into danger," said Chief Crandall. "Are you sure you know what you're doing?"

"Chief Crandall, my pappy and his brother ran moonshine in these parts during Prohibition. They supplied half the bathtub gin this nation drank. I was raised in these swamps, my boys too, hunting and fishing these waters since they could walk. I still have extended family that's never left. So you ask me if I know what I'm doing? Yes, sir, I do. Now we're wasting precious time. Are your men coming or not?" asked Quaid.

Chief Crandall turned and nodded at Agent Morose, and the police officers and FBI men, all heavily armed, took up their positions. Quaid climbed into a small skiff, and Francesco powered the boat out into the harbor where Quaid's Cessna 172 floatplane awaited. He would fly ahead and stay in radio contact with Chief Crandall, who would be in the first boat with Eli.

With Eli at the till, and Quaid in the air, the small regatta left the dock in search of his family.

*   *   *

Walker was sitting in a chair, blindfolded, with his hands tied behind his back.

"Walker. It's me, Dad. Everything is going to be all right."

"Dad. Get out of here! He's crazy!" shouted Walker.

"It's too late for that now, ain't it, boy?" Rath said, laughing.

Monty turned and saw Rath holding the briefcase with the letters. He rose to his feet and stood between his son and an approaching Rath. Rath pulled a gun from behind his back, held it an inch from Monty's face, and stared at Monty, his glare cold and heartless. Monty didn't flinch.

Rath blinked and stepped away, grabbed a chair, and set it in front of Walker.

"Where's Rose?" demanded Monty.

"Rose? That little tart? Don't you worry about her. She ain't here, so don't get no ideas. I'm keepin' her elsewhere for when we have some alone time. Now, Monty, have a seat," said Rath. "Let's the three of us get to know each other."

*   *   *

Though the sun had set, a late harvest moon lit up the early evening sky for Eli and the others. Eli and the Dawson boys split up and plumbed the coveys and hidden corners of the marsh in search of some sign of Rath or Monty. They stayed in radio contact and were never too far from one another.

Quaid flew over the treetops, his eyes peeled for anything out of the ordinary. The view was beautiful. Quiet and peaceful. He tried to relax and trust.

*   *   *

"I'm not going to ask you again, Monty. Who do you love the most? My wife, Rose, my boy, Eli, or your pathetic excuse for a son, Walker here?"

Monty lay on the floor, battered and beaten.

"Now, I'm just getting started, Monty old boy. Or do you prefer Montgomery? Does the beatin' I'm givin' you in front of your boy cause you some embarrassment? It would me, that's for sure. Just look at you. Not even fightin' back. And you call yourself a man? What a pussy."

Monty struggled to his feet and hobbled over toward Rath, standing toe-to-toe with him.

"Rath, you're the coward. Holding a gun as you beat me, with my son tied to a chair. You abuse and murder women. What kind of man are you?" Monty managed to ask.

Rath just stared at him.

Monty continued.

"Let me guess. Your momma didn't love you. You were a failure in your daddy's eyes, weren't you? Maybe a woman laughed at your tiny pecker. Yeah, Rose told me all about it."

"Shut up," he yelled and backhanded Monty with the hand holding the gun.

Monty fell to the floor. Rath grabbed a pad and pen off the table. Monty thought he heard a noise in the distance.

"Now you gonna do what I tell you to do. Write down on this pad who you love the most," demanded Rath.

Monty, back on his feet, said nothing.

"God damn you. Now you're gonna do what I say, or else I'll cut your balls off and shove 'em down your boy's throat. How'd that be for a father-son moment?"

Rath was near hysterical, thought Monty. And then he heard the noise again, closer this time. Yep, a low-flying plane. Rath heard it too and looked toward the sky, then turned and pointed the gun at Monty.

"You didn't do anything stupid, did ya, Monty? You didn't tell anyone where you was headed, did ya?"

A mixture of fear and panic crossed Rath's face, and Monty saw a glimmer of hope.

"You're done for, Rath. They'll find you out. Everyone will know you're a coward."

"SHUT UP."

"Hit me, Rath. Hit me."

"SHUT UP."

"HIT ME, YOU COWARD."

Rath fired his gun repeatedly past Monty's head and screamed at the top of his lungs.

"SHUUUT UUUPP."

Rath, fueled by fear, with all his might, still holding the pad and paper in his left hand and gun in his right, reared back to strike Monty with the back of his hand. But Monty knew it was coming and ducked at the last minute. Rath lost his balance, and Monty pounced, crashing into Rath's side, driving him into the corner of the table. The gun skidded across the floor, and Monty dove for it.

Rath came up swinging a bat that had been leaning against the back wall. Monty, still lying on the floor, fired but missed, and Rath's mighty swing shattered Monty's left knee. Blinded by pain and struggling to retain consciousness, Monty fired again, hitting Rath in his gut. Rath, wounded and bleeding, kicked the gun free from Monty's hand.

Walker was screaming, and Rath was pacing, holding his hand over his stomach wound. Monty pulled himself up on one leg and was leaning against the wall, the bat lying on the floor in the middle of the room.

"Now, I'm gonna smash your other knee and make you watch as I fuck your son with my gun."

Rath moved to pounce, and Walker, with all his strength, hurled himself, tied to the chair, into Rath's path as Monty lunged for the bat and came up swinging.

Everything slowed down, and Monty felt the bat cave in Rath's head. Rath fell to his knees. His jaw dislocated and hanging ghoulishly to the side, he picked up the gun and raised it to fire when the front door to the cabin flew off its hinges as Eli and Chief Crandall bounded in and emptied their rounds.

CHAPTER 56

Family Reunion

The gunshots had done the trick. Quaid was flying just over the tree line with his window open when he heard the shots. He called in his position to Eli, who, not too far away, sped to the location and confirmed the presence of two boats pulled onto the shore. Within minutes, the other boats arrived, and the men, hearing the screaming and crashing chairs, charged the cabin.

Quaid air evacuated Walker and Monty to a nearby hospital. The men on the scene began an all-out manhunt for Rose, as other law enforcement personnel and agents from the state wildlife game and fish department appeared on the scene to help navigate the area. Rose was found later the next day, still tied to a chair, hanging onto life by a thread.

Back at the hospital, a joyous celebration erupted when Rose, lying on a stretcher, was removed from the ambulance and wheeled toward the emergency room. Eli was standing behind his father's wheelchair, with Walker off to the side. Walker hesitated, then looked to Eli, who smiled and nodded before Walker ran to his mother.

Rose, inclined slightly on the stretcher, turned her head to receive Walker's embrace. Looking past Walker, she saw her husband, and then her gaze was drawn to the handsome young man standing behind him. The handsome young man smiled, and in that moment, she saw, for the first time, her eldest son. A wave of pain for all the lost years rushed through her for she knew then that she had loved Eli all along, but that her own deep-seated self-loathing had handicapped her and rendered her incapable of experiencing it, expressing it, or in any meaningful way loving herself or her offspring. And with sudden clarity, she also knew that if she died tonight, she would die a happy woman, knowing she was both loved and lovable.

CHAPTER 57

Freedom

It was the Saturday following Thanksgiving. Walker took off Thursday and Friday from his usual training. It was easy to take off Thursday, but Walker couldn't remember the last time he went two days in a row without running.

Eddie and Walker agreed to meet at the Edgarton plantation. Quaid Dawson owned the property and didn't mind if Eddie ran the trails that crisscrossed and circled the land. There were over twelve miles of trails, and Eddie knew every turn and stretch.

"So Eddie, what are we going to do? A three-miler with intervals? A five-miler at 80 percent pace? What are you thinking?" asked Walker.

Eddie, with a slight grin on his face, was stretching, taking things in, no hurry at all. He was wearing running shorts, floppy socks that were more gray than white, old, worn-in running shoes, and, despite the cool temperature, a sleeveless shirt. His tangled blond hair ran a little longer than usual.

"What? What's so funny? Why are you smiling?" asked Walker. Walker was standing with his hands on his hips. His attire was neat and orderly, and his shoes were fresh off the rack.

"You, man. I'm smiling at you," said Eddie. "Why are we doing this, Walker?"

"We're training. What do you think we're doing?"

"Come on. We train every day after school. We're friends, but something's up. So tell me."

Walker, uncomfortable with the questions, stared into the distance. Finally, breaking the silence, he opened up.

"Look. I don't get it. I train harder. I plan and run smart races. But I can't beat you."

"So?"

"Dammit, Eddie! That's what Isabelle said."

"Huh?"

"Isabelle! She said the same thing. That's why I'm here. It was her idea. She wants me to run with you. She said something about how it looks like you're having fun when you run, but when I run, it looks like work. She thinks I'll learn how to have fun if I run with you."

Eddie, still stretching on the ground, broke into a big grin, popped up, and said, "Well, all right then. Let's go have some fun."

And they set off down a trail. After a few minutes, they found a rhythm and settled into a pace at which they could easily talk without breaking stride.

"So how far are we running?" asked Walker.

"I don't know."

"I thought you said you knew these trails?"

"I do. Just don't know how far we're running this morning."

"Then how do you know whether you're running a fast or slow pace? How do you know when to pick up the pace for a strong finish?"

"Hey, Walker, how are things with you and Izzy?"

Walker didn't know how to respond. His other friends would never ask such a question, so he remained quiet.

"I really like her, and it's obvious she's crazy about you," said Eddie. "And there's something about her that is kind of cool. She's not caught up in a lot of the bullshit that goes around. Congrats to you."

"Uh, yeah. Okay. Thanks, I guess. But really, are we doing a three-miler, or what? I have to know."

"A couple of weeks ago, I was running out here and I jumped dozens of deer. It was awesome, so keep your eyes open," said Eddie.

They kept running, and Walker figured Eddie wasn't going to answer his questions. And he didn't. Walker kept checking his watch. They'd run for over an hour at the same pace. Eddie wasn't wearing a watch and showed no signs of resting or of being tired. Walker had no trouble with the pace, but not knowing how far they were going to run weighed on him, and he felt tired.

"Hey, Walker, do you want to rest?"

"Hell, no. I'm fine."

"Well, it's just that you keep looking at your watch, that's all. Thought you might be getting tired."

"I'm not tired. Look, I get it that you always beat me, but I'm as strong a runner as you are."

"Stronger, actually."

"Yeah, right. Then how come you always beat me?"

"Oh, that's easy. I stay close to you and then kick at the end. I let you do all the hard work. You know, thinking through the course, thinking you know when to hold back, when to sprint ahead. Me? I just stay close to you, and then run faster at the end of the race."

"Very funny."

"I'm serious, Walker. If you took off at the beginning and ran your hardest, you'd push through and leave us in the dust. But no, you overthink it, holding back to preserve your kick for the end of the race. Well, I have a kick too."

"But if I go out too fast, I'll hit the wall."

"How would you know? Maybe you'd hit the wall, or maybe you'd push through. Maybe you'd catch a runner's high."

"The runner's high is bullshit. A myth. No such thing."

"Have it your way."

And with that, Eddie took off. He picked up his pace, caught Walker off guard, and quickly put twenty yards between them. Walker didn't know what to do. Should he catch him now and risk not having anything left in the tank at the end of the run? How far were they running? When should he start his final kick? But the gap between them grew, leaving Walker no choice but to run faster now and try to catch Eddie. So he did.

After a couple of minutes at this pace, oxygen deprivation set in. Walker's breathing grew short, and he felt the burning in his neck and shoulders. But he closed the gap and was able to slow down slightly to keep pace with Eddie. Eddie, though, wasn't breathing hard; he was fine, still gliding over the trails. Walker didn't know how much longer he could keep it up but was determined to run until he dropped.

Walker was dying but kept pushing, one stride at a time, determined to ignore the pain. And then Eddie picked up the pace; he had another gear.

Walker started to cramp. A stitch. His shoulders ached, his sides ached and his legs felt heavy. He stood taller, took deep breaths, and held the air in, letting it out slowly, hoping to unravel the knots in his side. He shortened his stride as they ascended a hill. Walker lost any sense of what was going on around him as he was totally focused on pushing through. If he collapsed, so be it, but he would not slow down. He didn't fear pain anymore; it couldn't get any worse.

Then something happened. The stitch faded away, and he stopped growing tired. A calm overcame him. As he crested the hill, his legs felt lighter and his stride more powerful as the trail flattened out and descended ever so slightly. Gone was the heavy breathing. The aches and weariness subsided, and he was overcome with a sense of euphoria he couldn't explain. His energy was boundless, and he felt like he could run forever. A warmth enveloped him. He'd never felt this way running.

He passed Eddie somewhere along the way but didn't remember where. In the distance, over the tree line, the sun was breaking through, and a clear blue sky unfolded. Walker's senses were alive, and he was keenly aware of everything around him.

As he rounded a corner, a trail emerged from the sparse woods and into a clear field. Across the field, Walker saw their cars. He turned off the path and ran in that direction.

Walker had one last gear, and with a huge smile breaking across his face, he sped up and sprinted past the cars before slowing to a walk. He turned and walked back toward the cars, his breathing heavy but surprisingly under control as Eddie ran up alongside him. The two of them slowly walked around, alternating between their hands on their hips and their hands on their heads as they caught their breath, their heart rates returning to normal. Neither said a word. They knew something very cool had happened and didn't want to ruin it.

After a few minutes, Eddie broke the silence. "So, did you have fun?"

Beaming from ear to ear, Walker answered, "Yeah, I had fun."

*   *   *

For the remainder of their time in high school, Walker and Eddie dueled it out at cross-country meets in the fall and track and field races in the spring. Walker began to win, not all the time, but enough to challenge Eddie's dominance. Their races were legendary. They ran without fear. Sometimes

Walker would bonk and fall far away from the front of the pack, but he cared so much less because, on those days when he remained strong, he ran like a free spirit with nothing holding him back. Walker would remember this time of his life as one of the best. He had discovered something wonderful. The freedom to fail, the freedom to live without fear.

Freedom.

ACKNOWLEDGEMENTS

I wish to thank my first readers and editors: Lyn, Sarah, Jillian, Clarke, Mike, Dallas, Jim and Erin. I appreciate all the support, comments, and encouragement. I loved strategizing story lines, book titles and cover designs with you all. And, of course, David Aretha, Barbara Kois, and Andrea Vanryken. Your professional expertise and insight helped me take my story and turn it into a book. And finally, my thanks to Martha Bullen for helping me understand how the world of publishing works.

Paul was born and raised in the Atlanta, Georgia area. Paul and his wife, Lyn, met in college at Georgetown University and were married after Paul graduated from the University of Georgia School of Law. They moved to Phoenix, Arizona in 1988 where Paul embarked on a thirty-year business career before retiring so he could write fiction. Paul and Lyn raised three children together in Phoenix and now split their time between Phoenix and Charleston, South Carolina.

Blood in the Low Country is Paul Attaway's debut novel. Writing this book, along with the move to Charleston, is a coming home of sorts, a return to the South. The history and culture of America's South is rich, complicated, at times comical, sad, tragic, uplifting, and inspiring. Paul hopes that his novels capture even a small bit of this tapestry.

You can learn more about Paul, his upcoming appearances, and his next novel at
www.paulattaway.com.

Made in the USA
Columbia, SC
06 July 2022

62930763R00198